Wages of Destruction

Emmanuel Simon

Ukiyoto Publishing

All global publishing rights are held by

Ukiyoto Publishing

Published in 2024

Content Copyright © Emmanuel Simon

ISBN 9789367954928

All rights reserved.

No part of this publication may be reproduced, transmitted, or stored in a retrieval system, in any form by any means, electronic, mechanical, photocopying, recording or otherwise, without the prior permission of the publisher.

The moral rights of the author have been asserted.

This is a work of fiction. Names, characters, businesses, places, events, locales, and incidents are either the products of the author's imagination or used in a fictitious manner. Any resemblance to actual persons, living or dead, or actual events is purely coincidental.

This book is sold subject to the condition that it shall not by way of trade or otherwise, be lent, resold, hired out or otherwise circulated, without the publisher's prior consent, in any form of binding or cover other than that in which it is published.

www.ukiyoto.com

Dedication

I dedicate this book to God Almighty for his loving Kindness. I acknowledge these beautiful team of proofreaders for their many hours sacrificed to proofread this book. Perina Amini, Josephine Schembri, Joe Lowsley, Mary Acquah, Christine Collins-Campbell, Grace Briggs, Martin Evans, Euan Clark, Anastasia Korotkova, Adeola Johnson. Thank you Proofro team.

Contents

CHAPTER ONE	3
CHAPTER TWO	14
CHAPTER THREE	29
CHAPTER FOUR	39
CHAPTER FIVE	48
CHAPTER SIX	57
CHAPTER SEVEN	74
CHAPTER EIGHT	86
CHAPTER NINE	97
CHAPTER TEN	108
CHAPTER ELEVEN	118
CHAPTER TWELVE	130
CHAPTER THIRTEEN	137
CHAPTER FOURTEEN	147
CHAPTER FIFTEEN	154
CHAPTER SIXTEEN	163
CHAPTER SEVENTEEN	173
CHAPTER EIGHTEEN	187
About the Author	201

The conspiracy, action and thrill are about to begin. Fasten your seat belt for a dangerous ride.

CHAPTER ONE

ONE EARLY AFTERNOON OF A THURSDAY, some agents of death conspired, and two of them rode towards Allen Avenue, Lagos, to perform. Harsh wind rustled dry leaves across the sky, and forced them to dance to a silent dirge devoid of symphony. The two agents on motorbike got to Allen and pulled to a stop across the street and disembarked. They cut their eyes about to see if anyone was watching. The taller of them wore a dark t-shirt over a dirty jean trouser, he looked stocky and formidable. His head was clean shaven. The other wore a wrinkled gray jacket, white button down shirt over a faded blue jeans trouser, he has average body built. Their eyes were covered with dark sunglasses, and the one in dark t-shirt carried a blue tennis bag in his right hand. The men hastened across the street and headed to daxa parking lot, a little distance from Sabrina shopping complex. There were a large supermarket, fashion stores, souvenir shop and two restaurants in the shopping complex. The place was busy with shoppers entering and exiting the complex. The men signaled to each other and moved in different directions in the parking lot. The one in dark t-shirt casually stepped beside a red Mercedes 350e and stopped. He glanced about to see if anyone was watching. Seeing no one watching him, he brought out a single key from his trouser pocket and slid it into the keyhole of the front door. He carefully scanned the space to be sure no one was watching. No one watching him, he opened the front door and lowered himself into the front seat. From the bag he brought out a time bomb and affixed it in the car compartment and flicked on a switch. A few seconds later, he stepped out and closed the door and quickly moved to another car. The other man in wrinkled jacket rose from beside the fuel tank of another car and slid beside another car, a Toyota Camry. A shopper came out from the supermarket and walked towards her car, a wine-red Honda accord. She carried her shopping bags in a cart and stopped beside her car booth. The man in dark t-shirt pretended to be talking to someone on phone. The woman didn't notice him. She opened her car booth and dumped her shopping bags inside, and waited for a fraction of a second, looking inside her booth as if checking something, then she closed the booth and turned to the driver's door. She opened the door and lowered herself behind wheels. The wine-red Honda roared to life and she eased out of the parking space. There were some people in their cars either waiting for someone, or sleeping, some were waiting for their families that went shopping, but the two men avoided been seeing doing their act. The man in dark t-shirt opened the driver's door of a black Lexus jeep straight away as she drove off. It would be an easy job for them because there were no security guards at the parking lot. Two minutes later, the men left the parking lot and rode off, leaving their weapons of mass destruction behind.

Police agent, Mark ozara, exited Sabrina shopping mall with a nylon bag full of items he bought from the supermarket. He headed towards the parking lot where his car was parked. He was five-seven with average body, fair skin and in early thirties, a police agent with Lagos state command. As he got a little closer to the parking lot, without warning, an explosion rocked in the parking lot and two cars blown up into thick balls of flame. Mark threw himself to the ground for cover. Pandemonium broke, people scampered for safety, and all of a sudden, another explosion rocked another car and threw it upside down. Mark crawled away and rose to his feet and ran to safety. He crouched low by a store wall and watched as thick fire and smoke billowed up into the sky, several dead bodies scattered about. Some burning victims trapped in their cars were wailing in agony for help. Mark watched in devastation as burning victims cried out in pain and terror, survivors scampering away for safety. The heat from the fire was intense. Across the street, a man in brown blazer watched briefly from inside a white Toyota car. He smiled in satisfaction and drove off. The cries of the burning victims troubled mark's soul. He tried to reach a victim struggling to crawl away from the fire but another explosion stopped him on his track. Total of five cars got hit. People gathered, watching from a safe distance. Loud siren could be heard approaching the scene, and smell of the burning victims filled the air. A few seconds on, police cars screeched to a stop at the scene and policemen jumped down, guns ready in hand. Excited voices filled the air as policemen shouted instructions across to each other. Agent mark got up and dusted his clothes, and walked to the leader of the police team, police superintendent Paul. "I am agent mark" the officer grabbed his hand. "I am superintendent Paul." they shook hands. "Let's get to work." mark said. Paul only nodded and joined other policemen keeping people off to a safe distance from the revaging fire. More police cars glide to a stop across the street, doors flew open and the police cars emptied, more police agents poured out to help. The furious fire continued to rage, and the heat intensified. Tick dark smoke continued to rise to the sky from the burning cars. Another siren wailed in the distance approaching the scene. A few seconds later, fire vehicles pulled to a stop at a safe distance from the fire. Firemen jumped down and water hoses drawn, they attacked the fire with water. Suddenly another explosion rocked another car a good distance from the firemen. The firemen quickly withdrew to avoid been hit. A Bmw car went up in flames and some of its body parts blown into the air. Particles rose into air and descended to the ground. The firemen returned with vengeance trying to put out the fire to stop more carnage. Mark and other policemen were busy trying to keep people off to a safer distance and the firemen continued with their efforts as the fire raged on. Agonized cries of burning victims bit by bit died down and the fire finally reduced to a smoldering point. Agent mark, continued to help some injured victims. An injured lady trying to crawl away to safety saw him and cried out. "help me!" he got to her in no time and put his hand under her back and legs and lifted her towards a safe spot, his muscles protesting under her weight but he shut his mind to the pains and carried her to safety. Another siren wailed furiously towards the scene. A few seconds on, an ambulance eased to a stop across the street and paramedics jumped down and pulled stretchers. No other vehicular movement was allowed on the street. Mark straightened up and cut his eyes to a corner of the street and his eyes caught two dangerous-looking men watching him. One of them made a sign language to him. "You're a fool for even thinking it. One wore a rumpled shirt over a blue cotton trouser and the other was in an ash track suit. They looked very formidable. Suddenly the other made another sign language to Mark. Mark read him well. This is Just the beginning. Mark mumbled the sign and rubbed his eyes. Was he hallucinating? He looked again, the men were real. He suddenly dashed after them but the men ran from the spot. Mark chased them but they cut corners and disappeared into Ikeja train station. Mark missed them and ran into a fashion shop in hope to catch the men but saw two females discussing. They stopped talking and stared at him the moment he stepped into the shop. "Wrong place." he said to them and quickly exited the shop. Outside the shop he stood watching as people gather at a safe distance of the car bomb scene. It downed on him that he lost the fleeing men. "Damn!" he punched his palm in disappointment.

In the early morning of next day, mark woke from a troubled sleep and sat straight up in bed like a zombie. The curtains were drawn and the windows slightly open, but no breeze. His night was nightmarish, bedeviled with ugly pictures from the car bomb scene. The silence in his room was as heavy as lead. He was alone in another world where he went in search of answers. Only the tick, tick sound from a chronometer somewhere in the room could be heard. A driver of a passing truck blared it's horn somewhere in the street and that brought mark back to reality. He swung his foot down to the floor and bent low, his palms cupped his jaw and his knees on his elbows. His mind was befuddled by confused thoughts and questions seeking for answers. He sighed and stood up from the bed, his average body was aching. He went to the window and spoke to it incoherently. From the slightly open window, he could see the twilight from the horizon filtering in from the distant sky, calling the night a thief. He left the window and began to pace in the room, his mind searching for any clue, any answer to the reason or those behind the bomb incident. No immediate clue came to his mind, but instead his mind replayed what one of his superiors said to him some years back, "you're not a smart police officer, just an ordinary police agent with no fineness." mark shook his head and the voice faded away. He didn't let that faze him. Some of his colleagues respected him despite the impression his superior had of him. He looked at the chronometer on the wall and time said five o'clock in the morning. The thought of the men laughing and mocking him at the bomb scene crept into him like a thief and the sign language. This is just the beginning. Beginning of what? He asked in his mind. I have to discuss this with my superior in the office. He said to himself. A new day gradually broke and he needed to go to work as quickly as possible. He turned away from the window and snapped on the light switch; bright light glowed from above the opposite wall. He walked to the bathroom to brush his teeth. From the kitchen, the rotten smell of unwashed dishes hit his nostril. He covered his nose with his palm and managed to brush his teeth. He promised himself to do the dishes when he closed from work. He loved to cook meals when he could and hates to do dishes when he should. His girlfriend had complained on several occasions when she visited him and met the dirty dishes in the kitchen.

An hour and a half later, agent Mark got ready for work and stepped out of his apartment and locked the door. He descended the stairs and headed to where his Toyota Camry was packed. He stared at a paper pasted on his driver's door and read and reread it again. It was written in capital letters. MANY MORE WILL HAVE TO DIE, EVEN YOUR PREZ. He removed the paper and unlocked the car door and sat behind wheels. He read it the fifth times. Maybe some children pasted it on my car. My neighbor's children sometimes play too much. He thought and decided to warn them when he got back from work. He roared the engine to life and waited some seconds for it to warm, his mind on the paper pasted on his car door. What if it was not my neighbor's children that stuck the paper on my car door? He asked himself. He let his car engine idled away while watching the Street. Seconds on, he leveled the automatic gear to drive and eased the car out of the parking corner and drove towards the office.

Evening of the same day, at about five pm, agent Mark was in his office pecking at his computer when the door opened and all of a sudden a junior officer rushed into his office. Mark stopped pecking and looked up. "Bernard what is it?" "Sir I got a desperate call from Olowu branch of Savannah Bank that armed Robbers are robbing the Bank right now." Sergeant Bernard said in urgency. Mark sprang up from his seat and hastened towards the office of the Divisional police officer to inform him of the development. "Tell Joseph to get available policemen ready" He yelled instruction as he grabbed the door handle of the DPO'S office door. Sargent Bernard dashed off. Mark opened the DPO's door and stepped in, closed it gently behind him.

Few minutes later, Mark came out from the DPO's office and met the police team ready and waiting. He grabbed the front door of one of the vans and slid into the front seat and the van rolled off.

At the branch of Savannah Bank, along Greg Olowu Street, agent Mark opened the front door of a police van the instant it pulled to a stop across the street. He jumped down and pulled his gun. Two other police vehicles violently screeched to a stop and policemen jumped down from their vehicles and scattered in all directions, guns drawn in readiness. In a fraction of seconds, every one of them took positions, ready for gun battle with the robbers. The marauders were about to leave with their loots when the policemen arrived. They stepped back into the bank and began to look for a way to exit. Terrified customers and the bank staff lay flat on their bellies on the floor, hands spread in front. One female customer of the bank was shot dead before the police arrived. In deliberate and bold moves, two of the robbers gingerly stepped out from the front glass door of the bank and scanned the scene. Mark ducked lower behind a police van and watched from a tight space. All of a sudden one of the robbers opened fire on a police van as a show of courage. Hot Bullets whistled pass and shattered the windscreen. The team of policemen ducked lower. Mark fired at one of the Bank robbers; the bullet hit the target but bounced off and did not even make a mark. The armed robbers wore JuJu fortified cowry like chain bullets. The robber smirked and shot sporadically at the police vans. A bullet whizzed pass Mark's shoulder, inflicting pains. He winced in pain and threw himself down behind a police van. He scurried off to another position as his men responded to the robbers attack. He aimed and fired again but the robber just dusted his charm armored jacket and smiled again and shot at the police cars, some policemen crouched low while some scurried off to safety. The pain in Mark's shoulder was not much. He checked his injured shoulder and saw that blood soaked his uniform. Two more Robbers joined their colleagues from inside the bank and it became a war zone as policemen opened fire at the robbers and the robbers responded with their own firepower. That moment, a police backup arrived to help their colleagues. The armed men jumped down and attacked from another angle. Without warning, a bullet whistled pass and hit the fuel tank of one of the police vans. Instantly it exploded into a tick ball of fire, the windscreen caved in and scattered. Policemen scampered for safety as the fire escalated, thick black smoke billowing up into the sky. Two policemen got hit in succession and before you can say Jack, bullets ripped into the fuel thank of another police van and it went up in flames. A siren wailed from a distance, approaching the scene. Mark crouched low and ran to help a colleague that got hit. More ferocious shots rented the air as the police matched the robbers' bullet for bullet. Bullets could not penetrate the armed robbers; they seemed immune to bullet. Suddenly one of the robbers squeezed the trigger and the hammer clicked on an empty chamber. He turned to dash into the bank, but Mark scooped a little sand into the muzzle of his automatic and fired at the leg of the robber, he cried in pain and fell to the ground. Mark saw it worked. He felt happy he has discovered their Achilles heels. "Target their legs." He yelled to his men. Signals passed from policeman to policeman and the message was passed. The policemen scooped little sand into the barrels of their guns. Mark sneaked to another police van and aimed at the other robber's shoes and shot at the right leg. The robber yelled in pain and crashed to the ground, but still held his gun. Another shot from Mark and the robber's gun dropped to the ground. Three policemen ran to them, guns pointing, ready to fire. They handcuffed the robbers and took them to a police van. Mark signaled his men, and one ran to the Bank and slid to a wall. Mark ran in zigzag and slid to the left side of the wall of the bank. More police cars pulled to a stop and more policemen jumped down and scattered in different positions. Some of the robbers were inside with the hostages. "Surrender and come out. You are surrounded, no way of escape." Mark yelled. One of the robbers inside looked through the front glass door and saw the burning police cars, and his men were no longer holding the fire line. In anger he shot a lady in the head and blood splattered, her head blown up. Some of the bank staff and customers on the floor silently prayed for miracle. "Let them go! Mark yelled again. "You let us go or we kill all of them." The robber yelled back. He hit his chest like a Chimp in great anger, his eyes burning with anger. He shot a man in a suit in the head and slid by a wall and came closer to the front glass door. That should warn the police that they meant business. Seconds on, two fire vehicles pulled to a stop across the street, away from the police vehicles, and firemen jumped down and scattered and watched the happenings. "We go or they all die!" the bank robber said out aloud. A policeman ran towards the back of the building and slid by the wall near an iron door. "Why not come out so we can settle it man to man." Mark threw a gauntlet. Silence from inside. The robber went back to the female staff and grabbed her hand and jerked her up from the tiled floor. He signaled the other two of his men to do the same and they picked their victims and pointed guns at the base of their necks and warm to obey or die. The first robber in front with a female bank staff gently got close to the front door and stopped, the hostages were used as shields. Mark withdrew slightly from his hiding and waited. The robbers wore chains of juju-fortified cowries which ran from across their necks down to their belts. The first robber gently stepped out with the female hostage; gun pointed at the base of her neck. The other policemen that crouched low on the left side saw them and raised their guns to fire but stopped. Mark saw them and tried to shoot but stopped because of the female hostage. He ducked behind a car belonging to bank staff and yelled to his men to hold their fire. The robber scanned the waiting team of policemen. "Let us go! No need to waste the lives of these people." The robber said loudly, but the police remained in their positions, guns pointing in readiness to fire. The other two robbers stepped out from the front door and held their victims close with their guns pointing close to the base of the necks of the hostages. The robbers gradually pushed their hostages forward. Mark reasoned that it would be dangerous to try to take out the robbers because of the two female and male hostages. Suddenly the robber in the front stopped. "Let us go or I kill all of them." He yelled in anger. "Let them go and we let you go." Mark yelled back to him. The first robber smiled wickedly and suddenly he pushed away the female bank staff from him and turned and jerked his head sideway to his men to do the same. His men pushed away their hostages and the front man yelled at the temporary free female hostages to run. The two females dashed off towards the left where the policeman waited with his gun and the middle-aged male hostage scurried off in a different direction. The leader of the robbery gang threw his hands apart. "Can we go now?" He yelled at the policemen and suddenly a shot rang out from the police team and more gunshots joined and bullets hit the first robber, but he remained standing and without any scratch. He kept saying. "Not for me and not for my boys." He said as he used his hands to wade off the bullets. He raised his gun and opened fire on the policemen and killed two policemen instantly as they kept advancing towards the street. Mark aimed at the first robber's black shoes and fired. The bullet hit the target and the robber crashed to the ground and still held his trigger down until it clicked empty. More bullets hit the shoes of the other robbers and brought them down to the ground. In no minutes the robbers were apprehended and bundled into police vans and Mark went into the van as two ambulances glide to a stop, and paramedics jumped down and began to put dead bodies in a bag. A fire vehicle pulled to a stop across, a little distance from the burning vehicles, and red light flickered from the top of its roof. Firemen jumped down and began to pull water hoses. In seconds they began to put out the fire from the burning police vehicle.

Inside the Bank building, Mark with other policemen helped the survivor's and ordered them to go outside the bank for the police to begin to dust for finger prints and evidences. As Mark stepped into the manager's office, he saw her body on the ground, face-up, her eyes open in terror. At that moment, two ambulances glide to a stop outside and paramedics jumped down and pulled the stretchers. He signaled to one of his men and they checked from office to office a few minutes later, four bodies were carried out in a body bag by the paramedics and loaded in an ambulance. A paramedic walks to Mark and attended to his injured shoulder. "You're lucky bro." The paramedic said to Mark as he bandaged his wound. "You can say that again," Mark responded with a smile. The paramedic finished attending to his wound and smiled at Mark. Mark thanked him and the man left to join his colleagues in the ambulance. Mark instructed his men to string yellow tape to cordon off the robbery scene and thanked his team for a good job. The ambulances drove off with dead bodies and injured victims and the policemen began to climb onto a police van, and Mark stood and looked at the police cars which the skeletons were what remained. He walked to the leader of the fire team and spoke to him briefly and they shook hands. Mark sauntered to the waiting police van and grabbed the front door, he turned and looked at the burnt police vehicles and shook his head. He yanked the passenger's door open and slid in and closed it a bit hard. The driver rolled off and they headed towards the station. Mark looked in the side mirror and noticed that the fire has finally died down; only the skeletons of the two police vehicles could be seen. Firemen began to head back to their vehicle. He looked out the window to the carnage and shook his head. He looked cut his eyes to the front and watched in silence as the first police vehicle drove on. He remained silent with different thoughts rattling in his head.

As the police van pulled to a stop at the station, Mark alighted and looked at his men, his face expressionless as he walked towards his office. Darkness has begun to descend, and it was well passed his closing hour at work. It was almost closing hour when the desperate call came in from the Bank. Agent Mark got to his office and entered, a few policemen there greeted him and tried to inquire about how things went at the robbery scene, he excused himself and simply told them that he couldn't talk about it because he had a headache. He entered his office and sat in his chair. He wrote the report down on a paper and closed for the day and was ready to head home. The pain in his injured shoulder has gradually waned off, it was just a minor bruise because the bullet only whizzed pass and slightly touched his upper shoulder. He felt lucky. He stepped out of his office and closed the door and strode towards another office to say his byes to his colleagues. As he got close to the door of the office, he stopped in his track and slid by the wall to listen.

Two of his colleagues, agent Lawal and agent Anthony were talking in low voices, but Mark managed to overhear what they were saying. "We have an important assignment" Agent Lawal said, almost in whisper "What assignment?" Anthony asked in same low voice. I got a directive today to inform you that two of us have a role to play in a ploy to delete the prez". Agent Lawal drew closer to Anthony. He smacked his dry lips as if trying to soften it with saliva. "Tell it to the marine." Anthony countered his eyes wide with astonishment. "It's true, Tony" Agent Lawal assured him. "There's a big plan to assassinate the President of the Country so that a man from the Northern region would take over the seat of government" Lawal informed him with a faint smile on his lips. "Who are involved, any idea?' Agent Anthony asked. "I don't know the principal player but all I know and cared for is that, We're going to be rewarded handsomely." "I am in, pal. If the reward will be big, I would assassinate him myself. I hate him". Anthony said with bitterness. "Reward will be when mission is accomplished". Lawal said. Anthony nodded without a word. His mind eyes focused on an imaginary bag containing wads of crisp dollars notes being handed over to him by an unknown man. He smiled and touched Lawal's arm. "I am honored, to play a part in such important project" Lawal nodded in affirmation without a word. He felt happy and important too that two of them were recruited to make it happen. Mark stood and listened for more, but the men heard something, like shuffling of feet. Instantly they stopped talking and laughed at Lawal's effort to crack a joke, in an effort to create an impression of two officers minding their own businesses and sharing jokes. That moment Mark tapped at the door the men stopped laughing and turned to look at him, surprises on their faces. He said bye to them and they watched him as he exited the office. Lawal and Anthony whispered to each other and agreed to be careful. They believed that Mark eavesdropped on them and might have heard them. Mark strutted to his car and opened the driver's door and fell behind wheels. He started the car and headed home. Agent Lawal, and Anthony's discussion replaying in his mind as he drove home that evening. Mark knew that the Northern region hate Andy Ubih as President and would do anything possible to harm him. The Northern region claimed that it was their birthright to rule the Country. So, to them, it is wrong for a person from another region to become the President of the Country. Mark's mind rattled, full of thought on way he would protect the President. They're from same town; same kinsmen and it would be my added duty to make sure the President is safe. He weighed the danger awaiting the President in his mind and shook his head. He agreed to himself that what he overheard agent Lawal and Anthony discuss has laid credence to the premonitions he had. He must stop the conspirators planning to assassinate the president. But how would he go about it? It's like a battle against the unknown. He got to an intersection of Orile and Costain and slowed in the traffic. Some people are conspiring to harm the President and some men in uniform are being recruited in the conspiracy, he reasoned in his mind as the cars in front slowed to a crawl. Impatient drivers honk horns in the traffic, the rowdiness on the road couldn't distract Mark's thoughts. Finally, the traffic began to move, and he drove home in silence. The President would be coming to Lagos to commission a completed National Hospital on Wednesday and Mark was one of the police agents tasked to provide security that day. He weighed the option to alert the President, but how would he prove his claim, and by doing so he might let the evil people behind the ploy know that he knows, and they might lie low and change the plan which he might not know what they would come up with. I must keep watch and be alert and somehow find a way to stop them. He said to himself. Someone wants the Prez dead, and I must have to stop him.

It was a hectic Monday for Mark, after the tough battle with the daredevil armed robbers at the Bank, which was one of the biggest Bank heists in the recent history of Lagos. The police lost four men and it wasn't easy to apprehend the Bank robbers that seemed immune to bullets. When he got home that late evening about nine pm, he had his bath and retired to bed immediately without eating dinner. His mind was too fogged to even replay the picture from the robbery scene. He lived alone, not married and his girlfriend works with the Navy in one of the Southern states. Suddenly he saw himself being chased by two masked men with long guns. He dashed into a bush and the gunmen shot sporadically at him and bullets kept flying in all directions over him, ferociously tearing the shrubs and wounding the trees in front. Mark crouched low as he ran and manage to dodge the bullets. The footpath he took got to a dead end and the masked men kept running and shooting at him. He on impulse began to climb a hill nearby in a bid to distance away and escape from his pursuers. The men stopped near the foothill and looked up to where he was trying in desperate bid to escape. They glanced at each other in amusement and chuckled. They waited with their guns as he continued to try to get to the other side of the hill. Mark in desperation glanced back and saw them and cut his eyes at the other side of the hill for a quick escape but noticed it was a dangerous edge, and large dark snakes occupied the deep bottom. As he tried to maneuver through the dangerous edge suddenly the two men opened fire and he lost his grip and yelled as he began to precipitate towards the deep bottom. He made a weak and desperate cry in terror and woke with a start. It was just a dream. His heart pounded in rapid rhythm, his body covered in sweats. He touched his pounding chest as it hammered against his chest. He realized it was a dream.

He got up and snapped on the bedside lamp and sat straight up, his mind racing. He tried to balance his breathing. What a dream, what's the meaning of this dream? He reasoned in his mind. To him, the dream definitely was a bad omen, a premonition. He swung his foot down and sat on the edge of the bed. Mark was averagely built no fat, strong biceps, fair skin, his hair was crew cut and he stood at five-eight. He prayed in silence and lay back into the bed and switched off the bedside lamp. Sleep seemed far away as he lay in quietude in the darkness, his thoughts racing until he fell into the hands of Morpheus, three in the morning.

CHAPTER TWO

NEXT DAY, TWO CROWS CAWED as they flew across over the Aso Rock Villa, as if announcing the arrival of the number one citizen of Nigeria, Andy Ubih, to the Statehouse as the President's black Limo rolled towards the stopping point. The birds cawed again and flew pass, headed towards an unknown destination. The Nigerian President's Limo eased to a stop a few steps before the foot of the stairs that led up to the front door of the Presidential office, and a large built male with a thick chest in a gray suit and white shirt, red tie threw the passenger front door open and gingerly stepped down and hastened to the back door and yanked it open, waiting for the President to also alight. The President vivaciously alighted and smiled at the orderly. He looked incredibly happy, and it was evident on his face, his eyes sparkled with love and kindness. He bounced up the stairs that led to the door of his office and, from inside, the door swung open, and the President stepped in and merrily waved in response to greetings from his competent staff. Good morning, Mr. President. Good morning Mr. President. He was happy and they noticed that. He was known to be a happy man but occasionally in the privacy of his room, he precipitates into a mood swing. During such occasions, he prefers to be alone, and his wife does know when it happens and how to manage the moment and knows how long it last. So many people love him because he has proven to be no doubt, a nice man with amiable character. He ambled towards his office, opened the door, stepped inside and closed it. He removed his suit and hung it on the suit hanger and walked to the window and cracked it a little. He whistled an oldie tune as he slid into a burgundy leather office chair. A man of early fifties, average height, strands of gray hair covered his temple. A good husband, a father to three beautiful children, blessed with a beautiful wife in her forties. He leaned forward and clasped his hands together and closed his eyes. He said his prayer in silence before resuming properly for the day's work. That has been routine for him. After the orison, he brought out his mobile phone and punched some digits from memory. Lift the phone to his ear as it began to ring. He hungers to speak with his good friend, from way back in College, the President of the United States of America, Chris Griffin. On the third ring, his friend, Chris Griffin's voice came on from the other end. "Hey Andy, how are you doing over there?" the President asked as he relaxed back to the seat. "My good friend Chris, it's nice to hear your voice this morning".

Andy coolly responded in happy mood. "How're you and your family doing?" Chris asked, a smile playing on Andy's lips. "We're doing just great. Hope Hannah and the girls are doing fine?" "We're particularly good. How're things over there?" Chris asked. "God is faithful; everything's going very good." "Oh, that's good. I'm contemplating visiting Nigeria soon. In the summer" "Oh that'll be great; I can't wait to see you again; after I visited two years ago. We're starting re-election campaign in few weeks; your visit will be a good booster." Andy said happily. "Andy, I promise; I'll visit. Our official positions should be an advantage to both Countries. When I come, we'd discuss what your Country can do for America and what America can do for your Country." A Sudden light tap on the door and the Chief of staff to the President, Henry Usman opened the door and stepped into the office, and closed the door gently behind him. The President waved him to a seat and said goodbye to his friend and cut call. He smiled at Henry and rubbed his hands happily.

EVENING OF SAME DAY, THE 3RD MAINLAND BRIDGE; a black Mercedes car raced down the bridge which stretches down into the Island. High-rise buildings adorn the two sides of C- Street. Cars flying pass the busy road that connects Bank Anthony way. A few seconds on, the black Mercedes car pulled to a stop near the sidewalk of M- street and a white male threw the front door open and stepped out gingerly. He wore black jeans trouser and a white Reebok and white tee shirt, a black baseball cap and aviator sunglasses. He cut his eyes about and began to walk towards another Mercedes car parked a little distance from his. The front door of the Mercedes car opened a little and the man in black jeans trouser slid into the front seat and gently closed the door. An average looking male sat behind wheels. They shook hands violently and the man in the Black Mercedes E- class said, "Happy you came." "Uh I was contracted, so keep my word. The other man nodded in satisfaction without another word.

A few seconds Later, the Black Mercedes Benz pulled off Marina link and rolled to a stop beside a less busy sidewalk, and the white male in black jean trousers and the driver of the car threw open the doors and alighted and began to talk in low voices. The driver was light skinned and tall, about late thirties and he looked very athletic. He wore a brown suit and brown shoes. He occasionally glanced at his back and cut his eyes to make sure no one was watching. Some friends knew the driver of the black Mercedes as Peter while the white male in jeans introduced himself to his new client as Osmond, not his real name. The sun shone from above in the sky. Time was five-fifteen in the evening. The traffic has started to build up at various points because some businesses and shops have begun to close for the day. People were trying to beat the heavy hold-ups that hinder some people from reaching their homes until eleven at night, and occasionally midnight for those that live in far places in the densely populated city of Lagos. The sidewalk was busy with people walking to and from. Peter looked at the pro marksman before him and felt okay with what he saw. He was a good choice.

Osmond coolly watched and talked like a real businessman. He has been in such business deals on many occasions; He'd been in the killing business for ten years and still counting. His first kill was when he was sixteen. When he stabbed a schoolmate in the chest and hid his body inside the booth of an abandoned and dilapidated car. His second killing was his uncle who threatened to deal with his mother if she challenged his authority in the family again. He uses many pseudo names when he meets a new client and he has gone under the knife three times, in wanted list of four countries, USA, the United Kingdom, Germany, and Israel. All has been looking for him. He had assassinated three Presidents, an American President, John Olson, President of South Africa, Eddie Malambo, and President of kings Island, Peter Clarke. He had managed to cover his tracks in South Africa, Kings Island. Osmond has an American passport, Netherland, French, Algerian and Canadian passports. He speaks French and English, Dutch, German and Arabic very fluently. He is fluent in American English. His paternal grandmother was a little French woman, his grandfather an Arab from Algeria, and his mother was a honey-blond white American. His maternal grandmother was an Arab Dutch. Osmond looked formidable and handsome, a smooth talker with great pedigree and a professional Marksman. "How was your trip?" Peter asked him "I had a long trip; from Paris, to the Netherlands, before our plane landed in Nigeria, an hour ago." "Welcome. The job is expected to be quick and clean". Peter replied, "Yes if all details are accurate and no sudden change of plan." Osmond said and touched his beard. "All info will be given to you when you settle in. This operation has been well planned." Peter responded "Good. For now, I need to go catch some few minutes of sleep." "The target is expected back morrow; around 1600 hrs. The next day he will be coming to Lagos to commission the NHIS Hospital on Tuesday at about 1300hrs, then after that, he will meet with some party members and later dine with the Governor and some friends, and... "Very busy schedule" Osmond cuts in. The election is around the corner, you know." Peter said, looking serious and business-like. "Good, give me all the vital info and be sure no mistakes. It'll be swift and clean". Osmond said. "Okay. Everything is in other. You need to get some rest. We'd talk more in about an hour." Peter said, holding the open car door. "Where am I staying?" Osmond asked. "Blue Point, on Andrew Osagie Street; you're booked in as Zakari Broovenberg. Room D

773". "What a name." Osmond said with a small laugh. "The driver of that blue Honda over there will come to pick you up and drive you to your hotel immediately." Peter said and nodded to a blue Honda packed a few feet away. Osmond flashed him a warm smile.

Peter gave a thumb up and lowered himself behind wheels. He roared the Mercedes to life and rolled off onto the street, then headed towards a connecting bridge. The blue Honda started and eased to a stop near Osmond by the sidewalk. Osmond slid into the back seat and the Honda drove off into the evening.

Later that evening, the door of room 773 gently opened and Osmond quickly walked to the adjacent door, room D772, and gently tapped on the door. A voice came from behind the locked door of room 772 "Who is there?" A man's voice asked from behind the door ". "This is Mr. Broovenberg; and who asked? "I am Harold." The voice from behind the door said. Not real name. The door quickly opened, and a briefcase was pushed out to Osmond and the door closed back immediately. Osmond picked it up and went back to his room. He snapped the latch open and laid the Briefcase on the bed, and that instant the phone rang. Osmond lifted the receiver and spoke softly into the mouthpiece

"Yes" Opening the black briefcase, he lifted the black cotton cloth covering the equipment in the Briefcase. "This is Harold, everything you need has been taken care of; map, contact, and your getaway car". "I see the equipment and switchblade. Where would the contact be?" Zakari Broovenberg asked. "The contact would be waiting at the corner of Salami by Costain, a red Lexus car. Don't worry about the tag number. It's been taken care off." "Why is the wiring of the Zimbi delayed? And the agreed fee remains three Million?" Osmond asked, his voice tight. "It wasn't our fault; the wiring was delayed by something I can't explain on phone. The balance of three million will be wired to your account in the next forty minutes." "I won't lift a finger until the balance is wired, and I get confirmation". Osmond threatened. "You will get the confirmation before thirty minutes. How will you know when it landed?" "I have my ways". Osmond responded, a bit relaxed, knowing the balance won't be delayed. "Hold your peace. We keep to our words". "As you do, that's why there's the outstanding balance you're struggling to wire". He responded sarcastically. "Just get your job done and everyone will smile". Harold said. "I'm a professional, I'm accurate and quick. In a few hours I'd be out of the scene" "We know you are one of the best, that's why the boss agreed to pay such humongous fee." Harold responded. "Okay. I am done talking for now. Duty calls". He cuts call and lifted the long-range gun and inspected it. The long-detached barrel and optic lay side by side. A berretta lay in the large briefcase too. He doesn't need it; he can kill with a hand or even a pen, but anyway in case of an emergency. He went and sat on the only sofa in the room. On impulse, Osmond cut his eyes up the walls to check for security cameras. He smiled to himself; anyway, why bother about security cameras, because it has been taken care of. There was no need to check but just routine, in case someone failed in his duty. The people that hired him made sure the security camera in his room was disconnected. Osmond scanned the room, satisfied there is no circuit camera; he began to study the map. The air conditioner hummed by a corner, but he could feel a little heat in the room even when the ceiling fan spun on low from the ceiling. A thirty-six inch Led TV was on the wall and the volume was muted. He continued to study the map.

The next day, in the morning, agent Mark sat in the front seat of a police van that followed the President's limo and the Lagos State governor's convoy as they drove along Balewa Road. Mark watched carefully at the President's limo and his eyes darted from side to side of the road, trying to see all the going ons. The police van he was in drove two vehicles behind the last car in the Presidential convoy. Security agents scurried here and there to ensure the road was safe and there was no security threat. So many policemen and SSS, security agents in mufti, and even Local security operatives were there too to maintain law and order. The convoy headed towards the link to NHIS HOSPITAL. There were so many people on both sides of the road; Party Faithfull, supporters, waving and cheering as the convoys drove on. The President of the Federal Republic of Nigeria continued to wave to the people. The governor wave to the people that cheer and running frantically to get noticed. The president waved more happily with a sense of accomplishment. The election is around the corner, and he thought it the right time to start winning the confidence of more voters. He continued to smile knowing the people appreciated him. He has performed well as a president in this first tenure, so he hoped the people would smile and nod their support for a second time. He needed their support to consolidate on the gains of the first tenure. His only worry was about some opposition even from within his party, but from the show of love by the people waving and cheering, there'd be no doubt of another victory in the poll. He knew that some political wolves from other zones or regions do not like his face or region. He leaned toward his Chief of staff, Henry Usman, who sat with him in the back seat of the Presidential Limo. "Many of those people out there love me. Only the idiots have sleepless nights, trying to find a way to stop our re-election; burn their asses digging for my fall." He parted the Chief of Staff on the knee. The Chief of staff smiled. "We are not performing badly. All we need to do is add more friends to our circle and pacify some grunting groups. I am sure we will get re-elected." His chief of staff said, looking out the car window at the people who continued to cheer and wave. "Election is barely three months, the campaign kicked off yesterday. I think it is pertinent to discuss with our national and state party chiefs." "Yes, that is a good move. We'd try and gain their total loyalty." The chief of staff replied. "The swine amongst them would still play dirty by plotting against their masters." The President said. "That is one aspect of politics I hate and love." "How do you mean?" The President asked. "Some people serve as tools of advancement, while some serve as tools of destruction". The President smiled (He looked out the car window as siren wailed ahead of them. (He waved to no one in particular, as the convoy took the Kashimowo link and headed towards NHIS Hospital. The previous election had not been easy, with so many people working underground to undermine the President's effort to win, both within and outside the party. It came as a big shock to opposition and enemies within that Andy Ubih emerged winner after collation. Some agents of destabilization were hired by political power players from the North to rubbish the election by rigging it in favor of their preferred candidate from their zone. The thought of what happened during the Presidential campaign in one of the Northern states replaying in Andy's heart. Some political thugs were hired by the opposition to ferment trouble at the campaign ground. Tear gases were used, and chaos took over the campaign venue. Andy Ubih was smuggled out from the campaign ground. The President shook his head as the picture played vividly in his mind, how he was smuggled out through a back door.

The governor's convoy preceded the President's, as they drove into the Hospital Premises. The governor's convoy rolled to a corner, and then the President's own. Buildings with three and four floors were on the other side facing the Hospital. Osmond patiently waited in one of them. As the Presidential convoy rolled into the hospital compound, he watched with attention. He released the latch of the briefcase and unpacked the long-range gun. He screwed on the barrel and the optic and slammed the magazine into the chamber. He peered into the optic, picked the security People milling about. Suddenly a security aide of the Governor pulled the back door of the Governor's car open and the governor, Adewale Ojodu stepped out in great importance and people surged forward to greet him, to get noticed. Osmond watched patiently. He has been in here for hours. Patient is the name of his trade. In the killing business, one needs to be patient. It can take several hours of hiding and waiting in a closet, locker, or waste bin. He has done it before; it's not new to him. He was trained to be patient in other to succeed. As he looked, the back door of the President's car opened and a policeman stepped down and stood at attention in salute as the President stepped down. Agent

Mark jumped down from a police van and stepped closer to the President's limo and watched; his hand on his gun at his right hip. He was edgy. He felt something might happen. The president scanned the people and smiled rewardingly. So many people came into the premises to witness the commissioning ceremony. Up on the third floor of a building, opposite the premises of the NHIS building, Osmond relaxed and waited patiently. Everything seemed to be in order. A little distance away from the President's limo, Police agent Mark watched intently at the going on. His hand was still on his automatic in the holster on his right hip. He knew that some people tried to harm the President during the first Presidential campaign, and he since then made it a point of duty to watch carefully for anyone who might try to harm the President. Having in mind the obstacles the President went through to get elected. If the Northern region dislikes him, the Northern region may try to delete him, Mark reasoned to himself.

SOMEWHERE at another location in the city, Peter and a man by name, Solomon, watched the Television on the wall before them; the venue of the commissioning ceremony was shown live on TV. They watched with great conviction of the success of their plan. Peter laughed and said to Solomon,

"In a short while,' the nation would be thrown into mourning; sad news for a region and good news for another region." Solomon smiled and nodded. "It'll be mourning and partying in different camps." They roared into laughter and Peter said, "The ruling party will blame the opposition, No one will suspect inward." "That's the wonderful part of it. Once our man ascends, we shall be handsomely rewarded". Solomon responded with a warm smile. Only the two of them are in the house, no other sound could be heard in the house except the Television "He promised to make us special assistants." Peter said. "We would push for ministerial posts. Special assistant won't fly for me". Solomon responded, his eyes glued to the Television.

"Let's see how it goes, all I know is we're the big players in the plan. We stand a better chance for bigger rewards." Solomon turned to him and smiled with excitement in his eyes. "Yea some minutes of waiting; I can't wait to pop Champaign." Peter said with happiness. "I must confess, the men that handled the job at Allen did a pretty job. I think they should be used the more in subsequent jobs." "Oh it was a perfect strike, though I don't still see its relevance in our quest to remove the Prez." Peter confessed. "I heard from a source that oga wants to create the impression that the state is overtaken by terrorists." "Uh it wasn't necessary." Peter said. Solomon shrugged; his face emotionless. He said, "We can't change what has been done. It's his call

Right?" "Yea he pays the piper." Peter said in resignation and stood. "I am going to check on the other end to make sure things are in other." Solomon smiled and responded, "Okay. See ya later for the partying." Peter nodded and smiled at Solomon. He waved him bye and left feeling enthused on hearing the mention of partying.

At the NHIS venue, Agent Mark moved from one location to another, and carefully watched those that got close to greet the President. The President of the Federal Republic of Nigeria, Andy Ubih stepped forward to cut the ribbon. He stood about five-ten. He's not fat, not thin but average body built. He does take care of himself, exercises four days a week, jaw was clean shaven and his hair was crew cut, his eyes were brown, and grays could be noticed in some parts of his head especially the temple. Not old and not young, he was in his early fifties. The Lagos state Governor stood on the left side of the President, while other top party chiefs and Local Government chairmen stood a little distance away. Security people were positioned in different areas. The air was mild with light heat and the atmosphere controlled. The sun blazed down from the sky mercilessly. It was about one o'clock in the early afternoon. The President positioned the scissors to cut the ribbon,

"I am cutting this ribbon, in dedication to God Almighty, in the name of the Father, and of the Son and of the Holy Spirit. Christians amongst them chorused Amen and the President cut the Ribbon. People clapped and shook hands, even hugged each other. Osmond aimed from a slightly open window in the opposite direction of the hospital. As he tried to pull the trigger; that moment, a man steps forward to shake the President's hand. Osmond stopped in a fraction of a second, peered again into the optic as he took aim and peered again, then squeezed the trigger. That moment the man wearing a white Agbada, choose that moment to embrace the President and both laughed and hugged. Too late, a muffled shot flew out the gun and hit the man on the back. Pandemonium as the muffled gunshot woke the security operatives on the ground even with its almost no noise. The man slumped to the ground, dead.

Agent Mark moved, he withdrew his gun and looked up in the direction the shot came from. His eyes caught a figure of a man that quickly withdrew from the small opening of a window from the third floor of a house opposite, from across the Street. He dashed off towards the retreating man, his gun ready in hand.

The moment the bullet hit the victim, the President crouched low, and his security aids shielded him from danger and tried to move him out of the scene unhurt. Osmond quickly unscrewed the attachments. Excited voices rented the air as police and DSS people ran towards the direction the shot came from and agent Mark yelled and pointed in the direction of the window. Some Policemen dashed off. A police officer, ASP Lawal looked at Mark with a wicked eye as Mark ran pass him. Sound of an advancing Helicopter to the venue could be heard.

"Go! go!! go! Guns were drawn, ready to fire. Agent Mark ran off in that direction, others followed suit. Some policemen scurried off while some ran towards the direction the suspect retreaded from. State security service too headed towards the building. Osmond ran down the stairs with the briefcase containing the equipment. He dashed off towards the west end of the building in a bid to reach the getaway car. Agent Mark ran and entered through an open door of the building the gunman was spotted. He took the stairs in twos, gun pointing, ready in hand.

Osmond already exited the building; he cut corners and entered another short narrow part that connected to the getaway car. He yanked the door open and jumped behind wheels and threw the briefcase containing the weapon in the front seat and sped off. The Helicopter pilot spotted the escaping car and began to chase it. Radios went off and in little seconds three police cars joined in the chase. Osmond drove the car like a pro, turning bends sharply and cutting corners. He tore along Williams Road as if he had been living in Lagos for ages. Siren blast the air as the police cars flew to stop him from escaping. The Helicopter doggedly intensified the aerial chase. Oncoming drivers dodged the flying red Lexus car as Osmond drove in desperate effort to escape. Osmond got to an intersection and slowed, he in a ferocious move turned right, tires protested on the tarmac and he swerved away from a car moving on slow speed and headed towards Marine Road.

Agent Mark ran into the hall he saw the gunman earlier and met space. He ran down the stairs to meet other security agents as they got to the building and spread in different positions, guns ready in hand. Mark stopped and spoke to one of the police agents. "I believe the gunman already exited the building; send men to check the whole building, to be sure." "Yes sir! The police agent responded and signaled to some of the agents to take positions. Mark hastened off to continue to look for the gunman in another building.

Some Security agents shielded the President as people scurried off for safety in different directions. The President fell into the back seat of his Limo and the driver drove off. Police cars drove in front and back of his Limo as it rolled onto the road and headed away from the scene. Policemen with guns ready to fire tailed from behind the convoy.

At the venue, tension prevailed as people continued to scamper for safety.

Back to the President's car, the Limo quickly pulled to a stop and the back door flew open, the President stepped down and practically throttled to the chopper and quickly clambered in. A few seconds on, the chopper lifted into the sky and headed west.

The police cars blast their siren as the chase intensified. Osmond glanced into the rear-view mirror and noticed the police cars were a little farther aback. His mind racing in thought on what to do. Along a free Road, Osmond accelerated at a neck braking speed, hoping to get an opportunity to stop the car at a place that he could get a chance to escape. What a mess. He'd never been spotted like this in all the years of his career. As he got to Marina Bridge he raced down the road until he got to the end of the bridge and turned left and accelerated on in a bid to connect 3rd Mainland Bridge. The Helicopter kept on chasing from above. The police vehicles have missed him but their siren could be heard wailing and following. Before he could connect the 3rd mainland bridge the chance came. The pilot noticed that the red Lexus was a good distance from the nearest car and no other car was following. He concurred with a police agent sitting with him and they agreed on something. That moment the police agent opened fire at the red Lexus. Some bullets hit the back of the car and Osmond swerved in an effort to avoid been hit. Another shot from the Helicopter and the bullet hit the back tiers of the red Lexus and another landed close to the fuel tank. Instantly fire ignited and began to burn. The right back of the Lexus was on fire. Osmond hung on for miracle of escape. The car veered to the right but he managed to connect link with the 3rd mainland. Not deterred by the fire he drove the burning car without hesitation. The drivers of oncoming vehicles stopped in fear and watched from their vehicles the happenings. Osmond glanced to the water and his eyes caught a speed boat slowing down. He jerked open the driver's door as the car rolled on and threw himself out of the moving car and rolled to a stop. That moment, the Helicopter pilot fired at him, missing target because Osmond was so quick. The red Lexus crashed into the first car across the other lane. Before the driver could move, the car exploded into thick ball of fire. Other cars at the back got caught up too. Osmond used that moment of respite to jump into the lagoon. Pandemonium broke from the other occupants of yet to get hit vehicles on the line. Osmond managed to swan farther away from the scene and a thick rope was thrown down to him from the speed boat and he grabbed it with optimism. The speed boat raced on the water till it got to a safer point where a small cruise ship waits at a boarding point. Osmond clambered onto the loading dock and disappeared into the cruise ship. No other passenger was on it except a thin black helmsman. Few seconds later, the police vehicles screeched to a stop and policemen jumped down and scattered in various directions on the bridge.

The burning cars kept burning furiously, and policemen got to a safe distance to find a away. The driver of the first car had died in great agony from the fire. The noise from the Copter was deafening as the pilot began to descend. But one of the policemen on ground signaled him and he veered off away from the scene. Sounds of sirens could be heard in the distance, approaching the accident scene. Seconds later, two fire vehicles pulled to a stop a safe distance from the first burning car and began to put out the fire. The driver of the car burnt beyond recognition.

At the NHIS scene, the governor and his security agents were in his car as it drove away to avoid being hit. The governor hastened to his official car and slid low in the back seat, security men in their police van shielded the back of his car as it drove off in a hurry, and People continue to scamper away. No one would love to die, not in this way anyway. Mark glanced about but could not find the gunman. He checked from floor to floor and realized the gunman has already exited the environment. He headed back to meet others. When he stopped to talk to another police agent beside where ASP Lawal stood with another officer, Lawal and the officer cut their eyes at him and whispered to each other.

In the afternoon of the same day, Agent Mark sat in his office, his mind replaying the incident that happened at the commissioning ground at NHIS hospital. He stood up and began to pace in the free space of his office. The curtain is drawn; the ceiling fan spun from the ceiling and the door was closed. "Some people want Andy dead. Who are they? He said to himself as he continued pacing. He stopped pacing and perched his butt on the edge of the table, his face solemn. He brought out his mobile and punched some digits, put it to his ear, and waited for it to ring. It rang five times and stopped. He redialed it and puts it to his ear again. On the second ring, a voice came on from the other end. "Hey Mark, how are you doing? Long I heard from you." "I am fine Joshua, how busy are you? I would love to see you." "Hope all is well Mark?" Joshua asked in apprehension from the other end. "I can't say all is well, friend. There's something I want us to discuss; not on phone." Silence from the other end until Joshua said. "I am busy throughout this week and maybe next. I will see how I can sneak out to see you next week. You know our work; the IG demand that we go to all units and update officers on the latest security gadget procured to detect drug peddlers. Agent Joshua said. "Ok buddy, try to see me as soon as you can. It's important and kind of urgent." Mark replied. "You sound worried Mark, hope it's nothing serious?" "When you come, Joshua, I wouldn't talk about it here." "Okay, see you then, buddy. I am running off to attend to something." Joshua said and they both said byes and Mark cut the call and returned to his office chair, and started to peck on his computer on the table.

Peter and Solomon sat, and all looking sad Then Peter's phone rang, he grabbed his mobile and picked the call. He perched at the edge of a large table. "Hey Lalong!" "What happened? Honestly, this is sad news to all of us. Oga is devastated right now." Lalong said. "We're not happy at the turn of event. Someone decided to be a sacrificial lamb; the bullet hit the wrong person; the target was lucky." Peter replied. "What about the gunman?" "He escaped before the security could move; he's already left the Country," Peter responded. "It's not a happy ending at all. We have to switch to plan B." "Yes, we got to come together and device a new way on how to carry out plan B," Peter said and glanced at Solomon who watched and listened to him. "Yea we should. Listen Oga wants to see you immediately." Lalong said. "Okay, I would be in Abuja in the morning," Peter said and paused to listen. "Talk to you again when you come," Lalong said. "Okay! Till we meet again." Peter cut the call and turned to Solomon.

On a Tuesday morning, in a high-rise building in a high-brow area in the Asokoro area of Abuja, Aliu Issa sat listening to two other men by the names of Williams and Habib. The men talked without excitement in their voices. Habib's face looked tense as he listened to Aliu Issa talk. "If we fail to remove him from office now before the election in three months; it won't be good news. He has performed creditably and that will get him re-elected. That means new tenure; another waits before we try again to remove him." Aliu Issa said with sadness in his voice. He adjusted his bulky frame on the seat. "Our marksman was unlucky; one useless politician choose the moment the assassin pulled the trigger to hug the President, thereby providing cover for the Target, and got hit instead," Habib said. "We have to take to plan B; my only worry is the President might be scared now and might decide to withdraw from public functions for the time being," Williams said. "Not only that; the security will be beefed up; there are security agents loyal to him, they will be watchful and at alert. They are no dummies." Aliu said. "I suggest we lie low for a few weeks before trying again," Habib suggested. "I will have to discuss it with Oga when I see him today. Right now, he's very upset that the operation failed." Aliu said. Williams tried to speak but started to cough. He coughed a few times and stopped and asked. "What if plan B fails?" The office is large and expensively furnished with a black leather chair and a large mahogany table, brown and milk color curtains, the window was closed and the air conditioner was purring at a corner, providing coolness in the office. The office was merely a meeting place for such urgent matters like this. It was not a rented space; the owner of the building happened to be a big player in the political scene of the country, and he preferred to be silent and lie low in obscurity. He knew the meeting was going on and he would be briefed by a close link, Aliu. Meetings like this must be held because of its urgency and it was imperative to discuss ways to achieve the set goal. There are other units like this in other parts of the Country where some important members of the team converge for a serious meeting. Aliu sighed deeply and said to others. "Our marksman would return to take him out; I believe plan B would work." "I suggest we plant a local gunman to make sure the job got done. Say maybe a police mole, someone from the disadvantaged region." Habib suggested. "It would've been very easier to kill him if he had liked women. A beautiful woman would have been planted to fix him," Aliu said with a small laugh. "His Excellency is so faithful to his wife; we have tried on a few occasions to catch him cheating but to no avail. Inyamiri Banza." (Igbo Bastard) Others burst out laughing. The laughter served as a soothing balm to their frayed nerves and minds. It is good to laugh even when discussing such a heavy matter like this, yes, it is permitted Williams thought as he continued to laugh at the little joke. "When I meet Oga; he will let us know the next move and when." Aliu's voice called them back to attention to the discussion at hand. Williams looked at his watch and glanced at Habib sitting near him. "Gentlemen I think I have to run. I have another meeting to attend to in a couple of hours. You let us know oga's decision on the subject matter." He said, his eyes on Aliu. "Okay, talk to you again; messages shall be passed to all players in our team." Williams hauled his ass up from the chair and shook hands with others excitedly and exited the office, closing the door behind him.

NEXT DAY, in the Lagos state governor's office; the state governor sat deep in discussion. The door was closed, and all assistants were busy working in another large space in their offices. The time was ten on Wednesday morning. The governor resumed work barely ten minutes ago before his deputy walked into the governor's office, closed the door and began to discuss with the governor. "I couldn't sleep in the night as the picture of what happened at the commissioning ground replayed in my mind. We got lucky the gunman did not succeed. I nearly wet my boxer in fright." The deputy governor said. His look was intent. "It was a horrible experience. You know I was standing close to the President. Thank God I did not get hit." The governor replied as he lowered himself to the large leather chair of his office, behind a large mahogany table. "It happened like lightning, pandemonium broke out and people began to scamper away from danger. The security agents scurried away from danger also." The deputy governor said. "Who might want the President dead?" The governor asked. His deputy shrugged and relaxed on his chair. "It must be his political enemies; especially I don't trust some of our political members. Those disgruntled elements in our party that are greedy and want things to be done their way." Governor Adewale said. "Our political system is heated, and unfaithful members are scampering for one seat or the other, or do you think maybe, the opposition has a hand in this?" The deputy, Bada asked and leaned forward on his elbows on the table. The governor shook his head. "Who knows; but I doubt opposition has any hand in this, I might be a target too. I know those who don't like me but pretend to; they would give anything to see me dead." Governor Adewale said, he rubbed his hands together and raised them up in silent supplication to God. "Two dangerous and wicked enemies I know of are Bamidele Badmus and Akin Sofue." "Ah those two; I don't trust them any time any day. They are fetish and I know they are eyeing my seat; I am careful whenever they are around." "Their plastic smiles mean nothing to me. They are wolves in sheep's skin, pretend to be friendly while beneath them they continually plan to destroy people." Bada said. "My offense is they both demanded that I give their candidates choice ministerial posts; Minister for finance and minister for works and housing which I turned their request down and they became enemies and conspire to bring me down." "They aimed to dictate the running of government and find a way to siphon state money, we won't allow them," Bada said. "Not while I am alive as governor of the state. We must be upright and deliver our campaign promises to the people of Lagos state." "After our tenure, they can try again; but for now, no vacancy, Awan Ole." (Thieves) They both burst out laughing happily. "Let's me not forget; you are going to represent me at the coming meeting with our local government chairmen." "Okay no prob; do you have any engagement morrow? I want you to meet someone." "Who might that be?" Governor Adewale asked, eyes fixed on his deputy for an answer. "One of my friends from a neighboring Country wants to invest in our state." "Oh, that's good. I will be on seat." "He would be expected in the state house by two pm," Bada said as he rose from his seat. "Okay, I will be expecting both of you." Bada nodded and excused himself to return to his office. He grabbed the door handle and yanked it open and stepped out, closing it behind him. As the deputy governor left, the Governor leaned forward on the office large mahogany table and smiled to himself. 'Bada thought I trust him." He said to the office. I don't trust any politician; I know he's looking for ways to remove me as Governor of the state. He said in his mind. The political world is like a jungle and there's a saying that, No paddy in the jungle. He said in his heart. His intercom nipped, interrupting his thoughts. He stretched his hand and picked it. "Sir the commissioner of police is here to see you, sir." His personal secretary said from the other end. "Allow him in." He said to her and replaced the receiver. A Fraction of seconds on the office door opened and a trim tall man in uniform entered and closed the door gently. He saluted and the Governor waved him to sit. "Welcome, Commissioner. Hope you're doing ok." "Yes your excellency, sir" The commissioner of police, Nuhu Abass, responded with a warm smile on his face. "Commissioner, I sent for you because I am worried about the recent insecurity problem in the state." Nuhu shifted in his seat. "Gunmen, seems to be controlling our dear state now and the recent bomb incidents are worrisome. What are our police doing to stop this?" Nuhu cleared his throat and spoke, "Your excellency, sir. We are worried too, and we have mapped out plans to apprehend the perpetrators of the wicked act. "Our state is no longer safe." The Governor said. "My men have been digging and searching for the criminals. They won't escape." "How soon will you bring the perpetrators to justice?" The Governor asked, watching the police commissioner. "We are following a lead and soon we are going to make an arrest." "Better it be soon as you said. I can't watch Lagos state become a red spot, a city in siege by terrorists and drug peddlers." "I promise you sir; we are working on eradicating all forms crime from the state." The nodded and stood. The commissioner stood too. The shook hands and meeting ended. "We will come together again to talk progress on the matter." The Governor said. "Yes sir." Nuhu nodded. He exited the Governor's office.

CHAPTER THREE

FRIDAY MORNING, President Andy Ubih sat discussing with his chief of staff, Henry Usman at the west wing of the Aso Rock villa. The President relaxed on a burgundy single sofa while his chief of staff, Henry sat on a double. The space looked very expensively furnished with expensive golden curtains; the floor-tiles were expensive marbles. A glass table sat at the center of the space and a beautiful chandelier hung a few feet from the ceiling. The air condition unit hummed from a corner of the room. One of the curtains was parted slightly. President Andy looked at his chief staff and shrugged. "Thank God I escaped the attack. Some people want me dead; I need to find out who they are." "Yes, that's what I thought too. You know some regions are not happy we won the election; some of them hate the fact that you are on the coveted seat." "But it was the turn of my region to produce the President and I was collectively chosen to vie for the seat." "We would always have selfish people who want things changed for their selfish end." Henry said and crossed his leg. "We are performing well, and I hope our record will help us get re-elected in three months' time." Andy responded and crossed his right hand to his left shoulder "When are we kicking off the campaign?" Henry asked. "I would discuss with our party chairman; to see if we can kick start our campaign next week." Andy replied. "Mr. President, sir, I suggest you schedule a meeting with the security chiefs to instruct them to beef up security on all ends. I have an inkling those behind the bomb incident might try again. I suggest you call a national conference; we can use the opportunity to clear some debris." The President nodded and relaxed his hands. "I don't think they would be foolish to try soon. They know all security units are beefed up to fish them out." Andy responded and rose from his seat and began to pace in the room, many thoughts rattling in his mind. What would have happened if the enemies succeeded in assassinating him? His wife initially kicked against it when he agreed to contest the Presidential election. She wanted them to live their normal quiet lives devoid of media, camera, and front page. She wanted a simple life for her and her children; but after many rubbings of minds, allaying of fears and assurance that it would end in happiness, she reluctantly agreed that he vie for the presidential seat. He was asked to return from his base by some concerned citizens of his region, for him to represent. He had no option but to oblige his people. Suddenly he stopped pacing and turned to his chief of staff. "The people behind the attempt on my life must be fished out and dealt with decisively according to the weight of the law." He sat back on the sofa and relaxed, his arms relaxed on the arms- rest of the sofa. "I may have to reshuffle my cabinet; I don't trust some of them. Some moles might be amongst them." "Good idea; I hate things are like this. Some people would be removed and some would change seats. No government survives without moving staffs." Henry proffered. "You are right." Henry concurred. "All I want is to leave a good legacy of good governance." "Our government is performing well." Henry said. "We are going to do more." Andy said with optimism. "We are performing creditably well; there's enduring polity, all political mechanism is thrown in to make it work." Henry said. He rose and walked to one of the windows and parted it and peered out just to release cramped nerves. He turned and returned to his seat. "The economy is stable, and we are not going to leave any debt for the next set to inherit. We created many jobs; we are transparent in running the affairs of the Country and I plan to do more before I exit the office." The President said. "Our foreign friends are happy with us; we created more jobs and eradicated hunger, built more roads, and rehabilitated bad ones. We delivered the dividends of democracy, more human and in-fractural developments." Henry said proudly. "The majority of the people are happy with us and that matters to me." Andy said and yarned. "Your Excellency sir; it might be that because our government is not throwing money about that may be the reason the idiots are after you." "I don't and won't condone any corruption in my government. Anyone found wanting must be convicted in the competent court of jurisdiction." Two security aids stood at different locations; one by the door, the other stood at a corner away from the interlocutors, his ears listening to their conversation and his eyes glued to a spot at the wall. Suddenly the President rose and stretched and yarned and the chief of staff rose too; he understood the meeting has ended. He preceded the President towards the door. The security aid threw the door open as Henry approached, and the President ambled behind. The door thrown open and they stepped out. The security aid by the door walked in front while the other followed behind the President. A police van was waiting outside a little distance from the door where the President and his chief of staff were talking. Stern-looking policemen watched attentively as the President and his chief of staff emerged and headed to their cars. The car door opened, and Andy lowered himself into the back seat and the door shut. The President's official Black Land cruiser jeep began to roll away. A police van with policemen in front and a car with other policemen followed from behind as the small convoy headed to the Aso Rock villa, the main office of the President.

TWO DAYS LATER, a black Mercedes Jeep drove along Awolowo way Ikoyi, it was rush hour and there were many vehicular movements on the busy road. The driver of the Mercedes, a short thick man in his late forties concentrated on the road and a man of about late fifties sat in the back seat, his babariga almost covered the back seat of the jeep. The driver left the road and turned the corner of Dele Fasasi Street, off Awolowo way, drove towards a short lane to a large building and pulled to a stop. Another meeting point belonging to the conspirator. The back door opened and the man in the back seat of the jeep known as Alhaji Garba Indai stepped out gingerly. He adjusted his flowing Agbada on his shoulder as he headed towards the gate that led into the compound. The driver of the Jeep drove off. He would come back in twenty minutes as was instructed by Garba. Alhaji Garba got to a door and as he made to grab the door handle, it swung open inward. A police orderly saluted as he stepped into the richly furnished office. A man sat on the chair behind the mahogany table. "Greetings, Alhaji," he said, and they shook hands. The man behind the table whose name was Alhaji Gambo, Smiled coolly. "You are welcome; how is home?" Alhaji Gambo asked him. "Everyone is good. How is your home too?" Alhaji Garba asked. "Everyone is good; seat down" Alhaji responded and waved him to a sit. Alhaji Garba lowered himself onto the seat. "I spoke with Oga today." Alhaji Gambo said. "What's up? Garba asked. "He instructs that we wait till next month." Alhaji Gambo said. "It's good that way; the idiot must be assassinated," Garba responded. "Useless Igbo man; he must be killed before the election," Gambo said gesticulated, and made a sign of throat slash. "I came so we go to the office of the minister of finance," Garba said leaning forward. "Okay let's go," Gambo said risen rose from his seat. "Let me call my driver" he brought out his phone and punched the driver's number. A few minutes on, the driver pulled to a stop by the sidewalk and the two men entered the jeep and it rolled off.

The same day, the President, Andy, and his wife Victoria sat in their gorgeously furnished living room in the living quarter of Aso Rock. The president's wife, Mrs. Victoria sat close to her husband on a double sofa. Her mind was troubled. "Darling, I am very afraid. Some enemies want you dead." "I am grateful to God that their plans failed," Andy said and pulled her closer to him. "Please you should minimize attending functions until after the election." She said her eyes on his face. "It won't be easy my love; our party is preparing to kick-start the campaign next week." He smiled at her warmly, his hand on her shoulder. "Please instruct your security aides to be watchful. There are so many enemies, and we don't know whom to trust." "God is the one that protects," Andy said to her and planted a warm passionate kiss on her chin. "I am very afraid." She said again and held him tighter. "My life is in the hands of the Lord." "God please protect you, my love; I don't want to be a widow." "My God is alive forever. I will live to see the end of my enemies." Andy said and pecked her on the forehead. "Amen!" Victoria said.

One month later, at the campaign ground, some policemen moved from spot to spot as they checked the campaign ground for any explosives with a metal dictator. To make sure the venue is safe. The President's political party would kick start their Presidential campaign that day. Agent Mark amongst the policemen carefully checked the podium; check all corners to make sure there was nothing suspicious. Satisfied that the venue was safe, he headed to loudspeakers at a corner. The leader of the police team, Asp Lawal watched him as he moved about from spot to spot. When he noticed that Agent Mark was not close enough; he signaled to one of the policemen and the policeman hastened closer. Asp Lawal whispered to him and the man stepped away. He called the policemen together and asked. "Hei gather here everyone!." The policemen gathered except Mark who continued to check for any dangerous looking item hidden somewhere. "Anyone detects anything?" Lawal yelled. "No sir!" the policemen answered in unison. "Good; I assume the campaign ground is very safe. Now let's go!" The policemen began to file out of the campaign venue. Agent Mark felt satisfied, he walked away. Agent Lawal met with Mark and threw his hand over his shoulder and began to discuss with him as they headed out of the venue. The policeman agent Lawal spoke to earlier, Sergeant Anthony stepped to a corner and picked a black leather porch from a corner and waited until Lawal and Mark walked pass. He went back to the venue and headed to the podium and opened the black leather porch, a bomb the size of a small melon lay in it. Sergeant Anthony flicked on a switch and set the timer to 1430 and lifted the foot stand and placed the leather porch under it and let it drop back. The President is expected to start the campaign at about 1400 hrs. Sergeant Anthony quickly left the venue and entered onto a street, away from the route his colleagues followed and disappeared.

The president was expected to kick off his Presidential campaign in a few hours and he was expected to spend about thirty minutes or more addressing his party members and supporters. The police had barred people from entering the venue. It must remain so pending when the security agents at the gate would allow party supporters and members in proper.

As the time drew near, Andy in his living room sat while the clock ticked, he was counting the time to start going to the venue. He was eager and ready to be there on time. He was dressed in an Igbo traditional Isi Agu, the traditional wear of his people of the Igbo tribe special wear for the titled Igbo men, designed with the imprinted head of a tiger, and a red cap to match it sat on his head. The phone near where Andy sat began to ring. The President looked at it and slowly lifted the receiver and spoke into receiver almost in a murmur. He did not need to be troubled with phone calls. It was his direct line and only a few people have access to it. "Hello, he said softly into the mouthpiece and waited for the person at the other end to speak. Hello, your Excellency sir, this is Pastor John; your kinsman sir." "Oh, pastor John; how are you doing? It'd been a long time since we talked." "You're very correct; your Excellency sir, hope you and your family are doing great?" "God has been faithful to us. My party is starting our Presidential campaign in a few hours now and I am getting ready to go to the campaign ground." Andy replied as he relaxed back to the sofa. "That's the main reason I called, your Excellency sir." Andy listened attentively. Pastor John continued. "Sir, I had a revelation from God that some people want you dead and they are waiting to strike at the campaign ground. You shouldn't go to the venue where the enemies lie in wait for you." "Hmmm, I know something is not right. I woke up this morning worried and couldn't understand why." "My brother, Your God is alive. The enemies plan to eliminate you today. I suggest you send someone to represent you instead and don't give anyone a reason why you want to attend." "I can just tell my party chiefs that I am indisposed; the doctor advised me to rest," Andy said, feeling sick in the spirit. Why must anyone want to kill him? His people choose him to represent them, and it was the turn of his zone to produce the President. "Good, your Excellency sir; I will call back. Some people are waiting to see me." Pastor John said from the other end. "Thank you, my brother, for this message. I appreciate." "Glory is to God who reveals hidden things to his people." Pastor John said. "I bless the name of the Lord. Please call back later so we can talk better." Andy said a feeling of gratitude to God filled his heart. "Okay your Excellency, sir; by for now." Andy cut the call and put back the receiver and leaned forward with hands to his jaw and elbows to his knees. It should be right to alert my party chiefs; he reasoned, but no not a wise thing to do, he discarded the idea. That would be letting whoever wants him dead to know he knows. Who are the enemies and who are on his side? Right now, everybody is a suspect. All lizards lie belly flat so who knows the one with a belly ache? He said in his mind. Andy shook his head and rose from the sofa and began to pace in the living room mumbling to himself.

On the campaign ground, Agent Mark moved from place to place and carefully watched the going on. He suspects a cover-up, a conspiracy against the President. Someone in obscurity wants the President dead. He vowed to do his best to fish out those behind the nefarious act. An hour and a half later; at the campaign ground, party supporters and the Governor of Lagos state, so many Party stalwarts from other states. National Chairman, State, and Local Government Chairmen, and party supporters are in the venue chanting the party slogan, acrobatic display from enthused members. It was a beehive of activities. They wait for the arrival of the President while different groups, a women's wing, a youth wing, and other cultural groups kept the crowd busy with dance and cultural displays. After another hour of waiting, a man walked to the party chairman's seat and leaned close and whispered something to his ear and left. The Chairman then leaned close to a man sitting close to him and whispered to him. Because of the recent gun incident, the governor decided that it would be wise to sit far away from where the President would sit. Since he got lucky during the attempt on the President's life, the Governor thought it smart to sit a few distances from the number one man of Nigeria. Being cautious is not cowardice. The whisper got to the Governor and quietly it was agreed that the party chairman should kick off the campaign proper. The party chairman, Chief Remy Ojo slowly rose and tapped at the microphone in his front. He adjusted his all-white agbada lace on his shoulder and cleared his throat, just to call attention. The dancing and excitement quieted down and attention was given to him. "TPP" He yelled in great mood and the supporters responded. "Transparency!" He repeated and got the same resounding response. "He shouted another TPP, and the crowd rewarded him again with a loud response and cheer. He raised his right hand and silence prevailed. "Today is another beautiful day; we as great party members are gathered here to begin our Presidential campaign proper. I urge all to be of good conduct while we carry out our campaign. Unfortunately, I want to announce to you that the President has an urgent matter to attend to. I beg your understanding and solicit your unwavering support. Thank you and God bless you all." He waited briefly to let his words sink low. The people were gearing to go even without the presence of the President. "TPP! A loud response sounded from the people. He smiled and waved them to continue in their dancing and cultural display. He sat back to concur with other party big wigs on when to enter the next phase of the campaign proper. Allow the people some time to sing and dance, after all, that's part of it all. Local drummers, traditional dancers took over and excitement returned, party flags flew at different locations, and some elderly party members began to leave. The party chairman rose and addressed the party members and supporters; he solicited and advised everyone to vote the party back in the come Presidential election. Cited the achievements of the government and promised that the party would do more to make life beautiful for all Nigerians. More campaign promises, more cheering, more happiness in the air. The Governor and entourage left the campaign ground and some party chiefs stood to leave.

At another location somewhere in the city, an average built Indai and another player in the team, Gambo, watched the going on at the campaign ground live on a Led TV in a hotel suite. They watched with utter disappointment as people began to file out from the TPP Presidential campaign venue. Gambo turned to Indai and stared at him in amazement and sprang up. He began to pace angrily. "Hei Alhaji; what went wrong? The useless Igbo man didn't go to the venue. Things didn't go well." He said and shook his head in disappointment. In a fit of anger he grabbed a flower vase and threw it to the wall and it shattered into pieces. "Honestly Alhaji; I am very surprised," Indai responded with sadness in his voice, his head in his palms. "Oga must be very upset by now. In truth, the idiot is very lucky." Gambo said with bitterness. Sadness enveloped his heart. He tried to imagine it. The opportunity of a lifetime gradually slipped away from their grips. He had dreamt of himself as a minister and it seemed it might not come to pass. No, the Prez must die; if he remains alive there won't be a way for us to actualize our dream goal. It can only take a longer time, but he must not escape death. The team has invested too much time and energy in this, and our efforts must not be in futility. He said in his heart. He shook his head and held his head in his hand. As if remote controlled, he stopped pacing and went back to his seat. They continued to watch in silence the happenings at the campaign ground.

At the campaign ground, Agent Mark ran to help a man struggling for his last breath, the man's left leg got shattered by the bomb and people were desperate to leave the campaign ground, not minding the injured victims. "He held the man and tried to carry him away from the stampede, but the weight of the man was much for him. He pulled the man away from danger by his hands and returned to help another victim. Some other policemen joined him to rescue those in harm's way. In the pandemonium, Mark guided people out of the scene, and instructed other policemen to help guide the people out of danger. Afraid another bomb might go off. A question ran into his mind. He was among the policemen that inspected the venue and he made sure he checked every corner and he didn't saw any bomb. Who are the masterminds of these bomb attacks? It became obvious to Mark that some policemen are working for someone. The thought ran in his mind as he helped an injured woman to a safe corner, hoping that paramedics would arrive soon. He could hear the sound of a siren approaching from a distance. He dashed off to help more wounded victims.

At the hotel suite, Gambo's phone rang. He picked up call and Peter came from the other end. "Gambo, are you watching from that end?" "Peter, yes we are watching it life; this is another bad news for us." "We're all in shock over here, Alhaji. He keeps getting lucky."

Gambo's eyes watered and he looked at the television which has become a bit blurry to him. Suddenly an explosion rocked the podium and the living scampered for safety. Pandemonium broke everywhere as another explosion rocked; bodies were thrown up and crashed to the ground. Smoke and scattered debris rose into the air and dropped back to the ground. Anguish, crying, and excited voices filled the air. The bomb left many dead bodies and many injured ones. The survivors kept scampering farther away for safety, and Gambo and Indai watched in aghast, their mouth fell open and their eyes glued to the screen, all watching in shock at the happenings. It was expected that people would be sacrificed to assassinate the President successfully but no, things are happening fast and wrongly. Why did the target not go to the campaign ground? This is very devastating. Gambo bolted up from his seat and began to pace and Indai lowered his eyes to the floor, his eyes watered a little. He shook his head and looked at Gambo who paced in desperation, mumbling incoherently to himself. "This is unexpected and hurting. How come he got this lucky a second time?" he asked nobody. Gambo didn't even heard him as he continued to pace in exasperation, gesticulating in pain as he soliloquized and gradually awakening from his bitter and sad dream. Indai looked at the Television, sadness written all over his face. The pain was not that other people died in the process, no it was expected but where is the President? He continued to watch as police vans pulled to a stop at a safe distance from the bomb scene and policemen jumped down and a siren wailed from outside, three ambulances glide to a stop, paramedics jumped down and pulled out stretchers. Another siren wailed and a fire vehicle screeched to a violent stop and firemen jumped down and pulled the water hose. Indai's eyes returned to the floor. His watering eyes fixed on a small dirty spot on the floor-tiles of the hotel suite.

At the Presidential Villa, the President watched intently live footages of the happenings at the campaign ground. His wife sat close to him and watched in total shock. "Andy turned to his wife. "Jesus Christ. Darling, are you seeing what I am seeing?" "Hei hei hei; my God my knees are on the floor. Take all praises. You saved my husband." Her hands were up in supplication. "My Lord my God, who's like thee? Your mercy over me endures forever." He knelt beside his wife; his voice rose in supplication. His wife hugged him tight, and both held each other. She broke into tears and in seconds she began sob in gratitude to her maker. Tears of joy ran down her cheeks. A gentle knock sounded at the door and Andy and wife looked at the door in unison. They disengaged and gently rose and sat back on the sofa. Another gentle knock and Andy asked the person at the door in. The door opened and the vice President, Matthew Ochei stepped in with other men following him through the open door. He walked in to meet the President. The chief of staff was amongst them. President and wife silently watched them as they entered. The President's wife stood and welcomed the men and headed into another room to allow the men time together. The men picked their seats and the Vice President, Mathew Ochei looked at the President, and his face was bland. Many thoughts ran amok in his mind but he managed to conceal them with opaque screen and masked plastic smile. How the Prez can be this Lucky twice? He reasoned in his heart. His face revealed nothing as he spoke. "This is shocking, Mr. President; Glory is to God you are safe. I am shocked beyond words." he said. Andy shook his head in sadness. "I am still in great shock. The people that want me dead killed innocent people just to get me." "I suspect the opposition, Mr. President; their plan didn't work. God loves you so much. Two tries and you came out safe" Henry said. Vice President Mathew Ochei stole a glance at the Chief of staff and looked at the President who bent low, his head in his palms. "The perpetrators of this act must be apprehended. I will instruct the law enforcement agencies to as matter of urgency fish out the people involved." Mathew said. "Please organize a press conference to declare a national mourning for the victims of the bomb blast who lost their lives. I can't think straight right now". Andy said to his vice. I will do that immediately after I leave here. I will address them myself. Just relax and get your emotions together." The President nodded and rose from the sofa. "Gentlemen I am not in the right frame of mind to offer any entertainment." All the men agreed that the situation does not call for any entertainment. This is a tragedy, and the nation is mourning. "Mr. President, I hope your wife is taking this calmly. She might be in shock." Mathew asked in concern. "It's not easy on her but I believe she's strong enough to hold herself together." Andy responded and sat back on the sofa. Suddenly the phone by the sofa rang. He stretched his hand and lifted the receiver. A voice from his assistant came on from the other end. "Mr. President Sir; the Senate President and others are here." "Send them in" Andy instructed and replaced the receiver. A soft knock on the door and the police orderly beside the door pulled it open. All eyes to the door as the Senate President and his Deputy stepped into the living room with the Speaker of the House of Assembly through the door. All went to the President, shook hands with him and the seated men and picked their seats. No pleasantries. The Senate President, Alhaji Danbaba, and the deputy Ayo Ogundele looked concerned and worried. "Mr. President, this is a shock to all of us. What a tragedy." Danbaba said. "Glory is to God you are safe." "I am still in shock this happened in our dear Country." Ayo threw in. The speaker of the house, Mazansu Sheriff watched. Only the President wore a red senator while others are in different shades of traditional attires, Agbada, lace, and damask materials. Mazansu looked at the President and sighed. He said, "Allah is merciful. Our President is safe; what a national tragedy." "Those who want to kill me should've considered that innocent lives matters. It is a shame this happened." Andy said. Vice President kept quiet, listening. "The entire security chiefs must be summoned immediately. The situation must be nipped in the bud." The senate President said. "I am going to personally talk to the Inspector general of police. This is a very big dent on the Country's good image." The vice President said; his face hard. "Our Foreign friends might see us in a bad light. Not good news at all but a smear on a good clean spot." The President threw his hands up in exasperation. The Senate President said, "Gentlemen, right now I am troubled in my spirit; please I need time alone." All other men stood and shook hands with the President, some promised to check back on him. In the other part of the villa, the First Lady, Mrs. Victoria Ubih was on phone with someone in her well-furnished living room in another section of the Presidential Living quarter. "My sister, God saved my husband; enemies want him dead." She said as she lowers trim five-eight frames to the sofa. In the living room, the vice President and all the other men headed out the exit door and left the President to have time alone.

CHAPTER FOUR

A WEEK LATER, in the Presidential villa; the President of the Federal Republic of Nigeria, Andy Ubih, and all the security chiefs, including the minister of defense, Senate President, and Secretary to the Federal Republic of Nigeria in a security meeting. Time was ten on a Thursday morning. Andy wore an IsiAgu over a black trouser, no cap, and the security chiefs were in their uniforms. Andy looked at them and cleared his throat. "Welcome everyone; I called this meeting to discuss the recent bomb incidence and attempts on my life, and to find ways the government can improve security of lives and properties of this Country. This government is ready to do its best to better the security of this Nation. What are your suggestions on how best to improve our security outfits?" The police chief cleared his throat and spoke. His name was IGP Ahmadu Sanda. "Your Excellency sir, the bomb incident a week ago in your party's campaign ground really drained me emotionally. It was heinous and damaging. I promise to do my best to fish out the perpetrators of that wicked act. All my men are briefed and instructed to begin the search for the bad elements that did that." President nodded and continued to listen as the minister of defense began to speak. His name was David Clark. David cleared his throat and looked at the President. "Mr. President, I promise that all our security apparatus will work assiduously until the perpetrators are apprehended. I will have a separate meeting with our entire security chiefs" he said. The SSS chief Illiasu Daama adjusted his babariga on his shoulder and said, "Mr. President, sir, the bomb explosion on the campaign ground served as a wake-up call to us to tighten up any loose ends and I promise that I and my men will do our best to keep the Country secure." "We all know that this government has done well in different areas including the security of the Country. All our security apparatus will be thrown in to keep the Country safe." The Senate President said. The president nodded and closed his eyes in silence, waiting for another reassurance. A brief silence and the President spoke. "I thank you all for the work you have been doing and your promises to do more. We all know that the security of the people and Nation is paramount to this government. I urge you all to do all in your capacity to keep the Country safe. The pocket of gunfire between two ethnic groups in the Northern region must never be allowed to repeat. The terrorists disturbing the peace of our dear country must be located and stopped. All regions must be safe for every Nigerian to live in". Silence everywhere in the room, then the minister of defense cleared his throat and spoke. "Thank you, Mr. President, sir, for believing in us to deliver. On behalf of all security chiefs, I promise that we will keep the Country safer." "Thank you. I must say today marks another phase of our quest to keep Nigeria safe. Welcome, thank you, and goodbye." The President rose and shook hands with the men, and they began to file out of the office. The smile on the President's face was an indication that the meeting went well.

ONE WEEK LATER, Aliu Issa and Williams stood talking beside a parked red Toyota Venza. Time was ten on a Monday morning. "Oga called me last night; he instructs that we lay low for a while to re-strategize." "I agree with him; tension will cool down and attention will be diverted to other things," Williams said. "Oga got other plans in mind; something bigger," Aliu said. "Anything that must be done to remove the Prez must be done. Once he is deleted, our Oga would become the President." Williams said and his face hard. Aliu nodded in agreement and said. "His death would also open many opportunities for us." "I trust Oga would do all it takes to delete the Prez. I am ready to do anything demanded of me as long as we get rewarded generously." Williams said with a soft smile on his face. "From my understanding, Oga is looking at a bigger picture. There might be international involvement." Aliu said in confidence. "Oh, that sounds good. The coveted seat is worth all the trouble." "Yea, we all shall laugh last when the target is removed. The inner caucus is discussing with some kingmakers to make it happen once the target is deleted. The kingmakers would be used to block the Prez's region from appointing another person to step in to complete the tenure." Aliu said. "Sure, constitutionally Oga is rightfully empowered to ascend the throne," Williams said. "Let's wait and see what plan Oga would come up with. He is very keen to reach his set target." Aliu said and cracked his knuckles. "Our region is very much in support of his plan to remove the Prez. It would be a welcome development." Aliu added and watched Williams. "I can't wait for it to happen." Williams threw in. He put his hand forward and Aliu grabbed it. "I need to run; I have to see the director of operations before he travels," Williams said, standing up from his chair. They shook hands violently, each looking very enthused.

Williams waved as he ambled to his car parked at a corner and Aliu yanked the back door of the red Venza open and slid into the back seat and the driver rolled the mechine off.

That same day, an hour later, Agent Mark walked into the police building and two pairs of eyes looked at him and one pair looked down to the floor. He walked to the table of one of them and pleasantries were exchanged and he waved in greetings to the rest. The pair of eyes on the floor looked up and their owner, agent Lawal forced a smile and waved back. Mark headed to an office and immediately he closed the door, Lawal stood and walked out to a corner and cut his eyes to make sure no one was watching. He brought out his mobile and punched some digits from memory and put the mobile to his ear and waited for it to ring. It began to ring and on the second ring someone picked it up from the other end. Lawal said into the mouthpiece. "Listen, Anthony, Mark just entered our office. I want you to go to his house right now and find a way in. Wire his phone and quickly exit. Make sure no one sights you and no mistakes. He must be snooping around for info, and I know he knows. He is just playing low and watching." He listened briefly and added. "Alright, go now." He cuts call and returned to his seat and began to peck on a computer.

A few minutes later; Mark stepped out of the office and waved them bye and headed out. He suspects Lawal to be a player in the game. Lawal's body language and the little he has been able to find out. His instinct cannot be wrong about it. Lawal may be a smaller player in the big conspiracy to assassinate the President. He must dig until he comes up with good evidence. He understood how dangerous his digging and fishing are and he already knew he's been watched but prayed he would not be found out soon. All he knew was that the conspirators must be people of high connections and they won't waste time to delete him if they know he knows. The thought rattled in his mind as he headed to his car parked in a parking lot. He got to his car and opened the door, slid in and drove off. "There must be a way to unmask them." He said unconsciously as he drove to a connecting road.

Anthony went to his house as was directed by Lawal and with a lock pick he opened Mark's back door and sneaked in and fixed a transmitter in the mouthpiece and connected a magnetic device that would transmit to another transmitter hidden in the storage room and quietly closed the door and left. His calls would be listened to at a location somewhere in a temporary office in a hotel suite.

A few minutes later, at the Presidential villa, time was about one-twenty in the afternoon on a Monday. President Andy Ubih and the police chief, IGP Ahmadu Sanda sat, deep in talks in the west wing of the Presidential villa. A cup of apple juice sat on the table before the Police chief and Andy sipped from his orange juice and put the cup down on a small side stool in his front. He relaxed back to the sofa; his hands rested on the armrests. He wore a blue-white shirt over a pair of blue trousers. "Have the police made any brake in finding the people that carried out the bombings?" "We are yet to get any lead, your Excellency sir. About fifty of my men are on it, digging." "Any suspect?" "Sir, I am suspecting the opposition. I might be wrong, but we all know the opposition can do anything to tarnish your image and of this good government."

"I know the opposition hates me very much but look in other directions too. What if the person who masterminded it is in obscurity?" "We are not leaving any stone unturned, your Excellency, sir. You are right sir". "I want daily briefing and make sure you hand a daily report to the chief of staff." "Yes sir" Ahmadu responded, displeased about the task of coming to the state house daily to give a daily report but he managed to conceal his displeasure. He waved him to go and Ahmadu drained his apple juice and said bye to the President and headed to the door. The security aid at the door saluted as he approached and quickly threw open the door. Whether Ahmadu noticed the security aide or not he did not show it. He stepped out through the door, and it closed. The President lifted his orange juice and sipped a little and put it back on a small stool before him. He closed his eyes and rocked gently as his mind drifted into deep thought.

The evening of the same day, Mark drove home and parked his car and killed the engine and alighted. He walked to his door and unlocked it and stepped in, he cut his eyes to the street to see if anyone was watching. None, he shut his door and bolted it. He removed his shoes and unbuttoned his uniform and hung it in the wardrobe, leaving only a white singlet over his trouser. He sat on a single sofa and brought out his mobile, he dialed agent Joshua's number and wait for it to ring. It began to ring, and he waited. On the second ring, Joshua picked from the other end. "Hello Mark, how are you doing? I was planning to call you." "I am good J; when do you think you'd be visiting?" Then brief silence at the other end. "I am still up to my neck with deadlines, Mark. I will let you know as soon as I can; sorry for the delay." "Alright, buddy, not your fault." "Thanks, for your understanding, Mark. Talk to you later, the IG is waiting for me in his office." "Okay bye. Take care." Mark said and cut the call. He rose and went to his fridge and poured himself cold water from bottled water and went back to the sofa. He was hungry but lacked the zeal to enter the kitchen to cook a meal. He skipped dinner at a time like this when cooking became boring to him. He needs a woman in the house but wait, what was he thinking? He shook his head. His girlfriend works and she won't be home when he needs his dinner when they get married. Maybe I would later fix something to eat, he said in his mind. His phone started to ring. He got up and walked to it and lifted the receiver to his ears. "Hello" He said into mouthpiece without enthusiasm. His sister came on the line. "Hello Mark, how are you doing? Hope you're doing great?"

"Yes, sis, and how're you and your family doing?" "We're good over here. The kids are asking of you. I pray you to make out time someday and visit us in America." "Oh, honestly sis, I would love to, but my work won't allow me in the near possible time. Maybe if I can squeeze out two weeks leave by the end of the year." "Okay, that'd be better. We miss you a lot." "I miss you guys too. Please say my greetings to your kids." "I'll brother. Take care until we talk again." She cut call from her end and Mark replaced the receiver and went and lay down on the double sofa. The window was closed, and curtains were drawn, the only light in the living room was from a small blue bulb by a corner. He yarned and the hunger increased with vengeance. He had no other option than to get up and enter the kitchen to fix something to eat.

In the hotel suite about three streets away, a man in a suit removed a large earphone from his ear and smiled. Lawal and the other two men looked at him for an explanation. Some gadgets are on the table and the man in a suit without a tie, but a V-neck white shirt perched his ass on the edge of a table and looked at them. "He just received a call from his sister from the states. The transmission worked perfectly well." He turned and pressed a button and Mark's conversation with his sister began to replay. When it stopped, he punched another button the voices came crisp clear again. After two replays he punched a button and it stopped, he turned to them. "We will keep listening until something breaks. He must surely call, or someone may call him regarding the subject matter." He said assuredly. "We want to catch him pants down and we go from there." He's already on our watch list but we need evidence to delete him." Lawal said. "He's already marked like a Mark he is, he's not escaping us." The other man whose name was Yerima smiled. "Keep listening; we need to rub him off immediately after a link is established," Lawal said as he stood up. He put his hand forward to Yerima and he grabbed it and they shook hands, he did same with the man in a suit and headed out of the suite.

On an evening of a Saturday, Mark drove to a lounge somewhere along point road Apapa and eased his car into the parking lot and waited. The front door of the lounge opened and Anthony and another policeman in plain clothes stepped out. Mark watched them as they discuss and ambled towards a blue Toyota parked two cars away from him. Quickly Mark slid dark eyeglass to his face and slid lower in the driver's seat. The men stopped and the other man backed the blue Toyota as they talk. Anthony's voice dropped low almost to a whisper. "I don't know the real conspirators but the person I know is agent Lawal. He instructed me to put that bomb under the podium at the PPP campaign ground." "That was risky, Tony. What if you were caught?" the other asked. "I know it was risky; I needed the money they paid me to upset a bill," Anthony said. Mark listened attentively, his eyes low to the car floor and his ears open. "How much?" the man inquired. "A quarter of a million;'" Anthony said. "It was not worth it." The other man said. "I know but the deed is done, and I got my money." "And many people died," the other policeman said. "Yeah, I felt bad afterward," Anthony said. "Be careful; so that some powerful cabals won't use you to achieve their selfish end." The man turned and yanked the door open and leaned into the car and opened the compartment and removed a gun and pushed it into a holster on his waist. "I just got off duty and decided to come to have a few bottles of beer with you and talk. Let me run home to rest my nerves." "Thanks, for your concern. Please Victor let it be between us." "Ah, there are no qualms Tony. It's just a small secret between friends." They shook hands and Victor turned to the driver's side and slid in and roared the car to life and began to reverse. Anthony waved him bye and returned to the Lounge. Mark continued to wait in his car. He replayed their conversation in his head several times and decided that he was not going into the Lounge again. He started his car and drove away into the gathering night.

ONE WEEK LATER; at Victoria Island, along chevron road which connects to the Lekki axis. Peter in his car drove in the slow traffic. The time was eight pm. He followed the traffic and turned right off the road and pulled onto another road that links the admiralty way. His car, a wine-red jeep finally eased to a stop a few feet from a two-story block of offices. He threw the door open and alighted gingerly and closed it. He threw quick glanced, seeing no one he knows, he ambled vivaciously towards another car parked at the front, a few feet away. He got to the passenger's side door and the window began to wound down. He leaned in and the occupant of the car in the driver's seat was an elegant-looking lady of about thirty-five. She smiled as he flashed her a sweet mile. "Come into the car," she said. He obeyed and yanked the passenger door open and slid in. "Why do you want us to meet here?" Peter asked. "I won't be comfortable elsewhere except in my car, away from prying eyes. Don't know who might be watching or listening." She replied with a sweet smile. "Okay, what's the score?" He has lived in the states for some time and occasionally American English escapes him. "The first lady will be attending a fundraising dinner in two days. She is expected as a special guest, the governor's wife and other state governor's wives would be there." She said and smoothed her wig on her head. "Good. What time and venue?" Peter asked, looking at her apprehensively. "Six pm, Eko hotel and suites. But there's one other thing." "What?" Peter asked as he glanced out the window to see if anyone is watching. He returned his attention to her and waited. "She plans to be driven to the venue in a taxi. She specifically demanded that for security reasons and she plans to leave the venue unannounced." "Did you hear her discuss the bomb incident?" "Yea, she was discussing it with her childhood friend on phone. She's scared and I overheard her telling her friend that she didn't want to accept the fundraising dinner invitation, but the President encouraged her to go." "She instructed that her security aids would precede her to the venue and wait for her to arrive." Peter smiled. "Thank you, for the info. I will recommend you to Oga and inform him how helpful you have been." "Okay, I am promised an ambassadorial post and I hope he would keep to his promise." "Oga never forget his friends. They shall always be rewarded; he keeps to his words." "Let me take you by your words. I must be on the road back. I don't want to attract unnecessary suspicion." She roared the car to life and Peter smiled at her and she nodded to the door. He opened the car door and stepped out. She rolled the car away onto the connecting road and drove off into the young night.

Peter walked back to his car and entered and drove off. Many cars flew pass in the young night. He headed back to the road he came. A few minutes later, Peter's jeep eased to a stop a little meter away from SPICY MEALS. The restaurant was gradually filling up with customers.

Customers like to eat late in the restaurant. He sat at a table and waited for the waitress who already sighted him and began walking to his table. His eyes watched the entrance. He brought out his phone and beeped a number and waited. The waitress arrived to take his order. As she left to get his order, Peter looked at her bouncing heavy behind. He smiled at the heavy butts and looked away. Two men and two beautiful women at a table by the other end of the restaurant roared into laughter, Peter glanced at them and smiled to himself, and shook his head. Wine and women equal to a happy mood, he thought. A few minutes on, the front door opened, and a man entered and stood briefly and scanned the tables. He spotted Peter and walked to Peter's table and slid on an empty seat. Peter's order arrived and the man Ordered fish and beer. The man stared at the same set of big butts as the owner left to get his order. "Don't look too much" Peter said with a smile on his lips. The man known to Peter as Levi laughed smirked and smacked his lips. "She's very sumptuous and tempting." Peter shook his head and laughed a little in amusement. Immediately the service left, Peter spoke softly from the corner of his mouth as if he spoke to himself. "Listen" "I got few minutes to stay; so, be snappy?" Levi cut in. "The target is expected to attend fundraising dinner on Wednesday; time six pm. Levi nodded and continued to listen and watched peters mouth. "The subject is expected at the venue in a taxi and unescorted by security aides. The venue is Eko hotels and suites. She would leave unannounced." The man Peter knew as Levi, not his real name nodded again and quickly glanced about. "I would want the money to be wired to my numbered account before I lift a finger. Levi said. "The money shall be wired as agreed; just make sure the job is done as wanted." "I won't fail; I am a pro and, he stopped as he sighted the lady approaching with his order. Peter understood why he stopped talking and attacked the fish; and as the service put the order down on the table covered with red and blue checkered tablecloth and turned to leave. Levi glanced at her heavy buttocks as she headed to another table. He attacked his fish too and the men ate in silence. Levi looked at Peter, fish in his mouth. "You have nothing to worry about my performance. I won't fail unless the info is wrong." He said and continued to masticate the fish in his mouth. "All info is accurate; fresh from the right source," Peter said and quickly done eating the fish in a no long time. He grabbed the beer bottle by the neck and pulled a long drink. On three takes he drained the bottle and put down five crisp thousand naira notes on the table. "I should be on my way. Send a coded message if you need me to talk." "Okay. It may not be necessary unless there's a change in plan." Peter nodded and headed to the door. People were busy with their fish and beer, so no one noticed him exit the door. Levi devoured his fish and took a long drink of beer and put the bottle on the table. He wore a brown blazer over dark jean trousers. His eyes were covered with aviator sunglasses; his hair looked dark and trimmed low. His jaw was clean-shaven. New brown puma footwear covered his feet; he was trim and athletic, no fat, about five-eight. He looked young and strong, mid-thirties. He took another long pull and the beer reduced close to the bottom. He belched and drained the rest and put the bottle on the table. He beckoned to the waiter, and she walked to his table. He pointed to the money on the table, she picked them and flashed a sweet smile at him and turned to go. He smiled at her bouncing heavy behind and stood. He pushed back his chair and headed to the exit door.

TWO DAYS LATER, the First Lady, Mrs. Victoria, and her Friend, Ruth, were inside Ruth's air-conditioned car, deep in a tete- a- tete. The windows were rolled up to avoid their words been heard by wrong ears. Ruth sat behind wheels while the first lady sat in the front seat. The air conditioner purred on low and the car idled away. "My friend, how can you ever think of going to a function with a cab? When there're cars and drivers at your beck and call? Ruth asked looking at her friend in surprise. "I'm just being cautious. All these attempts to kill my husband scare me." Why not send someone to represent you if you are scared." Ruth suggested. "No, my presence is needed to raise enough funds." "I won't allow you to go in the cab. I will drive you to the venue." Her hand rose in protest. "I think a cab will be better. No one will expect me to come to the venue in a cab." Vitoria said. "My friend, please that is even more dangerous. Please don't put yourself in a precarious situation. Please stop arguing; I would drive you to the venue. You would have to disguise yourself as well." "Okay, I surrender. I am just scared." Victoria said with a smile. "I suggest you send a taxi ahead of us; maybe your assistant can be in the taxi. She is equally beautiful. She can be used to distract anyone lurking around." Mrs. Victoria smiled. "I like this plan." Still smiling, she tapped Ruth on her lap. "Let me make the arrangement. I will be back in a Jiffy" Opening the car door. "Okay, I am here waiting." Victoria threw open the door and slid out, closed it, and hastened off to the entrance door of the building. She wore a beautiful red gown and her hair loose and swaying at her back of as she walked towards the entrance door to her living quarters. She was beautiful and tall, a graduate of economics from Yale University.

CHAPTER FIVE

A FEW MINUTES LATER, along Aqua bay Boulevard, Victoria Island, Lagos. A taxi drove towards Eko Hotels and Suites. Other cars in front slowed down almost to a crawl in the traffic as they approached Wahab Folawiyo link. A lady with great look and importance sat at the back seat of the taxi, gorgeously dressed. The taxi was clean and new. Her eyes were covered with gold-rimmed sunglasses and she wore a long blue dress with gold embroidery. She was talking to someone on her mobile.

Ruth and the President's wife drove some good distance apart towards Victoria Island. Down the road, Levi appeared from a corner and stood by the road. His head was covered in a hood. Even in the heat of the evening. He stood and watched the taxi approaching in the slow-moving traffic. This must be her taxi coming, he suggested to himself. The description of the car brand and color design matched. He quickly slid a dark eyeglass unto his face and pulled up a stick in his hand, stretching it out longer into a walking stick. A black porch was in the left hand. He choose this spot because he knew the traffic was always slow here since the traffic lights are a few meters away. As the taxi started to approach, he began to hit the stick on the ground and began to try to find his way to cross the road. The taxi got nearer; he made to walk blindly across the road before the taxi, hitting the walking stick frantically on the ground. In the process, that forced the driver of the taxi to apply the brake in a bid to avoid knocking him down with the car. The driver of the taxi looked out through the door window and yelled at Levi as he deliberately stumbled and fell.

"What is the matter with you? Do you want to die Abi? Go tell them you no see me!!!." the taxi driver yelled at him in Pigin English. Levi slowly rose with difficulty from the ground, hands first. His walk stick lay a little foot away. He picked up his stick and propelled himself up from the ground and made his way to the front passenger's side of the taxi. The traffic started to move but Levi has already opened the driver's door and slid in. "You want to kill me with your beautiful car eeh? Oh, poor people like us shouldn't cross the road anymore. Abi?" "Get out of my car. If you want to commit suicide; go to another car. Get out!" he yelled, pushing Levi by the shoulder. The beautiful lady at the back of the taxi then spoke. She had been watching in silence since the taxi nearly hit Levi. "Gentleman; what's your problem? You know you were at fault. Just thank your God the car didn't hit you. Please get out of the car." Levi turned and looked at her and looked away. Car drivers at the back honked their horns in desperation, some blared their horns loudly from the distant back. The driver threw his door open in anger and turned to the front passenger's door. In great rage he yanked open the front door and trying to drag out Levi from the taxi. Levi grabbed the side of the seat refusing to be forced out. Some drivers of other cars behind threw their car doors open and began to approach in anger to ascertain the problem with the taxi. They yelled to the taxi driver to move his taxi. "Get out of this car or I call the police on you." The beautiful lady at the back of the taxi threatened. Her name was Mirabel. A traffic officer watched and began to walk to the taxi. Levi gently opened the door and dropped the leather pouch on the floor of the taxi, near his feet and rolled out of the front seat and slammed the door hard. He grabbed his walk stick and began to find his way, away from the scene. He began hit the stick on the ground as he headed across the road. The driver went and entered his cab and started it, and as he tried to drive off; the light turned red. He cursed under his breath. Levi in controlled haste crossed the road to the far side. This time the walk stick no longer hit the ground. A few seconds later; the traffic light turned green, and the traffic began to move. Levi quickly got into a waiting car which the engine was already running and the driver drove off that instant. A few minutes down the road, suddenly an explosion rocked throwing the taxi violently upside down. Other cars at the back applied brakes in desperation, to avoid been hit by the carnage, but a few cars that were close to the taxi got hit in the car blast. A white BMW car was tore almost apart and was thrown on its side. The occupants in the BMW car yelled out in terror

Pieces of shattered glasses scattered about and a woman in back of a car got injured. Another female passenger in another car got pierced by sharp objects in her throat and blood- stain covered the front upper part of her dress. Her head slumped sideway to the car door. Few cars caught fire as another explosion rocked again, and people scampered away in different directions. The taxi kept burning and the smell of burning skin filled the air. The taxi burned unabated until the fire began to simmer down. Sympathizers rushed to the taxi but the charred remains of the driver and the Lady at the back of the cab greeted their eyes. Mirabel and the taxi driver got burnt beyond recognition. A foot and an arm lay on the macadamized Road. Some people gathered to help the other passengers of other cars that got hit. From the other side of the road, a siren wailed and died down as two Police cars arrived at the scene. The road became inaccessible as cars jammed up along the road. Three cars were badly affected and four people were dead and many injured.

Somewhere along a road towards Eko Hotels and Suits, the President's wife and Ruth drove in Ruth's car, Ruth behind wheels, discussing and laughing happily as they slowed in the traffic building up ahead, oblivious of the car blast that happened some meters ahead of them.

Agent Mark watched the breaking news from his Led TV in his living room. He watched intently as the gory pictures played on the screen. The carnage displayed on the screen was disturbing, another bomb attack. What is the Country turning into? He asked himself. He got up from the sofa and switched off the Television and walked into his room and threw a T-shirt over his singlet and headed to the door. He walked to his car parked at a corner and drove off. A few minutes on, he pulled to a stop in front of a one-story house. He threw the door open and stepped out and walked to the front door. He rang the bell and waited. After a few seconds of waiting, the door opened inward, and a fair-skinned woman stood between at the door. "Good evening, sir." She greeted. "Good evening, is he in?" "Yes sir." She answered and stepped aside to allow him to passr. Mark stepped in and took the stairs in twos to the first floor and walked into a spacious richly furnished living room. A man sat on a double sofa, a cup of wine in his hand. The man smiled at him and welcomed him. They shook hands and the man waved him to a seat. A glass of the same wine was brought to him by the same woman, and she left them alone to talk in private. Mark sipped a little wine and the man looked at him and asked. "What's happening at your end, Mark?" Mark sighed deeply and looked at him. "How I wish I can answer that question properly. All I know is I suspect a big conspiracy to assassinate the President." The man stared in astonishment. He says "Assassinate the President?" "That's big. Any suspect?" Mark shook his head. "Not yet" he answered. The man hails from same town as Mark and the same kinsman as the President. He was rich and a very successful businessman. He would do anything to help his people. "I have something I came to discuss with you, Daniel." Daniel swallowed his wine and looked at Mark. "I am all ears, Mark." Mark crossed his leg. "I suspect a conspiracy by people in high positions to assassinate Andy and they are desperate to kill him quickly. The reason for those bomb blasts and gun attacks" "How do you mean? Daniel asked, looking at Mark. "I am still investigating but I have an inkling the conspirators may be of Northern blood." "If you suspect so, I think it's pertinent to alert the President." "No not yet. I don't have concrete evidence to present." "Then what do you plan to do?" Daniel asked in concern, his glass of wine abandoned. "One of the reasons I came. I have a police agent friend working at the Headquarters. I intend to seek his help. He's the one closer to one of my suspects, but he might need more than convincing." "Try all you can to bring him in to help. I shall pay him enough to work for us." Mark smiled a little. He knew Daniel would proffer to help financially. He adores the President and would do all in his power to protect him from his enemies. "Thank you, Daniel. I was hoping for that. It would be easier to make my friend work for us if he's paid. "I will pay him, just bring him in," Daniel said and lifted his cup of wine and drained it. "Thank you for agreeing to help. This won't be an easy job, but I am ready to put my life on the line in the cause of fishing out the conspirators." "And I am ready to bring out any amount it requires to fight the enemies," Daniel assured. Mark thanked him and they began to talk about other things. From a door the woman and the man's sister emerged from an inner room. The men changed topic and Daniel watched the women approach. "Are you ready to go shopping?" He asked. They nodded.

That same evening at the Presidential villa, time was eight-thirty. The wife of the President sat on the sofa, her hand held her husband's own tightly. She leaned on his left shoulder and sighed. "Darling, I am much shaken. The people that want to assassinate you are after me too. My God! If not for God; I would've been very dead now." "They want to hurt me by all means. They want you dead; just to kill the inner me." "Oh my God; so, Mirabel is dead." She began to sob softly. A large Led TV was on at the opposite wall. The volume was turned low and the news of the car bomb incident came on. Victoria sat straight that instant and watched intently as the news reporter warmed that the pictures that was about to be shown were disturbing. The clips were from on-the-scene reporting. The female reporter who reports from the scene of the bomb explosion stood some distance, away from the charred remains of the cars. Gory pictures of the dead and burning cars created an ugly picture. The President and his wife listened with attention to the news. The reporter said that from information gathered, the wife of the Federal Republic of Nigeria was the female occupant in the taxi involved in the car blast. Victoria hugged her husband and sobbed the more. Her husband did not try to stop her. His face registered sadness. He let her sob for a while and began to pet her. Seconds later, she quieted down, her hand wrapped around him. Andy looked at his wife and shook his head. What would've become of his joy if the enemies had succeeded in killing his beautiful loving wife? They've been through a lot together and she means the whole world to him, his joy and it was obvious the enemies knew how much he loves her, maybe the reason they attempted to kill her, but God in his infinite mercy saved her life. Thank you, my dear Lord. He said in his mind. Victoria sat straight and kissed her husband on the lips. "No one is going to separate us. God knows how much we love each other; he won't let the enemies succeed." She said with tears building in her eyes. "I am most grateful to God for sparing your life. I'd have been very devastated." He pecked her on the forehead and pulled her to him, his heart beating rapidly in his chest.

In his house, Mark sat watching the news on the screen. He felt disturbed by the gory pictures displayed on the screen. He picked the remote and killed the volume. He relaxed back to the sofa and crossed his leg back on the sofa, his mind raced in thought. The conspirators are now after my wife too. He mumbled to himself. They are desperate and ruthless. If the President dies, someone very close to the President may benefit or who knows; maybe someone in obscurity is fanning this amber of destruction. He thought. Suddenly his landline began to ring. He looked at it and gently rose and walked to it. He picked the receiver and placed it to his ear. Daniel came on from the other end. "Hello Mark, the news I just watched is disturbing." From outside a loud disturbing knock sounded at the door. Mark looked at the door and it came again, very rudely and persistent. He excused Daniel and put the receiver down to find out who was knocking at his door in such rude mannerism. In a hotel suite where the man in the suit was listening with a large earphone, he smiled at Yerima and removed the large earphone from his ear and Yerima looked at him for a comment. "Someone interrupted him. He promised to call the caller back." The man in the suit said.

Mark angrily walked to his front door and unbolted it and yanked it open. A young girl of about twelve years stood at the door. She was his neighbor's daughter and not known for such rudeness. "Anna, why are you knocking at my door like that?" Anna was taken aback by the sudden anger in his voice. She mustered courage and spoke. "Sir, my mother asks me to tell you that a man just sneaked out of your car." "My car; a man sneaked out of my car?" Anna nodded with vigor and Mark in quick move stepped out of his house and followed her down a corridor where Anna's mother was waiting. Immediately she saw Mark she stepped close. "Sir I sent my daughter to call you. I was out to pick something from the balcony when I noticed a man sneak out of your car. "But I locked my car doors." Mark protested. "I couldn't see his face; he was quick and all I noticed was he was in a dark long suit." "Thank you, madam, let me check my car." He smiled at Anna's mother and headed to the stairs. When he got to his car he grabbed the door handle and pulled. It opened without any event. He stepped into his car and began to check if the intruder stole anything. Nothing is missing, satisfied that nothing was removed from his car; he stepped out and closed the door, and relocked it. He walked back to his room and shut the door and walked to a sofa and sat. What did the man want in his car? He asked himself. He continued to wonder until his mobile began to ring again. He picked up his mobile from the table and Joshua is on the line. "Greetings Mark, listen I am speaking to you from a tight space, I called to warm you to be careful. Your car might be bugged." "Bugged? Mark asked in astonishment. "Yea, watch what you say in your car. I overheard your name be mentioned several times." Some people are watching and listening. And I advise you to watch what you say on your landline. It might be bugged too. I got to go, talk to you later. He cut the call quickly and Mark stared at his mobile. Instantly he remembered Daniel and punched his number on his mobile and put it to his ear and waited for it to ring. On the fourth ring Daniel picked from the other end. "Hey, Mark I had to replace the receiver on the cradle… "Yea yea" Mark cut in. "sorry about that. I had to attend to someone at my door. Please listen, Dan, don't call me on my landline until all this debris is cleared. I will explain later." "Okay, I think it would be better if we discuss it when we meet," Daniel said. "Good. Good night: we shall talk about it." Mark said. "Stay safe bro and good night," Daniel said and cut the call from the other end. Mark put the mobile down and walked into his bedroom.

Mark looked just like any other ordinary police agent. He had won medals in Police College, but his superiors saw him as not smart enough, and one day one of them was bold enough to tell him to his face. Mark felt bad but since he was not to challenge a superior, he swallowed hard and took it in good faith. There were some of his colleagues who think him smart and a good officer. Regardless of his superior's opinion of him, he knew he was well respected among his ranks. Though he was seen as an ordinary Joe by some other police agents but that did not faze him. You cannot be loved by everybody. He believed he got what it takes to fish in murky waters if it gets to that. He had been a tough kid growing up, with good street sense, smart amongst his peers. He knows his onions and can stare at trouble with a poker face. A few minutes on, he emerged from his room and sat on a single sofa, a cup of steaming coco in his hand.

He put down the steaming Coco on a table and went to the window and parted the curtain and peered into the night. He felt restless after the call from Joshua. Who wants to kill Andy? Who tapped his phone? These questions rattled in his mind, begging for an answer. It downed on Mark that the conspirators know he knows and if not what other reason does someone has to bug his phone and car? He asked himself. He went back to the sofa and lay quietly, thinking. The steaming cup of coco was forgotten for a while. "The police chief is not serious to investigate the bomb incident".

He mumbled to himself. "Something is going on, a cover-up". "A plot to eliminate the Prez" and I suspect the Police chief is helping someone". Mark kept muttering to himself. From the attempted gun attack on the President to the car bomb incident no arrest has been made. The police chief threw some officers to head the investigation teams; all officers knew the game that is played. The Police chief instructed them to look in the other direction. In pretense that he is working tirelessly in other to arrest the perpetrators. Mark definitely smelled dirt, an organized crime against the number one family of the Federal Republic of Nigeria. He must find a way to reach the President, he reasoned. But wait, he has no concrete proof yet against anyone. What would he tell the President and who would he say are the conspirators? He killed the idea of finding a way to talk to the President. He resolved to continue digging until he can gather enough evidence. He advised himself to be cautious; those that bugged his phone and car might also want him dead. Since they know he knows; the evil people behind this heinous crime can try to delete him too. He decided to watch his back, watch where he goes, and trust no one. Yea to survive in the jungle, especially in heated political terrain like Nigeria you got to trust no one. To survive the Country's security wolves and foxes he must watch every player on the field. He decided in his mind. He suddenly remembered the hot coco on the table, and he sat straight on the sofa and grabbed the handle of the mug and sipped some little and held it in his hands. His thought raced from one incident to the other. Silence crept in as the night got old, only the occasional sound of passing cars came from the street. Night lifers headed to various destinations to have their fun. Mark sipped more coco and then drained the cup and headed to his bedroom. The time was about ten-thirty in the night and then from the open window wind began to lift the curtain and he peered out through a slightly open window and noticed that the sky has turned to a dark shade of grey and the stars has disappeared and the sky began to get cloudy. Mark's spirit lifted. He loves the splatter of rain on the roof when it rains.

Somewhere in the city, Peter and Lalong sat on burgundy sofas, in deep discussion. It was Peter's hotel suites which he rented to stay for a couple of days. They wore only singlet over trousers and a bottle of red wine, and two cups of half-filled wine glasses were on the table. Peter lifted his glass and sipped slowly. They were happy. He placed back the wine glass to the table and smiled widely at Lalong. "By now it's mourning and crying in the Presidential villa," Peter said with a happy smile. "It was a brilliant idea to hurt the President this way. He had refused to be caught in the web; let me see how he's going to handle this." Lalong said smiling too. "Please lower your voice, people have started to come in for late drinks." Peter cautioned. The wine has loosened Lalong's tongue. Lalong nodded in agreement. They were tipsy and the wine has started its work, their tongues loosened slightly. "You know the Prez loves his wife; her death would devastate him," Peter said. "Whose idea, was it?" Lalong asked. "It was Oga's idea; of course." Peter chipped in. "Incredible! Oga is a genius, a master planner." His voice rose to the ceiling again. Peter shushes him and signals him to quiet down. Lalong obeyed and smiled. "No. Let's say he is the evil genius with a dogged determination to achieve his aim." They roared to hearty laughter, Peter's voice rose higher even above Lalong's. Lalong poured them more wine and lifted his glass to the mid-air. Peter did the same and they clicked glasses in cheers and Lalong drank his own in one take. The rain began to pour down in torrents, deafening their loud voices. "Oga is very cunning and smart too. He understands how to wrench power from a stubborn opponent." Lalong said and rubbed his face in a bid to rub off the wine-induced fog gathering in his eyes. "I can't wait to hear what the Prez would say," Peter said with a sheepish smile. "What do you expect he would say? He would mourn his wife forever; Mr. Lover boy." They both roared into long wine-aided laughter. They stopped laughing and Peter lifted his glass and took a long drink and put the cup down. "He won't know what hits him. He is up against a dangerous team." Peter said. "Oga has the entire security chiefs on his side. All of them want the Prez removed." "The Prez believes the police and SSS are serious with the investigation," Peter said. "Please buddy, any arrangement for young girls that will keep us company this night," Lalong said, changing the discussion. "I did not arrange for girls. If you want a girl, why not go down to the lobby; you might grab one." Peter suggested. "I thought you made a prior arrangement," Lalong said in disappointment. He sulked for a few minutes and grabbed the bottle of wine and poured some for himself. He gulped it down and began to whistle happily. Suddenly he stopped whistling and turned to Peter. "The most important thing is deleting the Prez. That's a priority." Suddenly thunder clapped and lightning flashed and shattered the darkness, and it began to rain heavily. The rain poured down in torrents and created almost a deafening sound on the roofs of houses it forced people to retire into their houses and those caught out outside scurried and hid under makeshift shelters and front of houses. Vehicular movements slowed as drivers parked to avoid their cars falling into a ditch.

That moment as it continued to rain heavily, a violent wind blew across; forcing the trees to begin to gyrate to the natural force of its unheard music. That moment, a man in dark jacket sneaked up to Sergeant Anthony's door and stopped. He removed a set of lock picks and quickly began to work on the key. He continued for a couple of minutes and stopped. He cut his eyes about; no one was watching, and no one was expected. It was planned that way; to strike in the rain and quickly disappear. The man grabbed the door handle and turned it. The door opened inward with a little creak. The downpour helped to cover the little noise from the old door that led into Sergeant Anthony's living room. The man in the black jacket sneaked in and gently flipped on a small torch which its light was like a dying candle. He stood and listened for little seconds. He could hear heavy snoring coming from what may be the bedroom. Anthony was not married, and no one was expected to be with him at that moment. He had been followed since early evening from a bar and no woman with him. The man entered the bedroom and pointed the dying orange light at the bed where Anthony lay sprawled on his back; the bed sheet was almost kicked to the floor and Peter continued to snore oblivious of the danger before him. The man quietly removed a nylon rope and drew close to the bed. He quietly put the rope under Anthony's neck and began to tie it in a knot. Anthony stopped snoring and his eyes flared open in terror and pain. The man inserted a short iron in the little hole of the rope and began to tighten the rope. Anthony kicked in desperation, the rope got tighter. He gasped for breath but the hand tightened harder. Anthony managed to look at the attacker, but he was only able only to see a large dark blurred figure. His breathing began to slow, and his life began to ooze out from him. The rope cut an artery and blood began to drip on the sheet. Anthony's grip on the gloved hand of the assailant dropped beside him and he made a weak effort for survival, to fight the assailant off but finally, he stopped struggling and lay still, dead. The man in the dark jacket stood over his body briefly to be sure Anthony has begun his journey to the dark slippery land of the dead. Satisfied he then moved, and in a few seconds, he left the scene and disappeared into the rainy night.

CHAPTER SIX

THE MORNING OF NEXT DAY, Mark dressed for work, opened his apartment door and stepped out. He locked the door and began to descend the stairs. He looked clean and smart in his uniform; his shoes were polished to a shining black. He reached the landing of the staircase and headed out to the street. A white car drove by in top speed nearly knocking down a commercial bike rider. The bike rider yelled obscenity at the driver. Mark flagged down a taxi and it pulled off the road and stopped a foot away from him. He leaned in and told the driver his destination. The driver nodded and Mark grabbed the back passenger door handle and yanked it open and lowered himself into the back seat, the taxi rolled off. He decided not to use his car for the time being.

A few minutes on, he arrived at the office and exchanged pleasantries with his colleagues and entered the office. As he was about to sit down and tried to switch on the computer on the table, a knock sounded at the door. He looked at the door and asked the person at the door to come in. The door opened and one of his colleagues, inspector Timothy entered and closed the door behind him. Mark stared at him. Inspector made a quick salute and stood. "Sir we just received a bad news a few minutes ago," Timothy said. "Bad news; what happened?" Mark asked in apprehension. "Sir, Sergeant Anthony was killed in his sleep last night?" "Anthony?" Mark asked in surprise. "Yes sir, Nat went to his house this morning after waiting for him at a place he was to report for surveillance; but when he did not show up, Nat called his line but no response. In curiosity, he went to his house and found the door open, and he decided to look in. He found him garroted in his bed." "He was garroted?" Mark asked as he rose from his chair. Timothy nodded. "Has our men combed the place for evidence?" Mark asked. "I went with some of our men to gather evidence and try to find any witness; a nylon rope was found round his neck and blood stains on the sheet, his larynx cut. It must be his blood. The killer left nothing. No hair fiber, nothing to link him. No need for an autopsy, it was a clear case of strangulation. His larynx was cut with the nylon rope. It was a professional job." Mark's mind began to race. They have silenced Anthony to make sure he won't live to tell. Maybe he's next on the hit list. I must be careful, he said to himself in his mind. The idiots are covering their tracks, he said in his mind. "His body has been deposited in the morgue and soon we will have the coroner's report, though the course of dead was evident," Timothy said. "Good job, Timo," Mark said to him and sat down. "We must find his killer." He said to Timothy. "Yes sir, we shall do all it takes to fish him out," Timothy assured. "Give me a few minutes; I will join you later." Timothy saluted and left, closing the door behind him. Mark began to think.

Later in the afternoon, Mark stood near a car parked along John Ade Street; he cut his eyes about and brought out his mobile and punched some digits from memory and put it to his ears and waited for it to ring. Someone picked from the other end and Mark spoke briefly into the mouthpiece. "I am at the place now." He cut call and went to sit on a bench in front of a prevision shop. A heavy-set woman stood inside watching him as he approached. Mark pointed at a long bench by the door of the provision shop. "Hello ma'am." Mark greeted her. The large woman only nodded. "Please may i?" I am waiting for somebody." "Okay" The woman only said and turned her attention to other things. After a few minutes of wait, a black Range Rover Sport drove off the Street and entered a free space and pulled to a stop a little distance from shop. Mark stood up and thanked the owner of the shop and walked to the Range Rover. He opened the front passenger's door and entered. The door closed. He turned to Daniel behind wheels. Pleasantries exchanged and Daniel said to Mark, "Why are we meeting here; why not my office or my house?" "Sorry I had to do it this way. I don't want anyone to eavesdrop on us. Walls have ears they say." Mark said. "What is so urgent we can't discuss in my secluded office? What's going on?" "One of my suspects was garroted last night in his home. He was paid to plant the bomb at the PPP campaign venue." "What?" Daniel said in shock. "I overheard the man confessing to his friend a few days ago. He was paid a quarter of a million." Just that little amount for the life of a President and many others." Daniel asked in astonishment. "The main thing is the conspirators are desperate to cover tracks. A few days ago; that same friend I intend to bring in called to warn me to watch my back. That my name has been mentioned on some few occasions, and that my phone and my car are bugged." "You don't say, my brother. They are watching you too?" "Yes, I believe my name is on the hit list." "What do you plan to do?" Daniel asked, looking worried. "I am cautious and watchful. Don't call my landline; you have to only call my mobile. I won't be using my car until things are sorted out and the nefarious people are apprehended." Daniel nodded. "Andy's wife is believed to be a victim that died in the car blast," Daniel said. "Yes, that's the general belief, but she's safe and I learned from a source that she's hidden away from the public," Mark said. "Are the police not investigating these crimes?" Daniel asked. The windows of the Range Rover were up. Mark looked out to the road and watched cars fly pass and pedestrians going to and from the sidewalk. "Bro from my source; the police are not investigating. The police chief threw in a few officers from his region to flash badges and pretend to investigate. There is a big game play going on; a deliberate move and cover-up." Mark said. "They might be working for someone," Daniel said. "I will put it this way; they may be taking orders from some powerful people to carry out a deliberate wild goose chase, by looking in the wrong places." "The people that want to kill the President might be in alliance with the police chief," Daniel said. "Yes, but more than that; the SSS is involved too in the conspiracy. I am afraid for the President and his family." "When is your friend coming; we need to do something as soon as possible," Daniel said.

In the Presidential villa, the president's beautiful wife, Victoria, entered the back seat of a blue Toyota Camry. The car drove off and headed towards the Presidential Chopper a few distances away. No other car followed. The driver has been warned to keep it to himself. Since the rumor of her death has spread across the nations. Phone calls and visits from political friends and enemies. The President decided that his wife should leave the Country to hide her from the public and those after their lives. The news of her supposed death was in all dailies, front page. Televisions, both local and international, like CNN, ALJAZEERA, FOX; BBC relayed the gory pictures of the car bomb scene, the charred bodies, and people believed the first Lady was in the taxi when the car bomb explosion occurred.

A few minutes drives, the Blue Camry pulled to a stop a few feet from the chopper. The President's wife alighted from the car and headed to the Chopper that was on and waiting; the rotor rolled rapidly in the air, and dust and dried leaves rose in the air and scattered about. The driver of the car drove off and headed back the way he came. Only him amongst the drivers knew of the travel and no other staff was let into the plan. It was the President and his wife's decision for her to leave the Country immediately. Those who want them dead might try again. Andy thought it pertinent to send his wife away to a safe place where she can stay with their children. It would be better to face the battle alone without the encumbrance of having to protect his family.

Immediately she climbed into the Chopper; the engine changed sound as it began to ascend up the sky, raising more dust and dry leaves into the air, and in seconds, it lifted into the sky and flew towards the Benin Republic where she will board a plane to Canada; where she would stay with their children until things die down and reality sets in, that she was not the woman involved in the car bomb incident. Her worry was for her husband who vowed to stay and defeat his enemies. She was ready to support him to relinquish power and stay safe to enjoy their lives. Politics comes with Baggage and only those willing to play the dirty game can withstand the heat of the game. Nigeria has witnessed low and high moments in her political scene. There had been times of political quagmire and civil war, near disintegration, and as long as there are suspicions among the people; one region or the other must continue to feel cheated and sidelined. There had been accusations of nepotism, sectionalism, and favoritism against the past President from the Northern region of the Country. Now some people want a power shift back to the North

THE NEXT DAY, on the morning of Friday; time was nine in the morning. President Andy Ubih and some government officials, some ministers, some party chiefs, Senate President, and the deputy speaker were in the Presidential villa. The visitors did the talking, paying their condolences to the First citizen while he kept quiet, no response but listened and watched. Occasionally he nodded his head. He lifted the 8x10 picture frame of his fair skin, tall, elegant wife beside him on the sofa and fixed his gaze to it. Dramatically he squeezed tears from his eyes, and they dripped down his cheeks. The men in the room suddenly surged towards his sofa, all trying to pacify him. "Don't cry, your Excellency! God knows why it happened." The Senate President said soothingly. "Hold your peace, your Excellency sir." The deputy speaker, Adamu said. "This is a national tragedy. May God give the Nation the fortitude to bear this loss?"

Minister of foreign affairs said. The President lifted his head and peered at him from under his reading glasses. The Senate President collected the picture frame from Andy and placed it back right beside the right side of the President, besides the sofa. The door opened and the Vice President came in almost bursting into the room, panting like he practically ran to the place. He exchanged quick pleasantries with the other men and went to the President and sat close to him. He lifted Andy's hand and held it in solidarity. "This is shocking news and a tragedy to the nation. I still can't believe it. The demise of your wife is a very big blow to us all. He threw a glance to the other men for support. Some nodded while some watched, their faces registered melancholy. President Andy's eyes watered dramatically and he spoke. "Gentlemen, thank you for your care and words of encouragement. I am not in the right frame of mind to speak more. I am devastated. Thanks for coming." He gently hoisted himself up from the sofa and headed into the inner chamber. All the men stood up to go, they understood his pain and how he felt. The door opened and they filed out, each got their cars and slide into the back seat and their drivers rolled off.

IN ALIU ISSA'S OFFICE, at Abuja; Aliu and Williams were deep in discussion. The morning was still very young, and the time was about 9 am. The Abuja office was not too important, but the gang used many outlets like the Abuja office, temporary offices where many players on the team work assiduously towards landing one appointment or the other when the Oga finally ascend the coveted seat. Aliu has been overseen the running of the Abuja office. He shifted his small frame on the leather office chair. "Oga called me a couple of hours ago; he instructs that everyone should lie low till after the election," Aliu said. "Why? But the Prez might be re-elected and that means we'd lose this fight." Williams countered. "Oga said he has a bigger plan to hit the Prez hard and dangerously," Aliu said. "I don't know what his plans might be, but my opinion is that, this is the right time to remove the Prez." "You know Oga is a good planner; if he says we wait then we wait. He knows what he's doing." Aliu said. "Delay is dangerous. I am not comfortable with this waiting." "Remember we can't do anything about it; Oga has the final say in this matter. After all, it's his game entirely. We are mere fiddle players in the game." Aliu reminded him. "If he says we wait we have no option but to wait. All I care about is getting what belongs to us." "Now you're talking. A little wait won't stop us from getting to the winning line." Aliu said with a smile. Williams joins him to smile too. Aliu stopped smiling. "Oga wants to hit him when he is already savoring the victory at the poll and relaxed to enjoy the new tenure," Aliu said. "Oga is crazy, I heard he said even if it's only a few months he stays as President of the Country that he would be satisfied," Williams said. "Forget that small talk Willy; Oga won't even leave after a second tenure. Power is sweeter than honey." A knock sounded at the door, and they stopped talking. Aliu asked the person at the door to come in. The door opened gently and Solomon and Lalong stepped in, Lalong closed the door behind him, and all walked to the table. Pleasantries were exchanged and they picked their seats. "Welcome gentlemen; we have been waiting." "Sorry we came late; our flight was delayed." "Thank God you arrived safely," Williams said. "Thanks," Lalong said. Aliu cleared his throat and looked at the men before him. "Hope you already got the message from Oga; that we should all lie low and wait till after the election?" "Yes, we did but I don't like the idea." I don't too" Williams chipped in. "There's nothing anyone of us can do about it. He's the boss, let's wait as he instructed." Aliu said. "Yea, he might have a bigger plan cooking in his head," Peter said. "Peter, Oga will send someone to us today for briefing; that was why I called this meeting. He preferred we meet here in Abuja instead of Lagos." "No problem; we're here now," Peter said, and the men changed their discussion to the President's family issue. "The Prez is not saying anything about his wife's demise," Lalong said. "He chooses to remain quiet about it. I expect him to address the nation." Williams said. A plane with noisy engine flew pass in the sky. It was a helicopter and the noise from its engine was almost deafening. "This copter should be off the air. It is old and not fit to fly our airspace, it's very risky to fly in that." Peter said. Light laughter from the other men. The copter flew farther away with its noise and the calmness returned to the sky. "The Prez is cool about it; he prefers to mourn in private." Aliu brought back the discussion. "You know he loves his wife so much; so, it must've been a very big shock and blow to him," Williams said. Suddenly the phone on the table rang; interrupting the men's gossip. Aliu lifted the receiver and spoke gently into the mouthpiece. "Hello; who's this?" He listened briefly and smiled at the men. He cut call and looked at them with a warm smile. "We won't wait for long; Oga's messenger is close by." They smiled and relaxed and forgot their gossip at that moment. Peter, Lalong, and Williams were in suits, only Aliu was in the traditional Hausa wear of babariga.

The next day, in the home of the President of the United States of America; time was one-twenty in the afternoon. The President's first daughter Alice, sat on her bed pecking on her laptop on her lap. Her red-blond hair hung loose below her shoulders, legs stretched in front, her laptop glowing on her beautiful smooth lap. She smiled occasionally as she chatted with someone. She had registered on a dating site to explore the other side of the world; in a bit to find a man who will love her without knowing her opulent background. Now there is someone who catches her fancy, a handsome man who claimed to live and travel around the world. She continued to chat with him on the mail, smiling, having fun, and many promises of endless love. She only told him that her father works for the government of America. He claimed his family members were all dead, and he was the only male survivor of a family of six.

She looked tall and beautiful, like a queen in a fairy tale; with a rebellious mind against the life her parents choose for her, a good lifestyle that befits a first daughter of an American President. She wanted to be allowed to be like an ordinary girl, a simple life devoid of the weight imbedded in a President's last name. She preferred to be known just as, Alice. She hated to be seen on Television or paper. She would do everything possible to avoid the media like plaque. Not many people knew her or how she looked. She preferred an obscure kind of life. He told her his name was Morcos, not his real name. Told her he knew some places in America, claimed to be a businessman, and was in charge of his father's estate. She smiled beautifully, feeling loved as they chatted. A soft tap sounded at the door and Alice's mum gently opened the door and walked in. Alice put the laptop down and gathered her long blue gown and headed to the living room where she met her mother as she sat on a sofa. Alice smiled at her and greeted. "Hi, mum. What's the matter? You look worried." Her mum didn't try to hide her worried look. She came to talk about a disturbing issue.

She continued to look worried and her face was wrinkled inconspicuously. Alice stared at her and sat on the arm of a sofa. She was eager to return to her laptop to continue her chat with Morcos. She watched her mum sigh and expected what would come next. They had done this before; in fact, on many occasions. Her mother had walked into her space like this morning and began admonishing her. Alice wanted a different life and her family wanted her to live a life good enough for her status as the daughter of the President of the most powerful Country in the world. Her mother's name was Hanna. Alice has other siblings, and their parents are not trying to control her siblings' lives; why her? She doesn't want that and would not allow her parents to choose for her the life to live. Her mother sighed again and looked at her. Alice waited. "Alice! How long will you live in self-seclusion? Why do you choose to ignore your family?" "How do you mean mum; I didn't ignore my family. Why do you accuse me of that?" Alice protested. "Your dad thinks you're avoiding him; you no longer eat at the same dinner table with us" "Mum, I don't like this at all. I made it very clear the kind of life I choose to live. You and dad want to dictate my life, chosen boyfriend for me, you want me to smile and pretend in front of cameras and want me to act important and regal and all stuff like that". "But you're regal; a beautiful daughter of the President of America." Her mother said in truth. "Mum, please! I don't wanna do this with you again. I want to be allowed to live my life, a simple life, just like an ordinary girl out there. I prefer to live in obscurity; just a few friends and no Press People hounding me with cameras. No paparazzo's, to live like an ordinary girl from downtown. Is that too much to ask?"

"You're our daughter and we love you, want the best for you. You go out at will without any security aide. You travel in cabs when you have drivers at your becks and call. I'm not comfortable with that. I'm worried for you." Her mother said without mincing words. "Mum! Please stop worrying, I'm sure there won't be any danger and I know what's good for me. Other girls from common homes travel in cabs. Why can't I do the same? Alice said in anger. "Because you're different, you're the daughter of the President of America," Hanna said to her and rose from the sofa and walked to Alice.

"Aww! What an important position, but mum unfortunately I don't feel that way. I am different, am just a common girl that love's simple life." "You're not a common girl Alice; you know that." "But I feel like one. I think I was made to be so. Please mum can you and dad get used to this fact?" "Your dad is not happy about it. The son of Senator White wants to marry you, but you aren't giving him any chance." "Oh, there you go again. Mum, please! Must we discuss the Senator's son any time you talk to me? I am tired of this; No mum, I want to marry a man of my choice, a man I love. You and dad should please get used to this fact. I am sorry."

Her father was behind Alice door, listening. He wanted to speak to Alice about the whole thing but decided to send his wife who Alice always listened to better than she does to him. He shook his head and sighed in disappointment and walked away. Mother and daughter continued inside "Think about all I said Alice; we want the best for you as our daughter." "Thank you, sweet mum, for your care; but please get used to the kind of life I chose to live. I need the freedom to choose what is best for me. I am not cut for such things. I feel uncomfortable in front of the press or cameras. I like to move without anyone watching me. I am different from what you want me to be. Sorry, mum. I can't help it." Her mum watched her briefly and shook her said in disappointment and turned; she grabbed the door handle and yanked the door open and stepped out, closing it gently. Alice felt sorry for her mother. She know her mom loves her, but she can't help it. She's just the opposite of who they want her to be. They'll come around to the fact. She said in her mind and hastened back to her laptop. She sat back on the bed and attacked the keypad. She began to type furiously; worried Morcos might have waited and logged out. To her surprise, he responded immediately her message was sent. She apologized for the brake, and they continued to chat happily.

ONE WEEK LATER, in the office of the Nigeria police chief. IGP Ahmadu Sanda and his subordinate, DIG Gusau, were deep in private talk. Time was eleven-twenty in the morning. Life has returned to normal in the Country and the conspirators were lying low, and the man in a suit with the gadgets continued to listen to calls from Mark's phone and everyone continued to suspect everyone.

"Oga is from our zone, our friend, and the right person for the seat. We must do all we can to assist him to ascend the coveted seat." Ahmadu said. "He is a few steps to get there. The only difference is that he wants to be there a long time to come." Gusau said. "I agree with you but there's nothing wrong with that. It's good to be in charge and dictating things." Ahmadu said with a wicked smile.

"The Prez has been so lucky, the bombs and the rest. He won't know what hits him next. He won't be lucky next time." Gusau said. "You know he practically instructed me to give him daily reports on the investigation," Ahmadu said. "And he is getting it daily? Gusau said with a wide smile. "Oh, yea he gets what I submit to him. We are chasing leads, watching imaginary suspects and over fifty of our men are out there interviewing people." He chuckled and Gusau chuckled too. "I wonder why he's not saying anything about his dead wife," Gusau said and became serious again. "He's still in shock. We all know he loves her very much. It must be very devastating to him." Ahmadu said. "I am thinking we can do something." Gusau proffered. "Like what?" Ahmadu asked in apprehension. "We can prove to him we have been working hard," Gusua said with a serious look on his face. "I am not following" He adjusted in his seat and watched and waited on Gusau to elucidate better. Gusau looked up to the ceiling and sighed. "Let's see it this way. We strike a deal with two men; the men would be from another zone. We instruct them to claim responsibility for the bomb blasts and we pay them handsomely. Then take them to court and the case is expedited and they get sentence. On the way to prison we allow them to run and disappear from the city. We replace them with some other condemned criminals. Then our arranged gunmen will emerge from nowhere and attack the prison van conveying the two condemned criminals we used as a replacement. The Prison van must be completely destroyed with a bazooka, all men burn beyond recognition, terrorists at work." He burst into laughter. "That's a brilliant idea!" Ahmadu said; a smile playing on his lip. "The only issue is, if press people show very much interest in the case," Ahmadu said.

"We won't allow press the opportunity to get very close. With oga's influence we can arraign them in Judge Garba's court; twist arms and get what we want." "The President would be convinced that we are working, and no one will look inward for suspects. Everyone will believe it is terrorists at work." Ahmadu said happily. "Yes! Sell them a dummy here and a dummy there, and everything will go well," Gusua said. "You are a small evil genius," Ahmadu said with a laugh.

"I am just learning the ropes. Oga is the main evil genius." Gusau said. They both roared into Laugher. Ahmadu relaxed back in his office chair, a huge office table before him. Framed pictures of him, the governor of Lagos state, and the Prez hung above his head on the wall. The Police flag and National flag hung at a corner in the office. Laptop, phone, and files on the table. "I will suggest your brilliant idea to Oga. I hope he would buy it." "I hope it will fly. That way it will send a signal that the enemies of the state or the gunmen who will attack the Prison van are members of the group who don't want their captured members to spill the bean." Gusua said. "I will call Oga this evening to discuss things with him. He informed me that he is planning something massive." "Okay. We wait to know what he thinks about the plan after you've told him of it." Gusau stood up and said he was going out to see his mum who called him some minutes ago.

Mark sipped his beer from a glass cup, at the bar of Willow Hotel. His eyes darted to and from the entrance door as he waited for agent Joshua. Seconds passed, Joshua walked in through the entrance door and stood awhile and scanned the bar and his eyes pick Mark at a table in the far corner of the busy bar, alone with a bottle of beer on his table. He walked straight to Mark's table and slid unto an empty chair. Pleasantries exchanged and Mark beckoned to the waiter to serve more beers. "Thank you for coming on short notice. I appreciate." Mark said to him. Joshua smiled. "It's my pleasure; I can do anything for you," Joshua said with a smile.

The waiter arrived with two bottles of beer and placed them on the table then left. Joshua opened his beer and poured some into the glass cup, took a long sip, and placed the cup on the table. "Mark, I don't have much time on my side. I need to get back to work." "You called me to warn me; that my phone and car are bugged. You are the only person I can trust with what I am going to tell you." Joshua nodded and watched Mark. "I believe there is a conspiracy by top security men to eliminate the Prez." Joshua remained silent and listened. Eyes half shut.

"The police chief and some other people I don't know are into a big conspiracy to assassinate our President." "You hinted it to me the other time. Like I told you on phone; I heard your name been mentioned several times and there is no doubt that you are been watched, and someone somewhere is listening to your phone conversations. In fact they know I am here." Joshua said. "Thanks for warning me on time," Mark said in appreciation. "I have this inkling that the IG is involved in this conspiracy," Joshua said. "I never wanted to tell anyone what I know; but since I am talking with you as my friend, I will tell you all I know," Joshua said. "Thank you for your confidence in me," Mark said and sipped his beer a little. Joshua leaned his elbows on the table and spoke in a low voice. "Yes, you are right about the cover-up and conspiracy to eliminate the Prez. I on one occasion overheard the IG Discussing with the DIG almost in hushed voices. I couldn't make out exactly what they were discussing, but I managed to hear IG saying "Oga won't rest until the President is removed." "Wow wow, that's it!. I suspected a big cover-up," Mark said. "I have been trying to find a way to hear more but you know our headquarters, it is always busy with activities."

Joshua said. "Now the question I may ask is, where is the oga hiding and who might he be?" Mark said. "That definitely requires deep digging," Joshua said.

"Now listens Joshua" Mark rubbed his palms together and continued. "You know the Prez is from the same town as me. I want to find a way to save the President from the people who want him dead." Agent Joshua poured more beer and lifted the cup to his lips and sipped, this time slowly. He gently placed back the glass cup on the table and watched Mark who stopped talking to allow his words to sinker. "What do you plan to do?" Joshua asked. Mark lifted his beer and took a long drink, this time not using the glass cup He gently placed the beer back on the table and looked at Joshua straight in the face. "I want you to be my ears, work with me to find ways to expose the wicked men and by that, we can keep the President safe," Mark said.

"Anything I can do to expose the wicked men I will. Some people are hell-bent on removing the President by eliminating him." Joshua said and relaxed back to his chair. "I have a friend who is willing to pay for all your troubles, for you to work with us to expose the Syndicate." "I will not do it for the money, my loyalty lies with justice," Joshua said. "All I want is for you to work with me because I can only trust you with this. It is a classified case." Mark said. "I am in. It's dangerous; our lives could be in danger if they find out what we are planning to do, but I am willing to risk it." Joshua assured. "Thank you, Joshua; I knew I could count on you. So, when are you coming to meet with my friend?" "Let's keep it this weekend," Joshua said and poured more beer into the glass cup. "Okay, would be expecting you by the weekend," Mark said. "Okay. See you then." He picked up his beer and gulped it down and stood up to leave. "Mark, I need to run; I have one or two things to attend to before I go home," Joshua said as he trusted his hand forward for a handshake. "Okay, Joshua; I appreciate your coming." Mark grabbed Joshua's hand and they shook hands violently. "See you on Saturday," Joshua said and walked towards the exit. Mark signaled the waiter to bring the bill.

THREE WEEKS TO ELECTION; President Andy was on phone; gesticulating as he discussed with his friend, Chris Griffin. "Chris, my wife is safe; she wasn't the woman involved in the car bomb incident but her assistant." "I'm happy to hear that your wife is safe. But why the news is all over the place that she's the one who got killed?" "I don't know how the people concluded that she died. The news of her presumed death spread, and I had no option but to keep quiet about it. Some people want me dead. Maybe same people tried to kill my wife in other to get at me." "With the issue of terrorism in Nigeria; I am worried for you. I promise, America will help in any way we can to keep your Country safe." "Thank you, Chris, I am very grateful." "I hate terrorists and my government will do all within our power to stop them from destroying the freedom to coexist," Chris said. "Every government and nation should all come together with one voice and purpose, to eradicate terrorism from the surface of the earth," Andy said. "The UN member Nations must all stand up against this evil called terrorism. Some member nations from the Middle East are hiding behind doors, not willing to condemn the evil act." Chris said. "That's true. The safety of citizens must be paramount to all leaders across the globe. It is like laughing, watching mad men throwing stones into the market. Who knows who might get hurt?" Andy said. "Yea you're right, Andy, I am happy your wife is safe. I advise you to watch your back and don't trust anyone." "Yes, I am doing that. Thanks, Chris for your concern." "Take care of yourself Andy; I have a meeting in ten minutes. We talk some other time." "You take care too; my regards to Hanna and the girls." "I will. Bye!" He cut call and punched his secretary's line."

THE ELECTION CONCLUDED AND as the results trickled in, the TPP Party led in 2third of the states the result has been collated. By the evening of the 10th of June, the TRANSPARENT PEOPLE'S PARTY swept the polls. The party won convincingly. The happiness and euphoria of the win filled the PPP camp. The President with the Vice President, Chief of staff, National Chairman of TPP and another top government official from the ruling party, members of TPP from ward to Local government celebrated the victory with a funfair, and the President and top members of his government from his party sat in the Presidential villa all in celebration mood. Torrents of congratulatory messages flooded in from home and away. Happiness filled the air, for a landslide victory at the polls. Re-election is another new tenure of power and being ahead of the opposition. The vice President rose to his feet and cleared his throat just to call for everyone's attention. Silence fell across the large room; all watched the vice, President. Mathew Ochei clasped his palms together and spoke. "Today is another great moment for our great party. Victory is sweet and this victory calls for a toast." With a smile on everyone's faces, Andy felt happy and relaxed, and a warm smile played on his lips. The National Chairman of the TPP party rose from his seat and chanted, his name was Ajayi Ojo. "TPP!" others responded, "Transparency!" TPP!! Others chanted again "Transparency!!!" He began "I suggest a dinner party in celebration of our victory." The President nodded and spoke.

"I thank you all for working hard for this success. Send a thank you message to all our wards, state governors, chairmen, and everyone who played some role to get us re-elected. I dedicate this victory to all people, especially our party members who were killed in the bomb blast during the kickoff of our Presidential campaign. I am going to instruct my press secretary to organize a thank you press conference. I want everyone to understand that this is another responsibility to do more for our dear Country. I urge everyone to help us, all hands-on deck to leave a good legacy before we exit the office." "We've already set a good standard for the incoming government. Our Party performed creditably well." The vice President said. Pocket of clapping bursted in the room. "That's why our party got re-elected." The party chairman said and shouted the party slogan. "TPP!" He shouted again and others responded. "Transparency!"

A FEW DAYS LATER, it was the morning of a Thursday; Aliu Issa and Williams, Solomon and Peter were in Aliu's office, they all looked happy as laughter filled the office. Williams raised his hand to call their attention to him. Silence fell in the office; the others watched him. "I am so elated about the victory at the poll. We are getting closer to our destination." He said. Peter nodded with a smile. "Oga is very happy. I spoke with his assistant last night." Peter said. "It calls for celebration. I happily slept like a baby last night." Aliu said. "I, out of great happiness drank myself to sleep and could not perform my manly duties to my wife." Solomon said. Others roared into laughter. "You can still fulfill your obligation tonight." Aliu said. More laughter filled the room. The camp of the conspirators is happy because the victory at the poll translates to still an open chance for the Oga to ascend the seat after the President dies. Even though it is not in the constitution of the Country for another zone to step in when a President from another zone suddenly dies, the camp of the conspirators has already perfected plans to twist arms to stop the zone of the current President from appointing a replacement in the case if their plan sails through and the lover man is deleted. It must be their Oga, or anarchy sets in. They are connected, working with the blessings of the king markers from their zone and the kingmakers are movers and shakers of the Nigerian political scene. Since the conspirators have their backings, the sky would be the starting point. The Country seems to be at relative peace for now, but it would be ungovernable for the lover man if he escapes the next attack. Aliu thought in his heart. He smiled to himself as evil plans against the Prez played in his mind. "I heard the American president would be visiting Nigeria today and oga planned a small gift for him." Williams gaped with his mouth open. "I know Oga's gift always comes with consequences." Williams said. Aliu chuckled. "Oh, I learned it would be like to using one stone to kill two birds." Aliu said. "I am not following," Williams said. Aliu rubbed his palms, a wicked smile playing on his lips. "Just watch and see; there would be great news in Nigeria and America." He said. "Oga is crazy." Williams said. "He's always crazy." Aliu said and laughed out and instantly became serious again. "To get to the winning line, sometimes it requires not playing fair." He said. Williams nodded as if he understood but his mind was busy with thought of appointment he has with a young girl that vowed to make him her number two. "I don't really know what oga plans to do but I smell danger." Aliu said. "If the President is killed; don't you think that might ignite war?" Williams asked. "Oga hates him with passion, so won't stop until Andy dies. The US President's visit will present an opportunity to assassinate the both enemies." "This sounds like a plan of a deranged mind, a psycho who has no human feelings." "It might sound a perfect plan." Solomon said. "All I want is results. Whatever or whomsoever must be sacrificed for us to win, I give my blessings to it." Peter said. Williams shrugged. "You're beginning to sound weak; should I inform the organization that you're no longer fit and capable to be a player on the team?" Aliu asked but indirectly he wanted to threaten Williams. Williams instantly smiled and shook his head. "No didn't mean to sound weak or reasonable; I just allowed the other side of me to get the best of my thought." He explained. "Listen, comrades, to get to the top, one needs to be brutal and merciless." "Yea, that's true." Williams concurred but deep in his mind, he was troubled, afraid of what might be the outcome of the plan. To him, all he knows was that it was a dangerous and crazy idea to kill two Country Presidents in one take. "The election has come and gone." Aliu said just to change the talk. Williams happily jumped at it, he prayed for a change in topic. "Victory is sweet, and the fat lady is singing." Peter said with a small laugh. "And I am singing too, soon everything will work out as planned." Aliu said. "We are a formidable team and I trust in our ability to deliver." Peter said and rose from his chair and yarned. Others took the cue and also rose. "As I am basking in the euphoria of our party's victory, I can't wait to get home." Solomon said. "Please do not wound your wife with your attacking method o!" Williams said with a laugh. More laughter in the room as everyone joined in the joke. The men were very happy.

That Same day, afternoon, at the Presidential wing of Murtala Mohammed International Airport Lagos, a tinny jet appeared in the sky and began to descend, and as it neared it looked bigger. The Presidential jet belonged to the American President, Chris Griffin. Andy smiled and watched as the jet rolled to a stop and the engine died down. A few seconds on the door of the plane opened and the step came down gently. President Andy Ubih and some government officials waited on his Friend, Chris. The red carpet lay straight in wait for President Chris Griffin and his entourage. The US security aids emerged from the Presidential Jet first, followed by the USA minister of foreign affairs, and he stopped and scanned the waiting men, a few seconds wait before he descended the steps. In another fraction of seconds, President Chris Griffin emerged from the plane. He descended the steps as President Andy Ubih moved forward to welcome the visitors. Handshakes and hugs were exchanged, and the Presidents moved towards the white Limo a few yards away. The two friends slide into the back seat of the Limo and US minister of foreign affairs; David Coleman entered the back seat of a black Cadillac. Security agents waited behind and ahead in the convoy, agent Mark was in one of the police cars in the convoy. He glanced into the side mirror and watched at the limo at the back. Doors closed and the convoy drove off and headed towards the Presidential Villa.

Some minutes later, the President's convoy pulled to a stop in the compound of the Presidential Villa. No Guard parades at the airport and only about a hundred people excluding security operatives were on the ground to welcome him at the villa. As the police car, Mark was in pulled to a stop, he threw the door open and stepped out gingerly. His automatic hung in a holster on his hip. Press people Scurried about to take pictures, but only a few of them were allowed in. After a few questions and answers, the US president and the Nigerian President stood for pictures. Other government officials and important people who came to the airport to welcome the US President joined the Picture session. Securities operatives Barred the Press people from advancing to the restricted area and in a few seconds, a little girl of about four feet, dressed in traditional attire of iro and bubba emerged from the door with a bouquet and started to walk to present the flowers the visitor and suddenly from a corner a thick hand grabbed her arms and pulled her inside and from the room, another smallish looking lady that wore the same color of iro and bubba emerged with another bouquet and headed towards the door. She looked like a girl of about ten, but she was above thirty. She confidently began to descend the few steps, her eyes fixed on the number two men that waited and, she walked with a flicker of an eyelid. She had instructions and must adhere to them. Mark watched and noticed that the small-looking girl was not a small girl but a very small-looking lady with a small girl's face. She was not walking confidently and suddenly she stopped, and Mark noticed she was jittery; her face looked tense and troubled. The two Presidents watched her with a smile as she approached. Click, flash the cameras kept snapping quickly. Mark kept watching the small-looking lady, suddenly a picture of an explosion flashed in his mind. On impulse he ran towards the girl, knocking people off his way and he made to get to her. The small-looking lady was a little distance from the President when Mark reached her and knocked her down to the ground, he dove away and lay flat on the ground as he yelled for everyone to get down. The two Presidents moved instantly and fell to the ground and the US security operatives covered them with their bodies. People panicked and threw themselves to the ground and suddenly as the small lady made to scramble up from the ground, an explosion rocked from the bouquet and blow flowers about. The small child-like lady got killed instantly. As the bomb went off, the people scampered for safety in all directions. The two Presidents were immediately protected until they entered through a door and into a room and the door shut. Mark stood up and pulled his automatic, he scanned the environment he was eyes not on the people that has started to gather in small groups, still confused and terrified. He stepped to where the body of the small lady lay in a pool of her blood, her right hand severed off and her belly opened as if knifed apart, and her intestine gushed out to the ground, her face almost unrecognizable, her iro and bubba soaked with blood. She lay on her back, her eyes with the terror of death. Other policemen joined Mark, and some went to talk to the people and calm nerves. From a corner agent, Lawal stepped forward and joined the others. He stole glances at Mark and pretended he didn't see Mark. Mark noticed him and also pretended not to see him join others. Lawal talked to some other officers and kept himself busy from going close to Mark. The body of the little-looking lady was quickly removed from the spot and two policemen went to search for evidence in the bomb spot. Lawal gently stepped aside from the rest and punched a number in his mobile and spoke briefly. "It failed sir". He paused and listened briefly and nodded, then spoke. "Yes sir, I will explain when we meet." He cut the call and returned to and joined the others.

Inside the room where the US President and Nigerian President sat, the two Presidents were still trying to come out of their shock of what happened. Their security aids milled about and watched the door and windows. Their guns were drawn and ready in their hand. President Andy wore his Igbo traditional Isi Agu over black trousers and black shoes. President Chris Griffin wore a gray suit over a white button-down shirt, black shoes, and a red expensive tie. Andy sighed and shook his head sadly. "I am very sad for what happened, Mr. President, and I'm grateful to God for spearing our lives." Chris looked at him, his face gloom. "I am still in shock, Andy. Some people have the temerity to try to kill me in your Country." "I suspect the opposition; they've never been happy since I became President." "You must ask the Country's law enforcement to fish out the perpetrator of this dastardly act." Andy nodded as if receiving a lecture from his tutor. "I am sorry Chris and I apologize on behalf of my Country." "You need not apologize, buddy; that was part of the hazards of governance." "Yea," Andy said, his mind racing in thought. What if they have succeeded? He asked himself in his mind. It would've been very disastrous for Nigeria if the enemies had succeeded with their plans. Who knows how America would have reacted? He reasoned in his head. Andy clasped his hands together and said a silent thank you prayer to God. He has been lucky on two occasions. Many thoughts rattled in his mind. He wouldn't resign. He erased the thought of resigning from his mind. The geo-political zone that chose him to represent them has faith in him to deliver. Therefore there is no going back. My enemies must not triumph over me. My God is with me. He said in his mind.

CHAPTER SEVEN

THE BIG BOYS MUST PLAY BIG DESPITE THE DANGER. Later in the day, at the Villa; President Andy Ubih and his visitors from America were in the west wing of the villa, in the richly furnished Living wing of the Presidential villa. The incident that happened a few hours ago was temporarily forgotten or put aside. Security was beefed up around the Presidential villa with serious-looking security agents. They could be seen milling about with their guns ready in hand and Mark was one of them. He contemplated on few times to seek the audience of Mr. President to tell the President the little he knew and his suspicions. On such occasions, he changed his mind about seeking the President's audience. He has no concrete evidence and that would be suicidal. He waved the thought out of his mind and continued to watch other policemen. He doesn't trust any of them and one thing he was sure of was that he doesn't know how many the enemies were, where they were fighting from, and who they were working for. The Presidents laughed and talked happily like old friends and Presidents despite the bomb scare that left every one of them terrified. Chris vowed to himself never to visit the Country again. "Congratulations on your re-election as President of the Federal Republic of Nigeria," Chris said. Andy beamed with a warm but troubled smile. "Thank you, my friend. The people are happy with us, and we are happy we delivered." Andy said. "It's difficult and at the same time easy to please the people," Chris said. "Yea, delivering gains of democracy is very important and Putting the people first by providing an adequate enabling environment," Andy said and relaxed on the sofa. He wore a royal blue senator suit. Chris wore a black suit and a white button-down shirt, no tie. "No matter how good you perform, there must be those who hate you and won't see anything good you've done," Chris said. "Even the righteous God has those that despise him," Andy said. I'll keep doing all I can for my Country. I know I can't please everybody but as the President of the United States of America, I want to leave a good legacy." Chris said. "Even in the face of danger to my life; I am not afraid but will do more for my Country". Andy said. "Let's discuss what our Countries can do for each other." President Andy stood up and his interlocutor did the same and they walked into another room to have more Private talks; US minister of foreign affairs followed behind.

Later in the evening, the Presidential convoy drove towards the Chopper, this time more guarded by security agents as the US President was ready to fly back to America. A siren blared in the air, a few meters ahead, the Presidential Chopper was ready, pilot waited. Reaching a little distance to the Chopper; the limo rolled to a stop and doors opened, the US president and his Nigeria counterpart stepped out from the limo. They hugged and shook hands, embraced each other with smiles on their faces. They parted each other on the back as if trying to say to one another, forget what happened earlier today. The US security aides had already checked the copter for any bomb and the bird was satisfied clean to fly. Chris Griffin briskly bounced to the Chopper and his men followed closely. The Copter engine roared to life and the blades propelled rapidly in the air. Chris Griffin turned and waved at his friend. Andy waved back with a big smile on his face. Chris Griffin climbed into the bird and his foreign affairs minister climbed in also, followed by two security agents. Seconds later, the Copter lifted into the air and flew towards the Murtala Mohammed International Airport, where the US Presidential jet and pilots were waiting, in the Presidential wing of the Airport.

The night of the same day, Mark took a commercial bike to Daniel's house and explained the situation to him. Daniel gladly gave him a room in one of his buildings somewhere in another part of the council to lay his head and urged him to stay there as long as he wanted until the whole problem was solved.

Two days later, in the late evening, time was eight pm. The SSS chief and the Police chief sat in deep talk inside a black jeep off Graham Douglas Road, Victoria Island. No other person was in the jeep, only the two security chiefs deep in discussion. Cars flew pass the busy road. The police chief sat behind wheels while Illiasu was in the front seat. "We've been following the minister of Finance and that crazy journalist, Dele Jimoh, and from our findings, the minister of finance has in his possession damaging info against our man. He has in his possession every detail of money our man siphoned." Illiasu said. "That's dangerous; we need to act immediately before he exposes Oga," Ahmadu said. "I am instructed to make preliminary arrangements to take them out," Illiasu said. "No, it might be too late; I think it is pertinent to delete them immediately. A stitch in time saves nine." Ahmadu said. "I will have to talk to our man about it; I agree with your suggestion." "Yea, to keep a secret safe, it should not be allowed to stay in the heart of an enemy." He made a throat-slashing sign. "I think I know what to do," Illiasu said and smiled wickedly. "From my end, we are watching a police agent who we believe knows too much. I got info from a good source that two of my agents are meeting in secret. My private eye saw them exit a bar last night; they are planning to do something damaging." Ahmadu said. "Then take them out immediately. Like you rightly advised; no one with damaging info should be allowed to live." "Yes, I plan to make it look like an armed robbery; or better like they were mugged. They won't know what hits them." Ahmadu said. "Good, let's nip things in the bud," Illiasu said. "Let's go to my favorite restaurant and eat some sumptuous meal; I am famished," Ahmadu said and roared the jeep to life and leveled the gear. They drove into the evening.

On the morning of November 8, some police Agents with two men, the men's hands were in cuffs, and guns lay a few feet away in their fronts. A small crowd of people including police agents and press people gathered. The men confessed to the crime and claimed responsibility for all the bombings and attempt to assassinate the President. Press people darted to snap pictures of the arrested men. The police barred them from interviewing the arrested men as the men were being led away by the police into a waiting police van. It became national news. The bad guys have been arrested and within two days they were arraigned in court. The news spread across towns and borders that members of a terrorist group have been arrested and they claimed responsibility for all recent bomb incidents.

Two days later, on November 10; a white jeep slowed down along a beautiful street in Ikoyi and rolled onto Parkview Boulevard. It was a cool evening. An average-built man sat in the back seat of the white jeep. The man was Nigeria's minister of Finance, and his name was Sunday Ige. He was late fifties, a product of Harvard; a Christian, a vivacious and dedicated workaholic and he was just returning from work. He wore a white suit and reading glasses sat on the bridge of his nose. His driver was a short and fat middle-aged man that almost covered the driver's seat. One car, a red Honda was packed a little distance up the Street, and no one was seen walking along the Street. Beautiful houses adorned both sides of the Street. As the white Jeep drove on suddenly the red Honda started and dangerously drove in front of the coming white jeep, forcing the driver of the finance minister to brake abruptly to avoid an accident. The front door of the red Honda flew open and a man in a black leather jacket, dark sunglasses, jumped out with a gun and pointed it at the driver and fired a muffled shot instantly. The bullet ripped the driver's chest open and he fell sideways in the driver's seat, blood splattered to the doors of the jeep. The finance minister yelled in terror and like lightning, the man in a black leather jacket yanked open the back door and fired two quick muffled shots on the chest of the finance minister and he fell, dead, between the back seat and foot space, blood stained the back seat. The man ran to the Honda and quickly slid into the front seat and the driver furiously reversed and drove away into the late evening. The eyes of the driver were covered with dark sunglasses too and he wore a red Tee shirt, and a red baseball cap covered his head.

On the morning of the next day, the Nation woke to the news of the assassination of the Country's finance minister, Mr. Sunday Ige. It became the front page, the Nation was thrown into mourning.

Somewhere in a hotel suite, in the highbrow area of the mainland, the SSS chief, Illiasu Daama and Peter sat in a private talk. A bottle of open Andre sat on the table before them and almost one empty wine glass waited for a refill on the table. "It was a well-executed job; it was clean and quick," Peter said. "Yes, I sent professionals who have been working for me for a long time now; they're good," Illiasu said with a wicked smile. "The finance minister fished in murky water; so, he got what he deserved," Peter said. "He messed with the wrong people. Our man at the ministry of finance was able to gather all the damaging evidence the money man had. Now the fat lady can sing to the Bank." Illiasu said. Peter chuckled and grabbed the bottle of wine and poured a drink for himself. He lifted it to his lips and sipped a little and watched the SSS boss from over the wine glass. He then put down the wine glass on the table and smiled at Illiasu. "Who's next?" Peter asked. "The paper man is dangerous, and we might pay him a surprise visit," Illiasu said. He doesn't drink alcohol because his religion abhors it, but he doesn't either condemn those that drink it. "Good, deleting our enemies and obstacles, that would help in keeping our plan safe," Peter said. "Oga is ready to kill half of the Country's citizens to archive his set goal," Illiasu said. "His victory is our victory, and his failure would also mean ours too," Peter said. "Yea, to get to the winning line; we all must work collectively until it becomes hurray," Illiasu said. "You're right," Peter said and looked at his watch. The light was on, and the air-conditioner hummed at a corner of the large space. The curtains were drawn, and the room was cool. "I got to go to my house. It's been two days I haven't slept in my house." Peter said. "Don't overdo things, how is your wife taking it?" Illiasu asked. "She's not complaining but I guess she's not happy about my frequent nights out." "I advise you to try to balance it. A happy home makes a happy marriage, and you should not sacrifice the happiness of your home for this cause." "You're right sir. Thanks for your advice and concern." Illiasu rose and Peter rose too; both men shook hands and headed to the door and exited.

NOVEMBER 11

Some policemen and the suspects walk towards the stairs that led into the courtroom. ASP Ango preceded them and some of his subordinates walked behind the suspects. Some press people scurried about trying get a better view and take quick pictures of the men, but more policemen blocked the front, making it impossible to get a clear shot. Quick clicks while the men are led into the waiting room. Suddenly the crowd thinned, and, in a few minutes, the press people started to leave to do other things. Policemen made it impossible for the press to get any good shot of the suspects. They were protected for a good reason.

In the courtroom, ASP Ango and his men sat discussing in low tones. ASP Ango leaned to his right to talk to IPO Clement Imoke. The Federal Attorney, Balarebe Bauchi hastily walked toward the police agents. Handshakes and pleasantries were exchanged, and the Federal Attorney picked his seat. The courtroom was already filled up, waiting for the judge, Judge Garba Kaura. The court orderlies and secretaries took positions in their various duty posts. Another court orderly stood at the far-left corner of the courtroom, his gun in its holster on his right hip. The two suspects were led into the courtroom in cuffs, they sat on a bench near the dock, and a policeman stood a few distances from them. People discussed in hush voices. The two suspect's faces looked bland. No heart pounding, no worries, no sign of fear but they sat in quietude and watched. Occasionally they leaned close and talked in hush voices.

From a corner, the orderly yelled "Court!" all people in the courtroom rose to their feet. Momentarily, the Judge stepped into the courtroom. The Judge, a diminutive man, stood briefly and scanned the courtroom. The courtroom was already filled. He gently walked and gently sat on his seat and coolly removed his reading glasses. He scanned the courtroom again and called for proceedings.

Somewhere in the city, Indai and Gambo sat discussing in Indai's office. Sometimes they like to discuss in English. They were educated and held different degrees in food Technology and Political science. They wore their traditional Babariga. Indai sat behind a large office table and the chairs were black leather. "I hope all plans will work out soon. I am itching to lay my hands on the monies". Indai said. "Aai Alhaji, I am praying, that in a few months from now everything should fall in place". Gambo said. "Oga is planning something big. I believe it will work out soon". Indai said. "He is keeping it to himself. He said it will be the final stroke, like a big blow to the lover man". Gambo said happily. "I don't know why Oga waited for the Lover man to get re-elected". Indai said. "You know Oga is a good planner. He must be planning something big, it may be deadly as an atomic bomb". Gambo exaggerated and adjusted his large Babariga on his shoulder. "Let's wait and see". Indai said

At Seabird hotels, where peter made his temporary home, Peter and Lalong stood outside in the parking lot of the hotel deep in private talk. "I think the sniper should be invited back to practice his trade," Peter said. He's in a dark brown suit, white shirt, no ties, and a black shoe covered his feet. Lalong wore a black suit, a white shirt over black shoes, and no tie. "I am becoming desperate to see the Prez dead. How long are we going to wait?" he asked. "I will have to talk to Oga about it. The year is almost ended". Peter said. "It's becoming too long a wait," Lalong said. "There's some debris that needed to be cleared, but I think it's the right time we attack. I will talk to Oga," Peter said. "You do that, since the dust has settled, I believe this is a good time for another dust to be raised". Lalong said. "Yea! I think so too. I will suggest recruiting more attackers". Peter said, "That would be good. I believe if we have more gunmen, it would be advantageous to the union". Lalong said.

Inside the Courtroom, Judge Garba Kaura looked at the plaintiffs and spoke in their direction. "No counsel representing the accused, i adjourn this case to the 30th of November, to enable the defendants to hire a lawyer. He removed his reading glasses and glared at the people in the Court. The Court orderly herded the suspects out, followed by a police sergeant. ASP Ango and the rest of his team filed out of the court as the court clerk called the next case.

The evening of the same day, Dele Jimoh boarded a flight to Saudi Arabia where he hoped to interview the lady he discovered the Vice President used as his drug mule. The lady agreed to talk to Dele after so much persuasion and assurance from him to not reveal his source. The Lady in question has been feeling nostalgia to return home to Nigeria. She was tired of hiding away in a foreign land. She was given enough money to last her a lifetime, she would never work or lack anything material. The only little sacrifice demanded from her was just her silence and secluded life in a foreign land where she is forbidden to reveal her identity as a Nigerian. A new name and a new passport from another African Country were provided for her.

Agent Mark was inside his temporary room at one of Daniel's houses, talking to someone on the phone when a knock sounded at the door. The time was seven-twenty-five in the evening. He glanced at the door and lifted his gun from a table and put it on the right side of the sofa where he sat. Another gentle knock and he covered the mouthpiece and asked the person at the door to come in. The door opened gently, and agent Joshua stepped into the room. Mark promised to call the person at the other end back and cut the call. He sprang to his feet and smiled at Joshua who just stepped in and held the door.

"Oh, welcome my friend," he said happily as he rose from the sofa to welcome Joshua. Agent Joshua closed the door behind him and cut his eyes about the room. The room was large and has only little furnishing, a four by-six-inch bed, a red and blue designed curtain and a small table at the center, a set of wooden drawers in a corner of the room, a refrigerator at another corner, and an thirty-six inch Led Television on the wall. The ceiling fan spun on low from the ceiling and the window was open and the curtain parted, the floor was tiled with expensive-looking tiles. They grabbed each other's hands and shook hands violently as they beamed with smiles. Mark waved his friend to the only double sofa in the room and sat next to Joshua. "What a nice place you've got here," Joshua said jokingly. "Thanks. Just a place to hide which my friend offered me." He got up and looked at Joshua. "What do I offer you?" Water will do". Joshua said and crossed his leg. "I have beer and wine, why water?" Mark asked. Agent Joshua smiled. "For now, water will do. I am going back to duty in an hour." He said. "Okay, but I invite you to dinner at my favorite restaurant tomorrow; hope you'd be able to come." He opened the fridge and brought him bottled water. The Led television on the wall is on; the ceiling fan spun on low, while cool breeze blew through the open window. The night kept growing old and car horns could be heard some distance from the Street below. "I can't promise you of coming to dine with you tomorrow; I am up to my neck with work but let's see how it goes. I might still make it." "Okay, I pray you would be able to come," Mark said as he handed the cold bottle of water to Joshua and slid onto the sofa beside him. Joshua unscrewed the cap and took a little sip of cold water. "Any plan of marriage soon?" Joshua asked with a smile. "No, my girlfriend is not thinking of settling down for now." "Why? is she not matured enough?" Mark chuckled. "She's more interested in her carrier, not ready until she attains a certain level in her choosing field."

"She is more carriers oriented," Joshua said, not a question. "She's with the Navy. I can't push but let her decide if she wants it or not. Any woman I am settling down with must be ready to commit to our marriage." "Marriage is for serious-minded people who are ready to do it together, with all their hearts and soul." "Yea you are right. That's why I demand full commitment." Mark said. "Before I married my wife, I practically spelt everything out and we agreed to lay it all on the table," Joshua said and sipped more water.

A yellow jeep drove off the road onto Kensington Street and slowly pulled to a stop off a sidewalk in front of a two-story building, adjacent to Occidental kitchens. The driver switched off the car lights and killed the engine. The car door opened and Daniel slid out of the driver's seat. He closed the door gently and stood and glances about momentarily. Nobody was watching, thick darkness was fast creeping into the young night. He wore a white jumpsuit and red sneakers, a red baseball cap. He was five-ten, thick-bearded and muscular. He walked towards the door to the stairs where Mark and Joshua continued discussing inside.

"That was wise. It helps to allow each other to make…. A knock at the door interrupted him. Their eyes cut to the door. "My friend is here," he said and rose from the sofa and walked to the door and opened it to welcome Daniel. Daniel smiled at him and stepped into the room. Mark quickly carried out the introduction, and Pleasantries were exchanged, then Daniel slid to a sofa. Mark perched at the edge of the bed. He offered Daniel beer, but he declined and went straight talking with Joshua. "Mark told me much about you. I am happy to meet you." Daniel said with a warm smile, his eyes on Joshua. "It's my pleasure. I am happy to meet you too." Joshua said. "Mark, you explained to him everything and why we are here?" "Yes, I did he's ready to work with us." "Good. Joshua, the reason I demanded to see you is to know anyhow you would want me to help." He said. "We are in this together for a good course. Like I promised Mark, I will do all I can to help. The President is a good man, and I can kill or die to keep him safe." Joshua said in truth. "Thank you, Joshua, for your sacrifice; we are putting our lives on the line to make sure the evil ones are exposed," Mark said. "I was trained to stand on the side of truth and justice," Joshua said. Daniel nodded and watched Joshua in admiration. "You're a good cop. I will always respect that." Mark said. Agent Joshua smiled and responded.

You are a good cop too, Mark, despite the impression our colleagues have about you." Mark thanked him and smiled. "Some officers see me as an ordinary Joe without much fineness." "I see you differently, Mark." "One officer said to me during our police courses that, my performance was insipid to him; if it should be compared to food," Mark said with a little smile playing on his lips. "Forget those arrogant officers; they see themselves as smartest." I hated my superior for such stupid belief." Joshua said with a serious face. Mark looked at Joshua and said. "Thanks for your compliment." Daniel cleared his throat and spoke. "I am pleased to be seated with two of the finest in Nigeria police. Gentlemen, I have little time to spend here. I have another important business meeting I must attend in thirty minutes." Agent Joshua glanced at his watch and the time said 8: 02 pm "I need to be on my way too. I must get back to the office in less than Twenty minutes." Joshua said. "Joshua, I promise to take care of all finances during the cause of this espionage. I will pay you two million to be our ears." Daniel said. Joshua smiled and looked at Daniel. He shook his head. "Oh! no need for that sir. I don't need to be paid to do what is right." "I decided to put you on my payroll. Don't reject my offer. Daniel said. "No need for that. I am content with my salary. I am paid by the government to do my job." "I can't wait to recommend you to The Prez," Mark said with a wide smile. He looked at Joshua in great admiration. "You are an example of the type of police we need in our Country. I am proud of you." He stood up and put out his hand and Joshua put out his, Daniel grabbed Joshua's hand and both men shook hands warmly and Joshua rose too, and Mark escorted them to the door.

NEXT DAY, evening, a flight from Saudi Arabia touched down and taxied to a stop at the Murtala Mohammed International Airport, Lagos. The time was six-zero-five pm. Dele Jimoh picked up his small luggage from the baggage claim and headed to the exit. He went through customs in a short time and exited the arrival hall. He was well known in the Country as the best investigative journalist, and he was also known by many politicians since he mingles with them. He does get into some politics too because he has the ambition of becoming a politician in the near future. Two immigration men greeted him, and he waved at them humbly and headed to the parking lot on the far-left side of the airport ground. A car and a driver were waiting for him. He got to the car and slid, and the driver drove off. A grey car following from a good distance

As the car he was traveling with turned right and headed towards the third mainland bridge. The car, a grey Honda civic continued to follow. The driver of the Honda Civic, the same beautiful lady that watched Mark and Joshua in a low-lighted bar was in black jeans trousers, a white T-shirt, and gold-rimmed sunglasses covered her eyes. She was known among her circle of small friends as Slick Queen. Slick queen with one hand dialed a registered number on her mobile and on the second ring, someone picked from the other end. Slick Queen spoke briefly into the mouthpiece. "The Newspaperman is back." She listened briefly and nodded, then cut call and continued to follow Dele's car. Dele relaxed in the back seat, his mind played and rewound the conversation he had with the lady drug mule in Saudi Arabia. This would be a bomb, one of the biggest stories recently and he intends to shock the nation with the hard fact about their vice President. The lady confessed to him how she had mulled cocaine on several occasions for the vice President. She told him she was tired of hiding in a foreign land and wants to come back to Nigeria. She told him she was paid enough money that can last a lifetime for her to keep quiet and stay away until she gets the green flag to return to the Country. Armed with this fact, Dele confidently returned to finish his war against his enemy. He sighed deeply and closed his eyes as the car slowed and joined the traffic at an intersection in Maryland.

He got home about twenty minutes later and went straight to up to his study after he greeted his family. He has work to do. He switched on his computer and began to peck the story that will shake the Nation of Nigeria. The night got older and he began to yarn in tiredness. He needed some sleep and there was enough time to write his story right and concisely. He switched off the light in his study and joined his wife in the bed. In less than ten minutes he fell asleep and drifted deep into the land of dreams. His wife did not bother to disturb him for a little cuddling before she fell asleep herself, she knew he was tired and got a lot on his mind.

The next day, Dele drove to the office by eight-zero- five in the morning. He worked with Sky Newspapers as a reporter. Sky Newspapers was one of the biggest Newspapers in Nigeria. He killed the car engine and stepped out and closed the door gently. Suddenly a strange feeling hit him, he stopped. He couldn't fathom the reason why such a thing happened. A silent voice advised him to enter his car and drive home, to forget about work that day but he ignored the voice and continued to walk to the entrance door of the high-rise building of Sky Newspapers. As he grabbed the door handle of the front door, it hit him again, like a forewarning, a premonition of impending danger. He shook it off and walked in. He waved at the receptionist and a secretary. They greeted him warmly and welcomed him back from his trip. He began to climb the stairs; he even forgot to use the lift at the moment of his little crisis. He shook the thought of going back home off and continued up the staircase to his office on the third floor. He was known as a gutsy journalist who doesn't look back in the face of challenge. He was not known to be afraid of anything. He knew that was the only atavistic sign he inherited from his father. He got to his office door and opened it and entered. He walked to the window and threw it open and slid into a leather office chair. He sat silently for a brief moment and switched on his computer. He didn't saw chief-editor's car and that of the assistant editor in the parking lot when he drove in. Maybe they were yet to get to the office he thought. He would check them in their offices later. He thought. He entered his office and lowered his plumb body on ta black leather office chair. A lot of works need to be done. He said brief silent prayer and switched on his computer on a table before him. The computer glowed and he opened a black bag he came with and brought out a long sheet of paper and read through it, then he began to peck on his computer. He needed to finish the work he left unfinished before he flew to Saudi Arabia. He concentrated on the work until an hour later, a knock sounded on the door, interrupting him. He stopped and looked at the door. He asked the person at the door in and watched as the door opened quietly and his son, Tunde, a seventeen-year-old boy stepped in. "Tunde, what are you doing in my office. He asked his son. Tunde was surprised to see his son in his office. The boy was a result of Dele's indiscretion from the past when Dele was very young and filled with youthful virility. Tunde smiled at his father and closed the door gently; a large brown envelope was in his hand and it was sealed with Nigeria coat of arm. "Tunde, what brought you here? Hope everything is okay." Tunde nodded and walked towards his father's table and sat on a chair before him. "Dad this was delivered to our house a few minutes after you left. I thought it might be important; so, mom asked me to bring it to your office." "A parcel who delivered it?" he asked as he put out his hand to collect the large brown envelope. The envelope looked bigger than the ones he had seen, and it was somehow heavy. The flip side was sealed with a large emblem of Nigeria's coat of arms. Dele looked at it a second time and began to open it. Suddenly an explosion rocked and threw him out of his chair, his stomach tore open by sharp objects, some of his intestine gushed out, and his son too got hit, thrown out of his chair and got injured. The computer on the table got damaged. The explosion which was not loud enough managed to attract the attention of his colleagues and they ran to his office and saw him very injured and his son on the floor with ripped hand. Dele lay almost dead on the floor and his son seriously wounded. Excited voices filled his office as everyone trying to help. The receptionist ran to her table and called an ambulance. Before their eyes, Dele struggled for a while to stay alive until he drifted off into unconsciousness. A few minutes on, an ambulance arrived. Father and son were rolled out of the office down to the lobby where paramedics lifted the stretchers into the ambulance and door closed. Some minutes later, the ambulance arrived New world specialist hospital. Blood and damaged pieces of the computer and other miscellaneous items were scattered on the floor of his office. As the ambulance pulled to a stop in front of the New world, nurses and paramedics rolled father and son to separate emergency hall. Doctor Abraham was called from a ward visit and he practically ran into the emergency hall where Dele lay in a theatre room. Dr Abraham checked him and straightened up and shook his head. "He's dead." About an hour later, the news of his death filtered in to Newspapers that Dele Jimoh was killed in a bomb blast in his office. The News said doctors could not do much for him. His case was precarious already when he was brought in. A team of doctors battled to save him, but their effort fell to the mud. Tunde still hanged in there, his case was equally bad, and doctors were not optimistic about his making it out alive from the operating room. Same day the news of Dele's demise spread like wildfire and all Television stations carried it. It hit the front page of evening and morning papers. The great respected, gutsy, and acclaimed best investigative journalist of an era has been assassinated in cold blood. The news continued to trend locally and internationally, and it became very obvious to those in doubt and those that reverence him that he has actually died. The remaining battle was to save his son, Tunde.

The SSS chief, Illiasu sat in his office pecking on a computer when his mobile rang. He checked the caller id and picked the call and said hello to the person at the other end. A voice came on from the other end. "Hello Illiasu, you did a good job." "Thank you, sir. Illiasu responded. "Liaise with Ahmadu to get rid of the other roaches trying to infiltrate our camp." "Yes sir, I am already on it. In no time they will be history, sir." Illiasu assured the caller. "It must be soon. We are losing time and we can't afford to allow any damaging witness to live." The man from the other end said his voice sounded hard and wicked all of a sudden. "That will be done, sir," Illiasu said. "Keep up the good work. You shall be rewarded." The man from the other end said. "Thank you, sir," Illiasu said happily with a faint smile, full of hope. "Goodbye, we'll talk again." The man said and cut the call. Illiasu looked at his mobile momentarily and smiled and put it down on the table and returned to his pecking on the computer.

CHAPTER EIGHT

ALL WORK AND NO PLAY MAKES JACK A DULL BOY. So early Saturday evening, Lalong and Solomon were sunbathing on sunbath beds after a good swim at BLUE CREEK HOTEL on Daramola Street off Airport Road Ikeja. A bottle of Hennessy and two wine glasses lay beside the Hennessy bottle. Life was good, even the sun was friendly and faithful as it gradually began to recede into the horizon, but the two men were oblivious of it. They were pretty occupied with other thoughts. Lalong's phone rang; he looked at it and lazily picked the call and spoke briefly into the mouthpiece. "You're here late" he paused to listen and said again "Yea we're still here." He cut the call and looked at Solomon who watched him, waiting for him to speak. "The girls are here." He announced. Solomon's face light up with a broad smile. He rolled off the sunbath bed and sat up, poured a drink for himself and gulped it down in one take. Swimmers in the Olympic size swimming pool began to get tired of swimming and some came out of the pool and began putting on their clothes back, and some went to their sunbath beds and lay down. Solomon sat up and poured a drink and sipped it gently, his eyes fixed on the entrance door, for the girls. In light mood he turned to Lalong and asked." What's the arrangement?"

"They'll be staying for the night." Solomon smiled and nodded at him and got up, threw a sleeveless shirt over his tanned naked body. He joined in watching the entrance door to the poolside. A few seconds later, two beautiful damsels emerged from the entrance door to the pool area. The girls entered through the door and stopped. The one in front, a plump light skin girl with heavy front and large behind stopped and scanned the pool area for a familiar face. She sighted Lalong and began walking towards him and Solomon. The two beautiful women were light-skinned, with very large breasts and large butts, the one in the front looked five feet-six and the other five-seven approximately. As the women approached, Solomon slowly whistled in the air and turned to Lalong. "Wow, how did you do it? I like these girls." "Piece of cake; I can get any girl of my choice in no time. Money can do many wonderful things." Lalong said proudly. The women finally approached and the first girl went to Lalong, smiling generously. A red leather bag hung on her left shoulder. She embraced him as he pecked her cheek.

The other lady smiled at Solomon who stood, watching the big breasts bounce towards him. On impulse, Solomon put his hand forward for a handshake. She grabbed his hand and shook his hand. Her hand was very soft.. "Hi, I am Solomon." "I am Sandra" She flashed him a beautiful smile and Solomon fell in love instantly. He began to feel something steering between his legs. "I'm happy to meet you, Sandra" He said, smiling back at her. "Ladies, give us a few minutes to get dressed, so we can go to the bar for drinks." Lalong announced. The other girl's name was Cindy. Cindy nodded and they watched the men quickly move to get properly dressed in their regular clothing which hung somewhere in a locker. Many eyes were watching the beautiful woman from some distance. A few seconds later, Lalong and Solomon emerged and walked toward the beautiful heavy-chested girls. Arms across shoulders and the couples walked off towards the exit to the bar.

2 DAYS LATER, ASP Ango and his team walked out into the court premises from the courtroom. All beaming with smiles. The arranged suspects have been sentenced. He stepped aside and dialed a number on his cell phone and spoke briefly. "They have been sentenced, sir." He paused and listened briefly and spoke again." Yes, sir, I will be in your office by noon." He cut call and walked back to others who already were heading out of the court premises.

THIRTY MINUTES LATER, a prison van conveying the two sentenced men to prison drove along Hubert Omolade Road, heading towards the prison. The road was not busy as few vehicular movements could be noticed. As the prison van conveying only the two men approached Tin Can link, suddenly a white unmarked sedan drove out from the next junction, a few meters from the main road and tactically forced the prison van to slow down drastically. Immediately the prison van was stationary, the doors of the white sedan thrown open and at the same time the police escort with the prison van jumped down from the front seat and quickly ran to the back of the prison van and unlocked its door. The two men at the back of the prison van quickly jumped down and the policeman pointed at the white sedan. "Run to that van." He yelled. The men already were running to the unmarked white sedan. The Sedan has no windows at the back and sides. Another policeman from the white sedan withdrew a gun from its holster and gestured to the other men in cuffs at the back of the sedan to run towards the prison van. They were condemned criminals. "Run to the van, you have gained your freedom!" The second policeman said. The condemned criminals in cuffs looked confused but yet obeyed. They had no choice, freedom was mentioned. The other men from the prison van quickly got into the back seat of the white sedan and the condemned. Criminals climbed into the back of the Black Maria and the policeman shut the door instantly and locked it with a key. The swap was quick and in less than two minutes; both vehicles drove away and headed in different directions. A few minutes on, up along Tincan link; suddenly a black Land Rover drove to a stop close to an intersection connecting Liverpool Road. In quick action, the doors flew open and two men stepped forward with machine guns. Another positioned a bazooka pointing at the prison van. As the prison van rolled by, the man with the bazooka aimed and blasted the prison van. The officers in the van got hit and the impact threw the prison van to its side and fire ignited and began to burn rapidly. Another shot from the bazooka, the prison van lifted and catapulted into the air and landed upside down. It exploded into thick ball of fire. The policemen, the driver and the other wailed in agony as their bodies began to burn. The fire became intense and ferociously gutted the van. Anguish wailing from the back of the prison van sent a chill down the spine of one of the gunmen as the condemned prisoners in the back of the prison van desperately beat the body of the prison van in pain and great anguish, calling for help, for someone to rescue them. Some minutes on, the wailing from the inside back of the prison van died down and the fire continued to blaze furiously. It was obvious there were no survivors and the bodies of the condemned criminals at the back of the van burned beyond recognition. Within seconds, the gunmen jumped into the Land Rover drove away. Motorists and a few pedestrians gathered to watch. Minutes later, the fire reduced to a smoldering point. All victims burned beyond recognition. The sound of a siren could be heard, wailing and approaching from a distance towards the scene. Some of the people that gathered earlier quickly disappeared to avoid police questioning. None would like to be called upon as a witness to this incident.

IN A CELEBRATION MOOD, the police chief and his deputy DIG Gusau sat discussing in the IGP's office. They looked happy and satisfied. Ahmadu smiled and said to Gusau. "It was a quick and clean job." "My concern is the men we lost." Gusau said. "It's unfortunate, but it had to be convincing you to know. Two of our men were sacrificed to make it look real." Ahmadu said. "The news is already on National TVs." Gusau said. "The President will take us very serious now when we say we've been working, snooping, digging to fish out the perpetrators." Ahmadu said. Gusau chuckled and said, "That's correct." "Have you heard from Oga?" He asked, leaning forward on a table. "No, I will see him this night as we have something important to discuss." "By the way, the Policemen we sacrificed; from which region were they from?" Gusau asked. "From one of the minority tribes; the Lagos commissioner of police played a big role in the game. He instructed some of his men on duty around the axis the play took place to disappear and look in the other direction while our men did their thing." Ahmadu said. "I learnt the men we used as dummies have already crossed the border." Gusau said. "Yea, monies were paid to them cash, no records. They will be staying in different West African Countries." Ahmadu said. "Good." Gusau said and smiled. "Lawal is due for a promotion." Ahmadu said. "Yes, and he is due for a transfer out of Lagos." Gusau chipped in. "I will look into it. Oga would be happy to hear he played a good role in the scheme." "Yea!" Gusau said. "By the way, I want us to go together to see Oga this night. Do you have any engagement with your girlfriend?" Ahmadu asked with a smile. "No, I have none. Anyway, she's off my list for now." Gusau replied. "What has happened; are you two quarreling?" Ahmadu asked in concern. "No, I just need fresh oranges." They burst out laughing heartily. "Bad guy you like them fresh." The police chief said with more laughter. "At my age, I need them fresh to rejuvenate my congealing blood." Gusau said and they roared into serious laughter. The news of the incident became hot like wildfire as it began to spread from city to city, and news had it that the convicted men who claimed responsibility for an attempt to assassinate the President were members of a terrorist group. It was believed that their members attacked and killed them to stop them from exposing the larger group. No questions were asked by the people, no video footages from the scene and there was no way Nigerians would fault the role of the police.

An hour later, agent Joshua sat in the reception hall at the police headquarters, waiting to see the IGP. The police chief invited him for a briefing on an assignment he was sent as a team leader to arrest drug peddlers doing their trade in the ghetto area of Masha. DIG Gausa walked out of the IGP's office and headed towards the stairs. Agent Joshua stood at attention and saluted the senior officer. The receptionist spoke on phone briefly and nodded to Joshua. "You can go in now" Joshua rose from the seat and smiled at the beautiful receptionist and walked to the IG's door and tapped on it gently. The police chief asked him in and he opened the door and stepped into the large office of the IG and closed the door gently behind. He saluted and IGP Ahmadu only nodded and waved him to a spot before the large office table. He stood at ease waiting. The IG rose from his seat. He was pressed. "Wait" He said as he hastened off towards a door. He needed to use the restroom. He walked entered the restroom and door closed. Joshua waited. He cut his eyes about the large office. On the huge table before him, the cell phone of the IGP was beside the laptop. He picked it up and hastily dialed his number, imputed some codes and linked his phone with the police chiefs. He placed it back on the table, exactly where he picked it up from. The gurgling sound of the flushing water warned him that the police chief was about to come out of the toilet. He stepped back to the spot and waited as his boss opened the restroom door and walked back to his seat. "So how did it go? "Ahmadu asked, sitting back on his chair. "All went well, sir. The commissioner is pleased with our contribution." "Good." "You will lead the team again to consolidate on the gains of the exercise." "Yes sir." "You can go" Ahmadu waved him off and Joshua saluted once more and headed to the door. He opened the door and stepped out and closed it gently behind. Ahmadu watched the door as it closed and picked up his mobile and punched some digits of memory. It began to ring, and he waited for it to be picked at the other end. Elias' voice came on from the other end. "Hey Ahmadu, how are things going?" "All things are going good and what about your end?" "Everything is going fine." Ahamdu responded. "It was a perfect job your men pulled off." Illiasu said. "Yes, it was quick and clean." Ahmadu said. "Yea, it was." Iliasu said. "Ilia, I am considering sending some men to pay a quick visit to agent Joshua and probably Mark too. I am not comfortable with the idea that they know. It's risky allowing them to continue to exist." "I agree with you. I suggest they be removed as quickly as possible. If they continue to live it seems like we are sitting on a time bomb." "I thought so too. If I may ask; would it not be wise to send some men from your end? At least people they don't know as policemen." "Good idea, I will send some men." "Thanks friend." "No need to thank me, we are chasing the same game." "Yea, but all the same; thanks for your help." "You're welcome." "Talk to you later, some men are waiting to see me." Ahmadu cut the call and relaxed in his chair; different thoughts began to play in his mind. NEXT EVENING at Maxada hotel suite, the man in suit and Yerima concurred and began to talk in low voices. Suddenly a knock at the door and Yerima went and opened it to allow Peter and the police chief in. Both men entered and headed straight to the man in a suit. "Did you hear anything from his end?" Ahmadu asked him. "Many calls came in, but they rang and stopped unpicked." The man in the suit said. "Maybe he did not sleep in the house." Ahmadu said. "I think since you believe he knows; what if he's avoiding his house? Maybe he's hiding somewhere temporarily." Peter said. "I agree with you. His house has been under watch, but he's not been sighted for days now." Ahmadu said. "Doesn't he report to work?" Peter asked. "He does report to work. I must send someone to follow him; to know where he's hiding." Ahmadu said. "Another thing is; if he knows his phone and cars are bugged, he might intentionally avoid them." The man in the suit said. Yerima nodded to this. Ahmadu turned to Peter. "From the investigation we carried out, the wife of the President was not the woman involved in the car bomb incident." Peter stared in surprise. "lai la ilalahu How true is this?" Yerima asked. "This is very bad news to me; though I suspect a foul play because the President kept quiet about her supposed demise." Peter said. "The aid to the first lady was the one involved. My men dug that truth out." "Does Oga know about this?" Yerima asked. "Yes, that is why I called for this meeting. He wants us to begin another phase of his plan." "What's the plan, sir?" Peter asked. Silence in the room as IGP Ahmadu cleared his throat to answer. "It is a long-term plan, in which all of us shall have various roles to play. They all waited and listened. "A camp would be established at the Prez hometown and some gunmen would be sent to warm it." "I am not following; let us get the clearer picture." Yerima said. Ahmadu scanned their faces. "This meeting should not be concluded without other team players. I suggest we reconvene another day to enable others to join us." Ahmadu said. "Any slight idea what Oga might be planning to do?" Peter asked, anxious to know even a little bit of info. "Uhmm Oga is planning to set up a unit at the Prez's hometown. Some of our gunmen would be sent ahead from the major group. Though he didn't elucidate everything to me, he's planning to hit the Prez hard. I believe it might be a ploy to cause a problem between the Prez and his good American friend." Peter smiled and nodded. "It's going to be big; I guess." He said. "I need to run; I have a meeting with some of my men." Ahmadu said and turned to go. "Peter, can I see you at the parking lot briefly?" Ahmadu asked without looking at Peter. "Sure," Peter said and headed out the door with Ahmadu. At the parking lot, Ahmadu stopped near his car and turned to take a glance at the entrance door of the hotel. "I didn't want to say this in there. Oga wants you and Lalong to travel to the Prez's hometown to find ways you can get a good location for the camp before the gunmen would be sent." He said between his lips and looked at Peter with a poker face. "How possible would that be? We've not been to the Prez's hometown before." Peter said. "I believe that won't be any problem. You just throw some money here and there I bet you would find someone willing to show you the deepest part of their bush." Ahmadu said. "Okay, the job must be done by us. No qualms: we would go as tourists just visiting to see the wonders of their nature; luck may smile on us quicker than expected." "That is the spirit; remember, no venture no success. Oga said it must be done as soon as possible." Peter nodded. "Get in touch with Lalong and pass the message to him and get ready to travel in a couple of days. Talk to you again." He grabbed the door handle of his Mercedes car and opened it and put one foot in. He preferred to drive himself to any secret meeting that requires only the team players to come. "The real game is about to begin." He said and grinned at him and disappeared into the car. He roared the engine to life and began to reverse. Peter waved him bye and headed back to the suite.

The next day, it was on Tuesday, time was about nine-thirty in the night. A man in dark clothes sat by a dark corner of the street across Wellington Street where Mark live. The man watched and waited. The building still looked busy with the movements of Mark's co-tenant. The man looked at the front window and the lights were still on, only the one at the left end looked dark. Maybe the occupants have retired to bed. The man kept waiting. To while away time, he brought out a pack of Malboro and pulled out a stick and lighted it with a lighter and held it between his fingers. A gun with a silencer was under his belt. He put the cigarette to his lips and dragged and blow smoke up to the sky. He was away from the view of passers-by. Car lights flashed a few meters away from where he hid. He continued to smoke his cigarette. A few minutes on, all of a sudden, the light went off and darkness fell across the building he was watching. He quickly threw the cigarette to the ground and rose. He stepped on it with his dark booth, and it went dead. He stared across the street for a moment, and watched, no light came on from the building and he quickly crossed the street and stopped at the sidewalk on the other side of the street. He looked at the building and counted twenty in his head and suddenly he hastened to the front of the building and gently pushed the Iron Gate inward and slid in. The darkness provided him a good cover as he slid into the house and stopped at the foot of the staircase. He was instructed to shoot any unfortunate person that might see him and raise an alarm. He waited for a second, but no unfortunate person showed up on the staircase. He took the steps in twos and his hard boots made it impossible to sneak up silently. It was an error on his part to wear a police shoe instead of sneakers. Luck was on his side, or the unknown unfortunate person and he got to Mark's door and stopped and listened. He could hear a family praying seriously as they prepare to retire to bed. No other sounds, every other apartment in the building was quiet. Maybe the occupants were tired to put on their generator sets and preferred to go to bed like that. The man in dark clothes brought out a set of lock picks and began to work on Mark's lock. A few seconds later, the lock clicked open. He grabbed the door handle and the door opened inward without a sound. He slid in and closed it gently behind him and removed a small torch from his trouser pocket and switched it on. The light from the small torch was dim like a fading orange light of a candle. The apartment smelled of thick dust. He pointed the light about in the room and its emptiness stared him blank. He pointed it to the floor and the floor looked dusty and dirty, no broom had touched it for days. He carefully walked to the bedroom and the bed was made, but it looked like no one had slept in it in recent days. He turned and went to the kitchen and an odor of rotten food hit his nostril. He withdrew and as he headed to the door, suddenly the phone began to ring. He stopped abruptly and contemplated picking it but changed his mind. It rang several times and stopped and began to ring again. An idea hit him. It would be good to pick up the call and just listen, maybe he might hear something. He walked to the phone and when he tried to grab the handle it stopped ringing. He stared at it and cursed under his breath. As he turned again to go, it started to ring again. Lunging forward, he grabbed the receiver and put it to his ear and waited. He managed to say hello on impulse and instantly blamed himself for such an error. A woman's voice came on from the other end. "Hello sir, sorry if I woke you from sleep. "No problem, ma'am." He managed to say. I'm Dele Jimoh's widow. My husband left an envelope for you, and he instructed me before he traveled to call you and give it to you. I think it might be important. He said you know what to do with it." The man in dark clothes said a thank you almost in a muffled voice and promised to come to pick up the envelope. He knew the man in a suit would be listening at the other end and must be proud of him for doing such a good job. He thought as he replaced the receiver on its cradle. He walked to the door and stood and listened momentarily. No sound from the outside. He gently opened the door and sneaked out and carefully descended the stairs to the foot of the staircase and slid out the front door into the night. He cut corners and turned right and disappeared into the night. A few minutes later, the man in black opened the door of the hotel suite at Maxada hotel where the man in suit and Yerima were waiting. He closed the door gently and walked to where they sat, a roi tan burning between the fingers of the man in suits. His name was simply known as Scooper. The man in black stood before Scooper and Yerima with happy smile on his lips. "He has not returned to that apartment in recent time." He said. Scooper nodded and dragged his cigar and blew the smoke to the ceiling. "You did well by picking that call. It was revealing." The man in black smiled at the appreciation. "I would have to inform Ahmadu immediately about it. The journalist's wife must be visited immediately." "Yes, I agree with you. It's urgent before she realizes she spoke to the wrong person." Scooper brought out his phone to place a call across to the police chief.

One week later, in the late afternoon, a man eased a blue Toyota Camry with a fake number plate a street away from the residence of late Dele Jimoh. Another young looking man sat in the front seat with him. The one behind wheels wore a police uniform and the other wore black jeans trouser and white Tee shirt. He was neatly dressed. The one in police uniform opened the driver's door and alighted. He scanned the buildings across, then bounced towards the gate. He wore a fake police uniform and he looked young, a man in Mark's age range. A fake police ID was provided for him yesterday in case it was demanded by the widow. A grieving widow might not have the mental balance to reason deep. Ahmadu had said to him. The man confidently walked across the street to the house of the late journalist. His eyes were covered with dark eyeglasses. The neighborhood was quiet; only one or two vehicular movement could be noticed. The man tapped at the gate of the house and a security man peeped through a hole in the gate and saw the man in police uniform. He requested identification. The fake policeman flashed his ID and stared hard at the gateman. "What do you want sir?" the gateman asked. "I am here to collect something from madam." "She's not in the house" The security guard said. "She asked me to come" the policeman insisted. "What is your name, officer?" The security guard asked. "I am ASP Mark" The policeman said. The security guard stepped aside and dialed a number on his mobile. He spoke into mouthpiece in a low voice. Not audible to the man outside the gate. Few seconds later, he returned to the gate. "Please wait officer, let me inform madam that you are here to see her." The man nodded and waited. It was expected. After the bomb incident that killed her husband, it was expected that his family would be more careful about whom they let into their house. After a few minutes of waiting, the gateman returned and opened the small side door of the gate and the man confidently stepped into the large compound. The evening gradually receded into the horizon and the operation must be quick and clean, at least that was the instruction. The gateman pointed to the first floor of a beautiful one-story house in the compound. The man ambled towards it, his right hand in his pocket. From the living room of the house, a beautiful black woman of about late thirties parted the curtain slightly and watched the man approaching the house. He got to the front door and entered and began to ascend the stairs. The woman dropped the curtain and walked back to the sofa. She was alone, her younger children had gone to school and her maid had gone to buy some stuff at the grocery store and her injured son was flown abroad for more medical treatment, as she stayed behind to mourn her dead husband. A knock at the door, she asked the person at the door to come in, and the door gently opened and the man in the police uniform entered. He greeted her and she greeted back and asked him to sit. "I don't have much time to wait, ma'am. My car broke down and I must find a way to get it repaired before night falls." He said. The widow watched him briefly and spoke. "Please why did you come? I don't remember having an appointment with you." The man looked rattled, but he quickly gathered his composure and smiled. "My name is Mark; you called me last night about an envelope your late hubby wanted you to give to me." The woman looked at a small paper by her side and looked at the man. "Please what's your phone number?" The man managed to hide his shock. He rattled his brain and smiled at her. "5656789" Thanks to the little rehearsal he had before setting out on this mission. The woman glanced at the paper and nodded. She rose and walked to a corner and opened a chest of drawers and brought out an official-size brown envelope and walked back and handed it over to him. He grabbed it and it disappeared into his pocket. Suddenly he brought out a pistol with a silencer and the widow opened her mouth in terror to shout but no sound came out. Instantly two muffled shots to her chest, she crashed to the tiled-floor and writhed a little, then lay still, dead. The man in fake police uniform quickly exited and descended the stairs and headed to the gate. Two quick muffled shots to the head of the gateman and the man exited and ran across the street and slid into his car and drove off instantly. He got back to the rendezvous of the players and handed the envelope to Ahmadu who quickly tore it open and read the content silently. The paper in the envelope contained damaging info and details of money laundering against an unidentified person in the paper and a small note had details about the cocaine business involving the person and some other people. No name but initials and codes. Ahmadu turned to Peter and others in the room. "If this had leaked out, it would have been very devastating. The reporter had some damaging info; a potent tool to fight his war." They agreed to let their man know about it immediately.

The next day, the news of the murder of the late journalist's wife spread and it became front-page news questions of who killed her arose, but no one provided an answer.

Three days later, President Andy Ubih walked down the few steps from the living quarter of the Presidential villa into the Garden. The evening was growing older by the seconds. The lights in the beautiful garden were on, casting a beautiful glow in the young calm evening. Andy wore gold-colored pajamas; he planned to retire to bed early. He missed his wife and her absence from the house made him feel very lonely. Two security aids could be seen standing some distance from him, one at the west end and the other at the southern end. He slowly walked to a wooden garden seat which was at the eastern side and sat quietly under a flamboyant tree. The lush garden bloomed with beautiful flowers. A table stood under a royal canopy and colored LED lights were under it and they shone in the young cool evening. Andy punched some digits on his phone to call his wife's mobile phone and put it to his ear and waited as it started to ring. On the fourth ring, she came on from the other end. "Hello, my good husband; how are you doing?" "I'm good and you?" "I'm good but it has not been easy on me because you're not here with us." She said "Same with me; I am missing you so much." "Darling please, visits us in Canada; I am very impatient to see you." "I will visit by the new year." "Okay good, how is Nigeria; are the people that tried to kill us arrested?" "Investigation is still on. Did you watch the news of the terrorist group the police arrested?" "Yes, I watched it on news. Their members killed them to prevent them from exposing the rest of the members of the group." "Yes, the police are intensifying their effort to arrest the members of the group." Andy said and crossed his leg. "Our country is becoming a breeding ground for terrorists."I hope you don't call anyone on phone back home."

"No. I don't call my friends on phone for now. I am very cautious." "Good, I don't want people to know you are alive, and where you are. People believe you're dead." "God forbid, I did not die but them. Darling, please do not bother about that; I don't go out in the daytime but only at late evenings to the stores." Okay, my love. Take care of yourself. I want to retire to bed." "Ooh darling, good night. I love you." She said. "I love you too. Good night." He cut call and relaxed on the seat. Cool breeze caressed his body; he closed his eyes and began to meditate. It had been a busy day and so much had happened that pricked him.

The next day evening: Ahmadu was relaxing in his living room when his mobile rang. He picked it and Gusau was on the line. "Hello big boy, how are you doing?" Ahmadu asked excitedly. "I am always good." Gusau said. In Mark's room, Joshua listened to the conversation between the two police heads. "I called Oga today and he told me of his plans to hire the pro assassin to perform in America. He wants him to kidnap the daughter of the American President." Ahmadu said. "That sounds like a big plan. I think it is very risky to accomplish; the FBI and CIA are there." Gusau said. In Mark's room, Joshua turned and looked at Mark and they continued to listen. The phone was on speaker. Back to Ahmadu's house, "Two of our men would be traveling to the Prez's hometown to establish a camp for some gunmen that would be sent there to warm it." Ahmadu said. "That sounds good. I like what I am hearing." Gusau said and they laughed softly. Joshua and Mark continued to listen at the other end. "The international gunman would play a major role in changing the settings. Oga knows it would be difficult and he's ready to pay any fee to get it done." Mark looked at Joshua in surprise and they continued to listen. "He wants to rattle the American Prez and in the long run that would cause friction between the two friends." "I like the smell of this." Gusau said. "Meet me in my office morrow, we have something to discuss." Ahmadu said and they said their byes and Ahmadu cut call. Mark and Joshua stared at each other in great shock at what they heard. This is becoming bigger than envisaged.

CHAPTER NINE

THE VULTURES GATHERED TOGETHER at a meeting point, somewhere in a secluded area in a large compound with a beautiful two-story building, belonging to Alhaji Gambo. Peter, Solomon, Lalong, Alhaji Indai, and the police chief were there. It was on a cool evening in mid-November. The men wore different shades of traditional wear except for Peter who wore his traditional suit. He got used to wearing suits since his days in The States and he preferred them to the traditional wears. Ahmadu cleared his throat and silence fell in the circle and the rest watched him. "Our men tried to locate our pain in the neck, but he seemed to have disappeared into thin air." Ahmadu said. "Doesn't he report to work?" Peter asked. "No, he has stopped coming to work." Ahmadu answered and sighed. "It's important he's located and deleted quickly." Lalong said. "Our men are still looking for him. We hope to find him soon." Ahmadu said sadly. "This proves that he knows he's been watched. "Peter said. "Ahmadu nodded. "Someone from my office is helping him and he too is nowhere to be found." Ahmadu said. "Both of them are dangerous and must be located as quickly as possible." Alhaji Indai said. "This is very disturbing; we should not allow them to be clogs in the wheel of our progress." Alhaji Gambo said. "Nothing to worry about; they have been placed on the hit list. I sent men to kill them, but the men couldn't find them in their homes." "We would have a full meeting soon; comprising all units." Ahmadu said. Silence fell across and others began to weigh options in their heart. Ahmadu looked at Peter and Lalong and waved them to step away with him from the group. They stepped aside and Ahmadu spoke. "When are you embarking on the journey to the Prez's hometown?" "Peter looked at Lalong."If all things go well, we shall travel in two days. Is that okay by you, Lalong?" Lalong nodded. "In two days is okay by me." Ahmadu nodded. "Oga practically asked me to tell you how important this is to the project." "No need to worry, it'd be done." Peter assured. "Good. The contact will meet you when you arrive. He's part of us and knows about the game. He would assist you." "Good," Lalong said and Ahmadu turned and went back to the group. "Oga wanted me to send the goons that carried out the car bombings at Daxa parking-lot but I gave him reasons why we shouldn't use them on this crucial adventure." Peter only nooded. "Let's rejoin them." They walked back to where others waited.

Ahmadu said, "Sorry, gentlemen, we stepped aside to discuss their travel to the Prez's hometown." Others nodded and waited for him to say more.

That night, Mark and Joshua sat in the temporary room that Mark hid himself away from prying eyes. Their guns lay beside them on the sofa. The knowledge that the conspirators are hunting them and the danger involved kept them at alert always. The conspirators won't waste time to kill them the instant they are located. They began to plot how best to wage this war to expose the nefarious elements that are involved in the crime. "At least we now know some of the conspirators. The IGP, SSS chief and DIG are working for someone in obscurity. It's a big plot, a collective intent to make someone benefit if the President is assassinated." Joshua said. "Yes, my question is who the oga is?" "That's a mystery to be solved. The game is getting harder, and the deadly and ruthless conspirators are desperate to advance to a dangerous line." Joshua said in sadness. "A dangerous edge you'd rather say. An edge where all of them would precipitate into a thoroughfare filled with the jagged edge of broken metals." Mark said.

Two days later, Peter woke up slowly and rolled to the other side of the bed in his hotel room. It was still very early in the morning. He was tired, after a long journey from Lagos to President Andy Ubih's hometown. He lifted his watch on the bedside drawer and managed to peer in to check the time. Time said four in the morning. He lay quiet and allowed his mind to settle and relax. He and Lalong got to the Prez hometown late in the night around 10 pm. They were instructed to travel by road, to look like other ordinary travelers without raising suspicion. They had arrived and asked questions about where to get lodging and two commercial bike riders took them to LION GARDEN SUITES. Peter asked the commercial bike riders to come back in the morning around 8 am to pick them up and show them the town. He claimed they were tourists and had heard so much about the town.

A few minutes later, Peter fell back to sleep and started to snore. About ten minutes on, the first ray of the sun began to rise in the sky. Some distance away, a chanticleer announced the new dawn, the beginning of another new day. The weather was calm without any breeze. Somewhere in the distance other chanticleers joined in announcing the new day. Peter just lay quiet in bed listening to the distant noises of the town's awakening. A church bell chimed somewhere in the far distance. Peter's thoughts left the distance and his ears tried to pick for any movements in the Hotel but heard nothing. The other lodgers were still enjoying their sleep. In another room, Lalong stirred in his sleep and remained still again. The lights were on. He hated to sleep without the lights on whenever he was in a new place. Slowly he began to open his eyes to the environment. He had no watch but as the cockerels were crewing, to him that indicated a new dawn. He yawned and stretched, yawned again and gently rolled off the bed and sat straight up and began to listen. He wore blue pajamas with some touch of stripes. Suddenly his cell phone started to ring. He picked it and looked at the caller id, then spoke briefly into it. "Yes" He said into mouthpiece. "Hello sir, one of the targets is in the net and one eluded us." A nervous voice spoke from the other end and paused to listen. A thick voice said to the man. "Extract the truth from him and make sure you delete him. Dump his body in dirty water." "Yes sir, he's about to receive VIP treatment." The previous voice said. "Good, get it over with." The other man at the other end said and cut the call. Lalong smiled to the room. That was Adamu's voice. He connected a conference call for them to hear it first-hand but it wasn't necessary. Lalong thought. Peter must have listened to to it too. As he put down his mobile on the bed and made to get up, his phone started to ring again. He lifted it and looked at the caller ID. Peter was on the line. Lalong picked the call and spoke softly, "Hey P" "You listened to the connected call?" Peter asked. "Yea. Good news." He said. "This is real exciting news." Peter said from the other end and quickly added. "I think we should start getting ready, the bike men will arrive soon." "Okay, I will shower and be ready in no time." Lalong assured. "Ok, see you in about half an hour." Peter said and cut call. Lalong stood and walked into the toilet to freshen up. Peter punched the digits of the contact Ahmadu gave him on his mobile and waited as it began to ring. It rang several times, but no one picked from the other end. He redialed and it rang till it cut. No response. He decided they would do it alone without the contact. He put a call across to Lalong to inform him. As Lalong mobile rang he tied a towel and stepped out from the bathroom to pick call. "What's up?" He said into mouthpiece, a shaving stick on his right hand. "The contact isn't picking call. We may go it without him." He said. "Anyway that works best." Lalong said. Peter cut call and entered into the bathroom to bath.

A FEW HOURS LATER, the two bike men arrived and went straight to the hotel reception and requested the receptionist to inform Peter and Lalong that they had come to take them to wherever they wanted to go in the town. A few seconds later, Peter and Lalong descended the stairs and the two bike riders greeted them and headed out to their bikes. Peter and Lalong joined them, and they rode into town. Peter and Lalong joined them, and they rode into town. Peter claimed they were tourists, and they came to see the town, the waters, and any other interesting part of the town. Peter claimed they were tourists, and they came to see the town, the waters, and any other interesting part of the town. The bike men set out on the assignment and began by pointing out the King's palace. The bike men set out on the assignment and began by pointing to the king's palace. From there, they rode to the far end of the town. From there, they rode to the far end of the town. The areas were uninhabited with slopes and small hills along the route to the stream. The areas were uninhabited areas with slopes and small hills along the route to the stream. Thick bushes covered many parts of it except the un-macadamized road that ran straight from the stream up into the main town. Thick bushes covered many parts of it except the un-macadamized road that ran straight from the stream up into the main town. Peter even noticed gullies and erosion sites in some parts of the town. Peter even noticed gullies and erosion sites in some parts of the town. The journey stopped at the top of a small hill that led downhill to a small brook. The journey stopped at the top of a small hill that led downhill to a small brook. Peter and Lalong stepped down from the bike and scanned the beautiful scenery. Peter and Lalong stepped down from the bike and scanned the beautiful scenery. Birds sang in the bushes around them, and the environment was calm. Birds sang in the bushes and there was this calmness about the environment. The cool sweet breeze occasionally stirred the leaves in the bush to dance to its silent sound. The cool sweet breeze occasionally stirred the leaves in the bush to dance to its silent sound. Something was soothing about the place. Something was soothing about the place. A serenity that encompassed their understandings; the place oozed with great equanimity. "Oh, this place is beautiful." Peter exclaimed. "Yes Oga, it is the best stream in our local government. This is the source of pipe-born water to all towns in our local government." The first man said. "Wow, splendid. Look at the slope, the surrounding is beautiful," Lalong said as he pointed downhill. "What is that small building down there?" Peter asked pointing to a small zinc house with only one door. "That is the engine room, sir." The second bike man answered. "We call it water board house, sir." The first bike man added with a smile." The state water cooperation used there as a substation to supply water to some of the towns in the local government." Peter nodded and scanned the environment again. "That high terrain we descended from on our way here; what is it called?" Lalong asked as he pointed in the direction they had come. "Oh, that place the road sloped like this Look at the slope, the surrounding is beautiful." Lalong said as he pointed downhill. "What is that small building down there?" Peter asked and pointed to a small zinc house with only one door. "That is the engine room, sir." The second bike man answered. "We call it water board house, sir." The first bike man added with a smile. "The state water corporation used it as a substation to supply water across to some of the towns in the local government." Peter nodded and scanned the environment again. "That high terrain we descended from our way here; what is it called?" Lalong asked, pointing in the direction they had come. "Oh, that place the road sloped like this. He demonstrated with his hand. "That place is called

Ugwu Nwosa." The first Bike man said. "Ugwu nosaa," Lalong attempted. The bike men laughed out loud happily and the second bike man shook his head. "No oga, not like that. It is Ugwu Nw..o.sa he pronounced it slowly for them to catch the correct phrase." Peter slowly attempted the pronunciation of the word again. "Ugwu Nw..o.sa." "Yes yes, you got it!" The second bike man said excitedly and the two bike men clapped for Peter who felt good. Every one of them laughed happily about it and a bond was created instantly.

Peter brought out his cell phone and recorded the word; he pronounced it slowly the first time and the second time he pronounced it correctly without stopping. The bike men clapped and cheered for him because he pronounces it perfectly. He put back the phone into his trouser pocket and asked the bike men to take them to any other place with bush, where they could see other beautiful scenes of nature. They clambered back onto the bike and rode off going back the way they came. Peter was satisfied by the scenery he saw. The bush would serve its purpose. Their journey had been fruitful.

SOME HOURS LATER, the two bike men rode back with Peter and Lalong to the hotel where Peter and Lalong thanked them for their help. Peter pulled out a wad of naira notes and counted out eight thousand naira and handed it over to the first bike man. "Share this equally amongst yourselves." The bike man collected the money smiling happily. "Thank you, sir, we are very grateful." "Thank you, sir" The second bike man thanked them. "Come in the morning to take us to the motor park where we can board a bus to Enugu," Lalong said to them. "It must be very early, so we can reach the airport on time." "Yes, sir," the first bike man said. They agreed to come at five in the morning to take them to the park. Two days later, in mid-morning; Peter and Solomon, Alhaji Indai, Alhaji Gambo, Lalong, and IGP Ahmadu Sanda sat in Alhaji Indai's Office. They were talking in low voices. "So, Peter, how did it go?" Ahmadu asked. Peter cleared his throat. "Everything went well. We saw some places I believe are good for the camp." Peter said. "Good. How is the town; how busy is it?" Ahmadu asked. "It is not a busy town; there are very quiet areas with few people." "There is a police area command in the town." "Yes, it is true sir," Lalong said. "Chief, the police contact that was supposed to help us didn't answer the call," Peter informed him. "Yes, sorry about that. He called me later apologizing that he was on duty, and that he lost his phone a couple of days before you arrived the town." "Okay," Peter said. "How big is the town?" Alhaji Gambo asked. "We can't say but the town has banks, motor parks hotels and restaurants, hospitals, and few recreation centers from what we saw." "The town is big then," Garba Indai said. "It's fairly large but not in terms of development. I have been there once when I went to commission the police area command."

Ahmadu said. "That is good to know." Solomon said. "My question is what is oga planning to do?" Sambo asked. "All I know for now is that oga has a very big plan to hit the Prez hard. He hasn't let me into full details." Ahmadu said and clasped his hands. "When do we start moving the gunmen?" Peter asked. "I will discuss with him tonight; I ask all of you to be ready and do what is required." Ahmadu said and looked from man to man. Gambo adjusted his Babariga on his shoulder and coughed a little. "I am ready to do what I can for us to archive our set goal." He said. "It won't be easy, but I am confident we will reach our set goal." Solomon said and rubbed his hands. "I like the spirit gentlemen. Let's work to reach the winning line." Ahmadu said and turned to Peter with a smile. "Everything will surely turn out good." Peter said. "The Prez must die for us to get to our destination." Indai added and rocked in his seat. "Gentlemen; I am itching for celebration, how long are we going to wait." Others laughed softly and then Ahmadu rose from his chair and silence fell in the office. "We will have to reconvene to discuss ways forward. But first, let me discuss with Oga." He rose from the chair and pushed it backward. "See you again; I must be on my way." He said and others rose too, and all began to head to the exit door.

Mark and agent Joshua, discuss in front of a parked car, along Trinity Road. Cars driving pass in the late evening. Darkness struggled with light as some light bulbs illuminate the environment. A woman walked pass and eyed them and walked on and Mark and his interlocutor did not notice her." I am happy you can come on short notice." Mark said to Joshua. "I managed to sneak out from my hiding; how are you doing." Joshua said and glanced about. "I am good, thanks. I learned something from my source at the state commissioner of police's end and he told me that the police commissioner is very close to the IGP." Mark paused to allow that to sink in. Joshua waited for him to continue. "My source suspects the police van incidence was not as the public was made to believe." Mark said. "So, what else does he know or suspect?" Joshua asked. "He said he overheard a phone conversation when the state commissioner of police was saying I will send two of my men from the south as sacrifices." Mark said. "Did your source say anything about dead policemen in the prison van incident?" Joshua asked and glanced about again as the car drove by. Darkness continued to descended and provided them a good cover., "Yes he said two policemen from their unit were involved, they were the ones burnt beyond recognition." Mark said and stepped closer to Joshua. "We can't go back to work for now; I suggest we find a way to stop them. We're being hunted by the conspirators, and they won't wait for a second to kill us the moment they lay eyes on us. Mark said softly as if someone was listening very close. A Honda Civic was parked a little distance from where they stood and inside, Sleek Queen watched them from behind the wheels of the Honda Civic. She lifted a radio and radioed someone, then continued to watch from the dark windscreen. From the opposite direction, a very sleek black car dangerously turned onto the street and pulled to a stop a little distance from where Mark and Joshua stood, the headlights switched off but the engine kept running. The two Agents stopped talking and looked at the black car in apprehension. The front and back door of the black car was thrown open and two men with guns stepped out. Mark on impulse dashed across the road but before Joshua could try to run the men ordered him to stop or they shoot him. They herded him into the back seat of the black Mercedes at gunpoint and one of the men fell beside him and the other slid into the front seat and the car drove off. Mark ran and hid behind a kiosk. The Honda civic had started the instant Mark ran off. Sleek Queen had u-turned in a bid to chase him but lost him. He got lucky. She drove on; her eyes darted about in an effort to find him. She rolled the car slowly, her eyes searching for him. He has escaped. She cut corners and entered another dark street and drove away into the night. The black car drove along a lonely rough road, entered left, and drove down another road. Mark came out from hiding immediately and ran to a commercial bike man that just stopped for a passenger to climb down. Mark flashed his badge at him and told him "Police. Please borrow me your motor-bike. It's urgent." The bike-man shook his head in reluctance. "I am working officer" He protested. "I know, I will bring it back to you in a short moment." The man disembarked from the motor-bike and Mark grabbed the handle and climbed on. "Thank you. I am coming back."He borrowed the motorbike and began to chase the black car from a safe distance. The car turned right and entered a less busy street. Mark followed. The car drove on and joined the expressway. Mark continued to follow two cars behind. Suddenly the car left the expressway and drove down a lonely rough road that was not lit. Mark killed the headlight of the motorbike and rode through bumps. The lights of the black car were on low, and no other vehicular movements were on the road. Mark continued to follow from a safe distance, almost at a crawl. Suddenly the black car slowed drastically. Mark stopped and watched. The car rolled before an iron gate and eased to a stop. Instantly the Iron Gate opened inward, the car drove in, and the gate closed. Mark stepped down from the motorbike, stood it, and ran to the right side of the road. He sneaked to the brick fence of the building, pulled his automatic out, and listened. The driver killed the engine. The gunmen stepped down and ordered Joshua out of the car, guns pointed at him. Joshua, in fear, rolled out of the car, his hands up in the air. The driver stepped out and walked behind them, a pistol in his hand. The men propelled him towards the front door of a small house, with a high brick wall. The neighborhood was quiet, and the next nearest house was about five hundred meters away. As they got to the front door it instantly opened inward. A huge man in a black jacket stood at the door. The other man that opened the Iron Gate waited behind the car and watched the gate. They entered and took Joshua to an empty room without any item of furnishing by the right, then bonded his hands and feet to a chair. The man in the black jacket stepped aside and dialed a number on his mobile. He put it to his ear as it started to ring. The man returned to his colleague and whispered to him. There was no ceiling fan in the room, no furniture; it was empty, and only a white bulb glowed from the ceiling. Mark checked the fence to see if there was any easy place to scale through but saw none. The wall fence stood at about twelve feet high. The huge man in the black jacket stepped in front of Joshua and slapped him hard. Joshua moaned in pain and stared at him hard. "Where is your friend, Mark?" The man asked but got no response. The man glanced at his colleague standing a little distance away and said with a wicked smile, "We have a hard guy here." His colleague smiled wryly and stepped forward. He looked tough and dangerous. He glared at Joshua and landed a slap on his face. Joshua yelled in terror; his lips were covered with blood. "Now for the second time; where can we find Mark?" The second man asked; his face hard. "I don't know where you can find him." Joshua answered and spat blood from his mouth. "How dare you lie to us?" The huge man in black jacket asked angrily and slapped Joshua again. The other man grabbed Joshua's neck and began to strangle him. Joshua struggled to breathe and a few seconds on the man freed his neck. Joshua gasped and tried to steady his breath. "Are you ready to tell us where Mark is, or should we touch you more?" The man in the black jacket asked. "Honestly I don't know where you can find him." Joshua answered and cut his eyes to the gun at the back of the other man. Mark sneaked to the gate. He looked through a small aperture in the gate and saw a man near the car. He gently tapped on the gate and slid by the wall, his gun pointing ready in his hand. The man heard it and turned to the gate. He walked to his gate, pulled out a gun, lifted a cover, and peered out into the night. He saw no one; only thick darkness. He walked back to where he stood earlier and lit a cigarette, dragged and blew thick smoke up to the air. All of a sudden another tap came at the gate. He listened attentively; his eyes watched the gate. Mark slid to a wall again and waited with his gun. The man inside walked to the gate and gently unbolted it. Some kids might be playing pranks again at the gate. It had happened before. He vowed in his mind to punish the kids that are disturbing him. The last time he let them go free but not today. As he pushed open the gate and peered out; instantly Mark hit him on the head with the butt of his automatic rifle. The man made a low painful sound and staggered, and at that moment, Mark jumped him and grabbed his neck and violently twisted it. It broke and the goon dropped to the ground. Mark picked up the man's pistol and put it into his trouser pocket and stepped into the compound. The man in black jacket signaled his colleague aside and whispered to him something and entered another room. The man withdrew his gun from his back under his belt and kissed its muzzle and waved it at Joshua. Joshua watched him. "Are you ready to tell me where we can find him or would you prefer, I pump a few bullets into your head?" he pointed the gun at Joshua. "I don't know where you can find him." The man shot at the wall in demonstration and pointed the gun back at Joshua. Suddenly the front door burst open, and Joshua and the man looked at the door. Mark somersaulted into the room and landed on one knee and shot the man in the chest before the goon could even try to squeeze his trigger. Joshua stared at the happening in surprise. Mark quickly withdrew the pistol belonging to the man at the gate from his trouser pocket and placed it into Joshua's hands and slid by the wall because there was not enough time to loosen the rope from Joshua's arms. He cut the rope from Joshua's arms with a piece of a broken bottle he had picked from outside. Joshua began to loosen the rope from his feet. The instant the gunshot rang out, the other men inside stopped drinking their beer and picked up their guns and ran towards the room Joshua was kept. As the first man appeared through the door Joshua fired at him and he crashed to the floor Mark opened fire through the open door and held the trigger down, bullets flew out rapidly and hit the second man that ran out from a room and he crashed to the floor, dead, blood splattered on the floor and wall. Mark stopped shooting and slid by a wall. Joshua freed himself and sprang to his feet and slid by a wall, his gun pointing forward, ready. From his calculation there remained a man inside unless more men were in the house before they brought him to the house. The remaining goon heard the gunshots from inside a restroom and quickly ran out and Mark saw him. Mark sneaked close before the goon could enter a room to pick up his gun. He pointed the gun at the man's head. "Freeze" Mark yelled, the man heard him and saw him, the gun pointing to his head. He stopped in his track and raised his two hands up in surrender. Joshua stepped forward and pointed his gun at the base of the man's neck. "Who are you working for?" He yelled at the man but no response. The man kept quiet and trembling. His breathing was heavy. "Didn't you hear him!? Who are you working for?" Mark yelled in at him. "I, I, I don't know him; I was recruited by another person." The man stuttered. "And who's the man that recruited you? Talk or I shoot you now!" Joshua jabbed the muzzle of the gun into the man's rib. The man winced in pain but remained silent. Joshua pulled the trigger and shot the man. He crashed to the floor, dead. Joshua turned to Mark. "Thank you for rescuing me." Joshua said. "You'd do the same for me, friend." Mark said. They walked through the door and headed to the gate. At the gate Mark stopped and watched for a brief moment if anyone would appear from a corner. No one, he slid his gun under his belt and let his shirt drop loose. They exited through the gate and Mark pointed forward. They went to the motorbike and rode off into the night.

SHE EXCITEDLY PREPARED TO MEET HIM. AT THE US PRESIDENT'S LIVING QUARTER, Alice walked out of the bathroom, a white towel wrapped around her beautiful body. Her big breast hid under the white towel. She headed to the dressing table and checked herself in the mirror. Her tall frame, and beautiful face, stared back at her from the mirror and her red-blond hair hid inside her shower cap. Her reflection in the mirror pleased her. She just had her bath, and suddenly a knock sounded at the door. She turned to the door and asked the person at the door to come in. She picked up her cream from where she kept her cosmetics and the door opened slowly her sister, Laura walked into the room and closed the door gently behind her. Alice glanced at her sister walking towards the sofa. She sat down and watched her elder sister apply the cream to her body. Laura looked sad and very downcast. A musical was playing on the Led Tv on the white wall. The large room looked beautifully adorned with blue-colored and a glass table. The blinds were closed to wade off the chill from the cold winter outside. The winter started early, and it could be noticed even on the windowpane. Alice said to her sister without looking at her." "Laura, what is it, did you just walk into my room to watch me?" Alice asked screwing the cover of the cream back. "Alice, I need your help." Alice turned and faced her sister, her hand on her cream. "You look worried kid sis, what's the problem?" Alice asked. Laura began to sob; she cupped her chin in her hands. Alice quickly got up and went to her and sat beside Laura on the sofa and she placed her arm on her shoulder. "Talk to me Laura, what's the problem? Why are you crying?" she nudged her playfully. Alice loved her younger sister and she hated to see her cry. Now it is obvious Laura is very troubled. Laura kept sobbing softly. "Laura, please talk to me. I hate to see you this way, what's bugging your mind sis?" "Sis it is Andrew." She said softly and continued to sob "What about Andrew; did you quarrel with him?" Alice asked, looking worried "He's cheating on me," Laura said and turned to look at Alice, tears ran down her cheeks. "He's cheating on you?" Alice asked in surprise. Laura nodded and sobbed, even more, Alice ran her hand over Laura's white-blonde hair and said to her soothingly. "Stop crying Laura, he is not worth it." "I love him very much. Oh, I'm heartbroken." Laura cried out sadly and shook her head. "How did you find out about this?" Alice asked anxiously. "I caught him kissing the daughter of Senator John in his car." Laura answered and sobbed softly; she rubbed her eyes and began to sniff. "Does he know you saw them?" Alice asked. "It took him some time to notice me watching them kiss. As soon as he noticed my presence, he quickly disengaged from her, and came out of the car and tried to explain that it was not what I thought; then I ran and did not look back." Laura answered in agony. "I never liked that guy, not for anything. This is one of the reasons I prefer to find my man. Not the one dad and mum arrange for me, not any son of any fucking Senator or what." Laura looked at Alice. Why did her sister use the F word? It's unlike her, Laura reasoned in her heart. "Andrew has been promising me love eternity." Laura lamented. "Aww fake love; you know how some of these young men do; they can promise heaven on earth just to lay you. Stop sobbing sis; he is not worth your tears or love." Alice said and put her hand across Laura's shoulder. "Is mum aware of this?" Alice asked. "No, haven't told her. I came to you straight." Laura answered. "You'll have to let her know. Let her know you don't wanna have anything to do with Andrew again." Laura nodded and rubbed her tears with the back of her hand. "Let me get dressed, just got out from the shower when you came in. Relax sis, everything is gonna be fine." Alice said to Laura and kissed her on the cheek; she stood up and went back into her bedroom.

CHAPTER TEN

MARK DROVE IN RENTED RED Toyota car, through busy Afolabi Street, in Lagos Mainland. He rolled the Toyota off Afolabi and entered the parking lot of DRIPPING FINGERS. He eased to a stop and killed the engine. There were Cars of different makes parked in the parking lot. He was very famished and needed to buy his food without much delay but the many cars parked at the parking lot were evidence of many customers in the restaurant. He waited for a fraction of a second in the car, contemplating to drove to another restaurant where might be less filled with customers. On a second thought he decided to go in to lunch. He glanced in the rearview mirror to see if anyone was watching. Seeing no prying eyes, he removed his Smith and Wesson .38 pistol and hid it under his car seat and opened the car door. He alighted and closed the door gently. Two men stood in different positions at the parking lot watching him. One of the men was short and bearded. The man was standing near a white Nissan car facing the exit road, and the other, at the north side of the parking lot. They continued watching him as he moved away from his car; their hands were buried in the pockets of their jackets. As he moved closer the entrance glass door of the restaurant and bar, he heard someone screamed from the inside of the restaurant. Gunshot went off right away and he heard a male voice shouted a command. "Everybody lie on the floor!" "Bring out your phones and monies!" Mark stopped abruptly and retraced his steps back to his car. Straight away, one of the men watching him from the north side of the parking lot nimble toward him as he grabbed his car door. The short man pulled out a semi-automatic. "Freeze", he yelled to Mark's back. Mark stopped his hand on the car door. "Bring out all your money and phones, your ATM Cards too." The man was to close for comfort, the semi-automatic pointing at Mark's back. Mark quickly brought out the cash on him and his credit card, he tried to turn. "Put them on the ground and lie flat on your belly. The man's hard voice stopped him. Mark complied. "Your hands stretched forward. Don't try to act smart or you will force me to waste you." The robber added, his face painted with a frown. Mark gently flattened himself on the hard ground, his hands stretched in front. The robber picked up his money, credit card, and his phone. "Lie still or you die!!" Mark lay still on the ground, listening as raised voices filtered from inside the restaurant. A couple of minutes passed, and two men rushed out from inside the restaurant, all armed. One of the robbers' who was bigger commanded. "Let's get out of here!" Their man at the white Toyota car slid behind wheels and started the car; the engine idled away as he waited for his colleagues to join him for a quick getaway. The leader noticed Mark on the ground and pointed at him. "Has he emptied his pockets?" The short and bearded robber still pointing a gun at Mark nodded "Yes boss, He has vomited all." He answered. The leader of the armed robbers flicked his head, and his men began to move quickly towards the waiting car. "Let's go, the leader yelled to the one still pointing a gun at Mark's head. "Boss, should I waste him?" The man asked. The leader stopped momentarily and turned, looked at Mark on the ground. Mark held his breath. This is it; this is how he lost all. He thought. He waited and prayed silently knowing his end was nigh. Suddenly the leader of the gang spoke, "No, I am not in the mood to kill anyone today. Let's go!" They both quickly moved to the white Nissan car and joined their colleagues, and the car drove into the road. The road has suddenly become less busy. People across the street scampered for safety. The robber's car accelerated toward an intersection. Immediately, Mark got up from the ground and cut his eyes at the entrance door of the restaurant. Some bolder People came out from the restaurant, and the terrified ones were still afraid the robbers might still be lurking around. All their phones and ATM cards were carted away. Mark yanked his car door and slid in and roared the engine to life and began to reverse. He leveled the gear to drive and began to chase the robbers. It was obvious to him he was taking a big risk. He has become a hunted man and the men after his life won't waste time to kill him the moment they caught up with him, and now he's chasing escaping armed robbers. If the robbers smell him trailing their car, they would waste him. He prayed for luck, and he won't dare show himself to the police as part of them. He was hunted by ruthless conspirators that would do anything to silence him because he knows too much. At the Surulere link road, the robbers' turned left and raced towards Mende, Maryland. Mark followed cautiously from a safe distance, trying not to lose the car ahead. If he could follow the robbers to their location, he would find a way to call Joshua for help and maybe find a way to pass info to the police where the robbers were. Suddenly a siren wailed from behind and headed his way. He glanced in the rear-view mirror and saw a police van approaching from behind. Good, he doesn't have to continue the chase; maybe the police got the info and are after the robbers. He slowed to allow the police van to fly pass. The police van with armed policemen flew pass and in chase of the escaping armed robbers. "You can have them guys," he said and slowed the car. He finally eased to a stop, took a U-turn, and headed towards Costain. A hunted man should tread softly. Mark relaxed and his thought shifted to the discussion he had with Agent Joshua concerning some of his findings. A source told Joshua that Lawal was quickly transferred to a northern state a couple of days ago. The conspirators are desperate to cover up and silence anyone that knows about their evil plot. Lawal was from the same region as the IGP and the DIG and some of the other conspirators, so the reason he was quickly transferred back to the north was to keep the secret safe. Mark has no doubt the bloodsuckers would do everything within their power to kill him. All of a Sudden his mobile began to ring. He slowed and brought out his mobile and he checked the caller ID, his sister was on the line. "Hello sis." He said into mouthpiece. "Bro Mark, how are you doing?" "Missing you, sis." Mark said. He eased off the road and finally pulled to a stop to talk with his sister. "He spoke with joy, gesticulating as he continued to talk with his sister on phone. A few seconds on, he said. "I will call you later. I am parked off the road. "He cut call and made to pocket his phone but changed his mind and decided to call his girlfriend. He dialed a registered number on his phone and waited for it to ring.

Somewhere in a house, Garba adjusted in his seat and watched Amadu. "Salem is coming to brief you about my plans and ask peter to contact our professional gunman. I want him to bring the girl down here." A confident hard voice said from the other end. "Yes sir," Amadu said, and the caller cut call. "Peter, Oga wants you to contact the international gunman." "When?" Peter asked without enthusiasm. Mark smiled and spoke into the mouthpiece. "Hey, my beautiful; how are you doing?" "I am fine sweetheart", she answered from the other end. "Hope work is good?" Mark asked. "Yea, I am planning to visit you by the weekend. I miss you so much." She said. "I miss you too babe, Emmm, I suggest you postpone your visit babe; right now, I am on an important assignment that would take me away from the city for weeks." "Oh, why now, I managed to get a few days permission to travel." She lamented. "Don't worry I would find a way to come see you myself. I miss you a lot." Mark said. "Okay, if you promise." She said. "I promise, Mandy." Mark assured her. Mandy sighed heavily from the other end and brief silence before she spoke again. "I can't wait to see you honey." She sounded disappointed. "I can't wait too, sweet. I love you." Mark said and blew her a kiss, and she blew him a kiss too and they said their byes, and Mandy cut the call. Mark began to think. I can't let her know, he reasoned in his mind. No, it's dangerous to let her into it. If I tell her I'd put her life in danger too, and if I allow her to visit, she will ask questions and I won't provide an answer. It is better to keep her from harm's way. He weighed these thoughts in his mind as he turned right and drove onto a connecting bridge. He drove towards Liverpool axis, his mind continued to ponder on how best to handle the situation, how to expose the conspirators. If he tells the President, it might be too early to open the can of worms, and the enemies are not going to wait until they delete him. He thought of talking to some officers in the police force to seek their assistance and find a way to expose the evil people. No that's too dangerous, he reasoned. Right now, Joshua is the only agent I trust, and right now two of us are hiding away. He said inside him. If they could locate them a couple of days ago, when they stood discussing off the road at Trinity link road, then the enemies have someone following them. He reasoned and looked into his rear-view mirror, but the closest vehicle was a little distance away and it was a yellow bus. Suddenly a thought struck him. He thought of phoning his sister in the States to help him get Victor's phone number. Victor was an FBI agent whose father was from the same town as Mark and President Andy Ubih. Special agent Victor visited his father's hometown three years ago, and he and Mark became acquainted. He ruled the idea off from his heart with the reason that if he tell agent Victor about what he and Joshua found out about a plot by deadly conspirators in the country's high position to hurt the American President and probably a member of his family too, how he would prove it would be another issue. He can't tell any policeman in Nigeria, except Joshua who knew already. The conspirators are deadly, and he wouldn't want an innocent person to get killed because of this secret he found out. He resolved. It's his war, and he will fight it with or without the help of Joshua. Suddenly a surge of confidence grew in his heart. He made up his mind to prepare for the impending war.

DECEMBER 5, morning. Peter and Alhaji Garba Indai knocked at a door, gently opened it, and walked into an office. Inside the well-furnished office, a large table and chairs stood a few feet away and a man sat on the large office chair at the other side of the table, his back to them. Peter and Alhaji Garba greeted, and the man simply said, "Sit down gentlemen." They slid to the chairs and waited. The man kept quiet, his chair rocking. Peter and Alhaji Garba looked at each other, unsaid words in their minds, and they watched in silence. A few seconds on; a tap sounded at the door and IGP Ahmadu Sanda opened the door, stepped into the office, and gently closed the door. He went to where the two others sat before the large table. Pleasantries were exchanged between Ahamadu and Peter, and then Garba Indai and the police chief picked their seats. The large leather chair behind the large mahogany table turned, and the man behind the table smiled at them. His name was Abudu. He oversees Oga's many interests as Oga's confidant and childhood friend. He has been out of the country. He was 50, tall and lanky, with light skin. He was irascible, and he has Fulani ancestry. "Welcome gentlemen I appreciate you coming on short notice." Abudu said, and others nodded and waited. "On the directive of Oga, I call you here to discuss the next plan and he instructs that we discuss the plan of sending some gunmen to the President's hometown." He adjusted his agbada and watched them. "How many gunmen are we looking at?" Ahmadu asked and crossed his leg. He wore a brown short sleeve shirt with pockets in front and trousers of the same color, black shoes Peter wore his usual suit but of gray color, and Alhaji Garba wore cream color long sleeve damask material over same color trousers. Abudu gently began to tap a pen on the table and looked at them calmly. "He is considering sending ten gunmen to the President's town." He said. "I suggest the men should travel individually to the town, and that way no one will suspect anything. Lalong and I will travel ahead of them to receive them when they arrive." Peter said. "Good suggestion. Since you know the terrain, it is pertinent you and Lalong receive and settle them in." Abudu said and lifted the receiver of the phone on the table and put it to his ears. He dialed a number, and it rang thrice, and he cut the call and replaced the receiver. He looked at the men before him and said. "The duty lies with us. The gunmen are ready to travel." "I have an officer who is very loyal to me at the Police Area command in the town. I will link him up to assist them." The police chief said. Garba Indai turned to Ahmadu, "Inspector sir, can he be trusted?" he asked. "Yes, he is very loyal to me. He can kill for me. He knows most of the nook and crannies of the town, so he will be of great assistance to this project." Ahmadu answered. "That's good. He will help make things easier over there." Peter said. "That settled, now what about the two police agents?" They managed to kill our men and escaped into the night." Abudu said. "They won't elude us for long." I have already sent in more men to locate them and there's a pro on their trail." Ahmadu said. "If it requires bringing in more goons from our Abuja unit to support, we must do it immediately." Peter said. "The situation is worrisome, Oga is not happy about it and with those men walking free, gentlemen we should not sleep with our two eyes closed. Abudu said. "I want to allay all your fears; tell Oga he should not worry much about the agents. In no time they would be food to the fish in the Lagoon." Ahmadu assured. Abudu shrugged and prayed in his heart that it be so. "IGP, I want you to plug all leaks, we can't afford another outsider to know of our great plan to assassinate the President. We can't allow the bomb to blow on our faces." Abudu said with a knot in his throat. "Yea, we already have done something about it and that was one of the reasons I transferred one of our junior players in this team, ASP Lawal, to the North." Ahmadu said. "Good, let's nip things in the bud. The plan is getting bigger, and it's expected of us to play bigger to achieve our aim." Abudu said. "Do you have idea how he plans to settle all of us?" Garba selfishly asked. A burning anger rose in Abudu's heart, and he shot up angrily and hit his hand on the table, startling others with his sudden outburst.

"Alhaji, I don't expect that stupid question from you. Are you more concerned about the reward or how to get the job done?" He yelled, breathing hard in fury. Ahmadu shot up to his feet to calm Abudu. Garba watched in bewilderment, surprised at the sudden outburst because of his harmless question. "Calm down, Abudu, we shouldn't allow unnecessary and damaging interest to infiltrate our heart and pollute our unity and collectiveness intent in our pursuit." Ahmadu said, trying to make Abudu sit. Abudu glared at Garba Indai and shook his head. "Gentlemen, I hope we are not counting our chicks before the eggs hatch?", he asked angrily and lowered himself back to the chair. He breathed and sighed heavily. Garba's eyes hit the floor. What was his offense; it was a harmless question which did not warrant such an outburst. Maybe Abudu was annoyed at home before coming to the office, he thought. Abudu relaxed and managed a smile. He leaned forward on the table as if they won't hear him when he speaks. "Gentlemen, are we ready to get the job done by removing the President?" He asked and watched them. Peter and Ahmadu assured him of their readiness to carry on and get the job done. Abudu looked at the face of the troubled and unhappy Garba Indai. "What about you Garba?" Abudu asked and watched him. Garba's facelifted "Insha'Allah, we will get him removed." Garba said. Abudu could see and feel Garba's pain from his word. "Thank you all for your dedication and we should pass the info to other members that could not attend this meeting." Peter nodded and Ahmadu looked at his watch; a signal to Abudu that he was itching to go. Abudu forced a smile. "The President would go on two weeks' vacation in a couple of days, and Oga said that the timing is right to begin the next phase of his plan. He instructs that every one of you should have to report to me for now. No phone calls and visits to him. He wants to execute this plan thoroughly without having any direct contact with us. I can only report to his younger brother who then reports to him." He said. Ahmadu managed a little smile. Ahmadu wants to play important to them. I can reach Oga any moment I choose to phone him. He said in his heart. "No problem, as long as we achieve our aim." Peter said. Garba Indai only watched and listened. He didn't want to be seen as selfish if he says something that might rattle the bee's nest "At the end, we will all gather to celebrate." The police chief said and rose and Abudu relaxed back in his chair. The meeting ended and they all stood up and shook hands. The police chief preceded them out of the office, and every man except Abudu headed to attend to other things. Immediately the last man closed the door. Abudu picked up his phone and punched a number and waited for it to ring. On the second ring, someone picked from the other end and Abudu began to discuss with the person at the other end.

TWO DAYS LATER, EVENING OF WEDNESDAY, Peter, and Lalong got to the President's hometown early evening in a chartered taxi. They had flew the next available flight from Lagos to Enugu, and from there chattered a taxi to Uga, the President's hometown. Peter phoned the two commercial bike riders with an unregistered line from his mobile and in no time, the bike men came and rode them to Ugwu Nwosa. Sergeant Musa, the contact was already waiting for them there as agreed. A few minutes on, the bikes stopped. Peter and Lalong were at Ugwu Nwosa where Sergeant Musa awaited their arrival. They asked the bike riders to ride farther down towards the stream. Sergeant Musa joined Lalong on the bike, and the bike men rode towards the stream. A little distance to the stream, the bikes stopped, and all men disembarked from the bikes. "Wait for us here, we will be back in a few minutes," Sergeant Musa said to the bike men as he, Lalong, and Peter stepped away from the bike men and headed farther right. Musa showed them the other side of the bush and they discussed briefly in hushed voices, agreeing on a particular side of the bush the gunmen will build their camp. A few minutes later, they headed back to the bike men and rode back into town. Immediately Musa moved away from the group and punched some digits on his phone and put it to his ear. He spoke to a man to arrange some men to go with him to clear the bush for the camp and erect two tents.

The next morning, time was about eight in the morning. Peter and Lalong stayed in their hotel room while Musa led the laborers to work at the chosen spots for the camp. The laborers were from the same region as Musa, and none of them knew or cared to ask the reason the bush was being cleared. Peter instructed Musa to tell them that it was where some workers would stay during a water project in case he was asked. Two hours later, the hired men cleared the spots in the bush and erected three good tents. Peter and Lalong met them in a lonely area in an abandoned building and paid them off. Musa warned them never to discuss the camp with other people.

THE NEXT DAY, the first two gunmen arrive, and one phoned sergeant Musa as instructed. Musa drove a beat-up car to the bus park and picked them up. The men were carrying thick sack bags and inside them were guns and clothes and other personal effects. Sergeant Musa drove them to the campsite, and they began to settle and wait for others. One after the other the gunmen arrived in the town and Musa drove them to the camp. From that moment Lalong and Peter decided not to show their faces. They don't want the gunmen to see or know them. Sergeant Musa was instructed to settle the men in. The settling in went on smoothly and unnoticed because that part of the town was uninhabited but only a few farms could be noticed. There was a functioning teacher training college in the area, but it closed up some years back when the military took over the federal government and the seat of power changed at the state level. The teacher's institute was still young then and it was starved of funding within one year the school closed. The gunmen settled in their new location and began training. They were sent from a bigger unit of a terrorist camp from the northeast and the instruction was for them to warm the camp and never to attack indigenes and to be seen in the other part of town. There would be enough supply of food and their other needs.

In the morning of

December 15, President Andy Ubih was in the back seat of his Limo as it drove from the Presidential villa to where his Presidential chopper stood. The Limo eased to a stop a few feet away from the chopper. The front door was thrown open and a security aid stepped down and quickly walked to the back door and opened the back door. President Andy Ubih vivaciously alighted and waved bye to his staff that came to see him off on his two-week vacation. The copter would fly him to the airport to board his private jet and from there it would fly him to America. The copter engine started, and the blades beat rapidly in the air. Immediately Andy stepped into the bird and the doors shut; it lifted into the air and headed towards the international airport.

SAME MORNING, Peter and Solomon sat discussing in Abudu's office. Suddenly a tap at the door and Peter asked the person at the door in. Lalong opened the door and stepped in, pleasantries exchanged and he picked his seat. Seconds later, another knock at the door, and Alhaji Garba Indai and Alhaji Gambo walked in. The men sat and everyone concentrated on the business of the day. Abudu left his office a while ago to attend to something, excusing Peter and Lalong. Now the team players are waiting in his office. "Welcome gentlemen. Amuda just stepped out a few minutes ago. He will be joining us soon. All nodded. A few seconds later a tap at the door and Amadu stepped into his office in haste. "Sorry gentlemen, I went to attend to something." He said as he headed behind his office table. He sat and rubbed his hands warmly. "I summoned you to this meeting on Oga's directive. He instructed that we should come together and discuss the next plan of action." He shifted his big body on his chair and watched them. "What is his next plan?" Gambo asked. "He wants me to contact the professional gun man" Abudu answered. "He wants him back here to perform?" Garba asked and suddenly he remembered the last meeting, the manner Abudu spoke to him when he asked just a simple question. It would be better to keep shut; I don't want to lose out. He advised himself in his mind. Garba know Abudu could easily get him dropped from the team because he, Abudu, was very close and connected to Oga. Abudu looked at him and killed a little smile that tried to form on his lips; he remembered the last incident but waved it away from his mind. They were all pursuing the same goal, so no need for friction. "No not here really; he wants him to operate internationally." Amadu answered and clasped his hands together. "Honestly I don't follow, what role does Oga want us to play in this?" Solomon asked and turned to Peter for support. Peter fixed his gaze at Abudu, ignoring Solomon's attempt to make him look in his direction. "Oga said he'd...suddenly the phone interrupted him, and he lifted the receiver from the cradle. "Hello!" He listened with concealed excitement as the person at the other end spoke to him. His eyes widened and a smile played on his lips as he continued listening to the pleasant voice from the other end. He covered the mouthpiece and smiled at them. "Oga was on the line. Yes the assassin would perform in American." Peter's eyes widened in bewilderment, and he stared at Abudu as if he didn't hear him correctly. "You are kidding right?" he asked, his eyes still fixed on Abudu. "No, I am not kidding; Oga needs him to rattle America a little." "How will that help the project?" Peter asked. "This sounds crazy," Ahmadu said and sighed heavily. "We are not permitted to argue over this, it's an order which must be carried out. Trust me; Oga knows what he's doing." Abudu said. Garba sighed and kept quiet. He has nothing to say about it. If the pro assassin should perform let him perform. He has nothing to lose, and after all, the instructions came from Oga. "Oga is willing to pay his fee as long as he would deliver." Abudu said. "Okay, I'll call our contact to reach him." Peter said. Garba and Gambo looked at each other with unsaid words in their mouths. "How is this possible? I mean with the FBI and CIA watching." Solomon said and shook his head. "Oga believes it's achievable. With money almost all things are possible." Abudu said. "This is a very long and dangerous plan." Lalong said and stood up; he paced in the office, deep in thought as he weighed the possibility of pulling this plan through. Though none of them knew what the plan was. "I don't know what the plan is, but I believe it will be the biggest job of its kind in that part of the world," Solomon said. "He is yet to give me full details about this plan, but I know Oga always comes out with something good." Abudu said confidently and rose from his large leader chair and perched half of his large butt on the table. "Gentlemen, let's discuss the camp." He said and watched them. Ahmadu looked at Peter. Peter cleared his throat. "The camp is ready, and the gunmen are well settled in." He said. "Good. Now listen, gentlemen, no calls and no discussion about this anywhere except here in my office. That has been our rule and we must adhere to it." Gambo coughed and interrupted Abudu. Then Abudu continued. "For now, Oga only talks to his brother on this and his brother is permitted to talk to me, then I call all of you here together to discuss." They nodded. "What about the police agents?" "Any tab on them?" He asked; his eyes on Ahmadu. "I sent in more men to locate them; our men are watching motor parks and airports, we believe they are still in Lagos." Ahmadu said. "The police agents know too much, and you have to find ways to fix things." He said with a serious face. "I have other plans on what to do which I can't disclose for now." Ahmadu said and cracked one of his knuckles. "Can't they be officially declared wanted by the police or SSS?" Peter asked. "No that's risky. Let's talk about other things; they would be taken care of." Ahmadu said. Abudu raised his hand as a signal to stop. He stood and put his hand forward as others rose and shook hands with him one after the other and filed out of the office.

SAME DAY, Peter sat in his jeep with the driver's door open. He was talking to someone on the phone and his left leg was a little out of the door of his black jeep. No one is seeing close anywhere to a one-hundred-meter radius. The evening was growing old, and people were already retiring to their manifold homes for dinner, and others headed to various activities. Lights from passer-by vehicles shone on his windscreen and pushed the darkness away. He wore a black suit and a white button-down shirt. "Osmond, the boss wants you to practice your trade again, but this time in America". "Oh, very unfortunate; I won't be able to do that. I got another job." Peter's countenance changed instantly "It's urgent and cannot be delayed. The Prez is on vacation right now," Peter said. "Don't worry; I have a friend who is very competent. He is a pro and knows his onion in the trade. He has links in America." Osmond assured him. "I will have to inform the boss." Peter said and looked in the rear-view mirror. "If you want to use him, know this; his fee is very high, but he is a professional marksman. He has ninety percent of success in the trade". "Okay, I will get back to you soon." Peter said, "Okay, make your decision quick before my friend is hired by another moneybag, right now he's oiling his gun." Osmond said. Peter smiled. "Okay." "Talk to you again." He said and cut call, smile still playing on his lips. He watched a lorry dodge a reckless bus in the far distance. He shook his head. Life is full of danger. He said in his mind and closed the car, the engine roared to life and he drove off.

CHAPTER ELEVEN

AFTERNOON, TWO DAYS LATER, Mark sat inside a small kiosk along park-lane road Apapa. The weather was humid and sunny. He lifted a cold bottle of plastic pepsi to his lips and sipped a little and watched the road as cars drove by. Suddenly his mobile started to ring, he swallowed the cold liquid and put the plastic bottle down and brought out his mobile out of his black jeans trouser pocket and checked the caller id. Daniel was on the line. He picked call. "Hello bro" He said. "I am here" Daniel said from the other end. He sprang to his feet and stepped close to the road. He wore a black jacket; red T-shirt over faded jean trousers, a black baseball cap, red puma, and dark eye glasses covered his eyes. A white Honda eased to a stop close to where he stood and Daniel looked out from the window. Mark bounced to the other side of the car and opened the front door and slid in the front seat, and the car rolled off. Along the road, Daniel entered a lonely Street and pulled to a stop, he turned to Mark. "How are you doing, Mark?" "I am managing, not easy but I have to do this." "You said you needed some money?" "Yes, that's one thing I lack now," Mark said. "How much do you need?" Daniel asked as he threw open the car compartment. "A hundred thousand would be okay," Mark said. From the compartment Daniel brought out wads of notes and handed them to Mark. "Here is two hundred thousand, you need enough money on you." Mark smiled and thanked him. "Watch your back and try to stay safe. The conspirators must be exposed." Daniel said. "Thank you, bro, for your care," Mark said, stuffing the money into his pockets. "Now I should be on my way. Take care of yourself." Daniel said. "And you too," Mark said and opened the car door and stepped out and closed it gently. Daniel drove off and headed towards the Island. Mark crossed the road and flagged down a taxi. The taxi pulled to a stop and he slid lower into the back seat and the taxi rolled off.

TWO DAYS LATER, a taxi pulled to a stop off a sidewalk at Olodi Apapa and Mark stepped out and paid the driver. He cut his eyes about to make sure no one was watching. Time was four in the evening. He saw no one he knew or suspected. He headed towards the front door of a cheap hotel. At that moment, sleek queen rolled her car and eased to a stop by the sidewalk and watched him as he pushed the front glass door open and entered. Mark went to the receptionist and paid for a room and collected his room key and took the stairs. White Eagle hotel was an old two-story building. The walls required repainting and some of the windowpanes are broken. Mark chose it because it won't attract attention. He took the stairs in twos and got to the second floor, without trouble he found his door.

Sleek Queen alighted from her car and in confidence she ambled towards the front door. She pushed open the front door inward and stepped in and went to the receptionist. Mark in his room stepped to the glass window and parted the curtain a little and looked out down the parking lot. The same two cars he saw when he got to the hotel were still there. He dropped the curtain and went and sat on the bed. He cut his eyes about, the room has only a six-by-six bed, a small television hung on the wall. The curtains color were mixture of gold and black. The bathroom door was a small wooden door.

Sleek Queen flashed a sweet smile at the young receptionist and the receptionist smiled back at her. "What room does the man that just entered here stays in?" with a smile on her face. The smile vanished from the receptionist's face. "Sorry ma'am; I am not permitted to give out such information." The sleek queen leaned on the counter and retained her smile. "I know I am not supposed to ask; please help me, that man is my boyfriend, and I came from another city, I didn't inform him I am in the city. Just want to surprise him, you understand how it goes, you are a woman." The young receptionist hesitated a little and glanced back to make sure no one was watching or listening. She can lose her job if the manager found out. "Room 34; Please I didn't tell you." "Thank you, girl; no, you didn't tell me." Sleek queen rewarded her with a thank you smile and headed to the stairs case. She stopped at the first floor and brought out a mobile. She dialed a number and waited for it to ring. "Scooper, inform him i am inches away from the target's hotel room." She cut call and continued upstairs. Suddenly Sleek Queen mobile began to vibrate. She stopped and brought out her phone from her jacket and picked call. It was Ahmadu on the line. "Hello sir" she said in a hushed voice and listened. She only nodded and put back her mobile into her pocket. She stopped at room 34 and gently tapped on the door. The sleek queen wore a blue jean jacket, a red T-shirt over a blue jean trouser, and red sneakers covered her feet, she was blessed with clean fair skin, a lovely shape, long legs, a beautiful face, and nice-sized breasts. She stood at about five-seven. She waited briefly, the door did not open. She tapped it again and waited. A few seconds on, Mark opened the door slightly and peered out through the little opening. "Who're you? He asked softly. "Sorry I was not told a new lodger is in the room. I vacated this room yesterday; I forgot my ATM in the room and have come to get it, please." Sleek queen said. Mark hesitated and weighed this in his head. His gun was in his right hand behind his back. He stepped aside, and it was a terrible decision. The sleek queen entered the room through the open door and Mark turned to watch her check the top of the table, look under the bed and she pushed the bathroom door and entered. Mark became disturbed by this delay and got close to the bathroom door and sleek queen inside the bathroom door pulled out a gun from her handbag and gently stepped out the door and pointed the gun at Mark. Mark at once moved to dodged, and she fired at him, and the bullet created a hole in the wall. Mark responded with a quick shot and the bullet hit her stomach and sleek queen crashed to the floor, her gun fell off and clattered on the tiled floor, a little away from her. Blood flowed from the bullet wound. Sleek queen writhed a little time and lay still, dead. Mark quickly grabbed his baseball cap on the table and anxiously checked the room. He must leave immediately; someone might have heard the gunshots and decided to come to check.

By the sidewalk, a car pulled to a stop and two men in jackets stepped out and headed to the hotel. They looked like cops and the first man has thick neck and broad chest, dark sunglasses covered his face. The second man was shorter but also looked strong and dangerous. They entered through the entrance glass door of the hotel and the taller of them went to the reception. He pulled out a fake police badge and flashed it across the young receptionist's face. She tried to read the badge as it wiped across her face, but it disappeared into the pocket of his jacket. "Police," he said. The other stepped closer and produced Mark's composite from his jacket and showed it to the receptionist. From a door, a middle-aged black male hastened towards the reception and stopped and looked at the two men. "Alice, what's going on? I heard a gunshot, gunshots from upstairs. The men looked at themselves. "You said you heard gunshots? The taller of the fake policemen asked. "Who are these men? The man whose name was Cliff asked the receptionist, his eyes on the composite. "Police," the shorter of the men in jacket said. Cliff looked at them. "Did you see this man in your hotel?" the shorter one asked the receptionist. She looked at it again and began to shake her head but suddenly stopped. She was reluctant, and that sold her out. The shorter of the two fake policemen understood the hesitance. The shorter of the two was known as Silencer amongst a few circles of friends. The other man behind the receptionist was the manager of the hotel and his name was Cliff. Cliff collected the composite and studied it. "Please can I see some IDs gentlemen?" Cliff said. Silencer wiped out his fake police badge and flashed it across Cliff's face. "Police, he announced. "We are looking for this suspect. He is a dangerous criminal. Silencer said. Cliff looked at the receptionist. "Did you sight this man in our hotel?" Cliff asked. The receptionist hesitated and slowly pointed upward. "He just lodged in today." "What's his room number?" Silencer asked apprehensively. "34," the girl said. "And you heard gunshots?" the taller of the fake policemen asked. His name was Handy Gun.

Mark opened the door of his hotel room and sneaked out and closed it gently. He hastened down the stairs to the first floor and suddenly he heard footfalls climbing the stairs. He stopped and slid to a wall and waited. The hotel had few lodgers and the bar was almost empty except for a couple of men discussing over some bottles of beer. The jacket men practically ran upwards to the second floor and pulled out their guns, and Cliff followed a few distances away, struggling to meet up as they bounced up the stairs. Cliff struggled with his breathing as he jogged upwards the stairs. He was the hotel manager, and he has been working there for ten years. Mark listened and waited. The men passed and continued upstairs. Mark quietly sneaked down to the first floor and ran down the stairs. The receptionist was checking something inside a drawer when Mark's foot touched the landing. He hastened towards the entrance door. Then the girl looked up and saw him as he grabbed the door handle and stepped out. "Hei, Oga please wait." The receptionist yelled and sprang up from her chair. Mark ran out to the front of the hotel and headed towards the Street.

Handy Gun and Silencer entered the room first, Cliff entered the room last and Handy gun saw her first. He dashed to where the sleek queen lay in a pool of her blood and tried to help her. Silencer got close and stood, the manager looked at the dead woman with terror. Handy Gun realized that sleek queen was already dead. He strengthened up and looked at Silencer. Unspoken messages passed between them. "He stepped aside and pulled out his mobile and punched a number. The hotel manager stared in terror at the body on the floor. "Sir, she's dead." He said into the phone and listened briefly for instructions, he then he cut call and returned to where Silencer and the manager stood over the body on the floor. "The man that lodged in with her killed her and escaped." Handy Gun said to the manager. "I am flabbergasted about this sir." The manager said with nervousness. "We'll find him. He must pay for this crime." Handy gun said. "He won't live to tell the moment I set my eyes on him." Silencer promised the air.

SAME EVENING, Mark phoned Joshua and informed him what happened, and he also phoned Daniel. Joshua informed Mark that he would be traveling to his town to see his sick wife in the morning, and they agreed to meet when he got back. Mark lodged in a new hotel at a new location. He lay on the hotel bed that night as he weighed the options in his head. This is a serious situation that needs a quick solution. He feared for the President's life, but he was incapacitated by the fact that he had no concrete evidence to present.

If he should inform the President about the conspirators planning to hurt him, he wouldn't be able to present concrete evidence, wouldn't feel safe by confiding in any other law enforcement agent. The fear of the unknown, the identities of all the bad eggs, those involved in the conspiracy were not known to him yet. So if he talks to another officer about it except Joshua the officer might be a member of the dangerous gang. He ran away to stay alive so he would find ways to expose the wicked men. Goons were hired to fish me out and silence me; I need to be more careful. He said to himself. He lay in bed in the dark hotel room, his thought raced furiously until he fell into a troubled sleep at about eleven in the night.

NEXT DAY EVENING, Joshua arrived in his hometown and got off at the bus station. He took a bike to his village and as the bike rider rode onto a lonely road with a brush on both sides of it, a man in black jeans trousers, and black T-shirt, white snickers stepped out from the bush and quickly shot Joshua and the bike rider dead and quickly disappeared into the brush.

AFTERNOON OF NEXT DAY, Mark watched the small led TV on the wall of his hotel room and suddenly an announcement of him came on the screen. The police declared him wanted for the suspected murder of his girlfriend, sleek queen. His composite was in all police offices and every policeman was instructed to fish him out. He watched the announcement in total shock. The conspirators from the police force are desperate to destroy him. He thought. He switched off the Television and lay in the dark. To complicate the issue for him, the police chief and his deputy conspired to make people believe that the lady he shot was his girlfriend. Instruction was passed to all police units to stop and search cars for the suspect. He lay in deep thought until sleep rolled his troubled heart into the land of dreams.

The next day Mark woke and stared at the ceiling. He was not sure what next movement would be. He yarned and stretched on the bed. The ceiling fan spun on low and the window curtain was drawn. He put his legs down and sat at the edge of the bed. Suddenly an idea hit him. To go out and get some food and return back to the hotel. They must be searching for him everywhere in desperation. I won't allow them get me that easily. He said in his mind. He stood and went into the bathroom to shower. Inside the bathroom he turned the tap and a cold rush of water hit him. "Ouch" he said as water gushed out on him. Fifteen minutes later, he stepped out from the bathroom, a white towel tied on his waist. He removed his trouser from a hanger in an old wardrobe and wore it. He slid his singlet on and walked to the window and parted the curtain slightly. He looked down to the parking lot. No suspicious car down there. He left the window and quickly threw a shirt over his body, and covered his face with dark sunglasses, a white cap for a little disguise. He checked himself in an old mirror that stood by the wall. Satisfied, he walked to the bed and lifted the pillow and picked his gun. He checked it and lifted his shirt and slid it under his belt and headed to the door. Suddenly he stopped and returned to the window and peered down. Seeing no one of interest he walked back to the door and cracked it open. He listened briefly, not footfalls, he then stepped out. He left the hotel carefully and hit the Street. At mount View Street, he walked to entrance door of a restaurant and stopped; he cut his eyes about and ducked into the restaurant. A fair-skinned girl walked to his table the moment he sat. "What should I serve you sir?" The girl asked him, a sweet smile on her face. "Stew rice with fish, garnished." He said. The girl curtseyed and left. A few seconds on, his order arrived. The girl put the garnished plate of rice on the table and Mark pulled out two thousand notes and handed to her. She collected it and smiled widely at him. She was hoping he would ask her to keep the change. Mark only attacked the food. The girl left and returned with two hundred naira change. Mark looked up from his food, spoonful of rice in his mouth. She smiled again in a last effort. He looked at her smiling face and waved her off. "Keep the change" He said to her and she instantly rewarded him with a big smile. She bowed and left. Mark concentrated on his meal. Some minutes later, he left the restaurant and began to walk back to the hotel. He walked with confidence towards the hotel, no glancing back, no cutting of eyes till he reached the entrance door. He grabbed the door handle and slowly turned to look back, no one was following. He pushed the door inward and walked towards the reception. The receptionist greeted him. Mark waved at her and walked pass to the staircase. The bar at the other end was empty. No responsible man would be drinking by such hour. It was past nine O' clock. He took the stairs in twos and got to the door of his room. He opened the door and stepped in and shut it. He removed his shirt and hung it back in the wardrobe and sat on a single sofa in the room. I will spend another night here and use the light sparingly so as not to attract attention. He said to himself.

It was ten-thirty at night, the ceiling fan spun on low from the ceiling and the lights were off and the Television was not on. He lay in total darkness; his gun was under the pillow in his bed. He kept thinking about the best way to expose the people that were trying to kill the President. To him, the whole police force and SSS were involved, and he could not think up of any security agent to trust with this. He wouldn't want to put any more live in danger by telling. He might have put Joshua and Daniel in great danger. The conspirators proved to be desperate to eliminate anyone that knows. He reasoned that the scheme and the schemers were larger than he suspected. A voice said inside his mind that it would be best to inform the President. No, how do I prove my claim? I am up against a formidable team of evil men,

men in high positions, and the worrisome part, I don't know other people involved in this. He reasoned. The worst part of this quagmire was that the top players he knew were high-ranking officers of the force. Top security chiefs. How do I wage this war and win? He asked himself. I'd been hunted by their henchmen; their goons and God knows how many they are. He said in his heart. He fell asleep later and in his subconscious mind, he was alert for a sudden attack.

MORNING OF NEXT DAY, Peter and the police chief were discussing inside Peter's hotel suite. It was about ten in the morning. Only two of them were in the suite. They sat and discussed over coffee. "I got a call from the man I sent to agent Joshua's town last night and he affirmed the news that filtered in. The operation was successful and right now the gunman is on his way back. Peter smiled handsomely. "This is pleasant news this morning," Peter said. "Yea it's really pleasant news." Ahmadu concurred. He fixed his gaze on Peter and said. "I had a brainstorm last night, an idea cooked inside my head," Ahmadu said. "What was the idea?" Peter asked apprehensively. Ahmadu cleared his throat and a small smile flickered on his lips. "I can send men to Mark's network provider; to pay a quick visit to the company with Mark's picture and find someone who can assist us with little info on his call logs, his current location, and people he talks to." He watched Peter for a reaction. Peter nodded vigorously like an agama lizard, a warm smile on his face. "Splendid, chief, this is a brilliant idea," Peter said. It was maybe the first time he called Ahmadu chief. "It'll work and that will save us time and energy in trying to locate him. He must die." Ahmadu said. "Please do send the men to get this sorted out as soon as possible," Peter said. "I was thinking to send you along with the men, you know. You are smart and you know your onion, things might require some convincing at the other end." Peter nodded, he understood. "I'm ready to go, chief. It is imperative to clear this debris before it grows to a burning hip." Peter said. "Good, get ready to lead the team to the company. I will provide you with an id; just get ready to go this afternoon." Ahmadu said and rose from his seat. Peter rose too and they shook hands and Ahmadu headed to the door and exited the hotel suite. That afternoon, at about twelve-fifteen, Peter and two other men entered through the glass entrance door of one of the big phone Network companies in the Country and demanded to see the manager. Identifications were flashed and the team registered their presence as a team of police officers. They were shown to the manager's office and Peter introduced them to the manager. The manager: a heavy-set woman of mid-thirties in all red skirt and jacket glanced up at the men momentarily from her pecking on the computer as they entered her office. She stopped pecking on her computer and looked at them. She nicely welcomed them and inquired how she could help them. She waved them to seat but only Peter slid to a seat and the rest stood behind him, with their hands behind their backs like serious officers. Peter looked at the woman with a serious face. "We are officers of the law, and we need your help, please," Peter said and watched her. "I am listening, sir." She said calmly. One of the men with Peter quickly produced Mark's composite and handed it over to her. She studied it. "This suspect is wanted by law for the suspected murder of his girlfriend in a hotel room. You must have seen the news recently." "Yes," she answered. "How do I help officer?" she asked and relaxed back to her chair. "We need info on his call log, the current location he made the call, and who he talks with." The heavy-set woman sighed deeply and leaned forward on the table. "We rarely do that but since it's demanded by law to assist law enforcement agents during the investigation; I will fulfill my duty." Peter smiled and the men behind him smiled too. The manager pressed a red button on the table and in seconds on, her office door opened and a man in a dark suit stepped in. Peter furnished him with Mark's phone number and Name and the man left the office. Peter and the manager relaxed and waited and after about five minutes the door opened and the man in a dark suit entered and walked to the manager and handed her a sheet of white paper with the required information. They thanked her and quietly exited her office and headed back to the agreed place to reconvene.

That afternoon, Peter, Ahmadu, and Lalong sat deep in discussion in Lalong's hotel suite. Ahmadu studied the paper containing Mark's phone call history in his hand. Ahmadu looked up from the paper and smiled wickedly at Lalong. "We have what we need here." He said as he waved the paper before them. "I will send some men to delete him tonight." He said and others nodded. "What about the other number he called regularly?" Peter asked. Ahmadu rose from his seat and began to pace, suddenly he stopped, his face hard. "I will send a man to locate him and pass the quick judgment on him." "Good, we can't let anyone connected to the police agent live." "We don't know if he told them or how much they know, but we can't take chances." "Allowing anybody with little info about our team is like maneuvering through a minefield with the hope that no mine will go off." "That settled; Peter, what is the final arrangement with the international gun?" He sat back in his seat and crossed his leg. "The main assassin is engaged with another assignment, but he linked me up with an equally qualified colleague. The new marksman is ready and waiting to perform." Ahmadu nodded and looked at his watch and gently stoop up. "Gentlemen, it's high time I left. I have so much work I need to finish." Ahmadu said as he put out his hand. Peter grabbed it and they shook hands violently, and Ahmadu shook Lalong's hand and bounced to the door. He grabbed the door handle and exited.

EVENING OF SAME DAY, time was five o'clock. Mark in black jeans and white T-shirt and white sneakers carefully stopped beside a road and cut his eyes about to make sure no suspicious person was watching, seeing no one watching him, he crossed the Street. The evening was gradually getting older, and the darkness has started to descend. It provided him a good cover from prying eyes. He wore a blue jeans trouser, white puma footwear and a white baseball cap. His automatic was under his belt and that gave him an added confidence, at least he could blast his way if they try to attack him suddenly. They can't take him out just like that. He reasoned. A car drove by as he crossed the Street, and the driver honked the horn. Mark was tempted to look at the passing car but no he changed his mind and walked on. Another car started a distance away and gently rolled towards him. It was a black Mazda 626. The car lights beamed straight to his face, disturbed his view. The mazda eased to a stop three feet away and a senile looking man opened the back door and stepped out. He looked eighty, with thick gray hair and beards, a walking stick, and he looked bent with lumber pain. The right back door of the mazda thrown open and an elderly-looking woman stepped out with more agility. She wore a gown, and her hair was gray. Mark noticed she looked trim and quick for her age. The car idled away, and the driver sat waiting impatiently behind wheels. The elderly-looking man wobbled closer and missed steps and nearly fell. Mark rushed forward and helped steadied him. The elderly-looking woman in more quick steps got closer to them and held the elderly man. In a tinny female voice, she said a thank you to Mark, Mark smiled and made to walk off but suddenly the woman pulled out a gun from her hip and pointed it at Mark. Mark flinched in terror and that instant the elderly-looking man pulled out a gun too and jabbed it at Mark's rib. "Move quietly to that car." The elderly female commanded her voice then sounded mannish and thick. "Mark hesitated briefly; he understood that to attempt any quick move would be suicidal. They have guns and he was in a disadvantaged position. A quick thought of attacking them and trying a quick escape crossed his mind but the driver in the car may have a gun too. Suddenly a hot slap blinded his eyes, he staggered, and a quick hand fell through his back and his gun was taken. They pushed him to the car and the back doors opened and she pushed him into the back seat and fell beside him. The door closed and the man fell beside him on the other side of the back seat and the car drove away.

The mazda drove off to a lonely Street and exited through a connecting road and entered the expressway. It raced along the expressway. Suddenly Mark picked up the sound of an approaching siren from the opposite direction. He hoped the police might have noticed his abduction and are coming to rescue him, but another thought hit him. The police declared him wanted and wouldn't rescue him, but instead they would arrest him. Different thoughts raced in his mind. He looked at the driver and thought of lounging forward and grabbing his neck from behind, at least all of them would be in danger of a fatal accident. "Don't try anything silly or we waste you, here and now." A thick voice warned beside him. How come, was the woman reading his mind? He thought. A little distance ahead, the car slowed and turned right onto a rough road that stretched down. It drove down and turned left again and entered another lonely rough road. No other vehicular movement was on the road. Both sides of the road were brushy, the car light piercing the darkness as they kept driving on to an unknown destination. At a pothole the car slowed and entered a sinister-looking warehouse and stopped. No other houses were within the eight hundred meters radius of it. The warehouse was used for storage by a manufacturing company that folded up years ago, and the warehouse became useless for the owner. One man was contracted to look for such a suitable place for quick use and he was paid handsomely for it. The mazda pulled to a stop and the doors thrown open. The elderly-looking woman slid out and pointed her gun at Mark. "Step out!" She commanded. Mark obeyed and stepped out from the back seat. The driver pulled a Berretta and stepped out and quickly turned to the other side of the car. The elderly-looking man slowly alighted and frowned at Mark. He preceded them, his movement became quicker and the lumber pain was gone. He stopped abruptly and hit Mark on the neck with the butt of his pistol. Mark winced in pain as a sudden pain shot through his head. He managed to to steady himself from falling. They took him to the inner part of the warehouse where a man sat and waiting before a little lamp light. The inner part of the warehouse was a bit covered with darkness. Mark could not see well in the warehouse because it was darker inside. There were couples of old abandoned plastic containers piled at the inner corners of the dilapidated warehouse. Some parts of the roof of the warehouse were rusty and leaking. In a flash, a slap landed on Mark's face, blinding his view momentarily. They pushed him to where the man sat before a small little lamp light. The elderly-looking woman kicked Mark's leg and Mark fell to the dirty ground. Without saying a word, the elderly-looking man removed his disguise and revealed a strong-looking young man with a broad chest and thick neck. The gray hair and beard fell to the floor and Mark stared in horror at him. The elderly-looking woman also discarded her disguise and a hard-looking young man with a clean-shaven jaw with a crew-cut hair stood before them. A dirty brazier held some dirty pieces of clothes in place on his chest. "You have been playing hard to get ah?" the other man asked. He rose from his sitting position and stepped close to Mark. He slapped Mark hard, and another man hit him. Mark rolled on the ground in pains as more hard kicked landed on him. They pounced on him and beat him mercilessly. Mark groaned in pains but it fell on deaf ears. His head ached and blood dropped from his head. His hand got bruised and it bled also. The hard looking man grabbed him and bounded his hands and feet together. The strong looking one of produced a dirty sack bag from a corner and they put Mark into it. Mark lay tired and wounded in the sack. He tried to struggle but was too weak and wounded to even do that. His breathing began to fail him. He got weaker and weaker until he slipped into unconsciousness. The man that sat before a lamplight beckoned to the strong looking. "Dispose his body properly" He said and they took him to the booth of their car and dumped him into it and the booth closed. Two of them entered the car and drove off. The driver drove with the car lights on dim and headed out to the main rough road and drove towards an unknown destination. The area was quiet and dark; the bush helped the surroundings look dreadful. A few minutes on, the driver pulled to a stop off the road, and doors were thrown open and they alighted and one of them opened the car booth and they lifted the sack and carried Mark and took him down a little slope. A river was run down the slope. They put him down and one of them pulled out a gun. In the bush, some little distance away from where the men stood, a woman crouched behind leaves on a farm and watched them keenly. The men began to argue in low voices. One was telling the one that pulled out a gun that it wasn't necessary to shoot Mark, that they already knocked him off to oblivion. "Better we throw him into the water." The man with the gun said to his accomplice. "His blood would attract fishes to feast on his flesh." He added. The other nodded in agreement, and he shot Mark in the leg. The pain woke Mark for a moment from his unconsciousness, and again sent him back to deeper and darker ebb. He began to descend the dark slippery road of the silent world of forgetfulness. One of them produced a tinny flashlight and with it, they carried Mark in the sack bag and went down to the river and dumped him into it. They climbed out and entered their car and drove off. The female on the farm overheard their argument and understood it was a man they dumped into the river. She quickly stepped out of her hiding and began to descend the slope to the river. A voice in her head told her that what she was trying to do was useless because the man was shot, and he was tied in a sack. He must be dead by now. She was in her mid-thirties, and heavy in the chest, she was about five-six. She descended the slope with ease. It was gradually getting dark, and the invading darkness meant nothing to her, she was used to it and she could operate well in the dark. It was in the twilight of day and night. She got to the water and dove in and began to swim in the direction she saw them threw down the sack bag. Time was running out and she must go against time to find him. Suddenly her hand touched something hard and rough, like scales. There have been stories of crocodiles in the water and a woman had been attacked. Suddenly as she made to touch it again something moved a little against her leg and fear crept into her. The water moved and it rubbed against her leg again, she realized it was the sack bag. She quickly began to loosen it. In a few seconds, she untied the sack bag and dragged the limp body out of it and pushed it upward, and then she began to swim towards the surface of the water. She pushed the body and swam until she emerged out of the water. Within seconds she pushed the body ashore and fell to the ground. She gasped for breath hard. She managed to steady her breathing and quickly untied the rope on Mark's hands and legs. She felt for a pulse and it was little. She tried to make him disgorge water and got little success. She began mouth-to-mouth resuscitation, but on two try Mark didn't move. He lay lifeless on the ground, blood dripping from the gunshot wound. The leg looked badly damaged by the bullet, she felt sad and disappointed.

That same night, time was about seven minutes before the hour of nine; a bike eased to a stop by the sidewalk along a Street at Apapa and a man in jeans trousers and a T-shirt climbed down from the back while another waited. Cars drove by along the Street and from a connecting road; Daniel drove out from the connecting road and headed home. He went for a beer at a bar in the neighborhood. The man on the back signaled the other and he quickly clambered back onto the bike, and they began to follow Daniel's car. They followed from a safe distance and down the road; Daniel turned right and entered another Street. The Street was less busy, with little vehicular movements. The bike rider rode furiously and overtook Daniels's car and suddenly slowed a few feet away, forcing Daniels's car to slow down and stop to avoid knocking the men on a bike with his car. Instantly the one on the back seat of the bike climbed down and pulled out a gun. Daniel didn't see him do that. He wound down the window glass and angrily put out his head and yelled at the men. "Gerroff the road!" The man approached and instantly fired two quick shots at Daniel's head and blood splattered in front of the car windscreen, Daniel fell sideway in the seat and the car jerked forwards and died down and the car headlamps shined on and picked the elongated shadow of the gunman as he ran to the bike and jumped onto the seat. They rode off quickly, cut corners, and disappeared onto another dark Street.

CHAPTER TWELEVE

AFTERNOON OF 2nd January, a cab pulled to a stop near the sidewalk on Pennsylvania Avenue, and the back door opened. The cloud was grey, and the sun struggled to shine from the thick grey cloud. Pedestrians walking to and from the sidewalk, all wore various winter clothes. Alice stepped out of the cab and closed the door gently and the driver drove off. That moment, her phone rang. She stepped away from the busy sidewalk and picked call. Men threw quick lustful glances at her. Her beautiful red, blonde hair hung loose on her shoulders, and a pink wool cap adorned her head. She wore black velvet pants, a Baby pink jacket with thick fur covered her shoulder and Mellon size breasts, and a baby pink leather boots covered her feet. The snow has been hitting hard in the winter and the New Year has many more winters to offer. Washington D.C was going to experience a very long winter period. Alice cut her eyes at a young fat black female talking on the phone a little distance from her. "Hello, who am I unto?" She asked into the mouthpiece. "Hey babe! This is me Morcos." A male voice responded from the other end. Hey babe, I'm happy to hear your voice. How're you doing?" She asked looking very enthused. "I'm doing just great. Guess where I called you from, babe." "I'm not good at guessing games, please tell me, Morcos." Alice pleaded. "I'm called from a phone booth, here in D.C." Morcos said from the other end. Alice yelled excitedly. "What? Oh my God, you mean you're here in America?" "Yes, babe, I'm right here in DC; I came in Last night" "Oh, I'm so excited, this is like a dream. I can't wait to see you," Alice said in excitement. "I'm hungry to see you too. I've come to see you briefly before I travel to Europe for business". "This is a pleasant surprise, you never hinted to me that you'd come." Alice said. A man walked by and stood and made passes at her. She walked farther away, still talking to Marcos. "I planned it as a surprise, emm can we go out on a date? Let's say morrow?" Marcos said. "Yes, that sounds good to me. Where and when?" She asked without thinking. "There's a restaurant in the Ocean city front in Baltimore, on the Boardwalk, 23rd Street. "BRENDAS KITCHEN, Time four o'clock." He said. "Babe, even if it's in Mexico, I will surely come to see you. Can't wait to see you, my love," she said smiling happily. A middle-aged woman stopped and looked at her and smiled, she understood how Alice felt. She knew that feeling once. The weather is chilly and more cold winter is expected. She cut call and quickly walked off to the next connecting street to see her female friend, looking very happy within. At another location, Morcos opened the door of the phone booth and stepped out, and a heavy-set white woman that had been waiting for him to finish the call glared at him as he stepped out and walked pass. He didn't care to notice the woman as he bounced on, hands in his trouser pockets. He wore a gray suit and white button-down shirt, black shoes and a red inner wool coat jacket, aviator sunglasses covered his face. He was trim and sportive and he walked smart and quick. His hair was dark crew cut and he carried a black lizard skin briefcase which had just a few contents, an old newspaper, and a map. He looked like one of the Wall Street young executives, but he was a pro, a marksman with high rating in the killing business. Alice knew him as Morcos and that was the much she cared. That was just one of the so many names he assumed. He was 168cm tall, handsome and trim. He hurriedly sauntered off, happy for things are going ok. He had little time to spend in America and he has business to attend to. The heavy-set woman glanced back at him again as she stepped into the phone y cubicle and closed the door to place her call.

NEXT DAY AFTERNOON, a cab eased to a stop by the sidewalk 23rd Street off Border Walk in Baltimore, and Alice gingerly slid out of the cab and ambled to the entrance of BRENDA'S KITCHEN; Inside, Morcos glanced at his watch and the time said 4:05 pm. He wore a black Italian suit and black skin shoes, a white shirt, and another red wool inner coat. A gold-rimmed Blanc Michelle polarized sunglasses covered his eyes. He impatiently checked his watch again and glanced at the entrance door. The restaurant had begun to fill with customers; some couples were eating at a table a few feet from him. A man sat alone, nibbling at a big turkey leg. A glass of wine on Morcos table was almost empty. He slowly picked up the glass cup and took a little sip and gently put it back on the table and looked at the front door again. Suddenly laughter erupted from the table at the other corner of the restaurant where three men and a beautiful brunet sat. Morcos threw a glance at them and returned his attention to the door. Laughter from the table again and Brenda, a middle-aged woman that ran the restaurant smiled and shook her head. Her customers' happiness and satisfaction was what mattered to her. The glass entrance door opened, and Alice entered the restaurant. She stood for a little while and scanned the tables for Morcos. The laughter stopped, and men watched her as she took few elegant steps into the restaurant. Morcos eyes settled on her. He recognized her, and that instant he stood up and smiled handsomely at her, removing his eyeglasses. He waved at her. He was not an Apollo, but he looked trim and cute. He was looking smart and attractive. The men with the blond kept looking at Alice;

all were arrested by her beauty. The continued to stare at gorgeous Alice until the blond with them coughed a little to call their attention back to her. She wore a black pant, a yellow jacket, a black luxury fur, bobble hat, her red blond hair dropped to her shoulder, and a black leather shoe covered her legs. She smiled richly at him and he grabbed her shoulder and hugged her in excitement. He pecked her on the cheeks and they both sat down. A waiter quickly approached to take their orders, and activities resumed at other tables. Alice ordered fish and chips and he ordered shredded chicken soup and red wine. "I can't believe you are here now." He said with a pleasant smile. "I am so elated to see you after all this while." Alice said with a sweet smile. "You look very beautiful; I am the most blessed man in the world to have you". Morcos said holding her hand across the table. "Thank you love; you are very handsome too." She responded with a smile, her eyes sparkling with love and excitement. Their orders arrived and they started to eat, while some men stole glances at them. "Look at the men stealing glances at you. You are cute and sweet looking." She smiled and held his hand across the table. Her nails were long and painted red. She smiled more and blushed. She was already in love with this guy. She felt lucky. "Thanks, for your compliment, I'm honored." She said, her eyes dancing all over him. Morcos sipped a little wine and put the glass of wine on table. "So, how's your family?" He asked. "My family is doing great. Dad and mum are fine. What about your family?" "They're all fine. My good friend sends his greetings." Morcos lied. "Oh, what's the name of your friend?" "Williams" Morcos answered. That's a beautiful name." Morcos picked up his wine glass and sipped slowly. He peered at Alice from the top of the wine glass. She looked very gorgeous and smart, but duty calls. She's worth his fee, which is slightly over ten million dollars. She looked at him and they both smiled. She was happy and he was happy. Everything was going well. He predicted a difficult job but it seems he would be able to pull it through in less than estimated time. He flashed her captivating smile and her heart melted. She was falling for him head over heel. "I can love you till the end of time." He said. She stopped eating and stared at him. "You are kidding, right?" She asked and watched him. "No, I ain't kidding; I'm in love with you." He assured her. She rewarded him with a beautiful wide smile. "I love you too." She said. "I'm happy to hear that from you." He said and rubbed his hands. They continued eating and when the plates were nearly empty, he picked up his wine glass and drained the remaining wine in his cup. She already stopped eating; her wineglasses were almost empty too. He called for the bill and threw a one-hundred-dollar bill on the table and asked the waiter to keep the change, as a gentle and generous man he was. They rose and pulled their chairs back and some hungry eyes hit her again, and silence fell across. Only the low music playing in the background could be heard.

Morcos held her hand and headed to the front door and exited. The hungry eyes returned to their plates and talking resumed. Few eyes glanced at them, she's gorgeous and he is a lucky guy to be her guy. Brenda watched them from the far counter as they exited the restaurant. What a beautiful couple. Outside the restaurant at 23rd Street on the Boardwalk, Ocean City front, they held hands and slowly walked toward the sidewalk. Morcos was not worried, no one would recognize him. It's been a long time since he visited America and he had gone under the knife since his last visit. He glanced at the watch on his right wrist. The time says five-ten in the evening. She glanced at hers too and suddenly realized she must start going. Not that her parents would admonish her for coming back late but she needed to be home before the night crept in. It would take less than one hour to get to Pennsylvania, if there was no serious traffic. "I dunno how busy you are but I'd love to go see places with you." He stopped and stared at her, she smiled. "I'm not too busy, can make out time for you, anytime." He nodded and grabbed her hand. "How long are you staying before flying to Europe?" She said looking into his eyes. The cold bit harder, cars drove carefully along the street, and they stood holding hands near the sidewalk. "I have a few days to stay before I travel fly to Germany." "Okay, so where do you plan to go, where do you wanna see?" she asked looking into his eyes. "I am thinking, maybe we visit Grand Cayman. I am not too comfortable in this cold." He said. "Oh, that will be fun I'd like it. I heard there are beautiful beaches in Cayman." She said enthusiastically adjusting the fur over her shoulder. The cold caressed her face. "Good, let's go enjoy their beaches and maybe go scuba diving or even snorkeling" He offered more. "What day do you intend?" She asked, her hands wrapped around his wrist. "Tomorrow is Friday, I suggest we travel on Saturday and come back Monday afternoon," he said. "Okay with me" He gently kissed her on her lips, and she blushed. "Lemme get going before it gets very dark." She touched his shoulder and smiled into his face, she was falling deeper in love, and he was gaining serious ground with his plan. "Okay babe, please stay safe, can't wait to see you on Saturday." He said. "Me too" She started to walk but suddenly stopped and stepped before him, kissed him on his lips and strode off She stopped by the sidewalk and flagged down a cab which drove by slowly along the Street The cab eased to a stop immediately and she leaned into the window and informed the driver of her destination. He nodded and she grabbed the door and yanked it open and slid in, she lowered herself into the back seat and waved to Morcos and he waved too. "I will call you" He yelled to her as he put his hand to his ear to make a phone call sign. "Okay!" She yelled back across to him as the cab drove onto the road and headed on Morcos stood momentarily watching the car as it drove on He waved again at the cab just for the fun of it, and the lonely figure at the back of the cab didn't notice He strode off, one hand in his trouser pocket and he whistled happily He's never failed in his mission He happily walked towards a corner of the Street to phone his contacts immediately Not much time to waste and everything must be well-arranged He headed off to a payphone some distance away, while a quick plan for the kill rattled around his head He headed off to a payphone some distance away, while a quick plan for the kill rattled around his head He headed off to a payphone some distance away, while a quick plan for the kill rattled around his head He smiled wickedly and felt very accomplished. Over ten million dollars cash was paid to him by his contractor from Nigeria before he agreed to lift his finger and he must deliver quickly. Some part of the money will be used to pay those that are helping him too. In the end, about seven million will be resting in numbered accounts in Bahamas, Cayman, and Swiss Banks. I can't fail and my rating mustn't drop, and this is going to be easy. He reasoned in his heart. She was rapidly falling in love with him and that was an added advantage. The day was fading into early night as he stepped out of the phone booth.

Mark painfully tried to roll to one side on a small bed but the pains in his bandaged leg and body warned him against it. He gradually opened his eyes and stared up at a dirty ceiling. He opened his eyes wider, and his eyes picked strange furnishing in the room. Where am I, he tried to say but his mouth could not voice the question. He relaxed back on the small bed with old beddings. The wooden window of the room was slightly open and from the opening, he could see it was early morning. He painfully swung his bandaged foot off and sat in the bed. He looked at his bandaged leg; it had a clean fresh bandage, with some blood stains. No electricity, no fan, and the room had only a few items of furnishing. Suddenly a tap at a door and he managed to turn to look at the closed door. He stared at it and the person at the door waited briefly and knocked again. "Who's it?" he asked. His head pounded like a mortar and pestle were at work in his head. The door opened gently and from outside a woman peered inside. She wore a nightgown and a wrapper tied from under her armpit. "Good morning, I came to check if you have come around." She said. Mark looked at her, and a million questions rushed into his head. "Who are you and where am I; why am I here?" She smiled softly and opened the door more and stepped in. "My name is Risi; I helped you when some men threw you into the river." She answered slowly. "Threw me into the river?" he asked, looking astounded. "Yes sir, they tied you in a sack and threw you into the river. I watched them from my hiding." She said. Suddenly he began to remember. Pictures of the men beating him in the dilapidated warehouse played back in his mind. He looked up at the woman who was barely in her mid-thirties, just a couple of years his senior.

Her hair was tied in a knot behind her neck, and it was obvious she just woke up and came to check on him. "Thank you, emm… "Risi" she helped him with her name. "Please help me up." He said and she helped him stand and the pain in his leg was not much as he envisaged. "What happened to my leg?" he asked trying to walk to the open door. "The men that dumped you into the river shot you before they threw you into the water." Mark shook his head as he gently and carefully dragged his injured leg towards the door. She followed him out the door and Mark noticed another door by the right and a slightly open door to his left. He stopped. "What about your family?" He asked without looking back. Risi walked to his front and turned to him. "I live alone, lost my father some years ago and I am the only child." "Sorry about your father." He said. She unbolted a door in front of her and threw it open. Mark saw that it was still early morning. The rays of the sun had started to splinter out from the cloud and the little darkness that still required a nudge or reminder that its time has elapsed waited to complete its circle. Suddenly a chanticleer crow somewhere some distance away. From the door, Mark could see the outside of the compound. A narrow road with shrubs on both its sides runs out from the front of the house to somewhere unknown to him. She watched him as he held the doorpost and looked outside. Few houses could be seen some distance away. Some were small and some little, larger. "What's the name of this community?" He asked. "Abojoro. It is a little far from the main city." Mark turned and looked at her. "What are you doing alone in Abojoro, aren't you afraid to live alone in this house?" She smiled and shook her head. "This is my family house, my parents lived and died here and besides I took over my father's profession." "And what was that?" Mark asked. "I am an herbalist. My father was one of the greatest medicine men that lived in this community." "You're an herbalist?" I don't understand. * You're too cute to be one." Mark said and watched her. "Yes, I went to college, but I was compelled by unseeing elements to step into my father's shoes." "I am flabbergasted to know that a beautiful lady like you is an herbalist." Mark said. "You meant it is not a noble profession?" She asked. "No, no that was not what I meant. I am just surprised to see a beautiful young lady practicing the profession." "Now you have seen one. I wanted to read law but like I said circumstances compelled me to become a medicine woman." "Not that I am against it; I was only surprised you are one." "What's your name, at least now you know my name?" She said. "My name is Mark; I am a policeman." Or was, Mark said in his heart. "Policeman; Emm why did those men tried to kill you?" She asked and watched him for an answer. "I don't know, and I never met the men." He said and stepped out the door onto the compound. The community has started to come to life as the sun has fully risen in the sky and activities have begun to go on in the other compounds. Mark looked at his injured leg and asked her. "Did the bullet do a lot of damage?" "The wound looked bad; deep hole where the bullet exited; but the bullet missed the most important mark. It will heal in a few days; I patched it up with herbs. She said. "With herbs you said?" He asked in surprise. "Yes, nature blessed us with so many potent herbs to do many things. It would have required surgery to fix it, but it was easy with herbs." Mark watched her with his mouth slightly open. "How long do you expect it to heal?" His mind began to think of how he must take the gauntlet that was thrown at him by those who tried to kill him. Earlier on, in the beginning, he once contemplated applying Fabian tactics against the conspirators since he could not think up a way to go up against them but now the situation has changed, he would've died if not because of God in his infinite mercy sent this woman to save him. "You will be okay within a couple of weeks." She said the news gladdened his heart. So, in a couple of weeks, he could go out to hunt for those who tried to delete him. He smiled at her. "That is sweet news to me." He said. "I pray you to hide so those that tried to kill you won't see you and try to put your life in danger a second time." She said. "My life has been in danger, and I am no longer afraid of danger. If we live in danger and walk through it daily; I am ready to face it again." She didn't say anything but watched him. She shook her head and said to him. "You spoke like my father; he was not afraid of anything; he was a warrior and an herbalist before he died." "We must face our fear and glare at it straight in the eyes, look at it with a poker face and damn the consequences." He said. "I know you must be hungry; let me prepare some food for you to eat." She said. Instantly Mark remembered his money and felt his trouser pockets. The monies were still there. He pulled out a little bundle and she watched him. "My attackers did not care for my money." He said. The naira notes were in hundred naira notes and were still sticking together because of the wetness. "Is there anyone that sells guns in this community?" He asked. She shook her head. "And what do you intend to do with a gun if you find one?" "I am a trained police officer; I am used to carrying a gun and right now I feel empty without it." He answered. "Let me prepare breakfast, I hate to have my breakfast late." She said and headed to the kitchen at the corner of the back of the compound. Mark tried to turn and stretch his body but the pain in his body, ribs, and head warned him against it. Instead, he sat on a little wooden chair by the wall of the small brick building and watched the birds chirp and fly about in the trees.

CHAPTER THIRTEEN

SATURDAY MORNING; AT US PRESIDENTIAL LIVING QUARTER, Alice brushed her hair the third time and looked into the mirror, she smiled softly to the mirror and tapped her cheeks gently She liked her reflection in the mirror. It was a special day for her because she was going out on a date with her new man, a man after her heart, a man that swept her off her feet the moment she saw him. She was sure mum would like him and be proud of her. She was going to travel to Cayman for the first time, with the man she loves, isn't it wonderful? She has waited for this moment when that special man will come into her life and sweep her off her feet and the time has come. She was in her bedroom getting ready to meet him for the trip. She wore a red dress and a black fur lay on the bed, Black lizard skin boots covered her feet. She softly sang a love song as she lifted a caron poivre perfume from the cosmetics table and was applying the sweet smelling fragrance under her armpit and other parts of her body. Suddenly a tap sounded at the living room door; abruptly she stopped singing and looked at the bedroom door. She got up and went to the bedroom door and yelled across to the person at the door to come in and returned to what she was doing. The door opened and her mum walked in gently and closed it. Her mum was still in her pink night robe, she has average height, blond hair, and beautiful average body. She looked beautiful and mid-forties. Time was just eight in the morning. They've done this several times. Her mum liked to talk to her in the mornings. Alice headed out from the room into the living room and saw her mum as she lowered herself into a sofa. "Good morning mum" "Good morning, Alice, how are you doing? Hope you slept well?" "Yes mum and you? How's dad?" "He's fine, getting ready for the office". "Okay mum, I may see him before he goes to work". "He's in a hurry to leave; he'd be in a meeting with the Nigeria President who will be visiting this morning." "Okay, no prob I'll have to see him when I get back" Hanna stared at her first daughter as she combined her hair. Hanna sighed softly; she has been worried about her daughter's kind of rebellious lifestyle and Alice doesn't take to her advice. She insisted on the kind of life wanted. Alice does go out and returned home any time she wanted, and her father and mother are worried about it. Alice checked herself in the mirror; and smiled to herself. "Mum, how do I look?" "You look good, babe. "Are going out on a date?" "Maybe later, Right now I want to go to my friends." She knew her mum was there to talk to her again. She silently prayed that her dad would call her mum's attention, which would at least give her a chance to escape the house. "Where do your friends live?" she asked without excitement and watched Alice. "In this DC" Alice answered casually. "A Males or female?" Her mum asked in attempt to know the type of company or friends her daughter keeps. "Mum, I'm simply going out to see a friend" She answered with little sparks in her eyes. "Alice, we're worried for you, your dad is not happy at all." "Mum, please don't start. I made things clear to you; why are we going back to it again? Honestly I don't like this anymore." She said and threw her hands up in exasperation, her brow wrinkled. "You made what clear to me Alice? I'm your mum and I feel unhappy knowing my daughter is rebellious." Hannah said softly, trying not to raise her voice. It might make her daughter angrier, and she may not want to listen to her again. "How am I rebellious mum? Is it because I decide to live a low life, a life devoid of opulence, razzmatazz, cameras and the press? Being a daughter of the President doesn't mean I'm better than the ordinary girl out there. Mum, please try and understand me, please allow me to live my kind of chosen life." She said pitifully her mum sighed in disappointment. She knew her daughter was stubborn with her decisions and their mother and daughter talks always hit a brick wall. "We only want the best for you." Her mother tried to explain to her. "I know mum, and I know you and dad love me; I am 24 and a grown woman, please allow me to make my own choices." Her mum relaxed on the sofa, defeated and sad. Alice looked at her and smiled sweetly at her mother. She threw her hand over her mother's shoulder and leaned close, almost touching her lips to her mother's cheek. "Maybe this might shore up your spirit mum". Alice threw in excitedly. Hannah looked at her daughter hopefully. "What is it?" Her mother asked sitting up straight in the sofa. "I have a new boyfriend, and I think I'm in love with him." Her mum smiled and stared at her daughter as she picked up her fur which lie on the sofa and put it on her shoulder; she stepped to the front of the mirror and admired the woman in the reflection. She liked the fur which she bought a few days ago in an expensive fashion store in Pennsylvania. She removed it and dropped it back on the sofa. "Who is he? Is he someone we know?" "No mum, you don't know him. In fact, I might see him today and I promised to bring him home to meet my parent's soon." she said, smiling happily "This is good news; I can't wait to see the lucky man you eventually accepted into your life." "Mum, he's so handsome and smart, I'm so happy I made a good choice." "This is good news; my daughter is in love finally." "Mum, wait until you see him, he's so cute you will be proud of my choice". "Okay" "I am going out to see him; from there I'm going to see one of my girlfriends in the city I may not be back today." Her mum rose from the sofa and watched her elated daughter. She smiled and started for the exit the door. At least there she received good news from her daughter this morning, something to hang on to. "Take care of yourself and be a good girl." Her mother said without turning as she grabbed the door handle. "I will mum; I've always been a good girl." Her mother turned and smiled at her and Alice smiled too, and Hannah opened the door and stepped out, closing it gently behind. Alice hastily picked up her handbag and hung it on her shoulder, wore her watch and covered herself with the fur; she opened her handbag to make sure her passport was inside. She decided to travel with her Canadian Passport which her family did not know about. She schooled in Canada and later procured their Passport, but hid it away even from her sister, Laura. Alice's only brother, Ben, lives in Europe, so no one knew about it but her and the Canadian government. She covered her eyes with gold-rimmed sunglasses and left the room.

A FEW MINUTES LATER, Alice hastily bounced to her red Audi convertible and opened the driver's door and slid in behind the wheel and turned the key. The engine of the cute car roared to life, and she allowed it to idle and warm for a few seconds. She had not driven the car in days and now she had to use it to get to a place she can easily take a cab she planned to park it maybe in a parking lot of a mall and then take a cab to meet with Davis. She hates her movement being monitored. She didn't like any chauffer from the house to drive her and she seldom drove herself. She liked to travel in cabs and occasionally trains. But this moment, she needed to drive at least away from Pennsylvania Avenue. One day she caught a security agent trailing her, on the instruction of her father the President She got so angry when she got home and that day and refused to eat with her family at the same dining table. It took her dad several days to pacify her with a promise that no Security Agent will be sent to follow her again. Since then no law enforcement agent follows her. She's a big girl and can take care of herself. A soft chill wind blew across her face immediately she wound down the window glass. She rolled it back quickly and put the gear to drive and slowly rolls out of the marked lot. Gradually she eased onto Pennsylvania Avenue and drove off. Morcos or Davis was expected to wait at Dulles Airport by 10 am and she requested they fly from Dulles to Atlanta, then from there, fly to Grand Cayman. That perfectly suits him; it'll help his plan and makes it less tasking to kidnap her. She drove on and a few minutes later, she eased the Audi convertible into a paid parking lot in D.C. and killed the engine. She yanked the door open and stepped out, closed the door gently, and hurried into the office. She stopped at the counter before a young black woman and inquired about the fee, and she paid the parking fee for four days. A few minutes on, she walked out of the office and flagged down a cab and slid in and the cab drove off to Dulles Airport. Thirty-eight minutes later, she got to the airport. The cab eased to a stop in the parking lot, and she paid the cab driver and hurried towards the arrival to purchase her ticket. Immediately Morcos sighted her. He sprang to his feet from a corner, where he sat waiting for her arrival. They hugged and kissed lightly and then proceeded to buy their tickets. He was relaxed and confident, not worried about cameras. Since he went under the knife a year ago, he has not performed, so his new face won't attract attention. He was just like an ordinary man out there, but the old Morcos lay in wait within. He smiled to himself, feeling good. She went to a ticket agent, a white lady at the counter of Atlanta Airs and the lady rewarded her with a lovely welcome smile. "Next available flight please" She said to the ticket agent who was already pecking at her computer. The ticket agent looks up and smiles at her and tells Alice the amount and Alice opens her hand bag and counted out some hundred dollar bills and put them before the lady. The next available flight to Atlanta would be leaving at 11:45. Morcos also booked his flight ticket for the same Atlanta Air which leaves at the same time; he went over to Delta Air and booked a flight to North Carolina which will fly at 11: 55 am. He wore a dark brown suit, dark brown shoes, a white shirt, no tie, and aviator sunglasses covered his eyes, and his hair was dark crew cut. He didn't approach the ticketing agent with Alice; instead, he stayed away some distance as if they were not together. He stepped to the Virgin Air Atlantics and purchased another ticket to New Mexico which leaves at 12:05 and all he paid with cash. From a corner, a beautiful brunette walked up to Alice and smiled at her. "You're very beautiful; I like your hair." smiling the more. "Thank you, you're beautiful too." Alice managed a smile. "You look familiar like I've seen you before." She sounds Southern, New Orleans. "Oh, I'm not sure we've met." Alice said, itching to move away because she doesn't want any familiarity, no one should recognize her. She was just an ordinary girl like others. "Yea, maybe; anyway, I am happy to talk with you. My name is Cindy." She puts out her hand for a handshake. Alice grabbed it and shook it gently. "I am Christiana; have a safe flight." She started to leave and Morcos watched from a little distance away. Cindy headed off to buy her ticket. A few minutes later, their flight was announced, and they filed to the boarding gate and began to board, within minutes their plane taxied on the runway, and in seconds it began to lift to the sky.

LATER THAT SAME MORNING, President Andy Ubih and his friend, President Chris Griffin discussing in another section of the white house. Andy Ubih wore a wine-red suit, white shirt, and black shoes. Chris Griffin wore ash colored Italian suit, a white shirt, and black shoes, no tie, and his hair was brushed back and oiled. A considerable heat burned from the fireplace to warm the large beautifully furnished space. Beautiful sofas and chests of mahogany drawers adorned the big room. Tableaus of the Prez and other Past Presidents of America hung on the walls. The blinds were drawn and a few security aides stood a little distance away, watching the walls with, their eyes half closed, and ears open to the talks going on between the two Presidents. "So, how's Nigeria?" Chris shrugged and smiled. "Things are going well; since your last visit, there have not been many changes except that my political enemies attempted to kill my wife." "Thank God your enemies did not succeed. It would've been a big blow if they had killed us in that bombing incident. It's very obvious some people want you and your fortune to hostages dead." "Yea, I would've been devastated. They know I love my wife, so they chose to settle scores with me by trying to kill her. They could not assassinate me because God said no." He rubbed his hands together and relaxed back on the sofa. "You have to try fish out those who wanted to assassinate us. It's not going to be easy but you've to make the security operatives sweat, to fish them out." "Yea, you're right, the Security operatives are digging. I hope they come out with some names soon" Chris Griffin nodded and remained silent. "I need to run; I have some people to visit before I travel to Canada to see my family." Andy said and stood, Chris rose from his seat too and they shook hands and hugged as friends. President Andy Ubih's chief security aides preceded him and another of his aides followed President Andy Ubih out of the door, joined by President Chris Griffin and three serious looking security agents.

ONE HOUR THIRTY MINUTES LATER, The DC airliner touched down at Atlanta, Morcos and Alice came down and went to a counter and purchased a ticket to Grand Cayman. Morcos flew from Dulles as Stephen Greenhill with an American identity card and purchased the ticket to Grand Cayman earlier yesterday with a Canadian Passport under the name of Bernard Shaw. They had no luggage with them and that made their movement easy to travel light. The flight will leave by 14:30. They have almost thirty minutes before takeoff. Morcos held her hand and they went to get something to drink.

THE SAME DAY, President Andy Ubih and his chief security aides were at hotel Willard Intercontinental in DC at the 12th floor. He waited as his security aide called lift. It slid down and Andy entered first, then his security aide, by name, Clifford Dinma. Clifford punched for the ground floor and they waited as the lift slid silently downwards. After a few seconds, the lift stopped at the ground floor and the door opened. They both stepped out and headed to the exit door. A rented white Limo and driver waited in the parking lot. Andy had phoned Dr. George Obi and informed him that he would be visiting. Henry, who was Andy Ubih's father, had been a very close friend to

Dr. George Obi, and they were from the same town, from the Eastern part of Nigeria. Nigerian- Americans and Dr. Obi have only one daughter. Both Henry and George attended the same school and were very close. When Andy's mother died, Andy and his twin brother were three years. Henry got heartbroken and started to drink. He got killed in a car wreck and since then, Dr. George Obi stepped into the father figure's shoes and became their father. He trained Andy and his twin brother in school and imparted knowledge to them and did not fail to teach them about Nigerian and Igbo culture. Andy's identical brother somehow got jealous of Andy, claiming that their father loved Andy more than him. Andy in school was so bright and smart. His brother David was equally smart and a darling of many girls. One day, Andy hit David for yelling obscenities at their foster father and it resulted in a big fight. David angrily left home, traveled to another city, and from there boarded a train and traveled farther away from his family. For close to thirty-five years, no one heard from him. He left home at fifteen and cut ties with family. Since then, has been living in a distant state, California. George was old, in his mid-seventies. He now spends most of his time caring for his sick wife in his home at Massachusetts Height Avenue, east end. He owns a hospital and many other businesses, a few horses in a stable, a retired surgeon. He vowed to die, loving his wife. Their only child, Victoria was married with kids. George's wife, Wendy was sick and weak. She was diagnosed with cancer, and she has less than ten months to live. Two of them were waiting for Andy and David to visit. David had called from the blue a few days ago and apologized for abandoning the man that trained him and promised to come to see them. They informed him that his identical twin brother, Andy, would be visiting also. Like the prodigal son, David was coming home to his family. He was married with kids.

President Andy and his security aids ambled towards the rented White Limo from the hotel. The driver, a black man of middle- age, middle- height, and fat hand, slid low in the driver's seat, eyes closed and as he waited, with his head covered with a fedora cap. The parking lot was full of different models of cars. The security aids leaned into the window and saw the driver napping. He tapped on the car window and the driver instantly woke and straightened up on the seat. He pressed a button by the side door and the door automatically unlocked. Cliff opened the back door for him and waited until he lowered himself into the seat. He closed the door and slid into the front seat. "Good morning, sir!" The driver greeted. "Good morning, hope you're good?" Andy asked. "I am good sir." The driver said and roared the limo to life. "Good, drive us to Massachusetts Height Avenue, East End." Okay sir, that'd be about 40 minutes' drive." The driver said and began to roll off. He closed the door and slid into the front seat. "Good morning, sir!" The driver greeted. "Good morning, hope you're good?" Andy asked. "I am good sir," The driver said and roared the limo to life. "Good, drive us to Massachusetts Height Avenue, East End." Okay sir, that'd be about 40 minutes' drive." The driver said and began to roll off. President Andy relaxed in the back seat and closed his eyes and began to replay the fight incident with his twin brother in his mind President Andy relaxed on the back seat and closed his eyes, and began to replay the fight incident with his twin brother in his mind. Clifford wore a black suit with a white inner jacket and black shoes Clifford wore a black suit with a white inner jacket and black shoes. His pistol was in his suit pocket His pistol was in his suit pocket. The second security aids was not needed during the journey. President Andy wanted only his most trusted security aid, Clifford, to travel with him. President Andy wanted only his most trusted security aid, Clifford to travel with him. Few people know of his foster father and the history. Only few people know of his foster father and the history. He doesn't want more people in his past. The driver rolled the Limo out onto the street and drove on and headed towards Massachusetts Height Avenue.

Same moment, in Nigeria; Mark enjoyed a meal prepared by Risi outside the front door of the building. It has started to get dark, and the people of the small community have begun to retire to bed Risi stood by his side and watched him eat. "I am retiring to bed; we sleep early here." He stopped chewing and looked at her. "Thank you, for the delicious meal." She smiled and nodded. "Good night," she said. "Good night." He responded. She turned and went into the house. Mark ate quietly; his mind raced in thoughts as he strategized on how to begin the war.

Some thirty-eight minutes later, the limo drove along a tarred road into Massachusetts Avenue, East End. President Andy Ubih stared through the car window at the beautiful-rich environment he knew many years ago. He grew up and went to junior high school in Massachusetts Height Avenue. Through the window, he watched pedestrians in the rich Neighborhood walking to and from on a less busy sidewalk. It was on a weekend and the neighborhood was busy with activities. Kids and adults playing in the background and some white females laughing happily under a tree, Elderly ones sat, talking, watching the younger ones enjoying the happy moment in the clean, rich, and peaceful Neighborhood. The Limo rolled by a church and Andy stared at it, memories' of his young years when he was one of the participants in Youths programs in the Church came rushing back. He smiled and relaxed, watching through the window as houses receded through the window. The Limo drove unto a bridge and rolled across it, the water below flowed slowly to another connecting brook elsewhere east. The limo got to

34th Street and Andy watched the houses. The beautiful two-story house of George Obi appeared some distance away Andy cut his eyes in all directions. The white Limo drove up to an iron fence and eased to a stop, a few feet to the stairs that led up to a thick carved wooden front door of a beautiful white-painted house. Andy looked at the house he spent his young age growing up. The house was painted white with some touch of red bricks in front.

A couple of hours later, at Grand Cayman; Atlanta Airlines touched down at Owen Roberts International Airport at Georgetown, Grand Cayman about 4:15. Morcos and Alice alighted and went through the customs, and in no long moment, they emerged at the arrival gate. Already a taxi driver was waiting in the parking lot. Morcos and Alice held hands as they walked. Heads turned to watch them; many eyes stared at the lovely couple in admiration. She looked very beautiful in her red dress and he looked cute in his suit. The weather was warm and cool; the breeze from the beach caressed them. Morcos sighted the taxi driver, he clenched his fist in a ball and the driver did the same. That was the sign; he was one of the players in the game. Morcos nodded and walked towards the taxi, hand in hand with Alice. Reaching the taxi, the driver roared the car to life and they slid into the back seat of the old taxi. The driver eased off from the busy parking lot and headed away. Morcos held her hand in the back seat and she smiled, he leaned towards her and kissed her on the lips. She shivered as his lips touched hers Alice stared out the window, her heart beating. She was rapidly falling head over the hill in love with Morcos and it has been her dream to feel the way she was feeling for a gentleman. She counted herself lucky. Joann her friend was out of a relationship, and she was trying to get her heart mended from the hurt she suffered because of the bad relationship. But look at how lucky she got with her new man. Morcos said to the driver, "Stop us at Roy's Car rentals. That's where our ride is waiting. "Okay Morcos," the driver said They drove in silence Alice watched through the window at beautiful lines of buildings some distance away Morcos still held her hand on the seat, and he began to think. A few minutes on, the driver pulled to a stop off the road and pointed to a small compound with a little office. "There is Roy's Rentals" Morcos brought out two five-dollar notes and threw them over the front seat and grabbed the door handle. Alice alighted from the right side of the car while Morcos took the left side. The driver reversed and drove off while Alice and Morcos headed towards Roy's Rentals, then Alice said. "The Island is beautiful." Her hand still clasped Morcos own. Hand in hand they walked to a waiting old model 280 Mercedes car. "Wait until you see the beaches, so much fun on the Island Grand Cayman is a fun-spot Many Americans and Europeans visit here on vacation and there are so many foreign Banks here.''What are the foreign Banks doing here?" "The Island is not big and I don't think there's a large population here," Alice said. "Grand Cayman is a tax-free country for all monies hidden here by people; this is where many monies are hidden from people of different Countries "It is tax-free. Wow, I like this place, I will visit here on my next vacation," Alice said in excitement. "I would like to spend my holidays here too, with you" He added with a warm killing smile. She looked elated as it was evident on her face. "That would be fun, I'd like that." She said enthusiastically. The driver of the rented Old Mercedes 280 sighted them approaching and clenched his fist in a ball and raised it out through the window. Morcos did the same and stopped before the car. The Mercedes started and the driver yelled a greeting and smiled at them. Morcos opened the back door for Alice and she sat on the worn-out leather seat. Morcos made to enter but stopped suddenly. Their hands locked again, the driver glanced into the rear-view mirror and eased away. There are other cars in the compound but no rental sign anywhere. What served as an office was just a little block house with aluminum roofing. "Good evening, welcome to Cayman," The driver said with a smile without looking at the couple in the back seat He was a young man of about twenty-seven, his body well-tanned, soft reggae music played from the car stereo, and he was middle-built with a broken tooth. Morcos smiled back and Alice smiled and nodded. "This is our rented car, couldn't get a fancier one Most cars were already rented when I called; Right, mom?" "Right" The driver answered. He continued to nod his head to the rhythm of the reggae music playing from the car stereo. Morcos frantically felt his pocket and said his credit card fell down on the ground. The driver pulled to a stop instantly and he stepped out and jogged back to where the car picked them. Without warning, the driver zoomed off, and fear gripped Alice. She was taken by surprise by this sudden event. At the back, Morcos yelled and pursued the car. Alice yelled at the driver to stop for Morcos, she desperately turned and saw him running a few steps, then stopped and bent low, panting, his head and eyes slightly up, watching the escaping car. Alice yelled at the driver again who seemed deaf to her yelling. Morcos straightened up and smiled to himself. Inside the car, Alice yelled again at the driver to stop for her to get down but the driver kept driving along the road. Morcos punched a number on his cell phone and spoke into it briefly. "Consignment is on the way, get ready to fly." He said and cut call, glanced around; no one seemed to be watching. A group of men, some distance away did not even notice what happened. They were busy with their rum punch and Jamaican Stripes beer on the table, laughing happily, and loud reggae song blaring out from a speaker. Morcos quickly throttled off back the way they came. Alice desperately yelled at the driver as he turned a bend and continued to race along the rough road. No other car was seen along the road. Both sides of the road were brushy, and a ditch could be seeing a little distance from the road. Further down the road, suddenly the driver pulled the car to a stop and a man emerged from the bush and yanked the back door open and slid into the back seat of the car and the car drove off headlong. Alice tried to open the car door but the other man grabbed her right arm and pulled out a gun from under his belt and pointed it to her head. She froze mouth open. She pleaded for her life out of fear. Morcos hastened away and disappeared round a bend. The transfer of the consignment was quick and compendious. Just a very easy job, one of the quickest and riskless jobs he has ever pulled through. In the car, Alice continued to plead to the man with the gun not to kill her. "Please don't kill me, let me go" "Please I beg of you". Keep quiet "Obey and you won't get hurt; understood?" The man with the gun said to her, his face hard and mean. He looked tough and dangerous Alice nodded slowly but struggled to be quiet. "Good," The man said to her and forced a small smile on his lips. The driver concentrated on the road, looking straight as if he doesn't know what was happening at the back of the car. The man in the back seat with Alice was bulky and black, with strong biceps. He was a fearless thug respected by colleagues. The Cayman mob respects him because he was good. From the opposite direction, a blue van drove past the rough road, raising dust in all directions. Suddenly the Mercedes car slowed down, turned right onto another rough road, and raced down another lonely dusty road. The Mercedes then cornered a bend and headed down to another long stretched road. No sign of any other human activity, no car was parked by, but just occasional sound of the birds. Bushy sides of the road stared in silence and leaves swayed to the rhythm of the breeze as if dancing to the symphony from an invisible orchestra band. The driver then slowed the car and then stopped instantly, he opened the car door and quickly slid out and dashed to the left-back door. He yanked it open and pulled out a wide blue handkerchief from his left pocket and gagged Alice, while the other man held her tight to the seat. She struggled to free herself because the grip of the man's strong hands pinned her to the back seat of the car. She tried to yell but only a muffled sound came out. The driver quickly slid into the driver's seat and opened the pigeon hole, brought out a loaded syringe. He turned to the back seat from between the middle of the front and back seat and injected her with ketamin. He leveled the gear to one and violently put his foot down on the accelerator, the back tires flinging dust and small stones up as the care tore away. Seconds on, as the car drove down the lonely road, she began to drift into unconsciousness

CHAPTER FOURTEEN

MASSACHUSETTS HEIGHT AVENUE, George Obi threw open the door, Andy and his security aids stepped into the large house. Cliff followed behind as they entered the large living room. Andy and his foster father, Gorge, hugged and held each other tight. George smiled and then both relaxed their grip. George brushed his gray hair back and smiled again, looking into Andy's eyes. His dark skin had started to wrinkle, and he was aging nicely. A retired surgeon and he owned his hospital. He was about five-seven, not fat, and his hair had not started to recede. "Welcome home son, how're you doing?" "I am fine sir, and you? How're you doing, sir?" Andy asked, beaming with a smile. "I am doing fine as my old strength can carry me." He turned and went and sat on the sofa. Cliff stood and watched the opposite wall. Andy lowered himself to a sofa and crossed his leg. "How is mum doing?" Andy asked. "My son, she's hanging in there, we're praying for divine intervention. She's got only ten months." "Oh my God!" Andy exclaimed. "I trust the Lord. There is nothing he cannot do." He added. He waved Clifford to a seat, but Clifford preferred to stand. Andy looked around the beautifully furnished living room where he spent the teen part of his life. The house has gone through many renovations since he left to live on his own, many years before he traveled to Nigeria to get baptized into the political brook. To him, it has never been a 'do or die affair like some politicians see politics as. One of his close party members once said to him that power is sweeter than honey, and another member of the opposition party said during a live television interview that once you are in power, you can only strive for power aggrandizement. To Andy, leadership is a call to serve, not for self-serving. The walls of the living room were painted white, the sofa was burgundy, and a large LED TV hung on the wall. A big sound system adorned a corner of the large living room, and a big chandelier hung a little distance from the ceiling. "She's sleeping in her room. She was so elated when I told her you'd be coming." Dr. Obi said, breaking the silence and interrupting Andy's thought. "Let her sleep; I will see her later when she awakens," Andy said and re-crossed his leg. "Okay, she needs rest, she couldn't sleep last night. Got so down-casted, I am worried for her." Dr. Obi said sadly. "Please don't worry dad, let's trust God. May the will of God be done." "I am hoping on God, I don't know anything I can do to make her live." Dr. Obi said. "God never fails. Don't punish your spirit; you have done all you can as a human." Andy said. Gorge relaxed on the sofa and sighed in sadness. He was troubled deeply but trying not to make it obvious. "How is your family doing?" "They're fine sir; I spoke with my wife a few days ago." Andy answered and glanced at the front door. "I watched the Telly and the news and happenings from home are very disturbing, attempts on your lives and that of your wife." Dr. Obi said and watched Andy. Clifford's eyes fixed on an invisible spot on the wall. "Yes, God is merciful; he spared us from our enemies." "Your enemies will not succeed over you." Dr. Obi said as he relaxed back on the sofa. "Emm, do you know who'd be visiting?" Dr. Obi asked, looking him straight to his face. "No, tell me, sir." Andy said in apprehension. "David is visiting today." Dr. Obi said happily. Andy stared at him dumbfounded. "I can't believe this; you mean my brother will be visiting?" Andy asked in surprise, Cliff shifted on his legs and pretended he was not listening. "Yes, he called a few days ago, real worried, and he asked me to forgive him. He said he made a mistake and wants to make amends before it is late." "This is heartwarming. Can you believe we've never talked with each other since he left home? He didn't call and I don't know how to reach him, don't know where he is. So, for close to 35 years, I will be seeing David again?" He stood up and clasped his hands together, feeling very happy. He paced a little and Dr. Obi watched him. "He might arrive any moment from now." "Oh, I can't wait to see my brother again." Andy said and sat back on the sofa and relaxed, feeling very happy. "Andy this is your house, my help did not come to work today. See if you can get us something from the bar to drink." Dr. Obi said and rose. "Let me order some food from the restaurant for us to eat." He added. Andy declined the food with the excuse that he was not hungry. "Alright, but get the drinks; and why is the man with you keep standing and staring at the wall?" "Clifford is my trusted security aide, he is from Oba. Don't worry about him, he loves to stand." He chuckles and Clifford cupped his hand to his mouth to prevent himself from laughing out loud. Dr. George chuckled. Andy rose from the sofa and made for the fridge to get apple drinks.

GRAND CAYMAN, a few minutes later, the old Mercedes 280 eased to a stop in front of a small house. The driver killed the engine and quickly alighted as the thug at the back known as Sneaky was already opening the back door. He stepped down and cut his eyes about the neighborhood. Everywhere was quiet, no noise could be heard about. Alice was almost lifeless in the back seat of the car. The driver and Sneaky lifted her from the back seat and with one foot the driver kicked the car door close, and they quickly took Alice towards a small house. When they approached, the front door swung inward. They stepped into the house and the door closed. Inside,

Morcos sat on a wooden chair, two other men watched as the consignment was carried into the house, thick smoke billowed up to the ceiling as the men dragged and puffed cigars. They looked tough and dangerous. The driver and Sneaky gently lowered Alice to a blue blanket spread on the floor. No other furnishing was in the small room. The room has a small window and no ceiling fan, and no blinds. Another door was slightly open and it led to the other part of the house. Morcos rose from the wooden chair and stared at the beautiful unconscious beauty on the floor. "It's unfortunate." He just said and shook his head, his face expressionless. One of the men smoking a cigar removed the cigar from his lips and blew the smoke to the ceiling. He was tall and bulky; an old scar ran through the side of his right lips down to his jaw. He looked at Alice, unconscious on the bed sheet. He was known as Dragon. "She's very beautiful, mon" Dragon said. Morcos nodded. "Yea, she is". He said and stepped aside. He brought out the mobile from the pocket of his suit and punched some digits and waited for it to ring. It started to ring; he put it to his ear and waited for it to be picked up from the other end. On the third ring, a voice came on from the other end. "Hello Morcos." "Hello, please listen. The consignment is ready and will lift into the air in a couple of hours." He quickly glanced back and stepped through the slightly open door into the inner part of the house. He lowered his voice to almost a whisper and spoke softly. "Make sure the courier-man is deleted to cover up tracks. He paused and listened briefly, then nodded. "Yeah, exactly, now you follow. Don't try to contact me again on this line; it won't be in use anymore." He cut call and re-joined the others. He said to Dragon. "Now it's your game right from here. I already called my contact in Nigeria, and they are waiting for you to deliver the consignment." Dragon nodded and dragged on his cigar once more. He opened his mouth slightly, a ring of smoke coiled out. "The rented jet is ready and waiting, the pilots have already filed the flight plan." "Yea mon." Dragon said. "Load her in a crater and inject enough of the stuff into her blood, and be careful, so you don't kill her." Dragon nodded. "Half of my fee was wired into the numbered account I provided you, what about the balance," Dragon asked coolly. "The balance will land in your account in the next few minutes before the plane lifts, you will receive confirmation of payment," Morcos assured him. "Good, now boys get her ready to fly, Knock her out with more of the hard stuff." The driver and Sneaky chorused. "Yes mon" Morcos glanced at his watch, the time said 5:15 Cayman time. "Now move her boys, we have no time to waste. The job is half done, Move it!" The driver and sneaky moved. Dragon entered into the other room and reappeared in seconds. The driver grabbed Alice by the hands while Sneaky grabbed her legs. They carried her out to the car and lowered her into the back seat. Morcos and Dragon shook hands and hugged each other and then disengaged. Good business. "The custom link is clear and our man at the control tower is waiting for the signal. This is the easiest job I have ever pulled off." Morcos said with happiness. They both smiled and all were happy. "In a few minutes from now, our bird will lift into the air." Dragon said. Morcos nodded nonchalantly. "Keep her unconscious until the final handover. It's your ball now; the contacts are waiting in Nigeria." "Yea I promise to deliver; what do you plan to do from here?" Dragon asked, watching him. "I'm gonna disappear; until I'm contracted again to perform." Morcos answered. The driver got into the car and started it. Dragon shook hand with Morcos and hastily joined them in the car and they drove off. The sun was gradually fading on the horizon and beachcombers has begun to come out from their lodgings to enjoy the beaches, the rum, and darts, Jamaican stripe beer, and barbecued fishes. The men were beginning to take strategic positions to watch some skimpy bikinis stroll by. The live band could be heard tuning their instruments, the crystal water of the beaches incessantly glared at the fading sun and invariably played with the waves as female tourists happily stepped out with their skimpy bikinis.

MASSACHUSETTS HEIGHT AVENUE, a knock at the door and Dr. Obi quickly got up from the sofa and went to the door He opened it and David, President Andy's identical twin brother, stood before it Dr. Obi smiled at him and excitedly stepped aside to allow David into the large living room Andy stood and watched his identical twin brother walk in Dr. Obi closed the door and hugged David and David hugged him too and held him tight Andy stepped close to them and hugged both, tears swelling in Andy's eyes He was very happy to see his twin brother again after so many years They held each other for some seconds and Clifford turned and stared in awe The two brothers looked very much identical Same height, hair color, same build, voice, same haircut One of them could easily pass for the other The only difference about them was David was irascible, smart and unfriendly while Andy was friendly and cool, patient and smart Suddenly they broke their holds and Andy spoke first. "Today is a special day for me, seeing you mean the world to me brother," Andy said. "I'm also happy to see you all. I am very sorry for my immature behavior when I left the house" David apologized. "Welcome home, son I missed you so much," Dr. Obi said. "I am very sorry dad, for my silly behavior," David said and gently rubbed off tears with the back of his hands. "It's alright, son, I understood," Dr. Obi said, his hands on David's shoulder, he silently battled to hold tears from his eyes. "What about mum, is she not in the house?" David asked Dr. Obi removed his hand from his shoulder and began to walk to the sofa Dr. Obi's happy mood dropped to a sad countenance instantly. "She's very sick; she's sleeping in her room," he said sadly and lowered himself onto the sofa. "Oh my God, what is the problem with her?" David asked, looking shocked Andy sat back on the sofa and bends his head. "Stage three cancers and she's got less than ten months, according to her doctor," Dr. Obi said. "Oh Lord my God, why her?" David exclaimed. "Sit down son; I leave it in the hands of God" Dr. Obi waved him to a sofa. "How is your family doing bro?" Andy inquired his face still down to the floor. "They're fine, bro, and you, how are yours?" David asked. "Everyone is fine." Andy said David sat down and sighed. He wore carton color jean trousers and a black tee shirt, with sneakers, and a black baseball cap. Dr. Obi stood up and coughed. "David, what drink shall I offer you? We ordered food and we're still waiting for it to be delivered." "Don't worry about food and drinks, dad I am filled with excitement to see you all today." Andy smiled and Dr. Obi beamed with a happy smile. "I follow almost all the happenings in Nigeria on news, you're doing great as president, bro." "Glory is to God." He glanced at Clifford. "This is Clifford; my most trusted security aid." Clifford turned and bowed. David looked at Clifford and nodded. The men continued in their discussion. Suddenly someone coughed weakly from somewhere inside the house. Dr. Obi bolted up from the sofa. "She's awake now." He quickly headed to a slightly open door and entered a room where his sick wife lay on a large bed. Andy and David followed. Andy stopped before the bed as Dr. Obi learned to attend to his wife. Andy and David greeted her, and she strained to recognize the men that stood before her bed. "It's Andy and David; they've come to see us." Her husband said to her, holding her hand. "You mean Andy and David, our sons?" She asked, excitement lit up her face. "Yes" Her husband answered. "How're you doing, mom?" Andy asked and took her hand in his. David stepped forward and held the other hand. She looked at them unable to remember which was Andy or David because they had grown into mature men with the same look. They noticed her confusion and introduced themselves to her. She held their hand tight, and a tinny line of tears ran down her cheek. The large bed was covered with white beddings and a low light glowed above, from a small chandelier. The blinds were drawn shut and a large wardrobe stood by the wall. A ceiling fan spun from above. A double blue sofa by the corner of the room and a standing mirror stood on the right. She lay under a cover, from the middle to her feet. The room was large and clean. She wore a pink night robe, and her head was blessed with grays. She was sixty-seven years of age, and her name was Wendy. "David, is this you, my son?" She suddenly asked. "Yes, mum; it's me. How are you doing?" David answered and her hand held his tighter. "You can see how I am doing." She said. "Mom, God will do his miracle in your life." Andy said and continued to hold her hand. "Amen." she said. "I am waiting for the Lord; my doctor said I got a few months." She added sadly and suddenly she began to cough hard, her eyes closed. She was tired and they both understood. Her husband watched in sadness. "Please get some rest; we're still around. We'd see you later mum." David said. Dr. Obi nodded at them, and they released her hand and left the room, allowing her to get some rest.

BACK IN NIGERIA, Mark carefully exercised in the room where he currently stayed in Risi's house. The pain had begun to wear off from him and he was feeling better and fitter. Suddenly Risi knocked at the door and entered and stood watching him do his little stretch and loosen up. "You are gearing to go." She said with a smile. "I must be fitter than I was; I am up against a formidable team. I want to be a new and improved me." He said. "Okay, we'll see how it goes in the morning. Good night." She said. "Good night." He responded. She turned to leave. "Thank you for all you've done for me." He said. She stopped and smiled at him. "Don't mention. It was destined to happen this way." She left and he continued.

SOME MINUTES LATER, at Cayman Island, the old model Mercedes 280 drove to a space housing the hanger and stopped. Its headlights were lights on in full and a black Lear Jet 35 waited for the flying adventure. The airstrip lay with lights illuminating the runway. A Land rover drove into view and eased to a stop behind the Mercedes car. Its headlamps pierced the early night. The drivers killed the engines and the headlights switched off. Doors are thrown open and men stepped down and doors closed, and from the back of the Land Rover, three men lifted a wooden crater with air openings and headed towards the plane. Immediately the door of the Lear opened and stairs descended. The men loaded the crater into the plane and instantly the engine roared to life. Dragon climbed the stairs of the Lear and the door closed. The pilot called the control tower and in seconds the jet rolled onto the tarmac in minutes it taxied and began to lift into the air, and Alice lay unconscious in the crater, in the belly of the plane, oblivious of the journey into uncertainty.

BACK TO MASSACHUSETT HEIGHT AVENUE, a FEW MINUTES LATER, Dr. George Obi and Andy strolled to the horse stable at the back of the house, where two horses stood chewing vigorously. Clifford followed from behind. As Andy and Dr. George approached one of the horses, the animal stopped chewing and watched them. One of the horses was white with mane and the other was a brown horse. "Beautiful horses; who rides them?" Andy asked casually. "Sometimes I manage to stroll with the white one," Dr. Obi said. "It's been a long time since I rode one; maybe I should ride the white one," Andy said. "Hey dad, you own horses?" David asked. Dr. Obi nodded at him proudly with a smile. Andy touched the brown horse and the horse seemed to enjoy his touch. Dr. Obi opened the door and led it out for Andy. Andy ran his hand on her and carefully mounted it. Andy kicked the horse and it began to trot off. Reaching the end of the track he turned and suddenly the horse galloped in full throttle, enthusiastic for the freedom and exercise. Suddenly the horse hit its leg on a stone and crashed to the ground, and Andy hit his head on a stone, fell half-buried in the ground and instantly lay unconscious David yelled first from some distance The horse got up and throttled back into the stable and watched them. Dr. Obi and Cliff instantly bolted towards the scene of the accident. Clifford got to his boss who lay unconscious on the ground, Dr. Obi got there too. They tried to help him get up but Dr Obi realized Andy was not moving. David stepped beside Clifford and tried to help but all effort seemed in vain. There was a gash in Andy's head where he hit his head on the stone and it was deep, blood could be seen on the ground and the stone. Dr Obi whipped out his mobile and dialed nine-one-one. He continued to try to see if he'd bring Andy around but Andy was not moving. Suddenly a siren could be heard approaching the house. David held a kerchief over his mouth as hastened off to meet the paramedics and direct them to the scene. The ambulance screeched to a stop and paramedics jumped down and pulled a stretcher out and followed Dr. Obi. They were led to the scene by Dr Obi David stood by the stable and watched the horses; he remained like that until Andy was put into the Ambulance and the door closed Clifford glanced his way, wondering why he chose to look away while his brother was being loaded into the Ambulance. David didn't want the paramedics to notice the resemblance; he acted on impulse and couldn't understand why.

CHAPTER FIFTEEN

MORNING OF NEXT DAY, President Chris Griffin replaced the receiver on the phone and stared blankly at the opposite wall. Suddenly a tap sounded at the door, and without waiting to be asked in, the DC police chief, Paul William ambles into the oval office, followed by his assistant, Joe Brook. The president waved them to sit, a solemn look on his face. He clasped his palms together and watched them. The two police chiefs took their seats and waited for the President to speak. "Good morning, Your Excellency, Sir." Paul William greeted. Chris nodded without a word. "Welcome gentlemen; something terrible has happened and I need your help." The police chiefs nodded and stared and continued to listen. "My daughter is missing" .The words hung in the air. "She didn't come home since yesterday and we have called all her friends we know, but none seems to know her whereabouts." Chris said. The two policemen reacted in shock to the disturbing news. "This is serious sir; has she slept out before?" The DC police chief, Williams asked. "Not to my knowledge. Paul, I want you and your men to find my daughter, and please I want it to be done quickly." "We'll swing into action immediately sir; relax your mind, your Excellency, she will soon be brought home." Paul said. The deputy of police, Joe Brook, then spoke for the first time. "Your excellency, Sir; our men will swing into action, and we promise your daughter will soon join her family." Chris Griffin nodded and stared at them for a while. "Please, for now, I want the press out of this." They can blow things out of proportion and come swarming all over here." Chris said. "We'll do as best as we can to keep it low. You know some of the press boys can peck for news" Paul said. "Swing into action and find my daughter as quickly as possible." Chris ordered. The President relaxed back into the large office chair and closed his eyes. His mind raced with wired and chaotic thoughts, with so many unanswered questions. He sighed and opened his eyes. "Relax your mind, your excellency sir. She'll be home." William said, feeling sorry for the President. He only nodded and waved them to go. They both sprang from their seats. They understood how worried he was. They filed to the door and exited the office.

NEXT DAY, IN NIGERIA, time was about eight in the evening; Peter was in a meeting with some of the gang. They gathered in a secluded part at a poolside of a hotel. No other person was allowed to enter the restricted area by some security men. Important personalities were in an important meeting session. Ahmadu was present, Solomon, Lalong, and the SSS chief, Illiasu. The meeting would be brief, and much discussion was not expected. "I got a call from the international assassin; he informed me that the parcel is on the way to Nigeria." Excited murmur escaped some of them. "This is good news. Oga will be elated. Everything is working out for us. Mark is out of the way and now America's first daughter is being flown down to our soil." "Exclusively to us, if I may say." Peter chipped in. Someone smirked and silence fell across. "Oga instruct that she be taken to the main camp in the Northeast where she would be kept for some days before she'd be transported to the Prez hometown." Ahmadu said. "Oga has performed a feat no one has ever archived in Nigerian history." Lalong said. "I wonder how the international gunman managed to kidnap an American President's daughter under the noses of their police, FBI, and the CIA." The SSS chief, Illiasu said. "He must have paid so many people to help him pull it through." Ahmadu said. "I doff my cap for him; I was told he was one of the best in the business." Peter said. "He's worth his fee." Iliasu said. "I know America will come charging in search of the President's daughter." Ahmadu said. "That's their cup of tea. Oga hates the west, especially America and her stupid prez. Oga did this to rattle them." Solomon chipped in. "I can say the rattling is working." Illiasu said with a small laugh. "Once our President gets back from vacation we try once more to take him out." Ahmadu said. They all agreed and Ahmadu called for the end of the meeting, and they shook hands and headed out to their manifold destinations in light mood.

THE NIGHT OF THE SAME DAY, the Lear Jet touched down at Maiduguri International Airport and glid down the runway. The time was five minutes past nine. A white sedan van drove towards the Lear as its door opened. Dragon stepped down from the plane and entered the waiting van. Another contact sat waiting inside the back of the white sedan. He waved Dragon to sit, and Dragon lowered himself to a low leather seat. The man remained silent and watched him until Dragon spoke. "Where is the chief receiver?" "He is waiting for you a few minutes' drive down the road" The man responded, his face looking very bland. He wore a black leather jacket over a wine color jeans trouser and his hair was long dreads, thick beard, his neck was thick, and his chest was broad as that of a weightlifter. He must be a regular visitor to the gym. Dark sunglasses covered his eyes. "I was instructed to hand the parcel to him." Dragon said. The man nodded and stared. Dragon wore a red blazer on black jean trousers; his head was clean-shaven and bumpy. A strong jaw and he looked taller than the two. Suddenly the man pulled out a pistol with a silencer screwed to it and instantly pumped two bullets into Dragon's heart. Dragon crashed to the floor of the sedan. "Sleep well, pal." The man muttered under his breath.

Peter liked Morcos' instruction to eliminate Dragon to erase the link, so a killer was quickly arranged to do the job. The Lear will simply refuel and fly to Egypt, from there back to Grand Cayman. Men hurriedly lifted the wooden crater from the Lear and suddenly lights at the airport went off and thick darkness fell across the airport. The men hurried and lowered the wooden crater, in which Alice has been confined for hours, and a hand tapped the side of the sedan and it rolled off. Alice gradually woke from her deep sleep. The van drove off and headed towards the exit gate. Just a few minutes of darkness and the light was restored. Bright lights flooded the entire airport. The white sedan exited the airport, drove down the airport road. Down along it cornered a bend then raced towards a rough road. A few seconds on, the van slowed down and entered another road and drove down a narrow part and pulled to a stop a few feet from a chopper. Men quickly jumped down from the front of the van and another two joined from behind the chopper. They opened the wooden crate, and Alice was awakening gradually. She stared at the faces with difficulty but could not make out anything about what was happening and the faces looking at her. The men were shocked to see such beauty inside the wooden crate. The back door of the sedan opened and the man in the black leather jacket jumped down and beckoned to the two men. They went to meet him and saw the body in the back of the van. The man in the jacket flicked his head as a sign for them to remove the damn body. In a few minutes, the body was removed from the back of the van and taken into the bush for a quick burial in a shallow grave and that was the end of Dragon. One of the men gathered Alice's hair and tied it with a black head-tie. Every face and movement was blurry to her. She tried to stir but it seemed like a heavy weight was placed on her. She shut her eyes and drift back to sleep. Two men gently lifted her from the wooden crate and the door of the chopper opened. They carried her inside and the helicopter started, then a few seconds later it lifted into the air and headed away.

FIFTEEN MINUTES LATER, off a lonely road with bushes on both sides, a van parked off a rough road started as the driver who sat behind the wheels heard the beat of the approaching helicopter in the air. Another man sat with him in the front seat, and it was a Land Rover van.

The sound of the engine grew louder and near as the chopper approached the landing point. Its lights gleamed in the darkness as it lowered and began to descend until it settled down. Immediately, the doors of the Land Rover van opened and the driver and the man in the front seat jumped down and throttled to the copter, its door slid open and two men carried Alice down. They quickly carried her to the Land Rover and put her in the back seat, a man sat beside her and threw his arms over her shoulder, and in seconds the Land Rover roared to life and drove off. The helicopter lifted into the air and headed to another location.

A few minutes later, the Land Rover van pulled to a stop at another location. Men with long guns could be seen milling about; some wore fatigues while some wore what looked like fake police uniforms. They communicated in strange language. The doors of the van were thrown open and the men jumped down, one opened the back door and the man with Alice tried to make her wake. She was beginning to come around and could see the going on around her. Two men held her by the hands and helped her alight from the van. They made her wobble towards one of the tent in the space. She was weak and confused. She tried to talk but no sound came of from her mouth. They made her seat on a mat and left her to her confusion. She tried to call the men as they walked away but her mouth seemed to be glued together and no sound came out. From the near tent two men entered and took different positions, their guns ready in hands. A tall man in fatigue whistled to one of the men in the tent and he stepped outside to meet with the other two. They spoke in low voices in same strange language. It was obvious he instructed them not to molest her but provide her with food and water only, because another man came out with a plate of food and water. The man pointed him to the tent Alice sat. The man came and put the food and water before Alice and left.

The evening of the next day, Mark ambled out from the front door of Risi's house, a red cloth tied around his waist and he wore no other clothing. A large long metal drum was on four little large stones a few feet from him, and fire was burning from under it, and thick smoke coiled up from the drum. From the bush, Risi emerged with herbs and added them to the drum. She motioned Mark to step close and he did. "Climb into it." She ordered him. Mark hesitated. "It's too hot and I would get burnt." Risi smiled and shook her head. "It's an order." She said with a serious face. Mark shook his head again in protest. "To be a hero you must go through process." She said with same serious look on her face. Mark stepped back nervously. Risi shook her head. "To be a hero, a man must face his adversary and come out victorious. Hero's welcome is not meant for the lily-hearted." She said to him. Mark took two steps and stopped. His fear grew. He would be in real trouble if he climbs into the hot drum with water and leaves. "What is your need, Mark?" She watched him intently and waited for his answer. "To prove that I am smart despite what some people think. To fill my inner need, do something remarkable." She nodded and smiled. "The Hero's Road is full of thorns, danger, and edgy bends; it takes courage and grit to pass it. Are you ready to pass through it?" Mark looked at her and answered. "I'm ready." "Tell me, Mark, what will happen if the President is assassinated?" Mark thought briefly. "If the President is assassinated, what happened before will happen again and what has been done before will be done again." He answered. "And what will happen if you stop them from killing the President?". If I stop them, what will happen has not happened before?" He answered and began to wonder the reason for her questions. Risi nodded again and stepped closer to him. She removed a thick ring of amulet and put it around his neck and asked him to enter the drum. Mark stepped back in fear. "If you want real transformation from who you are, now, you must climb into the drum." Mark cut his eyes to the drum and suddenly hit his chest with his hand and stepped close. "That's the spirit. Now climb into it." Risi commanded him. Mark grabbed the edge of the metal drum; he expected a sharp burning pain, but no pain was felt by his hand. He felt cool and Risi watched him with amusement. He climbed into the drum and the water was calm, not hot, and with no biting pain, yet the fire continued boiling. Suddenly Risi began to chant incantations; she swirled, and danced, performing more rhythmic movements, then she continued to chant almost to frenzy. Mark squatted low in the drum; his head was not visible from the top. Suddenly the fire died down and thick white smoke covered the drum and coiled upward. A few seconds on, she ordered him out Mark stepped out of the drum, wet with leaves stuck to his body. She put between his lips a tinny palm frond and began to chant incantations again. She cut his arms with a sharp object and Mark flinched in pain. He signaled him to climb out. Mark climbed out to the dirty ground and waited. She led him inside the house and made him sat on a wooden stool. Risi opened a small wooden box and brought out a little container. Mark watched her in silence. She opened the little container and applied some dark stuff to the cuts on his hands and gave him a piece of cowry. "Swallow this." She said, handing it over to him. Mark stared at it. "You mean I should swallow the cowrie?" She nodded. He collected it and looked at it. "You must swallow it without water." He closed his eyes and in one effort he put it into his mouth and swallowed it without. Risi rewarded hi with a smiled. She opened another wooden box and brought out a necklace of old cowries. She removed the thick amulet from his neck and put the necklace of cowries around his neck and hit his bare chest. "This belonged to my grandfathers, and it has been in the family for years. "It belonged to your ancestors?" Mark asked in bewilderment. "Yes. They wore it to war, and no bullet can penetrate the body of anyone wearing this". Mark watched and listened. "It is important to my family, so please return it to me in one piece."

"Are you telling me that I am now immune to bullets?" Marks asked the first question that came to his mind. "You are now empowered to overrun your enemies and not only that; this, she touched the cowries necklace on his neck. "This will help you know when your enemies are coming to attack you, and it'll also turn black when you stand close where they are." "Wonderful" Mark exclaimed. Risi turned and walked to her bedroom and bent low under her bed, she pulled out a long wooden box from under her bed and opened it. She jabbed her index finger twice on it and mumbled something unintelligible, and lifted something rapped in an old clothe. She ran her hand long the length and spoke to it. She held it in brief silence, then untapped it. It was a short double-barreled gun. She went back to where Mark sat. Mark saw the gun and reacted. "Where did you get that?" He asked. Risi shrugged handing over the gun to him. "It was my father's". Mark collected the gun and inspected it. It was a short magnum, covered with dust. He blew dust off it. It was evident it had not been used in years. The rust and the dust looked aged. "Are there cartridges?" She nodded and began to leave. She went back to her room and brought a pack of cartridges to him. "These are only what I could find." She said. "Thank you, these will do," Mark said with a smile and a feeling of gratitude filled his heart. "I want to attend to other things, will talk with you later." She said and left the room. It was evening and darkness has begun to descend. Mark looked out through an open window and noticed that it was breezy. Maybe it might rain tonight he thought. He stood up and called Risi's attention to help him with oil. She produced a bottle of oil for him and he went back into the room and began to oil the gun. Minutes later, Mark asked Risi if he could get a phone to make a call. Risi told him she has no mobile but promised to collect one from the nearest house which stood a good distance away. He lost his mobile when the goons attacked him. A large chunk of his money was in the last hotel room he stayed in before the men attacked and kidnapped him. He has no other clothing except the one he wore when they attacked him. The money remaining with him was slightly over thirty thousand naira, which can still sustain him for a while. He needed to phone Joshua to inform him what happened, and he also needed to call David. They are the only people in this with me. They might be worried and trying to reach me, he reasoned.

Massachusetts Height Avenue, Dr. Obi sat in his study, deep in thought. The light in the room is dim and the window was drawn close. He looks like an Italian Godfather waiting for his boys to return from an assignment. The door opened and David stepped in and gently closes it behind him. Silence prevailed in the room. Dr. Obi waved him to sit on a black leather chair before his reading table. David gently waited for the Godfather to tell him why he summoned him. Dr. Obi looked at him and sighed deeply. President

Andy was badly injured in the accident; he lay in a coma in a hospital bed battling for his life. The doctors said his injury was bad and won't predict when he would snap out of it. Dr. Obi sighed again and shook his head; a reading light on the table cast a low glow in the middle of the room. They were sitting across each other from the table. "David, Andy may be in a coma for months, the injury on his head is severe." "I am worried for my brother; I pray he snaps out of it soon." "I pray so too; but I am thinking, David. Andy has enemies that want to take over if he dies; I believe this might be an opportunity for them if nothing is done about it." "What do you think can be done, sir?" David asked. "David, I want you to temporarily step into your brother's shoes until he gets well and return to his seat." "I am not following sir." David said his eyes fixed on Dr. Obi. "You are identical twins; people can hardly know the difference between both of you." "Uh uh that sounds dangerous," David said and adjusted on his seat. "Listen, David, I have links to some of the people from our side in the Nigeria government. I can make some calls and all you have to do is play the President. "That's risky sir." "Life is full of risks; even doing nothing is risky too." "I do follow Nigerian politics and happenings in the news, but I don't know how this will work". David said. Dr. Obi sighed and closed his eyes, thinking hard. He opened his eyes and looked at David. "Son, just say yes and leave the rest to me" "I played a big role in Andy ascending the Nigerian coveted seat, I can make it happen." David lowered his head to his chest and began to think. "Son, think it over; and remember we have no time to waste."Our decision must be quick". David sighed and looked at Dr. Obi watching him. Then David asked, "What are we gonna do about his Security people that came to America with him? His chief security officer witnessed everything and knows things"." Leave that to me son; Andy told me Clifford is very reliable and he can keep secrets. I will do anything for you and Andy; I owe this duty to him." Dr. Obi smiles and relaxes back on the seat. "That's good son" Now I want to be alone "Give me a few minutes to make some calls" David stood and headed out of the study room Dr. Obi followed him and beckoned Clifford into his study. He explained things to Clifford and in no time convinced him to play a part in the big conspiracy. A few minutes on, Dr. Obi emerged from his study and beckoned David back into the study. The two men sit waiting Dr. Obi to speak. "Son, I explained things to Clifford, and he agreed to play his part and he supports our plan," Dr. Obi said. "Sir, I am fully into this" No one will notice the difference. You and the President have the same attributes "It is a perfect plan, and I am solidly behind it," Clifford said. David nodded and smiled at him. "I'll need your assistance in some areas, to help get me settled when I go to Nigeria," David said to Clifford. I'll assist in any way I can, and I promise that no one must know who you are. The other security aide is at the hotel, and he won't know the difference when he sees you." "Thank you, Clifford; I do appreciate it," David said. "David, I want you to prepare to travel to Nigeria as the President of the Federal Republic of Nigeria." David chuckled softly and happily, and he stood and went and hugged Dr. Obi and the Doctor parted him on the back and they exited the room.

A few hours later, Risi brought a mobile phone to Mark which she borrowed from a female occupant of the nearest house to her own, and Mark thanked her and collected it He dialed Joshua's number from memory but it was switched off, he dialed Daniel's number and it was also not available He became worried Why couldn't he reach them, it was so important he speaks to them He thought of calling his girlfriend but killed the idea instantly. She'd ask questions and may want to visit which he was not ready for at the moment. He thought of calling his mother or even sister that lives in the states, but no he should wait to sort things out he reasoned A thought crept into his mind to call his town's man who knows Daniel When the man picked up Mark inquired if the man saw Daniel and told him he needed to speak with him. The man whose name was Jeffry asked Mark which of Daniel he wanted to speak with. He informed Mark that Daniel was shot dead some days ago and the family was preparing for his burial Mark cried out sadly and his cry attracted the attention of Risi and she came running to him thinking maybe a snake bit him Risi anxiously asked the reason he was crying, Mark struggled to control his emotion but he could not control the tears that ran down his cheeks He felt really bad, sad and weak and blamed himself for being the cause of Daniel's death If he hadn't got Daniel involved in the dangerous effort to expose the conspirators, Daniel would still be alive now It was my fault He said sadly and shook his head. "Mark, please what is the matter?" Risi asked desperately, she was worried seeing a grown man shedding tears What could've happened She asked in her heart Mark didn't answer but bent low, his eyes to the ground Suddenly he lifted his head and looked to her face, his eyes red and agony was written all over his face. "They killed my good friend." "Who are they?" Risi asked Mark to cleaning the tears that flowed freely from his eyes. "I suspect the men who tried to kill me killed him, I let him into a dangerous secret and now I got him killed it's my fault." He said and more tears followed." "Stop blaming yourself. It was not your fault; remember you nearly lost your life also." "I would prefer to die alone in this fight than to get innocent people into trouble." He said and began to pace A thought hit him He must find a way to find out about Joshua, he became more worried and anxious about Joshua now that he knew what happened to Daniel He punched some digits on the mobile from memory and put it to his ear as it started to ring The number he called belonged to Joshua's neighbor and Joshua gave him the number in case if he failed to reach him on his mobile. "Hello," a male voice said from the other end. "Hello, please I tried to reach Joshua your neighbor, but his number was switched off, I want to speak with him." Silence from the other end, Risi stood watching him, and then the voice returned. "Who are you sir, and when last did you speak with him?" "I am his customer." Mark said. "Joshua is dead." The voice said. "Did you say Joshua is dead?" Mark asked, his heart beating against his chest, he felt his head spinning He felt his knees weakening and he leaned to the wall to steady himself, to prevent himself from slumping to the ground. "Yes, he was shot dead by gunmen when he traveled to his town to see his sick wife." The voice said. "Oh precious God!. Mark exclaimed and cuts the call. Sadness enveloped his heart. He hits the wall in frustration and Risi stepped close to him and gently touched his shoulder. He slowly turned to her; his eyes filled with tears. "They killed another of my good friends." He said sadly Risi shook her head sadly, not knowing how to soothe him. It took her some effort to make him enter the house Mark refused to eat and he just lay down on the small bed deep in deep thought He got up and paced in the room as darkness started to descend. "I am ready to fight this war, not only to save the President but to get revenge on Daniel and Joshua's killers." He said out loud and banged his fist on the wall. To destroy them and stop their evil plans, I must cut the Gordian knots He said in his heart and went and lay back on the bed This is war and I'm not afraid to fight it, after all, I'll have nothing to lose, my girlfriend can find another man if I die." He said out to the gathering darkness His mind was beclouded with anger and sadness, even from thinking of his mother and sibling, how they would feel if he got killed, He smiled in the dark After all I was killed but now miraculously, I live They should be the ones afraid of a man who has nothing to lose He reasoned in his mind.

CHAPTER SIXTEEN

THE GUNMEN WATCHED INTENTLY for invaders at the terrorist camp in the Northeast of Nigeria. Two of the terrorists entered the tent where Alice was kept under watch and took her to a waiting car outside the camp. A driver was waiting in the driver's seat when they brought her. They put her in the car and the two members of the terrorist group slid on either side of her with their guns. She was gagged and a long black hijab was thrown over her that covered both her face; and her feet were covered with black nylon socks. She was injected with a slight dose of ketamine to keep her almost unconscious on her feet and her eyes blurred. She could sleep on the flight, which would be fine. The car started and rolled off and drove along a lonely rough road. She was fed bread and tea, fried meat, and fish during the period she was in the terrorist camp. She had cried with so much regret in her heart the past night and blamed herself for not listening to her parent's advice. She wondered about the pain her parents would be in because of her disappearance and she was afraid for her life and how worried Morcos would be. The terrorist didn't hit her and none of them got close to molesting her. She prayed fervently for a miracle, for her father to send a rescue team. The car pulled to a stop a few feet from a chopper and the car doors thrown open. The men stepped down; their guns pointing and they took her to the chopper and made her climbed in. Another man with a gun sat in the seat behind the pilot. One of the men climbed in and sat beside her and the engine started, in a few seconds, the copter began to lift to the sky. Ten minutes later, the helicopter began to descend a little distance to the Maiduguri Airport. As it settled on its skids, another car drove to its side and eased to a stop and quickly Alice was transferred from the helicopter to the car then it drove off with another two gunmen. Few minutes later, they arrived at the Airport. The two men quickly alighted and took her through the back door into an office, and through a secret door they emerged at a boarding gate and was quickly taken into a waiting commercial flight that was about to fly to Enugu in about ten minutes. The airline was owned by one of the kingmakers from the north, a player in the conspiracy, and trusted staffs who were instructed to handle the arrangement, for his wife was flying for the first time and would not want people to see her face and notice that she had aerophobia. A handsome courier man, a member of the gang sat in the next seat with Alice, to keep her company and make sure the parcel was delivered without a hitch. Within ten minutes the plane hit the tarmac and taxied on the runway and began climbing up. It climbed and leveled, then veered right and headed towards the eastern route.

NEXT MORNING, MARK inspected the gun again, he was itching to go. The gunshot wound on his leg has healed quicker than he envisaged, and his body was fitter and stronger, the man in him had transformed into a gutsy and daring police agent, unafraid of bodily harm. They threw the gauntlet at him before, now it's his turn to throw at them. He was not sure if the protection Risi promised, the cowry he swallowed and the ones she put on his neck, and the ritual he went through, would protect him. He relied on his anger, hunger, and dogged determination to triumph over his adversaries, and he vowed to bring their evil conspiracy to acatalectic annihilation. He vowed to cut the Gordian nut. After all joy and sorrow are regular visitors to a hero's life. From inside the house, Risi emerged and watched him oil and check the gun. He saw her and smiled at her. "You have a high spirit this morning." "Yea, I am ready to face the demons." He said. He leaned the gun to the wall and threw his leg and jabbed the empty air; kicked and punched. He began to intensify training to get fitter. Risi stepped out into the cool morning and walked to the gun and lifted it. He stopped abruptly in fear. "Be careful; it's loaded." He said. Risi ignored him and suddenly pointed the gun at his chest and before he could react, she fired a shot. The bullet hit his chest and only bounced off. He stared in confused amazement and as he tried to move, she fired at his chest again and the bullet hit the target with no impact, no pain. She smiled and put back the gun where she picked it. "Amazing," he said with a smile. "You were doubtful." Risi said. Mark couldn't deny and couldn't accept the glaring truth. "You are good to go, but you need to wait for a few more days to allow your wound to heal better." She said and headed to the door. "I am feeling better and rearing to swoop." Mark said. She stopped and turned to him. "Wait a few more days." She said and Mark understood it was an order. She turned and continued into the house. Mark confidently worked up enough sweat and was ready to face the predators. He had never felt so confident to confront danger as he was now.

THAT MORNING, at Enugu international airport, the plane from Maiduguri carrying Alice touched down and ran along the tarmac and slowed, then eased to a stop. The steps rolled down and passengers began to disembark. Alice was quickly taken to a waiting blue Honda jeep in the parking lot. Nobody suspected anything; no one paid attention, and no one was interested in a hijab-covered passenger. The jeep slowly eased out out of the Airport parking lot in no minute and joined a smooth macadamized road. Then drove down and turned joined the expressway. Little seconds later, the

Honda jeep accelerated away. They must get to President Andy Ubih's hometown before dark.

THREE HOURS LATER, the blue Honda glid to a stop behind a parked black Lexus Jeep with tinted window glasses. The back door opened, and a man stepped out and walked close to the bush. He unzipped and pretended to urinate. His eyes cut two men sitting in the jeep. Peter and Lalong were in the black Lexus jeep, Lalong behind the wheels while Peter sat in the front. Peter signaled the man to follow the black jeep. Alice was gradually stirring awake from the drug-induced sleep. She tried to look through the small opening in the eye level of the hijab, but everything looked blurry to her. She was feeling weaker; it had been a long journey from the northeast to the south-eastern part of the country. She closed her eyes and fell back asleep. The vehicles took the next road by the right leading to Uga, President Andy's hometown. They drove along the expressway until they arrived at President Andy's hometown. Peter phoned Sergeant Musa to join them immediately after the small convoy reached the town. They got to the market route and everywhere was busy with people doing their buying and selling. No one paid special attention to the vehicles that drove by. The vehicles entered a dilapidated road and drove down and joined another tarred road that stretched down to the brook, the area where the gunmen were camped. They got to a point and parked the vehicles. The driver of the Honda jeep heard a disturbing noise from the shaft. He stopped and got out. He bent to the tire he heard the noise from but couldn't detect any problem with the shaft or tires. He slid back behind wheels and allowed the engine to idle. Students could be seen along the road, probably coming back from school, it was nearing one-thirty pm, and it was on a Friday. The vehicles continued to idle away as they continued to wait. A few seconds on, a man appeared from the back and trotted towards the jeep. He was dark and stocky. Peter looked in the rear-view mirror and saw him approaching. His name was Sergeant Musa. He grabbed the door and joined them in the jeep. Lalong roared the engine to life and rolled off, and the Honda jeep followed. They drove through a rough road until they got to Ugwu Nwosa and headed down to the camp. The area was quiet except for occasional sounds of birds chirping in the brush. The environment looked lonely; no other human was on the road. A few seconds later, the vehicles reached a point and stopped. Musa pulled out a mobile to pace a call. He spoke briefly on phone and a little seconds later, three men appeared from the the bush and trotted to the vehicles. The men in the Honda alighted and began to help Alice step out from the jeep. She was awake but she was still very weak even to say any word. She just stared into space from the little opening of the hijab She was conscious; the gag in her mouth inconvenienced her more. She needed to breathe normally. Two men held her hand and helped her step out of the car. They began to walk her to the camp and Musa instructed them on what to do. Peter and Lalong stayed behind in the jeep. They had no intention of going to the camp with the terrorist. A few minutes on, Musa joined them and the vehicles drove off.

AT THE WHITE HOUSE, the Morning of the next day, Paul William tapped at the door of the office of the President and the chief of staff opened the door and asked him in, and went back to his seat He continued what he was writing on a legal pad and ignored the police chief that just entered The time was ten in the morning The President had had a restless and sleepless night the night before Alice was not home yet He looked haggard and troubled Routine pleasantries and Paul William slid to a sofa and Chris Griffin only nodded The chief of staff, Tom Henderson, lifted his head and looked at him then continued what he was writing on the legal pad. "Welcome, Paul, any news about my daughter?" The President asked. Mr. President, thirty of my men are out there combing, digging to get a lead on your daughter's whereabouts, but no luck yet. The President shook his head sadly and said. "This is a very sad moment for me and my family." "I know how you feel" Mr. President; I'm hoping she'll be found immediately." The phone was blinking, and Ton picked up and spoke briefly into the mouthpiece He put back the receiver and turned to the President. "Senator Madison is here." The door opened and Senator Madison entered and walked to the table He said hi to Paul and Tom and looked at Chris. He was a middle-aged honey-blond, average body built, tall and handsome He wore a red suit over a white button-down shirt and a white shoe covered his feet. "Good morning, Mr. President what's this news about your daughter missing?" I heard the news and flew in last night." Senator Madison said and slid into a seat. "She left home two days now, and no one knows of her whereabouts." The President said sadly Senator Madison looked at the DC police chief. "Paul, any lead from your end?" He asked. "My men are still trying to find her, no success yet" "Her car was sighted, parked in a pay parking lot, ten minutes from here." "Is there no one with info at the parking lot?" The President asked. "The secretary at the company described her and said she was in a hurry to leave after she paid and no other information." Paul said. "Boss I suggest we call in the FBI to assist, she must be found before she gets hurt." The chief of staff said. "I've already done that; Oscar will soon arrive." Oscar Meyer was the FBI boss. He was tough and has served through four American Presidents. The President liked him, and Oscar also liked the President. The issue at hand calls for a collaborative effort to locate the President's daughter. "She'd be found" Mr. President I know how you and your family feel; I advise you to be strong and let our law enforcement agents find her." Senator Madison said as he rose from his seat. "I was in the neighborhood, so I decided to check on you." The President managed a smile. "Thank you, Madison, I appreciate your concern." The senator said his byes to Paul and Tom and Tom followed him to the door and closed it as he exited. He returned to his seat. "I believe your daughter will be found in no tim. The FBI involvement will be an added advantage." Paul said, and suddenly the phone began to blink. Tom picked up the receiver and spoke briefly into it "Let him in." He replaced the receiver and a fraction of a second, someone tapped on the door. The door opened inward and the FBI chief entered the office. The FBI chief, Oscar Meyer, was sixty-three years, bulky and he has a gruff voice, ten years before retirement. He has a volcanic temper but could suppress it. He was tough and a no pushover. He has served through past three US administrations. He was known for his no-nonsense nature. He was a man of few words, and he could play hardball too. Oscar bounced towards the president and said his pleasantries "Good morning, gentlemen, good morning Mr." President." He slouched behind a desk and cut his eyes to Paul, without looking at Tom. Tom sometimes thought the FBI chief to be an arrogant, but no doubt that he respected the chief. The belt around his rough black trench coat was tied loosely around his bulky frame; his head was crew cut and lots of grays adorned different parts of it He was the oldest in the office and he was on first name basis with the President. They play golf together and occasionally he dines with the first family. "Welcome, Oscar." The President said with a sad face. "You told me on the phone that your daughter is missing," Oscar said without blinking an eye. He tugged at the belt of his black wrinkled trench coat and watched the President. "My daughter is missing. Paul and his men are trying to find her; I know it's too early to get you involved but, Oscar, honestly I don't want to take chances." "If it requires throwing in all our security apparatus in other to find the first daughter of America, we must do that," Tom said. "Chris, relax your mind" "I'll send fifty of my men to find her and bring her home." Oscar said soothingly. "Thank you, Oscar; please, I want you all to keep this from the press" "If the news goes on air, it won't be good for my daughter's safety." "I promise, Mr." President, that it'd be handled with utmost secrecy." "I'm banking on you guys to find my daughter as soon as possible." "Sure. Mr. President." Paul said. Oscar looked at Paul William. "Paul, let's talk after this meeting." Paul nodded. "Gentlemen, I need a daily briefing. Thank you for coming. Please I need to be left alone." The President said, rubbing his temple, eyes half closed. The security chiefs stood and headed to the door and exited the office. Tom Henderson closed the door and slid back to a chair before the president. "Boss, I thought you assigned one FBI agent to follow her?" The President opened his eyes slightly. "I did, but when she found out she was followed the outcome wasn't pleasant for my family. She practically ignored me and her mum for days. Went on hunger strike until I promised to withdraw the FBI agent and promised not to send any security agent to follow her." "Hmmm. Different strokes for different folks. She's one of a kind. My daughter wants to be surrounded by security men, to show her status and flaunt her naked skin in front of cameras." "Not Alice, my daughter hates opulence, cameras, front page. All she wants is to live like an ordinary girl out there, from a poor background." The President said and closed his eyes. "Alice is a good girl; I pray she is not in trouble." Tom said and watched the President. He sensed the President wanted to be left alone. The President mumbled something and began to say a silent prayer for his daughter's safety. Tom hoisted himself up and went to continue work on a memo he was doctoring. He understood the President didn't want more talks.

COUPLE OF DAYS LATER, evening, Tim, an FBI agent sat in a bar with his reporter friend, Connor, discussing over some bottles of beer. The dimly light bar at has started to fill up with customers. They've been drinking since an hour ago and Tim must leave or get tipsy. He was a light drinker, so he doesn't have the ability to consume large quantity of alcohol and remain in control of his tongue. Alcohol makes him loose his tongue and his friend, Connor, knew this. Tim nearly got dismissed from the bureau a year ago for his loose tongue when he leaked a top secret to a reporter. Oscar was so furious about it and ordered for his lockup. Tim a ten year man with the bureau got some contacts, his politician contacts waded in on his behalf and Oscar changed his mind. Tim was placed on probation to clean himself up and become a good agent. Connor was known as a sleazy reporter with Washington post. He can smell news from a good distance. He had worked as private eye for a year before becoming a reporter. He was forty and looking trim. Tim belcher and his tick belly bounced, he slid his short frame lower in his chair, a colored light reflecting on his bald head. His tongue has loosened a bit cause of the alcohol and Connor was ready to milk the juicy info from him. "What's up, buddy?" You called me." Tim nodded. "What's the latest at the Hoover building?" "What's for me if I tell you?" Tim asked, half asleep. What do ya want in exchange?" Tim sat straight instantly and stared at his friend. "Uh uh I need money, plenty of money and other fringes." "How much do you want?" Connor asked coolly. Tim thought briefly. "Five grands, and an all-expenses paid weekend for two." "That's outrageous. Tim and you know it." "What I have in my news bank is big, I should have demanded higher." Tim said. Connor was known for a first-hand reporting. He gets to it before others. He pays for it and cannot reveal his source. He was a well-respected reporter, known for good investigate journalism. Tim cut his eyes to the entrance door. The bar has started to fill up with customers and he has started to feel unease. A colleague might see them together. "Okay how much are you willing to pay?" "A thousand-five and all expenses paid weekend for two at Resia hotel." "Resia is too cheap and dirty." Tim protested. "That's what I can afford." Tim weighed this in his mind. Not that he has any option for now. He needed the money and all expenses paid weekend. His new girlfriend wants a weekend date with him, and he needed to take her far from the prying eyes of his wife. "Do we have a deal? I need to run back to the office." Connor's word brought his attention back to him. "Okay, a deal." Tim said. "Okay, I'm all ears." Connor said and relaxed back to his chair. "The President's first daughter is missing." He began. "You mean the first daughter of US President?" Connor asked, looking surprised. Tim nodded and continued. Connor suddenly remembered his bottle of beer. He lifted it and took a long drink and placed it back on the table. "The President invited the FBI and we started digging. The CIA too got invited to help find his daughter. We're still digging." The team had a break and followed a lead. A coupla of days ago, footages of the suspect was gotten from Atlanta Airport walking hand in hand with the President's daughter." Connor watched and listening and recording every word, in his memory bank. "What happened next?" Connor needed to ask questions to keep him conscious. "The CIA chief called his friend in Cayman and his friend knew a contact. Footages of the same suspect exiting the arrival hall were gotten. That's all I know." Connor beckoned the service for more beer. He suspected Tim hasn't told him all he knows. The beer arrived and Tim grabbed a bottle and forgot that his colleagues might enter the bar and see him and Connor. "There's something you're not telling, Tim." Connor said with a convincing smile and waited. Tim put his palm forward for the money. Connor pulled out a wad of hundred dollar bills and counted a thousand and seven hundred and pushed it across the table to him. Tim grabbed it and pocketed it. "That'll all I know and that's juicy enough." He took a long drag and belched. Connor watched him. Tim raised the bottle to his mouth and downed the remaining beer. He placed the empty bottle on the table and rose to go.

The CIA chief, VINCENT COOK, a man with amazing track records in the agency who has achieved many feats locally and internationally sat in his office going through the morning papers. He stopped some Russian terrorists that tried to destroy an American spaceship and was instrumental in the apprehending of Islamic extremists who tried to ignite a jihad in the Middle East. A man of few words, packed with action and passion for his country. He was sixty, strong built and looking younger than his age. His head was cut low and he was five-ten. Suddenly his phone rang. He lifted the receiver and spoke softly into the mouthpiece. The voice from the other end belonged to his friend from UK's secret intelligence service- M16, Charles Wilson. "Greetings Bernard" Vincent Cook happily said his pleasantries and began listening attentively, he reacted and shifted in his seat, his eyes wide in surprise and he spoke occasionally. He nodded and rubbed his forehead. A few seconds on, he replaced the receiver and sat quietly in thoughts. He shook his head as if he had just woken from a reverie. He lifted the receiver and punched a number. "Come to my office, Ray." A Few seconds later, his deputy, Raymond Kirk walked into Vincent's office and slid his bulky frame onto a chair before a large office mahogany table. "I just got off the phone with the MI6 chief. They sighted Islami exiting Heathrow Airport a day ago through Grand Cayman. I believe he was the one that performed on American soil," Vincent said. Raymond listened in disbelief. "I can't believe this." Raymond said. "He was certain it was him." Vincent said and watched Raymond. "I suggest you let the President know of this immediately." Raymond said. "Yea, I will inform the Prez; but I want to request from MI6 to send Islami's current profile, for us to be able to check with the footages from the Atlanta Airport security Camera." Vincent said. "The camera footage from Dulles Airport showed the President's daughter walking hand in hand with a man." Raymond said and leaned his elbow on the table. "I believe that the President's daughter might have been kidnapped by the same man." Vincent said. He stood up and went to the window and cracked it. He began to pace. "I suspect so too." Raymond said. Vincent Cook picked up the receiver and dialed the White House number. He spoke to the President and cut call and phoned his friend at MI6.

The CIA CHIEF AND THE FBI chief sat discussing with President Chris Griffin in the Oval office. The FBI Chief wore his usual rumpled trench coat and Chris Griffin wore an ash suit with a white shirt, a red tie. The CIA chief was in a black suit with a white shirt, no tie. Vincent cleared his throat and said. "From our findings, the man that exited Atlanta airport to Grand Cayman is the same the MI6 sighted at Heathrow airport; and he was the same man holding hands with your daughter at the airport. His name is Islami and he has been on our wanted list. He's also on the wanted lists of some other countries. Oscar rubbed his temple to clear the migraine that was forming there. He relaxed back on his chair and said. "He's a dangerous man and a professional killer who can kill with his hand or any object. He has a link to Nigeria." President Griffin shook his head and sighed sadly. "I am beginning to have a migraine." The President said and touched his temple; he stared at the security chiefs. "Where do you think he might've taken my daughter to?" He asked with the hope that she was still alive and safe. He could not think of her death. The CIA chief sighed and said. "After we received the picture of him from MI6 yesterday, we contacted some of our links and CIA can confidently say your daughter is being held hostage in Nigeria." The President jerked in shock and the security chiefs watched him as the news settled in. "Nigeria!?" The President asked. His chief of staff, Tom, was attending to an important meeting somewhere in New York. Chris stood up from his seat and began to pace in thought, they watched him. They understood that the news would be devastating to the President, considering how close the two countries' Presidents were, and the Nigerian counterpart visited a few days ago. The President shook his head in disbelief. "Did you say my daughter is in hostage in Nigeria?" The President asked gently lowering himself to his seat. "Yes, Mr President, your daughter is hold hostage by a small unit of a bigger terrorist group in Nigeria." "I can't believe this. The country's President visited me a few days ago. I believe he's still in America." "Our paramilitary at West African Command should be instructed immediately to fly to Nigeria to rescue your daughter. Some of my men will join in the rescue operation." Vincent said. The President slowly rose from his chair and began to pace in silence. They watched him. Suddenly he stopped and said. "This is an insult to America, to our government." Others nodded without saying a word. The President is worried, and they would try not to add to his worry. "Do everything you can to bring back my daughter." The President said and sat back in his chair. "Good, I will immediately instruct our military commander to facilitate the rescue mission." Vincent nodded. They rose to go. The President stood and put his hand across the table and Vincent grabbed it first. "Good job gentlemen; thank you." The President said and shook their hands and they headed to the door and exited; Oscar closed it behind him. The President sat back in his seat and picked up his mobile on the table and dialed President Andy's number, but it was switched off. He put down his mobile back on the table and closed his eyes, grateful to God that his daughter was still alive. In the few days of her disappearance, he prayed for her safety and had a strong hope that she would be found alive. Her disappearance had caused so much pain to his family, his wife especially. He planned to call her later to inform her that Alice had been located. He would try to reach the Nigerian President to discuss things with him. "He's still in here." He said to himself.

NEXT DAY, AT MUTARLA MOHAMMED AIRPORT, the Nigerian Presidential jet touched down on the runway and taxied down, and slowly rolled to a stop. The plane lights shone on the tarmac and a deafening sound from another arriving plane filled the air. The door of the Presidential jet opened, and the stairs slid down. Clifford and the other security aid emerged from the plane and scanned the people waiting for the President. They began to descend, and the other two men emerged too at the door of the plane. Then David emerged and the men parted for him to pass. He gently climbed the stairs and began to shake hands with the people waiting on the ground. Clifford took him through it all. Showed him pictures of staff and who is who in the Presidency. He vividly could remember each name. He was confident about this. He has been following and reading, watching the news about happenings in Nigeria. He won't fail. He smiled richly as he shook each hand. That was how his brother does it. The presidential chopper started, waiting as he strolled to it and climbed in. It lifted into the air and headed to the Presidential Villa. The President has returned home.

CHAPTER SEVENTEEN

THE DEAD RINGER PRESIDENT, David, settled in at the Nigerian Presidential villa. Clifford helped him know things he ought to know about the inner places of the villa, and the names of members of the cabinet and they watched some important video clips made by the state house media team of President Andy and rehearsed in secret on other ways Andy ran the government, and even how to sign Andy's signature. Everything seemed perfect and going smoothly. In a little time, he would be the perfect President Andy. No one suspected anything because they were very identical. He settled in comfortably and began to run the government. Within a few days, David began to taste real power and he realized that power is sweeter than honey.

ABUDU AND SOME of the gang members sat in a large living room in a rich area of Ikoyi, holding a meeting. Present was the Nigerian police chief, Ahmadu, the SSS chief, Illiasu, Peter, Solomon, and Alhaji Gambo. The men wore different shades of traditional attire even Peter wore one; an all-black weaved half Agbada and trousers. The time to strike is here and the vultures must play the sound of death, after all, if the President got assassinated, what has been done before will be done again and what has happened before will happen again. He won't be the first to have been assassinated. He would only join his compatriots in the dark world of history. Abudu cleared his throat dramatically to call the attention of the men in the room to himself. Silence fell across and they watched him intently. "The prez is back from vacation and we are back to trying to take him out." He paused to allow that to simmer down. "Oga instructs that you get out soon, ready to attack." He said. "And when is the attack likely?" Ahmadu asked with a wrinkled brow. "Oga wants it as soon as possible; the white girl has been sent to the camp and it should be pertinent to crown our victory with his death." Abudu said and smiled wickedly at them. "I support we take him out as soon as possible. It's taken longer than envisaged." Illiasu said. "Then prepare the gunmen for the job." Abudu said. "He's scheduled to visit the capital on an official visit in two days. "Good. You are the SSS and policemen, the onions lie with you for the details." Abudu said. "I will arrange it. Don't worry gentlemen." Illiasu assured. Others smiled because of the assurance. Abudu stood up from the sofa and walked to a window. He spoke to the window. "We must not fail this time, Oga is losing patience and he's beginning to be agitated." "Assure him that the job would be completed soon. We're worried and desperate to pull it through." Peter said. Abudu slowly turned and watched them. Ahmadu has started to get pissed off about Abudu's tactical play of boss on them. Just because he was closer to Oga shouldn't give him the temerity to play boss on us, especially I who have many officers under my command. I will have to find a way to stop this nonsense. He said in his mind. He heard from a source that Abudu is rapacious and wicked. He might be scheming to run you off the project when it is complete. The source told him. The voice of Peter cut through his thought as he said. "The time is now and we're not going to relent until the Prez is deleted from existence." They all agreed, and the meeting closed. The nefarious idiots rose and shook hands and exited the room except for Abudu who stayed behind. Immediately the last man closed the door, he rose from the sofa and began to pace in the large space. He was troubled and sad, with many unanswered questions in his mind. The President keeps getting lucky. How long it will take the team to just remove one man? He reasoned. He went to the window and began to talk to it. "I can't wait for the appointment." He said softly to the window. Different wicked thoughts rattled in his mind as he continued to weigh things in his mind. "No, he won't escape this time around." He said loudly to the glass window. Oga had promised him a juicy appointment if the project is completed, and the target removed. "I have longed for this opportunity to be in government and no idiot or Inyamiri (Igbo man) will stop me from reaching the desired height." He said to his faint reflection in the glass window. He slowly turned and bounced toward the sofa. He sat on the sofa and smiled wickedly and crossed his leg. Soon the country will be thrown into national mourning. He said in his mind.

MORNING, MARK DISGUISED himself and covered his eyes with dark sunglasses, a fedora cap sat on his head and the magnum was in an old dirty black leather bag provided to him by Risi. He wore a black jacket over washed blue jean trousers. A black puma shoe covered his feet. He thanked Risi for the tenth time and promised to return the cowry necklace to her. He wanted to make sure that he thanked her properly for saving his life. Risi wished him luck and escorted him to a road where he would catch a bus going to the city. He saw no one on the road as they walked to the connecting road. "It seems there are few inhabitants in this neighborhood. I haven't met any since I arrived." He said. "This is just a small community of fewer than two hundred houses scattered about the place." The residents do their business in the main city and return here late in the evening. "It's a nice and quiet place to live." He said. As they stopped by the road, a bus drove-by towards his destination. Risi flagged it down, causing the driver to slow the bus, and eventually, it came to a stop. The driver yelled out his destination and Risi waved him to wait. Mark climbed into the bus and waved goodbye as the bus began to drive away. After driving for a few minutes, the bus slowed and entered a service station to get more fuel. Mark saw a shop at the corner of the road in the distance. He paid the driver and walked off the bus so he could get to the shop. He bought few items, a bottle of Pepsi, a pack of soda, detergent and two bottles of Coca-Cola. They might be useful to prepare a Molotov. He was not very far from the Lagos state seat of government. He stepped out by the road and began to wait for a bus. Suddenly it hit him again. A picture of a long car been attacked by gunmen but he could not see their faces. The men shot sporadically at the long car and people scampered away for safety. He shook his head and the picture cleared instantly Was it a premonition?. He stood by the road debating in his mind on what to do, suddenly a siren ailed in the distance, approaching from the opposite direction. He looked and saw a convoy of cars driving down the road. As the cars approached, he could notice a limo in the middle of the convoy. Time was eleven in the morning. As the first car in front drove past, suddenly from a connecting junction, a generic white Ford without windows at the sides drove out front, cutting the second car from passing, thereby forcing the driver to struggle to pull to a stop to avoid hitting the generic ford. The limo was forced to a stop and reverse. Suddenly the side door of the ford was thrown open and three gunmen in dark long jackets opened fire at the car in front of the limo The driver got hit and before the security operatives could respond, three policemen fell to the firepower of the gunmen People scampered for safety including some security aides in the car behind the limo. It was a Presidential limo and President David sat in the back seat, terrified by the happening. Timothy pulled out his automatic and pushed the front door of the limo open and crouched low, using the door as a shield. He stepped down and sneaked out and crouched low to open the back door so that he could help David. Mark scampered away and hid by a wall away from danger He cut his eyes at the cowry necklace around his neck and noticed it has turned black. Wow Wow the war has just begun earlier than he expected. He quickly put the leather bag down and unzipped it and withdrew the double-barreled magnum. He jammed cartridges quickly into the chamber and zigzagged to a safe corner a few distances from the Ford. Three security aides got hit and their bodies lay on the road. Mark attacked and shot down one of the gunmen from the Ford, and that threw the other gunmen into confusion. They withdrew into the back of the Ford and that provided a moment of respite to the Presidential security aides. Mark crouched low and fired more shots to pin the men down inside the ford. He sneaked close to the limo as Timothy threw the door open and began to help David out, shielded him with his body. Mark instantly recognized him and signaled him over. More bullets hit the back door of the Ford as two policemen opened fire on the generic Ford, and the door got riddled with bullet holes. Suddenly one of the dare-devil gunmen appeared with a bazooka and instantly fired. It flew and hit the car in front of the limo and angrily flipped it upside down and ball of flame erupted, metal debris rose to the air and began to descend. Fire and thick smoke covered the car as it burned furiously. Timothy and David dropped to the ground. Mark crawled to them and signaled to Timothy. Timothy pointed to dazed and terrified President David to Mark, and rolled off to face the attackers. One of the gunmen saw them and instantly fired at President David. The bullet hit him at the lower part of his shoulder, an inch to his chest and he crashed to the ground face down and lay in pain, blood covered upper the right corner of his safari suit. Mark shot at the gunman and the gunman fell backward into the Ford. David was seriously injured. Blood spread on his white safari suit and he began to moan in pain. Timothy sneaked toward the Ford, Suddenly the Ford tore away and he shot at it; bullets narrowly missed the back tire. The two men that were in the first car in the Presidential convoy abandoned their car and ran into hiding as the gunshots rented the air. Mark rolled David face up and fell to his knees beside him. The bullet wound was deep and his white safari suit was soaked with heavy blood. Timothy ran back to them. "Take good care of him and secretly find a way to take him to a small community called Abojoro, it's not far; a few kilometers from here, I need to go after the gunmen. When you get there, ask for a lady herbalist by the name, Risi, tell her Mark sent you and she would treat him. Never let anyone know you are there. The men that tried to kill him would try again to find him." Mark said quickly to Timothy. David had lost a lot of blood and was getting weaker and weaker with the seconds. He lay there unmoved on the ground, his eye closed, gradually drifting into oblivion. People began to appear from their hiding and the other policemen appeared too from a corner. Mark quickly looked around and saw a car just pull up a little distance away. He ran to the driver's side and spoke to the man sitting behind the wheels. "Police, I need your car." The man looked at him and hesitated. "I am driving to somewhere important." The driver said. "You will be rewarded" "No get out of the car." The man cut his eyes at the magnum in Mark's hand and quietly opened the door and stepped out. Mark jumped behind wheels and drove the Honda car to where Timothy and President David were. He left the engine on and threw open the door and stepped out. Timothy helped him put the President into the back seat of the car and Timothy fell behind the wheels. "Remember the Name of the place" Abojoro, and her name is Risi "I will meet you there." Mark said and Timothy rolled the car away. The owner of the car stood at arms akimbo and watched as his Honda drove off. Mark ran to the last car in the convoy behind the limo and yanked the door open and jumped behind wheels and put his gun in the foot space and roared the engine to life. He maneuvered out from behind the limo and furiously drove away towards the direction the Ford went. He raced the car along the road not knowing the direction to follow but he trusted his instinct. He will locate the gunmen. He got to an intersection and slowed, then turned right and headed south. At a connecting road, he slowed drastically and put his head out of the window to inquire from a passer-by. "Hello madam, please did you happen to see a white Ford pass this direction?" The heavy-set woman stopped and looked at him. "Yes, a few minutes ago a Ford drove dangerously past this road "It nearly killed a woman trying to cross the road." She said pointing. Mark thanked her and drove on. He couldn't fathom why he was doing this, trying to locate a car or gunmen that raced away long enough to have disappeared. He glanced at the cowry necklace on his neck but became doubtful it was potent enough to help him locate the gunmen. His thought drifted to the Bank heist here the police faced the dare-devil armed robbers and remembered their Achilles' heels. These things cannot be trusted; no power is like that of God which protects completely. He touched one of the cowries on his neck and sighed. He concentrated on the road and drove down and turned another bend. He slowed and inquired from other people and they pointed in the direction the Ford headed.

Timothy raced the car along the road and about ten minutes on, he got to a junction and slowed the car to inquire from a woman the direction of Abojoro. The woman pointed a road down the right and told him it was very near from there. He thanked her and drove on. President David lay in the back seat of the Honda; he was getting very weak from loss of blood. He needed an urgent attention. Timothy glanced in the rear-view mirror and noticed the President was dropping into the low ebb, his left hand limply dangled to the floor in the back seat. He said a silent prayer for David's life. He got to the road the woman pointed out to him and saw a sign that said Abojoro. He turned the Honda onto the road and drove down He watched two kids stroll in his direction. He slowed the car and eased to a stop beside them as they try to make way for him to drive past the narrow rough road. They stopped and looked at him. "Please I am looking for a lady herbalist, by the name, of Risi." One of them pointed. "Take that small road, sir." "The house is one small house." Timothy smiled in appreciation to them and rolled away. He got to the road the kid pointed and drove onto it, and drove down narrow grass covered part.. A small block house stood a little distance away and he saw a young lady in the front of the house standing watching as the car rolled towards the house. Timothy eased to a stop and quickly opened the door and stepped out. He went to her. "Good day, please I am looking for Risi." He said to her anxiously. He watched him briefly. "Who are you and why do you want to see Risi?" Timothy quickly explained to her and told her who sent him and pointed to the car as he talked, She moved to the back of the Honda in a few strides and Timothy yanked open the door. They carried David out from the back of the car and took him into the house.

Mark drove onto a rough road and slowly rolled the car along. His eyes darted from side to side and he noticed the area was brushy and he saw no other vehicular movement. Tire marks could be seen on the road ahead and it looked like just a few vehicles passed the road. He followed the tire marks on impulse until he got to a spot where the road deepens. He stopped and scanned the area. Suddenly he noticed that the cowry necklace on his neck has turned white and blinking shinny lights, he looked ahead and saw what looked like an abandoned warehouse. He drove on and from a safe distance of the warehouse he saw the white generic Ford packed in front of it. He pulled to a stop and picked the magnum and from his jacket pocket he removed some cartridges and jammed them into the chamber and corked it, he gently opened the door and stepped down. He crouched low and sneaked towards the dilapidated warehouse. Suddenly he recognized it as the place he was beaten and thrown into a car booth. He said in his mind, Revenge time, he smiled and held his gun ready for battle. Inside, two men sat on a dirty blue plastic drum smoking weed. Their guns lay beside their feet. The sun was high up in the sky and the heat has become more intense. He slid by the wall of the warehouse and listened. Suddenly someone made a desperate bird cry from somewhere and instantly the gunmen picked up their guns and sprang up from their sitting positions and quickly dashed into hiding in different positions. Mark waited a slight seconds more before he began to sneak into the warehouse. The old warehouse has no doors; its owner was using it as a good place to package contraband stuff for distribution to a few selected customers. Since after it became useless to the human owner, it became very useful to rats and roaches, and sometimes snakes do slide into it for warm shelter. Mark tip-toed forward, his gun pointing in readiness to fire. Suddenly a cold gun muzzle touched the base of Mark's neck. He froze and a thick voice ordered from behind him. "Put the gun down" Mark obeyed and a long dark jacket swirled behind him. Mark remained calm, his heart not racing in fear. "Gently walk into that space." The thick voice said and suddenly a painful jab landed at the back of Mark's neck. Mark staggered and managed to steady his balance so stop him from crashing to the ground. The other two goons heard the voice of their colleague and emerged from their hidings. "Wow wow wow" "Look who we have here." The man with the thick voice said. He was known as Furious agent by his colleagues. The second man known as Jackal smiled wickedly at Mark and said. "Honcho man, you got the liver to come looking for us, huh?" Mark stood in their midst, two guns pointing at him. "He's proven to be indelible, so have decided to pay us a visit." Furious agent said. Suddenly one of them shot twice on the ground, a little foot from mark's legs. Mark jumped and the man laughed happily. "He's afraid of bullets. How did you survive the last time" "Huh, and now you want to play hero, you fucking Jackal have the ginger to shoot down our buddy," Furious Agent said and angrily landed a dangerous blow to Mark's ear and' mark crashed to the ground. His ear buzzed with intense pain. He tried to stand but a black booth kicked him hard. Furious Agent angrily grabbed Mark's throat and began to strangulate him. Mark struggled, his legs began to kick the ground desperately but Furious Agent held tight and increased his grip. Suddenly he let his hand loosen and Mark began to gasp for breath. "Did you call this chap a hero" "He could not withstand even a little choking?" The other man said with a laugh. Jackal looked strong with a thick neck, thick head, strong arms, and biceps, about five-nine. He was new in the group. Furious Agent stood at about six feet, small head, covered with a fedora cap, and big eyeballs, and he looked strong and dangerous. His eyes were red with constant inducement from weed smoking. Suddenly they descended on Mark and began to hit him mercilessly. Mark cried out in pain, he tried to cover his eyes to wade off another punch to it but a kick threw his hands off and another deadly punch landed on his left eye, blinding him momentarily. He cried out in pain and suddenly the beating and kicking stopped. Furious Agent grabbed him by the neck and made him stand. "Since he loves to play hero, let's see how heroic he can be." He said. Mark's head pounded hard, his left eye tried to see but the pain advised against it. The man in front of him looked blurred to him. "The idiot has the effrontery to enter the lion's den" Now the lions will eat him raw." Jackal yelled angrily and raised his gun at Mark. Furious Agent waved him to stop. "I have another plan." He said. "Let's test his skills, it's been a long I practiced, I think it would be great fun to practice with a hero." "Yea yea". Jackal and the other goon concurred with amusement. "Hei Mr. hero, let's make a deal; If you beat me my men will allow you to walk; but if I beat you, you'd be cast into a furnace. Huh, what do you say?" He asked Mark mockingly. Mark remained silent. "Are you ready to kill this guy and walk or you've suddenly lost your courage?" Jackal yelled to Mark and Mark tries respond. His mouth suddenly fails the attempt to respond. Suddenly Jackal landed a dangerous and hard punch on his face and the force knocked him down. Furious Agent bent low and sneered at him. "Get up and fight, you mother fucker." He said and slapped Mark hard. Mark groaned and began to rise. "Jackal and the other goon began to clap mockingly. "Yea he's about to attack." The other goon said mockingly. Furious Agent stepped back and watched Mark as he began to stand, his legs could not stand firm but instead wobbled and nearly fell. "Wow wow this guy is even a dancer," Jackal said mockingly. Mark managed to steady his feet on the ground and suddenly swirled round and landed a punch at Furious Agent's chest, but Furious Agent stood unmoved. "Good, now you are providing me the practice I need." He said with a wrinkled brow. Like a lion, he attacked Mark and began to throw punches left and right, hitting targets, and in seconds Mark slumped to the ground. "Naw he's no match for me. He can't provide me with enough practice time." Furious Agent said, gently brushing dust off from the lapel of his long black trench coat. "Take him away and build a hanging bridge for him." He said and two hands grabbed Mark's jacket and he was dragged to a corner in the warehouse. Rumors had it that Furious Agent was deported from the US for drug and other criminal-related offenses and it was rumored he was a member of a dangerous cult in the states.

Jackal and the other goon looped a rope over a four-by-four wood and hoisted Mark to a small wooden stool and tied the rope around mark's neck. His hands were bounded behind his back and Jackal smiled wickedly at him. "Kick the stool and fall to your death." He glared at Mark and laughed out like a possessed animal. Jackal left and joined the others where they sat smoking thick weed, a bottle of whisky and three Styrofoam cups were in the middle. Jackal sat on a broken block and poured a drink for himself. The other man by name, Typhoon handed Jack a wrap of weed and lighted it for him with a lighter. They continued to smoke and enjoyed their whisky, occasionally bursting out laughing at a dirty joke. Mark struggled to balance himself on the small stool, his eyes ached and swollen, and his strength has started to fade away. The pains in his body felt like double. He hung there like that until evening came. He was weak and hungry; he had not much strength to attempt to free himself which looked impossible under the circumstance. If he slipped from the wooden stool it would be his end. He was hungry, weak, and injured, and his situation was hopeless because even if he screamed, no one would hear and come help him. He felt helpless in the jaw of death. Furious Agent stood up and stepped out from where they sat drinking and smoking. He brought out his mobile and punched some digits from memory and put the mobile to his ear as it began to ring and he waits for it to be picked up from the other end. At a location, Abudu and Ahmadu were in a meeting, planning, in a light mood, after Ahmadu got a call from Furious Agent informing him that the President has been assassinated. Jubilation in the camp of the evil conspirators, and calls were put across to share the good news amongst the team members. Ahmadu came on from the other end, he sounded happy. The phone was on speaker. "Yea, how's your end?" "Chief something came up but we are handling it easy and nice." "What came up?" Ahmadu asked, a little apprehensive, Abudu intently watching Ahmadu Ahmadu rose from the sofa and listened. "You mean agent Mark is still alive?" He asked, looking shocked. He shook his head. "Yes chief, he traced us to our den but was quickly spotted and incapacitated .There's a rope around his neck right now; I want to play the hangman, Chief. Just called to inform you what happened." Furious Agent said and dragged his weed and blew a ring of thick smoke up. "How did he survive, thought you said he was killed?" Ahmadu asked and began to pace about. Abudu listening. "Dunno how he pulled it off chief" Maybe he's a cat with nine lives." Furious Agent said. Suddenly Abudu snatched the phone from Ahmadu and Ahmadu jerked in surprise and glared at him. "Listen, boy, I don't care whether he is a cat with fifteen lives, I want him dead right now." He yelled into the phone. Furious Agent grunted. He felt anger well inside him, but he quickly suppressed it. He felt smattered for being spoken to so rudely by Abudu. When I collect my balance, I might tell that idiot to go to hell. He said in his mind. "You hear me, right?" Abudu's voice brought him back from his angry thought. "Yeah, I hear you right and clear." He replied, his voice low and angry. "Good" We're waiting for your call as soon as you fix him." Abudu cut the call and stared at Ahmadu. "I thought you said he's not smart." He yelled and Ahmadu yelled back. "He's never smart and I don't think there's good reason for you to yell." "I yelled and what about it, Eeh. He angrily threw a notepad to the wall and sprang up. "Calm down Abudu; things are under control. The president is dead and the fat lady is singing. We should rather be celebrating than yelling at each other." Abudu breathed heavily and stood before Ahmadu. Ahmadu watches him. He heard that Abudu has a volcanic temper and a tendency to attack anyone even at the slightest provocation. Abudu grabs Ahmadu's shoulder and says in a more relaxed voice. "I am sorry I yelled; I am at least comforted by the news of the President's death. If that police agent has not been captured by our gunmen, right now we would be talking damage control." "Yea, but it didn't get to that. He's in our net and the main target is dead." Let's celebrate' Mission almost accomplished." Ahmadu said. Nerves settled and they sat back on the sofa and began to discuss the next mode of operation which might require greasing of palms and arm twisting.

Furious Agent strode to Mark and poked him with a stick on his rib. Mark weakly and slowly opened his right eye and looked at him. The sun has gradually begun to recede on the horizon and a cool breeze rattling the leaves on trees nearby. Mark was weak and hungry; the pains in his body ached so much. He tried to move his legs on the little wooden stool and the stool shook a little as if about to fell down. He struggled to balance weight to avoid falling, and suddenly another poke to his rib. "Where is the President?" Furious asked with a hard voice and hard face. Mark was slow to try to talk. Furious agent got closer to him and hit him on the stomach with the stick. "I ask you, where is the President?" Furious agent asked angrily. "He was killed by your bullets." Mark answered weakly. Furious Agent smiled wickedly. "Who are your allies and where do they live?" Mark watched this moron. Like if he was going to tell him even if he has to save his momma's live. The idiot expected him to answer such a stupid question. Mark remained silent and began to think of what he would do to the bozo if he could wrap his hands around his neck. Jackal and Typhoon lay somewhere at a corner in the warehouse, almost stoned from weed and little snowflakes and rum. They were in the middle of substance-induced sleep, oblivious of the going on. Furious Agent furiously punched Mark on the belly and Mark winced in pain. "I asked you a question and I expect an answer from you, nigga." Mark spat on his face and that infuriated Furious Agent the more. He touched his face, his eyes wide in shock and surprise. "Oh, you fucking idiot still have the liver to annoy me." He said with a hard sneer. He brought out a switchblade from his pocket and flicked it open. As he moved to Mark, his long black trench coat swirled and his black booth crunched on some gravel on the ground. He cut the rope from Mark's neck and mark crashed hard to the ground. He dropped the switch blade to the ground and descended on Mark, and began punching him left and right, pummeling his face and Mark was incapacitated to defend himself because his hands were bonded behind his back. He managed to wedge Furious agent off with his elbow and tried to roll away from his attacker. Furious agent intensified his attack and suddenly with his last strength, Mark pulled his right leg and kicked Furious agent's groin. Furious agent stopped the attack momentarily and grabbed his groin in pain and that gave Mark a little respite. He used that moment to kick Furious in the face. Furious Agent fell back in pain and Mark locked his legs around Furious agent's neck and began to tighten. Furious agent struggled to remove Mark's feet but Mark tightened his feet lock the more with all his available strength and determination. Furious agent began to choke for breath. He gasped, and kicked furiously but his furiousness gradually began to leave him. His hands suddenly fell by his sides and he lay still. Mark quickly unlocked his legs and managed to stand. He searched for the switchblade and saw it lying about five feet away. He bended low and with his bonded hand he picked the switchblade and began to work on the rope tied around his arms. It was not easy trying to cut a tight rope at his back but he continued to work on it with all resilience until the rope was cut and he removed it from his arms and quickly moved. From the corner of the stoned men, Typhoon moved and suddenly became awake. He rolled to one side and got up and cast his blurry eyes to Jackal who snapped out of his sleep and staggered up like a security guard caught sleeping on duty. Typhoon picked up his gun and put his finger to his mouth as a signal to Jackal to keep quiet. "I picked a sound," Typhoon whispered to Jackal. Jackal rubbed his eyes and shook his head to clear the blur, trying to concentrate. He grabbed his gun from the floor beside his right foot and listened too to pick up the sound. Mark slid behind a plastic drum and waited. Typhoon sneaked close and signaled Jackal to another direction. Jackal thought it absurd, why would they be sneaking in their den, when they are in charge and their enemies is hanging on a rope, helpless. Besides, Furious Agent was out there when they went to their smoke; he alone can handle the insignificant police agent. He would personally see to it that they don't waste another time on the captive. He would shoot him dead. They have other things to worry about.

Typhoon sneaked close to where Mark crouched behind the drum. Suddenly Mark attacked with the switchblade and before Typhoon could realize what jumped at him, the switchblade sank deep into his throat. Typhoon winced and moaned in pain and his gun flew off his hand and clattered on a stone. Mark released him and his body dropped to the ground. He made a gurgling sound and twitched a few times and lay still, dead. He made a gurgling sound and then twitched a few times and lay still, dead. Blood flowed on the ground where he lay. Mark quickly picked up the gun and tip towed away to another plastic drum and waited. Jackal sneaked out from behind a drum in a deeper part of the warehouse and picked Mark him moving from his hiding. Jackal fired without proper calculation and the bullet pierced the plastic drum and missed the target. Mark hid in another corner and waited. Suddenly Jackal's blurred eyes cleared and he realized that something was amiss. Where are his colleagues and was that not the captured police agent, he saw a while ago. As he sneaked close, gun pointing, he saw Typhoon's body lay in a pool of his blood, a switchblade buried deep in his throat. He panicked and began to sneak toward the door. Mark saw him and fired, a bullet missed the target but cut out a chunk of wood from a wooden pillar. Mark boldly emerged from where he hid and Jackal sighted him and opened fire and torrents of bullets rained on Mark but without making any impact. They simply bounced off immediately after they hit his body. Mark looked at himself, no bullet marks, no pain, no injury, and no penetration He smiled to himself, it is working. Risi was right about the cowry necklace potency. Jackal momentarily stopped and stared at the figure advancing in his direction. As Mark raised his gun to fire, Jackal moved and dove behind two plastic drums. Mark sprayed bullets at the drum as Jackal from the other side frantically crawled away. He got up and began to run zigzag towards the white generic Ford. Mark fired again and the hammer clicked on an empty chamber. Jackal fired as he ran but knowing his effort was useless. He quickly grabbed the door handle of the generic ford, yanked it open, jumped behind wheels, and threw the gun under the seat. The engine roared to life, and he reversed quickly and pressed the gas pedal down along the rough road that led to the den. Mark threw the gun away, ran to the police car, jumped in, furiously reversed, and began to chase the ford. Occasionally Jackal glanced in the side mirror and noticed the ford chasing him. He raced along the rough road raising dust as he went, He got to the end of the rough road and turned right and joined the expressway and gunned down the needle until it pointed at one hundred and twenty.

Abudu in his office paced as he put a call through to Furious agent to find out if his order to kill Mark was carried out. The mobile rang several times but no response. He fumed and continued to pace, a million questions rattling in his mind without an answer.

Mark followed the generic ford at a good distance; he changed his mind about catching up with Jackal to kill him but decided to follow him from a safe distance so he might lead him to others. He must report to someone. His mind drifted to the President, if he was still alive, whether Clifford found Risi's place on time, and was the President saved. To Mark, President Andy was attacked and he must not die. He followed the ford until it slowed and entered another road and headed towards a busy intersection. Mark slowed the car and followed at a good distance, allowing three cars in front to conceal his car being conspicuous to Jackal. Jackal looked in the side mirror and didn't see the chasing police car. He smiled and began to relax; he has lost him. He decided to drive the ford to a spot where it won't easily be seen by prying eyes before he ran to inform the bosses.

IN AN OPULENT HOME, SOMEWHERE IN THE CITY, the predators gathered, they were in a celebrating mood. The President is dead, and it was the right time to divide the kill. Lalong, Peter, Solomon, and Williams were there. William was invited from Abuja, and he flew in an hour ago and there was a new man amongst them, the vice President of the Federal Republic of Nigeria, Mathew Ochei. The police chief, Ahmadu, and the SSS chief, Illiasu were there too. Happiness in the air, mission accomplished, and the vultures gathered to celebrate a hard-fought victory. The persons that were conspicuously absent were Abudu, DIG Gausa, Sambo and Alhaji Indai who had gone on other errands. Aliu and some other members of Abuja unit were back in Abuja to wait for further instructions Ahmadu and Illiasu whispered to each other and stepped aside a little distance from others. They talked in low voices without others observing. Everyone was happy, maybe, except the two security chiefs that shared a secret message between then and a moment on, they rejoined others. Illiasu cleared his throat and silence suddenly fell across the richly furnished large room. "Listen up everyone; today is a special day for us, and I say, congratulations to all the team members." Others responded happily in a cheerful mood. "The kingmakers are waiting to crown oga, president." Mathew beamed with smile and waved in response as the chant of Prez prez rented the air. "We fought and we came out victorious. It's time to complete the next phase of the project. You are all expected at a grand ceremony waiting for you in Kaduna. There the kingmakers will reward all accordingly." Illiasu said with s faint smile on his lips. "We have taken back what rightly belong to us. It's our right to rule the country. His ascension to power was a big mistake which would never happen again." DIG Gusua said. "It's our birthright to rule the country and we are ready to continue that assignment." Ahmadu said. "A private jet is waiting to fly you to Kaduna in about one hour; prepare your mind for the trip. We have no time to waste." Illiasu said. There was no need to remind them, they already had a hint of the journey and were itching to go.

Mark slowed as the Ford slowed and entered a narrow lonely road and eased under a low mango tree. Jackal killed the engine, picked the gun and slid it into his jacket pocket, jumped down. He cut his eyes about, seeing no one watching and no vehicular movement. He slammed the door and hastened away to another connecting narrow road. Mark watched all from a safe distance. He noticed Jackal moving away and gently rolled the car closer as Jackal flagged down a commercial motorbike and climbed up the back seat and it tore into the road. Mark began to follow, he was sure Jackal did not see the police car. Along the road, Mark allowed two cars to overtake his and stayed two cars behind. A few minutes on, the commercial motorbike slowed, and Mack slowed at a safe distance and concentrated, in a bid not to allow Jackal to lip out of his site. He eased to a stop and watched ahead as the Motorbike stopped by a sidewalk. From behind a van drove by, providing Mark a safe cover from the front because at that moment Jackal turned to see if any police car was in sight. He hastened off to a bar a little distance from the sidewalk. Mark killed the engine and slid out of the car and strode towards the bar. He had no gun on him; it became useless when it clicked on an empty chamber. Jackal entered the bar and waved at a man, who waved at him too. It was his joint and no one would stop him from heading to the rest room straight from outside. The evening began to get older, and darkness gradually fell. Mark stepped into the bar and stopped as he stepped in. He scanned and noticed the place has a cool ambiance with light music playing softly from a loudspeaker somewhere in the bar. He scanned and noticed the place had a cool ambiance with light music playing softly from a loudspeaker somewhere in the bar. Some customers were busy with their drinks; two lovebirds were busy whispering into each other's ears. The man that waved at Jackal noticed Mark step in. Mark scanned the bar and slid to a seat in a dark corner of the bar. Dim lights provided low lights from the ceiling. The man approached Mark's table to take his order. Inside the restroom, Jackal closed the door and wiped out a mobile. He scrolled the contact and placed a call across to someone. It was unavailable, he tried again, and it said the number was unavailable. He cussed and stood still. He thought briefly on the next step to take. Mark in the bar has ordered a bottle of small stout just to keep watch. The stout beer arrived and he sipped a little and waited. As he watched, Jackal came out in a haste and waved at the bar owner, and hastened towards the door. Mark gulped his beer in one take and threw some naira notes on the table and quickly made it to the door before Jackal flagged down another commercial motorbike. And in a second, they rode off. That instant Mark emerged from the bar and a red Toyota car eased to a stop by the sidewalk, he hastened to it and said to the driver. "Police, I need your car, I will bring it back in about an hour." The man looked at him and began to shake his head. "Sorry officer, I won't do that. I don't know you." Mark grabbed the door handle and yanked it open and before the driver could protest, he slid into the front seat and looked at the driver. "This is an emergency; please follow that commercial motorbike at a safe distance. You will be rewarded for helping the law." The man sighed and obliged. He began to follow the motorbike as directed. Jackal occasionally glanced back to see if the black car was following but saw no black car trailing. The red car was two cars behind other cars of different shades and make. The motorbike entered a connecting road and rode along Railway Street. Down the street, it turned left and rode towards a well-lit Mobil Road. The streetlights shone brightly from poles that lined the clean and paved street.

At a private hanger in the local wing of the Airport, some of the happy and celebrating members of the gang boarded a chattered black Lear Jet. Peter, Lalong, Solomon, William, and Oga, vice President Mathew Ochei with his personal trusted assistant were onboard. The other players, especially Illiasu, Ahmadu, and Gusua would be traveling with another jet. The king makers are waiting, they were informed. The Black Lear began to roll along the tarmac, and it hit the runway in seconds it began to taxi along and then began to climb for a takeoff. It climbed and leveled and veered off and headed towards the North.

CHAPTER EIGHTEEN

AT THE LARGE OPULENT HOUSE, Illiasu, Abudu, Gambo, Indai, and Ahmadu were joined by two other men. One of them was the Senate President; Alhaji Danbaba The other man wore an air of immense authority about him. He was tall and light in complexion, a pointed nose and stern face. His name was Issa Moibo. He owns vast businesses and the last descendant of a Dynasty which ruled and controlled the Northern Nigeria. He is respected and he commands great authority. He sat on a single blue sofa while others sat on double sofas about six meters from him, watching and waiting for him to talk. Moibo silently watched them, and the silence became a little heavy, then he smiled in their direction and they smiled too. "The chosen ones are here to cement things," he said and waited for that to sink in. "The fools never knew what was coming. They never know we are masters of the political game. They were used to clear the way for the right man here, Danbaba." The President is dead and in a few minutes another bad news will grace our screen." He smiled wickedly and others noticed it was permitted to smile too, they joined in the smile. He continued. "Danbaba as the Senate President will take over as the Country's President because the President is dead and his stupid vice will blow up in the air, his body scattered over the water." Abudu smiled and spoke. "I doff my cap for you, Alhaji; you've proven to be one of the brainiest of all men." Moibo smiled and nodded at this acknowledgment. Danbaba cleared his throat and rose. "I must say thank you all for your resolute support to make me the President of Nigeria. Alhaji may Allah bless you for your unwavering support towards this course." Moibo nodded with warm smile, looking very pleased and relaxed in his sofa. Gambo cleared his throat to speak. "Alhaji, my question is how you managed to convince those Christians to join the team?" Moibo leaned forward and rubbed his hands. "It took me time to find a man that managed to sell the idea to them and brought them into the fold, you know desperate men play desperate games, and they would do anything to achieve their selfish ends. I figured if they were promised choice positions, they would do everything to make the project successful." "Alhaji honestly you are a genius," Indai said in reverence. "Now let's wait for the breaking news, we can go from there. Danbaba, prepare to ascend to the seat of power; all the players from our inner caucus must be rewarded." He said and relaxed back. "Yes Alhaji, you are my Godfather, I will bring the list for appointments for your approval when I am done drafting it," Danbaba said. Illiasu clasped his hands together and asks, "Alhaji, how many Senators know about this project?" Moibo crosses his legs. "We have some Senators from our region who are aware of this project and are working underground to bring it to fruition. Some of our people in the House are in support and we have players in the judiciary too, in fact, all arrangements are ready for Danbaba to become President." He said and looked at Indai and Gambo. "Alhaji, Gambo, and Indai, you have not been much utilized in this project. I planned it so, now I want two of you to plan a smooth take over for Danbaba. You will have to work with Ahmadu and Illiasu to make it a success. You will meet Senator Guzama to begin the arrangement." Gambo and Indai nodded without words. Suddenly Illiasu's mobile began to ring. He pulled it out from his pocket and silence fell as he picked up the call. A nervous voice stuttered from the other end. "Oga a man here wants to see you urgently." A man with a gun inside the front door said. Jackal nervously cut his eyes as he stood by the front door. The goons were not permitted in the neighborhood. Mark watched from the parked red Toyota off the road. He quickly stepped out of the car and signaled the driver to roll away. He crouched low and ran and hid behind a black jeep parked near the opulent house. Darkness was fast covering the sky and it provided him a good cover. The house has an iron gate, tall fence and a tree in the compound. A few seconds of wait, Jackal slid in through the door and it closes. The man with a gun looked tough and stocky, he wore police fatigue and his face was hard with rough old wounds marks on his left chin. He looked at Jackal and pointed to a slightly open door. "Follow that door and take the stairs." He said. He looked at Jackal and pointed to a slightly open door. "Follow that door and take the stairs", he said. Jackal went in through the door and saw a staircase. He stopped and listened briefly and picked a sound coming from a room upstairs. He took the stair in twos and got to the top, a door was closed before him. He gently tapped on the door and waited. His eyes darted about, other doors led to the west wing, a beautiful chandelier hung from the ceiling. The door opened from inside and Ahmadu stood before him. "What's up, why are you here?" He asked, unpleasantly. Others in the large room watched him as he spoke to Jackal. "Sir, something terrible happened, and I have come to warn you." "To warn me; what the hell has happened?" he asked, his voice hard and menacing. He still stood at the door, blocking Jackal from entering. "Sir the Police agent managed to escape." He stuttered. Ahmadus eyes flew open, and he glared at Jackal. "How the hell did it happen? You were instructed to kill him immediately." His voice raised and Abudu and the others heard him. Abudu went to the door, his face angry and eyes red with rage. He tapped Ahmadu on the back gently. "Let him in." he said Ahmadu turned and looked at him with unsaid words in his mind. Abudu nodded at him as to say I understand It was against the rule to allow the goons to their meeting place and there was supposed to be no direct contact. Ahmadu stepped aside for Jackal and he stepped into the room and the door closed. The other men watched him as he stopped some distance to where they sat. The room was large and richly furnished with the finest make of curtains and sofas, two mid-eastern chandeliers hung at different locations from the ceiling. The rug was maybe Egyptian made. Mark cut his eyes about and saw no one watching, the neighborhood was quiet and rich No car drove by at that moment. He grabbed the Iron Gate and climbed to the top of it, carefully avoiding the tips of metal on top. He dropped to the ground like a cat without much sound. He had done it many times during his police college days when they do some tactical and physical training. He crouched low and ran to the front door and tapped at it and waited in readiness to swoop. He was not conscious of the pains in his body for the time being because the battle was about to begin, and he believed Jackal came to the house to meet the person he was working for. The man in police fatigue hissed and went to the door. Who the hell was at the door? He was instructed not to allow anyone in, or maybe another friend to the man that just went to meet the chief had just arrived. He wondered as he grabbed the door and unbolted it to take a look and suddenly a hard punch to his face sent him staggering backward. He missed his balance and crashed to the floor and instantly Mark slid through the door and dashed in and fell on the man in police fatigue. A hard kick to the head and the man groaned and his head wobbled, he tried to go for his gun but Mark was quicker, he landed a hard punch to the man's face sending him into a momentary daze. Mark fell to his right knee and locked his arms around the man's neck and broke his neck bone. A dying grunt escaped the man and he lay still, dead. Mark grabbed his legs and dragged him away to a corner because anyone coming down from the stairs would notice the body instantly. He picked the long gun and took the stairs in twos, ready for a gunfight. Inside Abudu sneered at Jackal and yelled. "You incompetent fools allowed him to escape and you have the temerity to come here to warn us, as you said." He vibrated, body tensed in anger, suddenly he slapped Jackal hard on the face and Jackal stepped back in terror, stars danced in his eyes. Abudu was making a good show of it; he needed to demonstrate to Moibo how efficient he had handled the whole operation. Suddenly he turned to Ahmadu. "You said that police agent was insignificant and not smart. Now who is smarter, he or you?" "You hired stupid and incompetent goons who could not kill just one police agent." Ahmadu made to yell back but controlled his anger because Moibo was watching and making a mental calculation. Mark listened from the other side of the door. Moibo gently rose like a heavy-fed king and waved Abudu to retrace back. He adjusted his white babriga on his shoulder and looked at Jackal. "Calm down everybody. This is not the time for yelling and apportioning blame. We should be talking damage control." He waited for that to sink in. He stepped forward to Jackal. Under serious pressure, Moibo can be cool when he chooses to and has the grandfathering approach to a difficult situation, He was cunning and dangerously wise.\"Young man, you and your team messed things up, but how do you think he can be located?" His voice suddenly dropped to a mellow tone and the tension in the room subsided. \"Sir, please give me a few hours to find him. I need some new men to comb the city for him." "What happened to the other men; where are they?" Abudu threw in. "They are dead, sir. He killed them." Jackal answered in jittery Abudu glared at Ahmadu. "That's wonderful. Your disparaged agent has suddenly become very dangerous and elusive. You underestimated him." Ahmadu looked at him with anger burning inside him, but he still managed to hold it in check. I will deal with this idiot later. He said in his mind. "How many men do you need to find him?" Moibo asked in the direction of Jackal. "Three competent men will do, sir." He answered. Suddenly Mark pushed the door open, the gun in his hand pointing. Sudden tension rose in the room as legs shifted and some tried to dash, but it was quick and sudden, so all eyes stared at Mark in terror and the gun. "No need for that I am here now." Mark said. All stared at him in terror. Illiasu tried to shift close Moibo but Mark looks at him hard and he movement ceases. He stood still, almost trembling, but as a trained officer he must act. He carefully put his hand into his trouser pocket and tries to remove a pistol. Mark was not fazed. Suddenly Illiasu moved aside and fired at Mark. The bullet hit target and bounced off. That kind of woke the concealed animal in Mark. He fired at Illiau and instantly Illiasu dropped to the rug dead. The other terrified men, Gusau, Gambo, Indai and Moibo tried to move Mark waved the gun at them. "Lie down on your belly and your hands in front where I can see them." He yelled. Others instantly flattened themselves on the rug. Danbaba looked terrified, why this hitch, this should not be happening at this moment in time; when he was almost to the winning line, a desperate moan escaped from him as he flattened himself to the rug, head low. Ahmadu choose not to be ordered by his insignificant officer. He suddenly whipped out his service pistol concealed under his large gown and fired two quick shots at Mark. Mark staggered under the force of the bullets and stood still. He shot Ahmadu in the head and he fell backward and hit his head on a sofa and lay still, dead. Blood flowed out from under where he lay and began to stain the beautiful Arabian rug. Mark stepped to where Ahmadu's gun lay and kicked it away to a far corner. "Now tell me why you want the President dead." He said with the authority of a man with a gun.

Dead silence. "Is there no one willing to talk?" He asked his voice hard and angry. Jackal made a mental calculation. Mark was standing a little distance away from where he lay. If he dives faster, he could reach his right leg before Mark noticed him. He know his employers would count on him to attempt to save them. He was trained to take risks and this moment is one of them. Mark turned to Moibo and jabbed the tip of the muzzle at his head. "Now talk." He ordered him. In that instant, Jackal dove at Mark's leg, which threw Mark off balance and he crashed to the floor and the gun flew out of his hand and smashed into a glass table and shattering it to pieces. Jackal jumped onto Mark and grabbed his neck and began to squeeze the life out of him. Mark struggled with the strength in him to stay alive, he tried to remove Jackal's hands locked around his throat but Jackal pressed harder other men noticed that the dice had turned their way and they quickly got to their feet and Gusua picked up Illiasu's gun. Gambo and Indai step closer to the door and Moibo followed, with a slim hope of them winning this fight. Danbaba went for Ahmadu's gun but the pistol slid under a sofa and he couldn't see it on impulse Danbaba went to where Mark lay and with his fingers, he pressed Mark's nostrils together in a bid to help Jackal kill him quickly. Mark gasped for air, and weakness set in and his breath began to fade away. His legs desperately tried to kick but his breath and strength failed him. In a last effort his hand began to search for piece of a broken glass. He feebly groped until suddenly his hand touched a broken glass. He locked his finger on it and with the strength in his arm, he slashed Danbaba's face and he yells in great sharp pain and fell backward on his butt, blood flows down his left cheek. Then Mark, with the last strength left in him, buried the broken glass into Jackal's left rib and instantly, Jackal yelled painfully, and his hands flew off Mark's throat. He made a grunting sound and moaned in pain. Mark pushed Jackel off him and began to stand. Gusua watched in terror, he dashed to get to the long gun a little distance away from Mark. Jackal was still alive but weak as blood flowed from his side where the broken glass sank in. Mark staggered and almost felt dizzy, his throat hurt. He saw Gus ua move and did the only thing that came to his mind. He dove at Danbaba's leg to stop him from reaching the gun first but as Danbaba fell he quickly dragged himself to where the gun lay and his hand locked on the metal. He swung it hard and its butt hit Mark and threw him off balance. He got up to his feet and pointed the gun at Mark. He has still got his reflexes as a trained police officer. Other's watched with a rush of hope that the enemy has no chance of winning this fight. Mark managed to grabbed the rail to stop himself from crashing to the floor, but before he realized what was in Gusau's hand, Gusau fired a shot and the bullet hit Mark on the chest but just bounced off, he staggered and steadied himself from falling Gusua fired again but the bullet again bounced off. He threw the gun away and made a dash for the door. Pandemonium broke in the room. Gambo, Moibo, and Indai followed as they dash for the door Mark somersaulted to where the long gun lay, grabbed it, and landed with one knee on the floor. He shot Gusua in the back and the bullet hit him and his legs lifted and he hit the floor hard and Gambo stumbled over his body and crashed to the floor A bullet hit Moibo and he fell backward and twitched a few times and lay dead. Gambo scrambled up to his feet and began to run down the stairs, his white babariga lose as he ran. Mark turned to Jackal and finished him off with a bullet. Indai had already ran out through the door and was escaping through the stairs. Mark stepped onto the top of the stairs and aimed. He squeezed the trigger again but it clicked empty. He threw the gun away and ran after them. Gambo slipped and fell as he tried to get to the foot of the stairs. Indai scaled over him and ran toward the front door. Mark grabbed Gambo and punched him furiously and he doubled over and desperately tried to scramble up in a desperate bid to continue running Mark hit his face and Gambo crashed to the floor. Mark locked his hand round Gambo's neck and broke it. He let the limp body fell on the floor and quickly ran to catch up with Indai who already exited the front door and ran into the quiet compound. There was little light in the compound, only from two low light bulbs at different corners on the wall. It was designed so, little light was required to conceal the movement of the conspirators when they leave the meeting venue in the night. In the dimly lit compound, Mark stopped and cut his eyes about for Indai. His eyes picked a shadowy movement upward of the tree in the compound and there was a sign that someone was disturbing the tree Mark ran to the tree and looked up. He was able to see a man in a big flowing gown trying to get to the upper part of the branch. Mark began to climb after him. He got close and tried to grab Indai's right leg and Indai kicked in desperation. In the distance, sound of siren could heard approaching the neighborhood. Someone heard the gunshots and called Nine-one-one. The police siren grew louder, heading towards the area. Mark heard it and Indai heard it also. In a desperate bid to get farther away up the tree from Mark, Indai miscalculated and his foot slipped. He began to fell and tried to grab Mark but missed and only succeeded in yanking off the cowry necklace from Mark's neck. It cut and the cowries scattered in different spots in the dark. Indai hit the ground head first and lay still, dead. Instantly blood flowed from the back of his neck, and his life drifted into the Cimmerian slippery world of the dead. Mark quickly and carefully climbed down from the tree; he touched his neck and noticed the necklace was gone He tried to search for it in the darkness but knew it was useless. It was like trying to find a lost coin underwater in the dark. The sound of sirens grew louder, approaching close. He could pick out red and blue lights flickering towards the building. He ran to the other side of the wall and climbed out and strutted to a dark street and began to walk normal. Car lights flashed in his direction as he hastened away from the vicinity, He saw a taxi and flagged it down and as the taxi eased to a stop he leaned into the front window. "Silverbird Hotel," he said, and the driver nodded. He grabbed the door handle and yanked it open, and slid into the back seat. The taxi rolled off and Mark slid lower and covered his eyes. Is the war over? Or are there other obstacles? He asked in his mind. The time was eight-thirty-eight when he alighted on the sidewalk in front of Silverbird Hotel. He had only about eighteen grand left on him and he prayed they will have a cheap room he can rent and rest his aching body and soul. He strode to the front glass door of the hotel and the glass door automatically slid open and he stepped into the lobby. He knew he looked dirty, but that was his problem to worry about. He needed a good rest, food, and time to heal. He went to the reception and a beautiful young female smiled warmly at him. "How much is your cheap room?" he inquired without returning the smile. The receptionist looked at the key rack and said to him. "Ten thousand" And only one room is vacant." Mark put his hand into his pocket and brought out some money. He counted ten one thousand notes and handed them to her.

As he entered his hotel room, he threw himself across the bed and closed his eyes. His eyes ache, his throat has a burning sensation, and the pains began to work against his resolve to catch a good rest. A sudden thought of the cowry necklace flashed in his mind. He became worried. What would he tell Risi? He had promised to return the cowry necklace to her. She had helped him, and he would disappoint her she told him how important the necklace was to her family, and she made him promise to bring it back. He felt sad and disappointed with himself for his failure to keep his promise. He thought maybe to go back to the compound tomorrow to look for it but shook his head in frustration. That would be suicidal he thought. He sighed heavily and slowly and sadly got up from the bed and entered the bathroom.

NEXT MORNING, Mark sat on the only single sofa in his hotel room and watched the morning news on the screen. He had a few hours to stay before he vacated the room. The news came on about a plane crash involving the Nigerian vice president and other men traveling with him to Kaduna. More details were expected as the investigation was still going on to ascertain the course of the crash, but from an unquoted source, there's suspicion that the plane exploded in the air over water. Names of other passengers travelling with the vice President were given as Williams, Lalong, Peter and Solomon. Mark sighed and killed the power with a remote. He began to think again, how to talk to Risi about the necklace and suddenly he sat up. He needed to go see her and to find out if the President made it out alive He walked to the door and unbolted it and stepped out His heart was more relaxed and rested, he had no fear of a sudden attack or anyone lurking around waiting to swoop on him. Inside him, he felt stronger as if a big load has been lifted off him. As he headed to the reception, his heart raced from his girlfriend to mother, siblings. They would be very worried after not hearing from him for a while. He decided to find a way to phone them when he gets to Risi's place. He thought.

THAT MORNING, two military helicopters belonging to the U.S paramilitary flew towards President Andy Ubih's hometown from their West African command. There were five paramilitary men, one FBI special agent on board. The special agent was Mark's kinsman working with the FBI. He was asked to lead the team to his hometown to rescue the US President's daughter held captive in the terrorist camp. The beat of the helicopters filled the air. They began to descend along a long stretched deserted rough road that led to the stream along Ugwu Nwosa. The birds finally landed on their skid and men in paramilitary uniform began to jump on, their guns ready in their hands to perform Agent Fred climbed down and scanned the environment The leader of the military men, Colonel Jack, shouted a command over the engine noise and his men scrambled in different directions into the bush. The helicopter engines died down and he and agent Fred talked briefly and Colonel Jack put the telescope hanging from his neck to his eyes and peered into it. His men crouched low in the bush as they sneaked towards the inner part of the bush. Jack pointed out a narrow footpath to Fred, and he made a low whistle sound and the shrubs moved as his men began to maneuver forward. At the terrorist camp, one of the terrorists called for the attention of his colleague and whispered to them. Others were summoned instantly, and they scattered and hid in wait.

The US rescue team quickly spread, and from both sides of the bush, they began to advance towards the dangerous area. A little distance to the end of the footpath to the camp, a hot bullet flew through the air and missed the target. The US Rescue team flattened themselves to the ground and waited. A gunman appeared at the enemy's side as he tiptoed forward, his eyes darted about. From a corner, ferocious shot rang out and a bullet hit a man, he crashed backward and lay dead. The US Rescue team crawled on their bellies towards the camp. More men appeared from the enemy side with guns. Angry gunfire shot cried out and two terrorists lay dead in the pool of their blood. Excited voices could be heard in the camp as the remaining terrorists yelled across to one another with instructions. They responded with their fire but the US paramilitary team kept advancing. Sensing they were no match, two of the terrorists raised their hands in surrender. Jack yelled at them. "On the ground, and put your hands where I can see them". The men quickly complied and flattened themselves on the ground. Two tents could be seen farther down. Jack gave a command sign to two of his men to cut to the left side, and another two to the right towards the tents. Agent Fred crouched low and ran towards the tent. Another US man followed as a backup. In an instant, the two terrorists removed automatics from their pockets and began to fire at Fred and his backup. The backup got hit on the thigh and he crashed to the ground with a painful moan. Jack signaled the rest of his men to attack. The US men shot and killed the two terrorists and quickly began to advance as more gunfire roared out from the other part of the bush at the back of the camp. Agent Fred went to help the injured man. He put his hand under the soldier's arm and helped him away from danger. A bullet hit a US soldier on the shoulder and he fell to the ground in pain. The US team replied and began to shoot sporadically forcing the enemy to duck and retreat. Two US men crouched low in the bush and ran zigzag into the first camp and saw Alice bonded to a thick log of wood. She looked dazed but managed to recognize her country's army uniform as the men began to untie her. In a little second they freed her and led her out through the other side of the bush. Alice walked tiredly as they helped her to the other side where the US team was waiting. Four more terrorists got killed and the camp area became quiet. No more response, all of them was killed. Alice cut her eyes to the faces of her countrymen who rescued her. Tears flowed down her cheeks in gratitude and regret. She was partly ashamed of herself and partly proud of her Country's military for their sacrifice to rescue her from the jaw of death. After the gun battle, only two US soldiers were injured.

The two military men led her out towards the road while the wounded US soldiers quickly received first aid attention from one of the soldiers that doubled as a doctor. Jack glanced at the wounded soldiers and looked at Alice and asked her, "Are you okay?" She nodded and looked down at her feet, ashamed of herself. She looked up and said feebly, "Thank you, gentlemen." Operation complete, they headed to their Helicopters and helped her climbed in. A few seconds on, after the hugs for a successful rescue mission, the US Paramilitary men climbed into the Helicopter and lifted into the air and began to fly back to the US West African Military command.

THAT SAME MORNING, Mark got to Risi's place and noticed the front door was closed. He tapped on the door and waited, his eyes darted around him. Few seconds of waiting the door opened and Risi stood in the door. She yelled in excitement and on impulse she ran and hugged him. He smiled like a just returned victorious soldier from a long war. She disengaged and looked at him. "You made it back alive; oh I'm happy." Mark nodded but his mind became troubled immediately after she appeared at the door. How would he begin to explain the loss of her family necklace? "Let's go into the house," she said stepping aside to allow him in. "Did the men I sent here find you?" Mark asked, Anxious with hope to hear in the affirmative. Suddenly a door at the right opened and Clifford stepped out. He and Mark hugged and Risi watched them with amusement. "How's the President?" Mark asked. Clifford nodded. "He's recovering real fast, thanks to God and thanks to this angel. She performed a delicate surgery with herbs on him to remove the pellet." Mark turned to Risi. "Thank you, honestly I can't thank you enough for all you've done for us." "The glory is to God, Almighty." She said. "Can I see the President?" Mark asked. "He's sleeping right now." Mark nodded and excused himself. He held Risi by the hand and they stepped outside. Mark tried to speak but the words failed him. Risi watched him intently as beads of sweat began to form on his forehead. "I.. I failed you, I failed to keep my promise to return the cowry necklace. An enemy tore it off my neck in a desperate bid to escape and I couldn't find them in the dark." Risi smiled and shook her head. "You don't need to worry; you brought back the most important thing." "Are you not mad at me?" Mark asked and stared at her in surprise. She shook her head and touched his shoulder. "Look, Mark, I asked you to bring it back because I felt if you could bring it back, you would come back alive." Mark hugged her excitedly and she hugged him back. "You're wonderful. I owe you my life. You don't know what you've done for me, for the country, or justice." Risi held him by the shoulders and looked into his eyes. "Mark, we are nothing but pencils in the hand of the creator. Every one of us is called to perform different tasks in life. I am proud of you for what you managed to accomplish." She said and patted him on the shoulder. "I can't wait to tell my family about you. You're one in a million." He said. She smiled and bowed. "Welcome" she said with a smile still playing on her lips and turned and entered the house. Mark watched her until she disappeared into the house. Mark turned and stood looking at the scenery, happiness crowded his heart. He went, saw, and conquered. He felt so fulfilled in his heart. The ordinary Joe has become somebody. Those who disparaged him would have to have a rethink. He felt stronger like a new man. Refreshed and full of vigor. In his heart, a song of gratitude to God for saving him, using him and helping him throughout the period. Clifford appeared at the door and watched him. He ambled to Mark and Mark looked at him happily. Clifford noticed the happiness in him because it was so evident on his face. "Mark, I have something to tell you." Clifford said. Mark watched him and waited for him to continue. "President Andy called me this morning and informed me he would be flying in today." Mark looked at him in surprise.

"What're you talking about bro? But you said the President is sleeping. Which President are you talking about?" Clifford held his hand. "Mark, it's a long story and I will tell you all if you step to that corner for us to talk." He pointed farther around the house. As they stepped aside to a spot, he began to tell Mark all that happened during their trip to the US. When he was done, Mark said "wonderful, wonderful. This is like in the movies." Clifford smiled and they hugged each other in excitement. As if nature had been listening to them, it began to get cloudy, and the wind blew across the earth making leaves gyrate to the silent music played in the air. The two men disengaged from their hug and headed back into the house. A few minutes later, the thunder announced the coming of the rain, and it came in torrents and began to beat on the rusty zinc of the little house where David, Clifford, and Mark took refuge, sipping hot cocoa prepared by Risi. Mark introduced himself to David and told him all he knew about the conspirators and what happened. Risi rose quitely and entered her room and closed the door. She stood at the centre of her room, eyes to the old ceiling in her room. Suddenly she crouched, her hands grabbed her head. She moans painfully and slumped to the floor. Her skin began to shrink and her eyes have death and horror all over them.

Outside, Clifford stepped to a corner to urinate and Mark entered the house and suddenly stopped on his track. Risi may be in danger, he reasoned and on impulse he barged into her room and saw her drifting away into the dark slippery land of silence. "Risi! Risi!!. What's the matter?" Oh noooh" He desperately called her as he shook her in an effort to help her live. "Risi please don't do this. It's a fat joke, Right." Risi managed to touch his hand. "Go! "You must leave right now" she said feebly. "I can't leave you to die" Mark yelled, trying to help her stand up from the bed. You can't stop me

. Me eee. She managed to say. Now go before it's late. All of you must go now." She said in between coughs. Clifford entered the door and heard them. He rushed into the room and saw Mark sitting on the floor, his head in his palms and he was sobbing softly. Clifford rushed to him. "What's the problem, Mark?" .Mark shook his head, tears ran down his eyes. "Mark, you are confusing me. Talk to me, what happened to her?" "I heard her moaning in pain and I ran in, I met her dying". Mark answered sadly. Clifford stepped beside her bed and touched her hand for a pulse. There was weak pulse. Mark joined him with anticipation of a sudden burst of laughter from her. Hoping she will just tell them it was just a prank. He leaned low to her but her weight became like a thick dead wood. "Go now" her lips moved. Both men heard the faint command. Suddenly her hands went limp and she left the present into the silent world of the oblivion. Mark rushed to her and grabbed her hands, trying to make her wake, but all in futility. Suddenly the thunder roared fiercely across the sky. Mark and Clifford stared at her body, dumbfounded. Mark rubbed his eyes to clear invisible cobwebs. No she's not dead he reasoned in his mind. The rain poured in torrent, wind blew and the leaves of the trees dance to the silent rhythm of a fierce wind. Mark closed her eyes and signals Clifford to follow him outside, into another room.

"What a sad end" Mark said softly to Clifford. "I'm torn apart, Mark. What caused her death? She wasn't sick." "I don't know I believe she sacrificed her life to save me and the President" Mark said, sadness enveloped his heart. "She knew she would die if I lost the necklace. She told me there was no problem that i lost it." "It must be a very important to her" Clifford said sadly. "She told me it belonged to the family. It was passed over from older generations" Mark said and began to pace restlessly, his mind thinking many disturbing thoughts. The rain continued to fell in torrents on the old zinc of the small house, creating a silent beat, a dirge for the body under it. Mark suddenly stopped pacing and listened. He heard a sound or a noise. "What's it?" Clifford asked, looking at Mark as if he has gone bananas. Mark shushed him and tip-toed towards the door to Risi's room. The rain beat ferociously on the roof, and thunder struck, causing a deafening sound. He touched the door and it seemed locked from inside. Clifford on impulse sneaked closer behind Mark. Mark again tried the door handle but the door didn't yield. He tried to force it open but it was as stuck. From another connecting door, President David emerged and the two men noticed his presence. Mark almost jerked when the President entered the room. "What's up gentlemen?" He asked coolly. His white shirt is unbuttoned to the third button, his long sleeve folded. Clifford smiled and shook his head. "Your excellency, sir. We have a bad situation at hand." "What situation" He asked in apprehension. "Sir, the girl died a few minutes ago" Mark said with pain in his heart. "What! how come. Was she sick or did she die accidentally?". "No sir, nothing like that. She just died". David drew closer and held him by the hands. "Tell me this is a joke. It's a big joke right?" No answer. Clifford and Mark lost the will power to speak. Neither Mark nor Clifford would be able to explain it. Suddenly Mark found his voice. "She sacrificed herself to save us" He said. "I don't follow and don't like it either" President David said honestly. Clifford left Mark to do the explaining. He knew more than him in this matter. "It's a long story which I will tell you later. Right now we must find way to take her body to the hospital for proper confirmation that she's actually dead". The rain has started was heavy. Mark went to the door of her room and began to apply more force. The door began to crack inward until it crashed inward. Mark stepped into the room and stood in shock as others joined him. The wall of the room has crumbled outward and rain fell into the room. But one other thing caught Mark's attention. Her body was not on her bed. It was there. Mark is very sure of that. Suddenly Clifford pointed to the distance. "Look, over there". The men rushed quickly stepped closer to the fallen wall and look to the distance. Mark sighted two moving figures draped in immaculate white carting something on their shoulders, one leading the front. Something like a wrapped log of wood wrapped in immaculate white wool clothe lay stretched across their shoulders. They wore all white caftans. On impulse Mark dashed off after them along a narrow bush part. As he got closer he hit his leg against a stone and fell hard, but quickly got up to his feet. "Hey stop. Who are you? Where are you taken her body to?" They stopped. Mark could not see their faces because they were facing front and their backs to him. "Who are you? Put her down. She was my friend and it's my duty to bury her". "No she belongs to us. We are taking her body to join her ancestors. Go back now, young man." One of them said, his voice has a hollow echo to it. "Now go! Run out of that house before it's too late. The rain began to pour down in more torrents. It was obvious it wasn't going to abate soon. Thunder clapped in the distance sky and more rain poured. Mark was fully drenched. They men began to move again. Mark stood watching their back as they moved deeper into the other side of the wood. Mark hit his chest in anger and wailed with loud voice, in agony for her. Confusion enveloped him as he turned and headed back into the house in great melancholy. Mark egged Clifford and President David to get out of the house immediately. He doesn't know why the men in white robes asked him to leave the house that instant but he must obey them, even if it's for Risi. Mark preceded others out of the house. Within a few seconds they stood outside in the front of the house, a fierce wind started to blow. Before their eyes the wind lifted the entire roof of the house and it fell away. The downpour intensified, forcing them to run under a tree for cover. Another Thunder roared, igniting fire which began inside of the house. Mark watched in bewilderment as the fire continued to burn as it rained. In a few seconds, the fire grew and the walls of the little house started to crumble. The rain and fire continued until the house was totally destroyed. From a narrow footpath, a small elderly looking woman appeared and walked towards them. They watched her approach. Her face was wrinkled and her hair was white as wool. She was holding an old umbrella. The rain wet her old wrapper In spite of the old umbrella she was carrying. They greeted her. She smiled and asked, "Are you surprised?" Her eyes were on the burning house. They didn't know whether to affirm or not. None of them answered her question. She said, "They served the gods of fire and thunder. Rain and fire pay their last respects whenever any of them dies and she's the last of them." "I am confused mama. What... "My Children, leave here immediately. Now!" She cut in. Without waiting for another word

Mark and the others scurried off in the rain towards the main road. The tone of her command sounded serious and they understood she must be obeyed. That instant, an earth shaking thunder roared across the sky and the fire gradually began to simmer. Another thunder shattered the symphony of rain pouring in torrents, followed by a lightning and a rumbling sound that announced the transition of the last in line of a family tree, into perpetual oblivion.

THE END

About the Author

Emmanuel Simon

Emmanuel Simon, also known as Zazamuza, is a produced screenwriter with over ten years of experience. He is also a musician with several albums and holds a diploma in music from the Jim Eskor Music Institute, Kaduna. He previously served as Vice President of both the Performing Musicians Association of Nigeria (AJIF chapter) and the Actors Guild of Nigeria (AJIF chapter).

www.ingramcontent.com/pod-product-compliance
Lightning Source LLC
LaVergne TN
LVHW041707070526
838199LV00045B/1240